THE PURSUIT

Relive the romance

Three complete novels
by one of your favorite authors!

LYNNE GRAHAM
THE PURSUIT

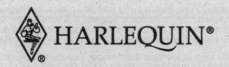

HARLEQUIN®

TORONTO • NEW YORK • LONDON
AMSTERDAM • PARIS • SYDNEY • HAMBURG
STOCKHOLM • ATHENS • TOKYO • MILAN • MADRID
PRAGUE • WARSAW • BUDAPEST • AUCKLAND

HARLEQUIN BOOKS

by Request—THE PURSUIT

Copyright © 2003 by Harlequin Books S.A.

ISBN 0-373-18514-6

The publisher acknowledges the copyright holder of the individual works as follows:
THE VENGEFUL HUSBAND
Copyright © 1998 by Lynne Graham
CONTRACT BABY
Copyright © 1998 by Lynne Graham
MARRIED TO A MISTRESS
Copyright © 1998 by Lynne Graham

This edition published by arrangement with Harlequin Books S.A.

Visit us at www.eHarlequin.com

Printed in U.S.A.

CONTENTS

THE VENGEFUL HUSBAND

CHAPTER ONE

A SLENDER fragile beauty in a silvery green gown. Translucent skin, a mane of vibrant Titian hair and spellbinding eyes as green as peridots behind her flirtatious little mask. A hoarse, sexy little voice, sharp enough to strip paint and then sweet enough to make honey taste bitter...

'No names...no pack drill,' she had said.

'I don't want to know,' she had said, when he had tried to identify himself. 'After tonight, I'll never see you again. What would be the point?'

No woman had ever said that to Gianluca Raffacani before. No woman had ever looked on him as a one-night stand. The shock of such treatment had been profound. But her eagerness in his bed had seemed to disprove the dismissive words on her lips...until he'd wakened in the early hours and found his mystery lover gone and the Adorata ring gone with her. And then Luca had simply not been able to credit that some unscrupulous little tart had contrived to rip him off with such insulting ease.

His memory of that disastrous night in Venice almost three years earlier still biting like salt in an open wound, Luca surveyed the closed file labelled 'Darcy Fielding' on his library desk, his chiselled features chillingly cast. With the cool of a self-discipline renowned in the world of international finance, he resisted the temptation to rip open the file like an impatient boy. He had waited a

9

long time for this moment. He could wait a little longer. 'It is *her* this time…you're sure?' he prompted softly.

Even swollen with pride as Benito was at finally succeeding in his search, even convinced by the facts that he had to have the right woman, Benito still found himself stiffening with uncertainty. Although the woman he had identified matched every slender clue he had started out with, by no stretch of his imagination could he see his famously fastidious and highly sophisticated employer choosing to spend a wild night of passion with the female in that photograph…

'I will only be sure when you have recognised her, sir,' Benito admitted tautly.

'You're backtracking, Benito.' With a rueful sigh that signified no great hope of satisfaction, Luca Raffacani reached out a deceptively indolent brown hand and flipped open the file to study the picture of the woman on the title page.

As Luca tensed and a frown grew on his strong dark face, setting his pure bone structure to the cold consistency of granite, Benito paled, suddenly convinced that he had made a complete ass of himself. That bedraggled female image sported worn jeans, wellington boots, a battered rainhat and a muddy jacket with a long rip in one sleeve. More bag lady than gorgeous seductress. 'I've been too hasty—'

'She's cut off her hair…' his employer interrupted in a low-pitched growl.

After a convulsive swallow, Benito breathed tautly, 'Are you saying that…it *is* the same woman?'

'Was she got up like this for a fancy dress party?'

'Signorina Fielding was feeding hens when that was taken,' Benito supplied apologetically. 'It was the best the photographer could manage. She doesn't go out much.'

'Hens...?' Bemusement pleating his aristocratic ebony brows, Luca continued to scan the photo with hard, dark deepset eyes. 'Yet it is her. Without a doubt, it is her...the devious little thief who turned me over like a professional!'

Darcy Fielding had stolen a medieval ring, a museum piece, an irreplaceable heirloom. The Raffacani family had been princes since the Middle Ages. To mark the occasion of the birth of his son, the very first *principe* had given his wife, Adorata, the magnificent ruby ring. Yet in spite of that rich family heritage, and the considerable value of the jewel, the police had not been informed of the theft. Initially stunned by such an omission, Benito had since become less surprised...

According to popular report within the Raffacani empire, some very strange things had happened the night of the annual masked ball at the Palazzo d'Oro. The host had vanished, for one thing. And if it was actually true that Gianluca Raffacani had vanished in order to romance the thief with something as deeply uncool for a native Venetian as a moonlit gondola tour of the city, Benito could perfectly understand why the police had been excluded from the distinctly embarrassing repercussions of that evening. No male would wish to confess to such a cardinal error of judgement.

In spite of the substantial reward which had been dangled like bait in the relevant quarters, the ring had not been seen since. Most probably it had been disposed of in England—secretly acquired by some rich collector content not to question its provenance. Benito had been extremely disappointed when the investigator failed to turn up the slightest evidence of Darcy Fielding having a previous criminal record.

'Tell me about her…' his employer invited without warning, shutting the file with a decisive snap and thrusting it aside.

Surprised by the instruction, Benito breathed in deep. 'Darcy Fielding lives in a huge old house which has been in her family for many generations. Her financial situation is dire. The house is heavily mortgaged and she is currently behind with the repayments—'

'Who holds the mortgage?' Luca incised softly.

Benito informed him that the mortgage had been taken out a decade earlier with an insurance firm.

'Buy it,' Luca told him equally quietly. 'Continue…'

'Locally, the lady is well-respected. However, when the investigator went further afield, he found her late godmother's housekeeper more than willing to dish the dirt.'

Luca's brilliant eyes narrowed, his sensual mouth twisting with distaste. In an abrupt movement, he re-opened the file at the photograph again. He surveyed it with renewed fascination. What he could see of her hair suggested a brutal shearing rather than the attentions of a salon. She looked a mess, a total mess, but the glow of that perfect skin and the bewitching clarity of those eyes were unmistakable.

Emerging from his uncharacteristic loss of attention, Luca discovered that he had also lost the thread of Benito's report…

'And if the lady pulls it off, she stands to inherit something in the region of one million pounds sterling,' Benito concluded impressively.

Luca studied his most trusted aide. 'Pull what off?'

'The late Signora Leeward had three god-

daughters…possibly the god-daughters from hell.'
Benito labelled them with rueful amusement. 'When it
came to the disposing of her worldly goods, what was
there to choose between the three? One living with a
married man, one an unmarried mother and the other
going the same way—and not a wedding ring or even
the prospect of one between the lot of them!'

'You've lost me,' Luca admitted with controlled impatience.

'Darcy Fielding's rich godmother left everything to
her three godchildren on condition that each of them
find a husband within the year.'

'And Darcy is one of those women you described.'
Luca finally grasped it, bronzed features freezing into
charged stillness. *'Which?'*

'She's the unmarried mother,' Benito volunteered.

Luca froze. 'When was the child born?'

'Seven months after her trip to Venice. The kid's just
over two.'

Luca stared into space, rigidly schooling his dark face
to impassivity, but it was a challenge to suppress his
sheer outrage at the news. *Cristo*…she had even been
pregnant with another man's child when she slept with
him! Well, that was just one more nail in her coffin.
Luca swore in disgust. Whatever was most important to
her, he would take from her in punishment. He would
teach her what it was like to be deceived and cheated
and humiliated. As *she,* most unforgettably, had taught
him…

'As to the identity of the kid's father…' Benito continued wryly. 'The jury's still out on that one.
Apparently the locals believe that the child was fathered
by the fiancé, who ditched the lady at the altar. He figures as a rat of the lowest order in their eyes. But the

godmother's housekeeper had a very different version of events. *She* contends that the fiancé was abroad at the time the kid was conceived, and that he took to his heels because he realised that the baby on the way couldn't possibly be his!'

Luca absorbed that further information in even stonier silence.

'I shouldn't think the lady will remain a single parent for long,' Benito advanced with conviction. 'Not with a million pounds up for grabs. And on page six of the file you will see what I believe she is doing to acquire that money…'

Luca leafed through the file. 'What is this?' he demanded, studying the tiny print of the enclosed newspaper advertisement and its accompanying box number.

'I suspect that Darcy Fielding is discreetly advertising for a husband to fulfil the terms of that will.'

'*Advertising?*' Luca echoed in raw disbelief.

> *Country woman seeks quiet, well-behaved and domesticated single male without close ties, 25-50, for short-term live-in employment. Absolute confidentiality guaranteed. No time-wasters, please.*

'That's not an advertisement for a husband…it's an ad for an emasculated household pet!' Luca launched with incredulous bite.

'I'm going to have to advertise again,' Darcy divulged grimly to Karen as she mucked out the stall of the single elderly occupant in the vast and otherwise horse-free stable yard. She wielded the shovel like an aggressive weapon. Back to square one. She could hardly believe it—and that wretched advertisement had cost an arm and a leg!

Standing by and willing to help, but knowing better than to offer, Karen looked in surprise at her friend. 'But what happened to your shortlist of two possibilities? The gardener and the home handyman?'

Darcy slung the attractive thirty-year-old brunette a weary grimace. 'Yesterday I phoned one and then the other in an attempt to set up an interview—'

'In which you planned to finally spill the confidential beans that matrimony was the *real* employment on offer.' Karen sighed. 'Boy, would I like to have been a fly on the wall when you broke that news!'

'Yes, well…as it turns out, I shan't need to embarrass myself just yet. One had already found a job elsewhere and the other has moved on without leaving a forwarding address. I shouldn't have wasted so much time agonising over my choice.'

'*What* choice? You only got five replies. Two were obscene and one was weird! The ad was too vague in one way and far too specific in the other. What on earth possessed you to put in ''well-behaved and domesticated''? I mean, talk about picky, why don't you? Still, I can't really say I'm sorry that you've drawn a blank,' Karen admitted, with the bluntness that made the two women such firm friends.

'Karen…' Darcy groaned.

'Look, the thought of you being alone in this house with some stranger gives me the shivers!' the brunette confided anxiously. 'In any case, since you didn't want to risk admitting in the ad that you were actually looking for a temporary husband, what are the chances that either of those men would have been agreeable to the arrangement you were about to offer?'

Darcy straightened in frustration. 'If I'd offered enough money, I bet one of them would have agreed. I *need* my inheritance, Karen. I don't care what I have to do to get it. I don't care if I have to marry the Hunchback of Notre Dame to meet the conditions of Nancy's will!' Darcy admitted with driven honesty. 'This house has been in my family for four *hundred* years—'

'But it's crumbling round your ears and eating you up alive, Darcy. Your father had no right to lay such a burden on you. If he hadn't let Fielding's Folly get in such a state while *he* was responsible for it, you wouldn't be facing the half of what you're facing right now!'

Darcy tilted her chin, green eyes alight with stubborn determination. 'Karen...as long as I have breath in my body and two hands to work with, the Folly will survive so that I can pass it on to Zia.'

Pausing to catch her breath from her arduous labour, Darcy glanced at her two-year-old daughter. Seated in a grassy sunlit corner, Zia was grooming one of her dolls with immense care. Her watching mother's gaze was awash with wondering pride and pleasure.

Zia had been blessed at birth, Darcy conceded gratefully. Mercifully, she hadn't inherited her mother's carroty hair, myopic eyesight *or* her nose. Zia had lustrous black curls and dainty, even features. There was nothing undersized or over-thin about her either. She was a strikingly pretty and feminine little girl. In short, she was already showing all the promise of becoming everything her mother had once so painfully and pointlessly longed to be...

Zia wouldn't be a wallflower at parties, too blunt-spoken to be flirtatious or appealing, too physically

plain to attract attention any other way. Nor would Zia
ever be so full of self-pity that she threw herself into
the bed of a complete stranger just to prove that she
could attract a man. Pierced to the heart by that painful
memory, Darcy paled and guiltily looked away from her
child, wondering how the heck she would eventually
explain that shameful reality in terms that wouldn't hurt
and alienate her daughter.

Some day Zia would ask her father's name, quite
reasonably, perfectly understandably. And what did
Darcy have to tell her? Oh, I never got his name because
I told him I didn't want it. Even worse, I could well
walk past him on the street without recognising him,
because I wasn't wearing my contacts and I'm a little
vague as to his actual features. But he had dark eyes,
even darker hair, and a wonderful, wonderful voice…

Beneath Karen's frowning gaze, Darcy had turned a
beetroot colour and had begun studiously studying her
booted feet. 'What's up?'

'Indigestion,' Darcy muttered flatly, and it wasn't a
lie. Memories of that nature made her feel queasy and
crushed her self-respect flat. She had been a push-over
for the first sweet-talking playboy she had ever met.

'So it's back to the drawing board as far as the search
for a temporary hubby goes, I gather…' Releasing her
breath in a rueful hiss, Karen studied the younger
woman and reluctantly dug an envelope from the pocket
of her jeans and extended it. 'Here, take it. A late ap-
plicant, I assume. It came this morning. The postmark's
a London one.'

To protect Darcy's anonymity, Karen had agreed to
put her own name behind the advertisement's box number. All the replies had been sent to the gate lodge
which Karen had recently bought from the estate. Darcy

was well aware that she was running a risk in advertising to find a husband, but no other prospect had offered. If she was found out, she could be accused of trying to circumvent the conditions of her godmother's will and excluded from inheriting. But what else was she supposed to do? Darcy asked herself in guilty desperation.

It was *her* duty and *her* responsibility alone to secure Fielding's Folly for future generations. She could not fail the trust her father had imposed on her at the last. She had faithfully promised that no matter what the cost she would hold on to the Folly. How could she allow four hundred years of family history to slip through her careless fingers?

And, even more importantly, only when she contrived to marry would she be in a position to re-employ the estate staff forced to seek work elsewhere after her father's death. In the months since, few had found new jobs. The knowledge that such loyal and committed people were still suffering from her father's financial incompetence weighed even more heavily on her conscience.

Tearing the envelope open, Darcy eagerly scanned the brief letter and her bowed shoulders lifted even as she read. 'He's not of British birth...and he has experience as a financial advisor—'

'Probably once worked as a bank clerk,' Karen slotted in, cynically unimpressed by the claim. A childless divorcee, Karen was comfortably off but had little faith in the reliability of the male sex.

'He's offering references upfront, which is more than anyone else did.' Darcy's state of desperation was betrayed by the optimistic look already blossoming in her expressive eyes. '*And* he's only thirty-one.'

'What nationality?'

In the act of frowning down at the totally illegible signature, Darcy raised her head again. 'He doesn't say. He just states that he is healthy and single and that a temporary position with accommodation included would suit him right now—'

'So he's unemployed and broke.'

'If he wasn't unemployed and willing to move in, he wouldn't be applying, Karen,' Darcy pointed out gently. 'It's a reasonable letter. Since he didn't know what the job was, he's sensibly confined himself to giving basic information only.'

As she paced the confines of Karen's tiny front room in the gate lodge five days later, Darcy pushed her thick-lensed spectacles up the bridge of her nose, smoothed her hands down over her pleated skirt and twitched at the roll collar of her cotton sweater as if it was choking her.

He would be here in five minutes. And she hadn't even managed to speak to the guy yet! Since he hadn't given her a phone number to contact him, she had had to write back to his London address and, nervous of giving out her own phone number at this stage, she had simply set up an interview and asked him to let her know if the date didn't suit. He had sent a brief note of confirmation, from which she had finally divined that his christian name appeared to be a surprisingly English-sounding Lucas, but as for his surname, she would defy a handwriting expert to read that swirling scrawl!

Hearing the roar of a motorbike out on the road, Darcy suppressed her impatience. Lucas was late. Maybe he wasn't going to show. But a minute later the door burst open. Karen poked her head in, her face filled with excitement. 'A monster motorbike just drew up…and this absolutely edible hunk of male perfection took off his helmet! It has to be Lucas…and Darcy, he is *gorgeous*—'

'He's come on a motorbike?' Darcy interrupted with a look of astonishment.

'You are *so* stuffy sometimes,' Karen censured. 'And I bet you a fiver you can't work up the nerve to ask this particular bloke if he'd be prepared to marry you for a fee!'

Darcy was already painfully aware that she had no choice whatsoever on that count. She *had* to ask. She was praying that Lucas, whoever he was and whatever he was like, would agree. She didn't have the time to readvertise. Her back was up against the wall. Yesterday she had received a letter from the company that held the mortgage on Fielding's Folly. They were threatening to repossess the house and, since she already had a big overdraft, the bank would not help without a guarantee that she would in the near future have the funds to settle her obligations.

Darcy winced as the doorbell shrilled. Karen bolted to answer it. Bolted—yes, that was the only possible word for her friend's indecent eagerness to reach the front door. Face wooden and set, Darcy positioned herself by the fireplace. So he was attractive. Attractive men had huge egos. She grimaced. All she wanted was someone ordinary and unobtrusive, but what she wanted she wouldn't necessarily get.

'Signorina Darcy?' she heard an accented drawl question in a tone of what sounded like polite surprise.

'No…she's, er, through here…er, waiting for you,' Karen stammered with a dismayingly girlish giggle, and the lounge door was thrust wide.

Blinking rapidly, Darcy was already glued to the spot, a deep frown-line bisecting her brow. That beautiful voice had struck such an eerie chord of familiarity she was transfixed, heart beating so fast she was convinced it might burst. And then mercifully she understood the source of that strange familiarity and shivered, thoroughly spooked. Dear heaven, he was Italian! It was that lyrical accent she had recognised, *not* the voice.

A very tall, dark male, sporting sunglasses and sheathed in motorbike leathers, strode into the small room. Involuntarily Darcy simply gaped at him, her every expectation shattered. Black leather accentuated impossibly wide shoulders, narrow hips and long, lean powerful thighs. Indeed the fidelity of fit left little of that overpoweringly masculine physique to the imagination. And the sunglasses lent his dark features an intimidating lack of expression. And yet…and *yet* as Darcy surveyed him with startled eyes she realised that he shared more than an accent with Zia's father. He had also been very tall and well-built.

So what? an irritated voice screeched through her blitzed brain. So you're meeting *another* tall, dark Italian…big deal! The silver-tongued sophisticate who had got her pregnant wouldn't have been caught dead in such clothing. And if she hadn't had such a guilt complex about her wanton behaviour in Venice, she wouldn't be feeling this incredibly foolish sense of threatening familiarity, she told herself in complete exasperation.

'Please excuse me for continuing to wear my sunglasses. I have been suffering from eye strain…the light, it hurts my eyes,' he informed her in a deep, dark drawl that was both well-modulated and unexpectedly quiet.

'Won't you sit down?' Darcy invited, with an un-
characteristically weak motion of one hand as she
forced herself almost clumsily down into a seat.

But then Darcy was in shock. She had hoped he
would be either sensible and serious or weak and bid-
dable. Instead she had been presented with a rampantly
macho male who roared up on a motorbike and wore
trousers so tight she marvelled that he could stand in
them, never mind sit down. With what she believed was
termed designer stubble on his aggressive jawline, he
looked about as domesticated and well-behaved as a
sabre-toothed tiger.

'If you will forgive me for saying so…you look at
me rather strangely,' he remarked, further disconcerting
her as he lowered himself down with indolent grace
onto the small sofa opposite her. 'Do I remind you of
someone, *signorina?*'

Darcy stiffened even more with nervous tension, and
she was already sitting rigid-backed in the seat. 'Not at
all,' she asserted with deflating conviction. 'Now, since
I'm afraid I couldn't read your signature…what is your
full name?'

'Let us leave it at Luca for now. The wording of your
ad suggested that the employment on offer could be of
a somewhat unusual nature,' he drawled softly. 'I would
like some details before we go any further.'

Darcy bristled like a cat stroked the wrong way. She
was supposed to be interviewing him, not the other way
round!

'After all, you have not given me your real name
either,' he pointed out in offensively smooth continuance.

Darcy's eyes opened to their fullest extent. 'I beg
your pardon?'

'Before I came down here, I checked you out. Your surname is Fielding, *not* Darcy, and you do *not* live here in this cottage; you live in the huge mansion at the top of the driveway,' he enumerated with unabashed cool. 'You have gone to some trouble to conceal your own identity. Naturally that is a source of concern to me.'

Stunned by that little speech, Darcy sprang upright and stared down at him in shaken disbelief, her angry bewilderment unconcealed. '*You* checked *me* out?'

He lifted a casual brown hand and slowly removed the sunglasses. 'The light is dim enough in here...'

He studied her with a curiously expectant quality of intensity.

And without warning Darcy found herself staring down into lustrous dark eyes fringed by glossy, spiky black lashes. He had the sort of eyes that packed a powerful punch. Gorgeous, she thought in helpless reaction, brilliant and dark as night, impenetrably deep and unreadable. With the sunglasses on he had looked as if he might be pretty good-looking, without them he zoomed up the scale to stunningly handsome, in spite of the fact that he badly needed a shave. And she now quite understood that hint of expectancy he betrayed. This was a guy accustomed to basking in female double takes, appreciative stares and inviting smiles.

But Darcy tensed and took an instantaneous step back, her retreat only halted by the armchair she had vacated. Yet the tiny twisting sensation of sudden excitement she had experienced still curled up deep in the pit of her taut stomach, and then pierced her like a knife with sudden shame. Her colour heightening, Darcy plotted her path out of the way of the armchair behind her, controlled solely by a need to put as much distance as possible between them.

Throughout that unchoreographed backing away process of hers, she was tracked by narrowed unflinchingly steady dark eyes. 'Signorina Fielding—'

'Look, you had no right to check me out…' Darcy folded her arms in a defensive movement. 'I guaranteed your privacy. Couldn't you have respected mine?'

'Not without some idea of what I might be getting into. It's standard business practice to make enquiries in advance of an interview.'

Darcy tore her frustrated gaze from his. Antipathy darted through her in a blinding wave. With difficulty, she held onto her ready temper. Possibly the reminder had been a timely one. It was, after all, a business proposition she intended to make. And this Luca might think he was clever, but she already knew he had to be as thick as two short planks, didn't she? Only a complete idiot would turn up for an interview with a woman unshaven and dressed like a Hell's Angel. A financial advisor? In his dreams! Conservative apparel went with such employment.

Bolstered by the belief that he could be no Einstein, and rebuking herself for having been intimidated by something as superficial and unimportant as his physical appearance, Darcy sat down again and linked her small hands tightly together on her lap. 'Right, let's get down to business, then…'

The waiting silence lay thick and heavy like a blanket. Settling back into the sofa in a relaxed sprawl of long, seemingly endless limbs, Luca surveyed her with unutterable tranquillity.

Her teeth gritted. Wondering just how long that laidback attitude would last, Darcy lifted her chin to a challenging angle. 'There *was* a good reason behind the offbeat ad I placed. But before I explain what that reason is, I should mention certain facts in advance. Should you agree to take the position on offer, you would be well paid even though there is no work involved—'

'*No* work involved?'

Darcy was soothed at receiving the exact response she had anticipated in that interruption. 'No work whatsoever,' she confirmed. 'While you were living in my home, your time would be your own, and at the end of your employment—assuming that you fulfil the terms to my satisfaction—I would also give you a generous bonus.'

'So what's the catch?' Luca prompted very softly. 'In return you ask me to do something illegal?'

A mortified flush stained Darcy's perfect skin. 'Of course not,' she rebutted tautly. 'The ''catch', if you choose to call it that, is that you would have to agree to marry me for six months!'

'To...*marry* you?' Luca stressed the word with a frown of wondering incredulity as he sat forward on the sofa. 'The employment you offer is...*marriage?*'

'Yes. It's really quite simple. I need a man to go through a wedding ceremony with me and behave like a husband for a minimum of six months,' Darcy extended, with the frozen aspect of a woman forcing herself to refer to an indecent act.

'Why?'

'Why? That's my business. I don't think you require that information to make a decision,' Darcy responded uncomfortably.

Lush black lashes semi-screened his dark eyes. 'I don't understand... Could you explain it again, *signorina,*' he urged, in a rather dazed undertone.

You certainly couldn't call him mentally agile, Darcy thought ruefully. Having got over the worst, however, she felt stronger, and all embarrassment had left her. He was still sitting there, and why shouldn't he be? If he was as single as he had said he was, he stood to earn a great deal for doing nothing. She repeated what she had already said and, convinced that the financial aspect would be the greatest persuader of all, she mentioned the monthly salary she was prepared to offer and then the sizeable bonus she would advance in return for his continuing discretion about their arrangement after they had parted.

He nodded, and then nodded again more slowly, still focusing with a slight frown on the worn carpet at his feet. Maybe the light was annoying his eyes, Darcy decided, struggling to hold onto her irritation at his torpid reactions. Maybe he was just gobsmacked by the concept of being paid to be bone idle. Or maybe he was so shattered by what she had suggested that he hadn't yet worked out how to respond.

'I would, of course, require references,' Darcy continued.

'I could not supply references as a husband...'

Darcy drew in a deep breath of restraint. 'I'm referring to character references,' she said drily.

'If you wanted a husband, why didn't you place an ad in the personal column?'

'I would have received replies from men interested in a genuine and lasting marriage.' Darcy sighed. 'It was wiser just to advertise my requirements as a form of employment—'

'Quiet...domesticated...well-behaved.'

'I don't want someone who's going to get under my feet or expect me to wait on him hand and foot. Would you say you were self-sufficient?'

'Si...'

'Well, then, what do you think?' Darcy demanded impulsively.

'I don't yet know what I think. I wasn't expecting this kind of proposal,' he returned gently. 'No woman has ever asked me to marry her before.'

'I'm not talking about a proper marriage. Obviously we'd separate after the six months was up and get a divorce. By the way, you would also have to sign a pre-nuptial contract,' Darcy added, because she needed to safeguard the estate from any claim an estranged husband might legitimately attempt to make. 'That isn't negotiable.'

Luca rose gracefully upright. 'I believe I would need a greater cash inducement to give up my freedom—'

'That's not a problem,' Darcy broke in, her tone one of eager reassurance on that point. If he was prepared to consider her proposition, she was keen to accommodate him. 'I'm prepared to negotiate. If you agree, I'll double the original bonus I offered.'

Disconcertingly, he didn't react to that impulsive offer. Darcy flushed then, feeling more than a little foolish.

Veiled dark eyes surveyed her. 'I'll think it over. I'll be in touch.'

'The references?'

'I will present them if I decide to accept the…the position.' As Luca framed the last two words a flash of shimmering gold illuminated his dark eyes. Amusement at the sheer desperation she had revealed in her desire to reach agreement with him? Darcy squirmed at the suspicion.

'I need an answer very soon. I have no time to waste.'

'I'll give you an answer tomorrow…' He strode to the door and then he hesitated, throwing her a questioning look over one broad masculine shoulder. 'It surprises me that you could not persuade a friend to agree to so temporary an arrangement.'

Darcy stiffened and coloured. 'In these particular circumstances, I prefer a stranger.'

'A stranger...I can understand that,' Luca completed in a honey-soft and smooth drawl.

CHAPTER TWO

'SO WHAT sort of impression did Lucas make on you?' Karen demanded, minutes later.

'It's not Lucas, it's Luca... My impression?' Darcy studied her friend with a frowning air of abstraction. 'That's the odd thing. I didn't really get a proper impression—at least not one I could hang onto for longer than five seconds,' she found herself admitting in belated recognition of the fact. 'One minute I thought he was all brawn and no brain, and then the next he would come out with something razor-sharp. And towards the end he was as informative as a brick wall.'

'He didn't accuse you of dragging him down here on false pretences? He didn't laugh like a drain? Or even ask if you were pulling his leg?' It was Karen's turn to look confused.

Darcy shook her head reflectively. 'He was very low-key in his reactions, businesslike in spite of the way he was dressed. That made it easier for me. I didn't get half as embarrassed as I thought I would.'

'Only you could conduct such a weird and loaded interview with a male that gorgeous and not respond on any more personal a level.'

'That kind of man leaves me cold.' But Darcy's cheeks warmed as she recalled that humiliating moment when she had reacted all too personally to the sheer male magnetism of those dark good looks.

Karen's keen gaze gleamed. 'He *didn't* leave you stone-cold...did he?'

Cursing her betrayingly fair skin, Darcy strove to continue meeting her friend's eyes levelly. 'Karen—'

'Forget it... I can tell a mile off when you're about to lie through your teeth!'

Darcy winced. 'OK...I noticed that Luca was reasonably fanciable—'

'Reasonably fanciable?' her friend carolled with extravagant incredulity.

'All right.' Darcy sighed in rueful surrender. 'He was spectacular...are you satisfied now?'

'Yes. Your indifference to men seriously worries me. Now at least I know that you're still in the land of the living.'

Darcy pulled a wry face. 'With my level of looks and appeal, indifference is by far the safest bet, believe me.'

Karen compressed her lips and thought with real loathing of all the people responsible for ensuring Darcy had such a low opinion of her own attractions. Her cold and critical father, her vain and sarcastic stepmother, not to mention the rejections her unlucky friend had suffered from the opposite sex during her awkward and vulnerable teen years. Being jilted at the altar and left to raise her child alone had completed the damage.

And these days Darcy dressed like a scarecrow and made little effort to socialise. Slowly and surely she was turning into a recluse, although the hours she slaved over that wretched house meant that she didn't know what free time was, Karen conceded grimly. Anyone else confronted with such an immense and thankless challenge would've given up and at least sold the furniture by now, but not Darcy. Darcy would starve sooner than see any more of the Folly's treasures go to auction.

'I get really annoyed with you when you talk like

that,' Karen said truthfully. 'If you would only buy some decent clothes and take a little more interest in—'

'Why bother when I'm quite happy as I am?' Visibly agitated by the turn the conversation had taken, Darcy glanced hurriedly at her watch and added with a relief she couldn't hide, 'It's time I picked up Zia from the playgroup.'

As Darcy left the gate lodge, however, that final dialogue travelled with her. Demeaning memories had been roused to fill her thoughts and unsettle her stomach. All over again she saw her one-time fiancé, Richard, gawping at her chief bridesmaid like a moonsick calf and finally admitting at the eleventh hour that he couldn't go through with the wedding because he had fallen in love with Maxie. And the ultimate insult had to be that her former friend, Maxie, who was so beautiful she could stop traffic, hadn't even *wanted* Richard!

That devastatingly public rejection had been followed by the Venetian episode, Darcy recalled wretchedly. That, too, had ended in severe humiliation. She had got to play Cinderella for a night. And then she had got to stand on the Ponte della Guerra and be stood up like a dumb teenager the following day. She had waited for ages too, and had hit complete rock-bottom when she finally appreciated that Prince Charming was not going to turn up.

Of course another woman, a more experienced and less credulous woman, would have known that that so casually voiced yet so romantic suggestion had been the equivalent of a guy saying he would phone you when he hadn't the slightest intention of doing so, only *she* hadn't recognised the reality. No, Darcy reflected with a stark shudder of remembrance, she had been much happier since she had given up on all that ghastly embarrassing and confusing man-woman stuff.

And if Luca, whoever he was, decided to go ahead and accept her proposition, she would soon be able to tune him and his macho motorbike leathers out entirely...

Perspiration beading her brow, Darcy wielded the heavy power-saw with the driven energy of necessity. The ancient kitchen range had an insatiable appetite for wood. Breathing heavily, she stopped to take a break. Even after switching off the saw, her ears still rang with the shattering roar of the petrol-driven motor. With a weary sigh, she bent and began laboriously stacking the logs into the waiting wheelbarrow.

'Darcy...?'

At the sound of that purring, accented drawl, Darcy almost leapt out of her skin, and she jerked round with a muttered exclamation. Luca stood several feet away. Her startled green eyes clung to his tall, outrageously masculine physique. Wide shoulders, sleek hips, long, long legs. *And* he had shaved.

One look at the to-die-for features now revealed in all their glory struck Darcy dumb. She wasn't even capable of controlling that reaction. In full daylight, he was so staggeringly handsome. High, chiselled cheekbones, sharp as blades, were dissected by an arrogant but classic nose and embellished by a wide, perfect mouth. Even his skin had that wonderful golden glowing vibrancy of warmer climes...

'Is there something wrong?' An equally shapely ebony brow had now quirked enquiringly.

'You startled me...' Heated colour drenching her skin as she realised that she had been staring, Darcy dragged her attention from him with considerable difficulty. As her dazed eyes dropped down, she blinked in disbelief at the sight of her cocker spaniels seated silently at his feet like the well trained dogs they unfortunately weren't. Strangers usually provoked Humpf and Bert into a positive frenzy of uncontrolled barking. Instead, her lovable but noisy animals were welded to the spot and throwing Luca upward pleading doggy glances as if he had cast some weird sort of hypnotic spell over them.

'I wasn't expecting you,' Darcy said abruptly.

'I did try the front entrance first...' His deep-pitched sexy drawl petered out as he studied the sizeable stack of wood. 'Surely you haven't cut all that on your own?'

Threading an even more self-conscious hand through the damp and wildly curling tendrils of hair clinging to her forehead, she nodded, aware of the incredulity in those piercing dark eyes.

'Are there no men around here?'

'No, I'm the next best thing...but then that's nothing new,' Darcy muttered half under her breath, writhing at her own undeniable awkwardness around men and hating him for surprising her when she wasn't psyched up to deal with him.

Forgivably thrown by that odd response, Luca frowned.

Darcy leapt straight back into speech. 'I assumed you would phone—'

'Nobody ever answers your phone.'

'I'm outdoors a lot of the time.' Stripping off her heavy gloves, Darcy flexed small and painfully stiff fingers and averted her scrutiny from him, her unease in his presence pronounced. What on earth was the matter with her? She was behaving like a silly teenager with a crush. 'You'd better come inside.'

Hurriedly grabbing up an armful of logs, Darcy led the way. The long, cobbled passageway that provided a far from convenient rear entrance to her home was dark and gloomy and flanked by a multitude of closed doors. Innumerable rooms which had once enjoyed specific functions as part of the kitchen quarters now lay unused. But not for much longer, she reminded herself. When she achieved her dream of opening up the house to the public all those rooms full of their ancient labour intensive equipment would fascinate children.

And she *was* going to achieve her dream, she told herself feverishly. Surely Luca wouldn't take the trouble to make a second personal appearance if he intended to say no?

She trod into the vast echoing kitchen and knelt down by the big range at the far end. Opening the door, she thrust a sizeable log into the fuel bed. 'Did you come all the way from London again?'

'No, I stayed in Penzance last night.'

Darcy was so rigid with nervous tension, she couldn't bring herself to look at him as she breathed tautly, 'So what's your answer?'

'Yes. My answer is *yes*,' he murmured with quiet emphasis.

Her strained eyes prickled with sudden tears and she blinked rapidly before slamming shut the door on the range. The relief was so immense she felt quite dizzy for a few seconds. Feeling as if a huge weight had dropped from her shoulders, Darcy scrambled upright and turned, a grateful smile on her now softened face. 'That's great...that's really great. Would you like some coffee?'

Lounging back against the edge of the giant scrubbed pine table, Luca stared back at her, not a muscle moving in his strong dark face. It was a rather daunting reaction and she swallowed hard, unaware that that shy and spontaneous air of sudden friendliness had disconcerted him.

'OK…why not?' he agreed, without any expression at all.

Darcy put on the kettle and stole an uneasy glance at him in the taut silence. She didn't know where the tension was coming from, and then she wondered if his brooding silence was a kind of male ego thing. 'I suppose this isn't quite the sort of work you were hoping to get,' she conceded awkwardly. 'But I promise you that you won't regret it. How long have you been unemployed?'

'Unemployed?' he echoed, strong features stiffening.

'Sorry, I just assumed—'

'I have never been employed in the UK.'

'Oh…' Darcy nodded slowly. 'So how long have you been over here?'

'Long enough…'

Darcy scrutinised that slightly downbent dark glossy head, taking in the faint darkening of colour over his sculpted cheekbones. He was embarrassed at his lack of success in the job market, she gathered, and she wished she had been a little less blunt in her questioning. But then tact had never been her strong point. And when she had interviewed him she had been so wrapped up in her own problems that it hadn't occurred to her that Luca must have been desperate to find a job to come so far out of London in answer to one small ad. Furthermore, now that she took a closer look at those leathers of his, she couldn't help but notice that they were pretty worn.

Sudden sympathy swept Darcy. She knew all about being broke and trying to keep up appearances. She had looked down on him for wearing motorbike gear to an interview, but maybe the poor guy didn't have much else to wear. If he hadn't worked since he had arrived in the UK, he certainly couldn't have financed much of a wardrobe. Smart suits cost money.

'I'll give you half your first month's salary in advance,' Darcy heard herself say. 'As a sort of retainer...'

This time he looked frankly startled.

'You probably think that's very trusting of me, but I tend to take people as I find them. In any case, I don't have a lot of choice *but* to trust you. If you were to get the chance of another job and decide to back out on me, I'd be in trouble,' she said honestly. 'How do you like your coffee?'

'Black...two sugars.'

Darcy put a pile of biscuits on a rather chipped plate. Setting the two beakers of coffee down on the table, she sat down and reached for the jotter and pencil lying there. 'I'd better get some details from you, hadn't I? What *is* your surname?'

There was a pause, a distinct pause as he sank lithely down opposite her.

'Raffacani...' he breathed.

'You'll need to spell that for me.'

He obliged.

Darcy bent industriously over the jotter. 'And Luca— is that your first and only other name? You see, I have to get this right for the vicar.'

'Gianluca...Gianluca Fabrizio.'

'I think you'd better spell all of it.' She took down his birthdate. Raffacani, she was thinking. Why did she have the curious sense that she had come across that name somewhere before? She shook her head. For all she knew Raffacani was as common a name in Italy as Smith was in England.

'Right,' she said then. 'I'll contact my solicitor, Mr Stevens. He's based in Penzance, so you can sign the pre-nuptial contract as soon as you like. Those references you offered...?'

From the inside of his jacket he withdrew a somewhat creased envelope. Struggling to keep up a businesslike attitude when she really just wanted to sing and dance round the kitchen with relief, Darcy withdrew the documents. There were two, one with a very impressive letterhead, but both were written in Italian. 'I'll hang onto these and study them,' she told him, thinking of the old set of foreign language dictionaries in the library. 'But I'm sure they'll be fine.'

'How soon do you envisage the marriage ceremony taking place?' Luca Raffacani enquired.

'Hopefully in about three weeks. It'll be a very quiet wedding,' Darcy explained rather stiffly, fixing her attention to the scarred surface of the table, her face turning pale and set. 'But as my father died this year that won't surprise anyone. It wouldn't be quite the thing to have a big splash.'

'You're not inviting many guests?'

'Actually...' Darcy breathed in deep, plunged into dismal recall of the huge misfired wedding which her father had insisted on staging three years earlier. 'Well, actually, I wasn't planning on inviting anybody,' she admitted tightly as she rose restively to her feet again.

'I'll show you where you'll be staying when you move in, shall I?'

At an infinitely more graceful and leisurely pace, Luca slid upright and straightened. Darcy watched in helpless fascination. His every movement had such…such *style,* an unhurried cool that caught the eye. He was so self-possessed, so contained. He was also very reserved. He gave nothing away. Well, would she have preferred a garrulous extrovert who asked a lot of awkward questions? Irritated by her own growing curiosity, Darcy left him to follow her out of the kitchen and tried to concentrate on more important things.

'What did you mean when you said you were the next best thing to a man around here?' Luca enquired on the way up the grand oak staircase.

'My father wanted a son, not a daughter—at least…not the kind of daughter I turned out to be.' As she spoke, Darcy was comparing herself to her stepsister. Morton Fielding had been utterly charmed by his second wife's beautiful daughter, Nina. Darcy had looked on in amazement as Nina twisted her cold and censorious parent round her little finger with ease.

'Your mother?'

'She died when I was six. I hardly remember her,' Darcy confided ruefully. 'My father remarried a few years later. He was desperate to have a male heir but I'm afraid it didn't happen.'

She cast open the door of a big dark oak-panelled bedroom, dominated by a giant Elizabethan four-poster. 'This will be your room. The bathroom's through that door. I'm afraid we'll have to share it. There isn't another one on this side of the house.'

As he glanced round the sparsely furnished and decidedly dusty room, which might have figured in a

Tudor time warp, Darcy found herself studying him
again. That stunningly male profile, the hard, sleek lines
of his muscular length. A tiny frisson of sexual heat
tightened her stomach muscles. He strolled with the
grace of a leopard over to the high casement window
to look out. Sunlight gleamed over his luxuriant black
hair. Unexpectedly he turned, dark eyes with the dramatic impact of gold resting on her in cool enquiry.

Caught watching him again, Darcy blushed as hotly
as an embarrassed schoolgirl. She was appalled by her
own outrageous physical awareness of him, could not
comprehend what madness was dredging such responses from her. Whirling round, she walked swiftly
back into the corridor.

As he drew level with her she snatched in a deep,
sustaining breath and started towards the stairs again.
'I'm afraid there are very few modern comforts in the
Folly, and locally, well, there's even fewer social out-
lets…' She hesitated uneasily before continuing, 'What
I'm really trying to say is that if you feel the need to
take off for the odd day in search of amusement, I'll
understand—'

'Amusement?' Luca prompted grimly, as if such a
concept had never come his way before.

Darcy nodded, staring stonily ahead. 'I'm one of
these people who always says exactly what's on their
mind. I live very quietly but I can't reasonably expect
you to do the same thing for an entire six months. I'm
sure you'll maybe want to go up to London occasionally
and—'

'Amuse myself?' Luca slotted in very drily.

In spite of her discomfiture, Darcy uttered a strained
little laugh. 'You can hardly bring a girlfriend here—'

'I do not have a woman in my life,' he interrupted, with a strong suggestion of gritted teeth.

'Possibly not at present,' Darcy allowed, wondering what on earth was the matter with him. He was reacting as if she had grossly insulted him in some way. 'But I'm being realistic. You're bound to get bored down here. City slickers do...'

Brilliant eyes black as jet stabbed into her. A line of dark colour now lay over his taut cheekbones. 'There will not be a woman nor any need for such behaviour on my part, I assure you,' he imparted icily.

They were descending the stairs when a tiny figure clad in bright red leggings and a yellow T-shirt appeared in the Great Hall below. 'Mummy!' Zia carrolled with exuberance.

As her daughter flashed over to eagerly show off a much creased painting, Luca fell still. Interpreting his silence as astonishment, Darcy flung him an apologetic glance as she lifted her daughter up into her arms. 'My daughter, Zia...I hadn't got around to mentioning her yet,' she conceded rather defensively.

Luca slid up a broad shoulder in an infinitesimal shrug of innate elegance. The advent of a stray cat might have inspired as much interest. Not a male who had any time for children, Darcy gathered, resolving to ensure that her playful and chatty toddler was kept well out of his path.

'Is there anything else you wish to discuss?' Luca prompted with faint impatience.

Darcy stiffened. Minutes later, she had written and passed him the cheque she had promised. He folded the item and tucked it into his inside pocket with complete cool. 'I'll drop you a note as soon as I get the date of the ceremony organised. I won't need to see you again before that,' she told him.

Luca printed a phone number on the front of the jotter she had left lying. 'If you need to contact me for any other reason, leave a message on that line.'

A fortnight later, Darcy unbolted the huge front door of the Folly and dragged it open, only to freeze in dismay.

'About time too,' Margo Fielding complained sharply as she swept past, reeking of expensive perfume and irritation, closely followed by her daughter, Nina.

Aghast at the unforewarned descent of her stepmother and her stepsister, Darcy watched with a sinking heart as the tall, beautiful blonde duo stalked ahead of her into the drawing room.

She hadn't laid eyes on either woman since they had moved out after her father's funeral, eager to leave the privations of country life behind them and return to city life. The discovery that Darcy could not be forced to sell the Folly and share the proceeds with them had led to a strained parting of the ways. Although Morton Fielding had generously provided for his widow, and Margo was a wealthy woman in her own right, her stepmother had been far from satisfied.

Margo cast her an outraged look. 'Don't you think you should've told me that you were getting married?' she demanded as she took up a painfully familiar bullying stance at the fireplace. 'Can you imagine how I felt when a friend called me to ask *who* you were marrying and I had to confess my ignorance? How dare you embarrass me like that?'

Darcy was very tense, her tummy muscles knotting up while she wondered how on earth the older woman had discovered her plans. The vicar's wife could be a bit of a gossip, she conceded, and Margo still had friends locally. No doubt that was how word had travelled farther afield at such speed. 'I'm sorry...I would've informed you after the wedding—'

Nina's scornful blue eyes raked over the younger woman. 'But of course, *when* it's safely over. You're terrified that your bridegroom will bolt last minute, like Richard did!'

At that unpleasant and needless reminder, which was painfully apt, the embarrassed colour drained from Darcy's taut cheekbones. 'I—'

'Just when I thought you must finally be coming to your senses and accepting the need to sell this white elephant of a house, you suddenly decide to get married,' Margo condemned with stark resentment. 'Is *he* even presentable?'

'With all this heavy secrecy, it's my bet that the groom is totally *un*presentable...one of the estate workers?' Nina suggested, with a disdainful little shudder of snobbish distaste.

'You're not pregnant again, are you?' Margo treated Darcy to a withering and accusing appraisal. 'That's what people are going to think. And I *refuse* to have my acquaintances view me as some sort of wicked stepmother! So you'll have to pay for a proper wedding reception and I'll act as your hostess.'

'I'm afraid I haven't got the money for that,' Darcy admitted tightly.

'What about *him?*' Nina pressed instantaneously.

Darcy flushed and looked away.

'Penniless, I suppose.' Reaching that conclusion, Margo exchanged a covert look of relief and satisfaction with her daughter. 'I do hope he's aware that when you go bust here, we're entitled to a slice of whatever is left.'

'I'm not planning to go bust,' Darcy breathed, her taut fingers clenching in on themselves.

'I'm just dying to meet this character.' Nina giggled. 'Who is he?'

'His name's Luca—'

'What kind of a name is that?' her stepmother demanded.

'He's Italian,' Darcy confided grudgingly.

'An immigrant?' Nina squealed, as if that was the funniest thing she had ever heard. 'I do hope he's not marrying you just to get a British passport!'

'I'll throw a small engagement party for you this weekend in Truro,' Margo announced grandly with a glacial smile. 'I will not have people say that I didn't at least *try* to do my duty by my late husband's child.'

'That's very kind of you,' Darcy mumbled, after a staggered pause at the fact that Margo was prepared to make so much effort on her behalf. 'But—'

'No buts, Darcy. Everyone knows how eccentric you are, but I will not allow you to embarrass me in front of my friends. I will expect you and your fiancé at eight on Friday, *both* of you suitably dressed. And if he's as hopeless as you are in polite company, tell him to keep his mouth shut and just smile.'

Her expectations voiced, Margo was already sweeping out to the hall. Darcy unfroze and sped after her. 'But Luca…Luca's got other arrangements for that night!' she lied in a frantic rush.

'Saturday, then,' Margo decreed instead.

Darcy's tremulous lips sealed again. How could she refuse to produce her supposed fiancé without giving the impression that there was something most peculiar about their relationship? She should never have practised such secrecy, never have surrendered to her own shrinking reluctance to make any form of public appearance with a man in tow. In her position, she couldn't afford to arouse suspicion that there was anything strange about her forthcoming marriage.

'I'm so glad you've finally found yourself a man.' Nina dealt her a pitying look of superiority. 'What does he do for a living?'

Darcy hesitated. She just couldn't bring herself to admit that Luca was unemployed. 'He...he works in a bank.'

'A clerk...how *sweet*. Love blossomed over the counter, did it?'

Utterly drained, and annoyed that she had allowed her stepmother to reduce her yet again to a state of dumbstruck inadequacy, Darcy stood as the two women climbed into their sleek, expensive BMW and drove off without further ado.

'Luca, haven't you got *any* of my other messages? I realise that this is terribly short notice, but I do really *need* you to show up with me at this party in Truro...er...our engagement party,' Darcy stated apologetically to the answering machine which greeted her for the frustrating fourth time at the London number he had left with her. 'This is an emergency. Saturday night at eight. Could you get in touch, please?'

'The toad's done a bunk on you with that cheque!' Karen groaned in despair. 'I don't know why you agreed to this party anyway. Margo and Nina have to be up to something. They've never done you a favour in their lives. And if Luca fails to show up, those two witches will have a terrific laugh at your expense!'

'There's still twenty-four hours to go. I'm sure I'll hear from him soon,' Darcy muttered fiercely, refusing to give up hope as she hugged Zia, grateful for the comforting warmth of her sturdy little body next to her own.

'Darcy...you have written to him as well. He is obviously not at home and if he is home, he's ignoring you—'

'I don't think he's like that, Karen,' Darcy objected, suddenly feeling more than a little irritated with her friend for running Luca down and forecasting the worst. From what she had contrived to roughly translate of her future husband's references, one of which was persuasively written by a high court judge, she was dealing with a male of considerable integrity and sterling character.

Late that night the frustratingly silent phone finally rang and Darcy raced like a maniac to answer it. *'Yes?'* she gasped with breathless hope into the receiver.

'Luca... I got your messages this evening—all of them.'

'Oh, thank heaven...thank heaven!' Just hearing the intensely welcome sound of that deep, dark accented drawl, Darcy went weak at the knees. 'I was starting to think I was going to have to ring my stepmother and say you'd come down with some sudden illness! She would've been absolutely furious. We've never been close, and I certainly didn't want this wretched party, but it is pretty decent of her to offer, isn't it?'

'I'm afraid we have one slight problem to overcome,' Luca slotted softly into that flood of relieved explanation. 'I'm calling from Italy.'

'Italy...?' Darcy blinked rapidly, thoroughly thrown

by the announcement. *'It-Italy?'* she stammered in horror.

'But naturally I will do my utmost to get back in time for the party,' Luca assured her in a tone of cool assurance.

Darcy sighed heavily then, unsurprised by his coolness. What right did she have to muck up his arrangements? This whole mess wasn't his fault, it was hers. After all, she had told him she wouldn't need to see him again before the wedding. Obviously he had used the money she had given him to travel home and see his family. 'I'm really sorry about this,' she said tiredly, the stress of several sleepless nights edging her voice. 'Look, *can* you make it?'

'With the best will in the world, not to the party before nine in the evening…unless you want to meet me there?' he suggested.

Aghast at the idea of arriving alone, Darcy uttered an instant negative.

'Then offer my apologies to your stepmother. I'll come and pick you up.'

Darcy told herself that she was incredibly lucky that Luca was willing to come back from Italy to attend the party at such short notice. 'I really appreciate this…look, you can stay here on Saturday night,' she offered gratefully. 'I'll make up the bed for you.'

'That's extraordinarily kind of you, Darcy,' Luca drawled smoothly.

CHAPTER THREE

Zia was spending the night with Karen in the gatehouse. Returning to the Folly to nervously await Luca's arrival, Darcy caught an unsought glimpse of her reflection in the giant mirror in the echoing hall…

And suddenly she was wishing she had spent money she could ill afford on a new outfit. The brown dress hung loose round her hips and flapped to an indeterminate length below her knees. The ruffled neckline, once chosen to conceal the embarrassing smallness of her breasts, looked fussy and old-fashioned. She was much more comfortable in trousers—never had had much luck in choosing clothes that flattered her slight and diminutive frame…

And in the back of her wardrobe the green designer evening dress which had been Maxie's wedding present three years earlier still hung, complete with shoes and delicate little beaded bag. Maxie, no longer a friend and always rather too reserved and too confident of her feminine attraction for Darcy to feel quite comfortable in her radius. As for the dress, Darcy hadn't looked near it once since her return from Venice. She needed no reminder of that night of explosive passion in a stranger's arms. Yet somehow she still hadn't been able to bring herself to dispose of that exquisite gown which had lent her the miraculous illusion of beauty for a few brief hours.

The Victorian bell-pull shrieked complaint in the piercing silence, springing Darcy out of a past that still felt all too recent and all too wounding. In haste, she yanked open the heavy door. There she stopped dead at the sight of Luca, her witch-green eyes widening to their fullest extent in unconcealed surprise.

He was wearing a supremely elegant black dinner jacket when she hadn't dared even to ask if he possessed such an article. And there he stood, proud black head high, strong dark face assured, one lean brown hand negligently thrust into the pocket of narrow black trousers to tighten them over his lean hips and long powerful thighs, his beautifully tailored jacket parted to reveal a pristine white pleated dress shirt. He looked so incredibly sophisticated and gorgeous he stole the breath from Darcy's convulsing throat.

'Gosh, you hired evening dress,' she mumbled, relocating her vocal cords with difficulty.

Luca ran brilliant dark eyes over her, a distinct frown-line drawing together his ebony brows. 'Possibly I'm slightly over-dressed for the occasion?'

'No...no...not at all.' Never more self-conscious than when her personal appearance was under scrutiny, Darcy flushed to the roots of her hair. Her attention abruptly fell on the glossy scarlet Porsche sitting parked beside the ancient Land Rover which was her only means of transport. 'Where on earth did you get that car?' she gasped helplessly.

'It's on loan.'

Slowly, Darcy shook her curly auburn head. It would be madness to turn up in an expensive car and give a false impression of Luca's standing in the world. Margo would ask five hundred questions and soon penetrate the truth. Then Luca, who could only have borrowed the car for her benefit—and she couldn't help but be touched by that realisation—would end up feeling cut off. 'I would really love to roar up in the Porsche, but it would be wiser to use the Land Rover,' she told him in some disappointment.

'*Dio mio*…you are joking, of course.' Luca surveyed the rusting and battered four-wheel drive with outright incredulity. 'It's a wreck.'

Darcy opened the door of the Land Rover. 'I do know what I'm talking about, Luca,' she warned. 'If we show up in the Porsche, my stepmother will get entirely the wrong idea and decide that you're loaded. If we're anything less than honest, we'll both be left sitting with egg on our faces. We want to blend in, not create comment, and that car must be worth about thirty thousand—'

'Seventy.'

'*Seventy* thousand pounds?' Darcy broke in, her disbelief writ large in her shaken face.

'And some change,' Luca completed drily.

'Wish I had a friend willing to trust me with a car like that! We'll park the Land Rover out on the road and run away from it fast,' Darcy promised, worriedly examining her watch and then climbing into the driver's seat to forestall further argument. 'I'd let you drive, but this old girl has a number of idiocyncrasies which might irritate you.'

'This is ridiculous,' Luca swung into the tatty passenger seat with pronounced reluctance, his classic profile hard as a granite cliff in winter.

As she stole a second glance at that hawkish masculine profile, Darcy found herself thinking that he had a kind of Heathcliffish rough edge when he was angry.

And he *was* definitely angry, and she didn't mind in the slightest. It made him seem far more human. Posh cars and men and their egos, she reflected with sudden good cheer. Even *she* understood that basic connection. 'Believe me, you're about to cause enough of a stir tonight. You're very good-looking...'

'Am I really?' Luca prompted rather flatly.

'Oh, come on, no false modesty. I bet you've been breaking hearts from the edge of the cradle!' Darcy riposted with a rueful sound of amusement.

'You're very frank.'

'In that garb you look like you just strolled in off a movie set,' Darcy reeled off, trying to work herself up to giving the little speech she had planned. 'Do you think you could contrive to act like you're keen on me tonight? No...no, don't say anything,' she urged with a distinctly embarrassed laugh. 'It's just that nobody can smell a rat faster than Margo or Nina, and you are not at all what they are primed to expect.'

'What are they expecting?'

'Some ordinary boring guy who works in a bank.'

'Where do you get the idea that bankers are boring?'

'My bank manager could bore for Britain. Every time I walk into his office, he acts like I'm there to steal from him. That man is just such a pessimist,' Darcy rattled on, grateful to have got over the hint about him acting keen without further discussion. It was so unbelievably embarrassing to have to ask a man to put on such a pretence. 'When he tells me the size of my overdraft, he even reads out the pence owing to make me squirm—'

'You have an overdraft?'

'It's not as bad as it sounds. The day we get married, I will have some really good news for my bank manager...at least I hope he thinks it's good news, and loosens the purse-strings a little.' She shot him an apprehensive glance, wishing she hadn't allowed nervous tension to tempt her into such dangerous candour. 'Don't worry, if the worst comes to the worst, I could always sell something to keep the bank quiet. I made a commitment to you and I won't let you down.'

'I'm impressed. Tell me, have you thought of a cover story for this evening?' Luca enquired with some satire.

'Cover story?'

'Where and how we met, et cetera, et cetera.'

'Of course,' she said in some surprise. 'We'll say we met in London. I haven't been there in over a year, but they're not likely to know that. I want to give the impression that we've plunged into one of those sudden whirlwind romances and then, when we split up, nobody will be the slightest bit surprised.'

'I see you're wearing a ring.'

'It's on loan, like your Porsche. We can't act engaged without a ring.' Darcy had borrowed the diamond dress ring from Karen for the evening, and her finger had been crooked ever since it went on because it was a size too big and she was totally terrified of losing it.

'Don't you think you ought to fill me in on a few background details on your family? My younger sister is the only close relative I have,' he revealed. 'She's a student.'

'Oh…right. My stepmother, Margo, was first married to a wealthy businessman with one foot in the grave. They had a daughter, Nina, who's a model,' she shared. 'Margo married my father for social position; he married her in the hope of having a son. Dad was always very tight with money, but Margo and Nina could squeeze juice out of a dehydrated lemon. He was extremely generous to them. That's one of the reasons the estate is in such a mess…I inherited the mess and a load of death duties.'

'Very succinct,' Luca responded with a slight catch in his voice.

'Margo and Nina are frantic snobs. They spend the summer in Truro and the rest of the year in their London apartment. Margo doesn't like me but she loves throwing parties, and she is very, very conscious of what other people think.'

'Are you?'

'Good heavens, no, as an unmarried mother, I can hardly afford to be!'

'I think I should at least know the name of the father of your child,' Luca remarked.

The silence in the car became electric. Darcy accelerated down the road, small hands clenching the steering wheel tightly. 'On that point, I'm afraid I've never gratified anyone's curiosity,' she said stiffly, and after that uncompromising snub the silence lasted all the way to Truro.

Some distance from her stepmother's large detached home, which was set within its own landscaped grounds on the outskirts of town, Darcy nudged her vehicle into a space. And only with difficulty. They walked up the sweeping drive and Darcy's heart sank as she took in the number of cars already parked. 'I think there's going to be a lot more people here than I was led to expect. If anyone asks too many probing questions, pretend your English is lousy,' she advised nervously.

'I believe I will cope.' Luca curved a confident hand over her tense spine. Her flesh tingled below the thin fabric of her dress and she shivered. He bent his glossy dark head down almost to her level, quite a feat with the difference in their heights. The faint scent of some citrus-based lotion flared Darcy's sensitive nostrils. Her breath tripping in her throat, she collided with deep, dark flashing eyes and her stomach turned a shaken somersault in reaction.

'*Per meraviglia…*' Luca breathed with deflating cool and impatience. 'Will you at least smile as if you're happy? And stop hunching your shoulders like that. Walk tall!'

Plunged back to harsh reality with a jolt, her colour considerably heightened, Darcy might have made a pithy retort had not Margo's housekeeper swept open the door for their entrance.

And entrance it certainly was. Margo and Nina were in the hall, chatting in a group. Their eyes flew to Darcy, and then straight past her to the tall, spectacularly noticeable male by her side. Her stepmother and her stepsister stilled in astonishment and simply stared. Suddenly Darcy was wickedly amused. Luca was undeniably presentable. How unexpectedly sweet it was to surprise the two women whose constant criticisms and cutting comments had made her teenage years such a misery.

Retaining that light hold on her, Luca carried her forward.

'Darcy…Luca,' Margo said rather stiltedly.

After waiting in vain for Darcy to make an introduction, Luca advanced a hand and murmured calmly, 'Luca Raffacani, Mrs Fielding…I'm delighted to meet you at last.'

'Margo, *please,*' her stepmother gushed.

Nina hovered in a revealing little slip dress, her beautiful face etched with a rigid smile while her pale blue eyes ran over Luca as if he was a large piece of her own lost property. 'I'm surprised…you don't look remotely like Richard,' she remarked. 'I was so sure you'd be horsy and hearty. Darcy always did go for the outdoor type.'

'Richard?' Luca queried.

'Oh, dear, I do hope I haven't been indiscreet,' Nina murmured with a little moue of fake dismay. 'Sorry, but I naturally assumed you would know that Darcy was engaged once before—'

'Left at the altar too. A ghastly business altogether. That's why it's so wonderful to see you happy now, Darcy!' Margo continued.

Darcy cringed as if her dress had fallen off in public, unable to look anywhere near Luca to see how he was reacting to this humiliating information. Her stepmother took advantage of her disconcertion to rest a welcoming hand on Luca's sleeve and neatly impose herself between them.

'Oh, do let us see the ring,' Nina trilled.

Darcy extended her hand. An insincere chorus of compliments followed.

They moved into a large reception room which was filled to the gills with chattering, elegantly dressed people. Margo turned to address Luca in a confidential aside. 'I'm really hoping that marriage will give Darcy something more to think about than that pile of bricks and mortar she's so obsessively attached to. What *do* you think of Fielding's Folly, Luca?'

'It's Darcy's home and of obvious historic interest—'

'But such a dreadful ceaseless drain on one's financial resources, and a simply *huge* responsibility. You'll soon find that out,' Margo warned him feelingly. 'Worry drove my poor husband to an early death. It's always the same with these old families. Land-rich, cash-poor. Morton was almost as stubborn as Darcy, but

I don't think he ever dreamt that she would go to such nonsensical lengths to try and hang on to the estate—'

'I don't think we need to discuss this right now,' Darcy broke in tautly.

'It has to be said, darling, and your fiancé *is* part of the family now,' her stepmother pointed out loftily. 'After all, I'm only thinking of your future, and Luca does have a right to know what he's getting into. No doubt you've given him a *very* rosy picture, and really that's not very fair—'

'Not at all. I have an excellent understanding of how matters stand on the estate,' Luca inserted with smiling calm as he eased away from the older woman and extended a hand to Darcy, closing long fingers over hers to tug her close again, as if he couldn't quite bear to be physically separated from her.

'That's right. You work in the financial field,' Nina commented with a look of amusement. 'I can hardly believe you're only a bank clerk...'

'Neither can I. Darcy...what *have* you been telling this family of yours?' Luca scolded with a husky laugh of amusement. 'Pressure of work persuaded me to take what you might call a sabbatical here in the UK. Meeting Darcy, a woman so very much after my own heart, was a quite unexpected bonus.'

'How on earth *did* you meet?'

'I'm not sure I should tell you...' Luca responded in a teasing undertone.

'Feel free,' Darcy encouraged, already staggered by the ease with which he was entertaining and dealing with Margo and Nina. Yet he had been so very, very quiet with her. But then why was she surprised at that? Her soft mouth tightened. Here he was with two lovely, admiring women hanging on his very word; quite naturally he was opening up and no longer either bored and impatient.

'OK. It happened in London. She reversed into my car and then got out and shouted at me. I really appreciate a woman with that much nerve!' Luca divulged playfully, and Darcy's bright head flew up in shock. 'You do everything behind the wheel at such frantic speed, don't you, *cara mia?* I wanted to strangle her, and then I wanted to kiss her...'

'Which did you do?' Darcy heard herself prompt, unnerved by his sheer inventiveness.

'I believe *some* things should remain private...' To accompany that low-pitched and sensually suggestive murmur, Luca ran a long brown forefinger along her delicate jawbone in a glancing caress. Darcy gazed up at him, all hot pink and overpowered, every muscle in her slender length tensing. Her tender flesh stung in the wake of that easy touch, leaving her maddeningly, insanely aware of his powerful masculinity.

'To think I used to believe my little stepsister was painfully shy,' Nina breathed, fascinated against her will by this show of intimacy.

'Hardly, when she's already the mother of a noisy toddler,' Margo put in cuttingly. 'Do you like children, Luca?'

'I *adore* them,' he drawled, with positive fervour.

'How wonderful,' Margo said rather weakly, having shot her last bitchy bolt and found him impregnable. 'Let me introduce you to our guests, Luca. Don't be so possessive, Darcy. Do let go of the poor man for a second.'

Darcy yanked her hand from Luca's sleeve. She hadn't even realised she had been hanging onto him. Feeling slightly disorientated, she watched as he deftly reached for the glasses of champagne offered by one of the catering staff.

She studied those lean brown hands, the beautifully shaped long fingers and polished nails. She recalled the smoothness of that fingertip dancing along her oversensitive jawbone, sending tiny little tremors down her rigid spine with an innate sensuality that mesmerised. And for the shocking space of one crashing heartbeat, as she met those astonishing dark golden eyes in concert, there had been nobody and nothing else in the room for her.

'You're not making much effort, are you?' Luca gritted in her ear.

'I never challenge Margo if I can help it,' she whispered back. 'She fights back with my most embarrassing moments. I learnt that lesson years ago.'

'Strange…you didn't strike me as a woman who lies down to get kicked.'

Darcy flinched at that damning retaliation. 'Excuse me,' she muttered, and hurried off into the cool of the less crowded hall.

'You won't hold onto that guy for ten seconds,' a sharp voice forecast nastily from the rear. 'I can't think what he imagines he sees in you, but he'll soon find out he's made a big mistake.'

Darcy swung round to face her stepsister. 'Time will no doubt tell.'

'Luca's not even your type,' Nina snapped resentfully. 'How long do you think you're likely to hold off the opposition? He doesn't look dirt-poor to me either. I know clothes, and what he's wearing did not come out of any charity shop.'

'Luca likes to dress well.' Darcy shrugged.

'A peacock with a dull little peahen fluttering in his

wake?' Nina sneered. 'He'll soon be out looking for more excitement. No, if there's one thing I'm convinced of now that I've seen him, it's that he's playing a double game. It *has* to be the British passport he's after...why else would he be marrying you?'

Why else? Darcy repeated inwardly as Nina stalked off again. What a huge laugh Margo and Nina would have were they ever to discover that Luca was no more than a somewhat unusual paid employee, prepared to act out a masquerade for six months. And every word her stepsister had spoken was painfully true. In the normal way of things a male of Luca's ilk would *not* have looked at her twice.

'Darcy...' Luca was poised several feet away, a slanting smile for show on his beautiful mouth and exasperation glittering in his deep-set dark eyes. 'I wondered where you had got to.'

He could act. Dear heaven, but he could act, Darcy found herself acknowledging over the next few hours. He kept her beside him, dragged her into the conversation and paid her every possible attention. Yet increasingly Darcy became more occupied in watching and listening to *him*.

In vain did she strive to recapture the image of the far from chatty male in motorbike leathers. For Luca Raffacani appeared to be a chameleon. With the donning of that dinner jacket, he appeared to have slid effortlessly into a new persona.

Now she saw a male possessed of a startling degree of sophistication and supremely at his ease in social company. He was adroit at sidestepping too personal enquiries. He was cool as ice, extremely witty and, she began to think, almost frighteningly clever. And other people were equally impressed. He gathered a crowd. Far from blending in, Luca commanded attention.

At one in the morning, he walked her into the conservatory, where several couples were dancing, and complained, 'You've been incredibly quiet.'

'And you're surprised?' Darcy stared up at him and stepped back. In the dim light, his lean, dark face had a saturnine quality. Brilliant eyes raked over her as keen and sharp as laser beams. 'You're like Jekyll and Hyde. I feel like I don't know you at all—'

'You don't,' Luca agreed.

'And yet you don't quite fit in here either,' she murmured uncertainly, speaking her thoughts out loud and yet unable to properly put them together. 'You stand out too much somehow.'

'That's your imagination talking,' Luca asserted with a smoky laugh as he encircled her with his arms.

He curved his palm to the base of her spine and drew her close. Her breasts rubbed against his shirt-front. A current of heat darted through her and she felt her nipples spring into murderously tight and prominent buds. She went rigid with discomfiture. 'Relax,' he urged from above her head. 'Margo is watching. We're supposed to be lovers, not strangers…'

The indefinable scent of him engulfed her. Clean and warm and very male. She quivered, struggling to loosen her taut muscles and shamefully aware of every slight movement of his big, powerful body. She wanted to sink in to the hard masculinity of him, but she held herself back, and in so doing missed a step. To compensate, he had to bring her even closer.

'I'm not a great dancer,' she muttered in a mortified apology.

'*Dio mio*…you move like air in my arms,' he countered.

And in his arms, amazingly, she did, absorbed as one into the animal grace and natural rhythm with which he whirled her round the floor. It was like flying, she thought dreamily, and the reflection could only rekindle a fairy tale memory of dancing on a balcony high above the Grand Canal in Venice. No wrong steps, no awkwardness, no need even for conversation—just the sheer joy of moving in perfect synchronisation with the music.

'You dance like a dream,' she whispered breathlessly in the split second after the music stopped, and she found herself as someone unwilling to awake from that dream, plastered as surely as melted cheese on toast to every abrasive angle of his lean, hard body.

Somehow her arms had crept up round his neck, and her fingers were flirting deliciously with his thick silky black hair. Unnaturally still now, she gazed up at him, green eyes huge pools of growing confusion. Dear heaven, those eyes of his. Even semi-screened with luxuriant black lashes, their impact was animal direct and splinteringly sensual.

As his arrogant dark head lowered, her breath feathered in her throat. But she was still stunned when he actually kissed her. He parted her lips with his and took her soft mouth with a driving, hungry assurance that blistered through every shocked atom of her being with the efficiency of a lightning bolt. In the very act of detaching her fingers from his hair she clung instead, clung to stay upright, vaguely attached to planet earth even though she was no longer aware of its existence.

Heat engulfed her sensation-starved body, swelling her breasts, pinching her nipples into distended prominence and sending a flash-flood of fire cascading down between her quivering thighs. As his tongue searched out the yielding tender sensitivity of her mouth, raw excitement scorched to such heights inside her she was convinced she was burning alive.

Luca lifted his hips from hers, surveyed her blitzed expression and dealt her a curiously hard but amused look. 'Time to leave,' he informed her lazily. 'I believe we've played our part well enough to satisfy.'

As Luca spun her under the shelter of one seemingly possessive arm and walked her off the floor, Darcy was in shock. Her legs no longer felt as if they belonged to the rest of her, and she was still struggling to breath at a normal rate. In the aftermath of that passionate kiss she was a prey to conflicting and powerful reactions, the craziest of which was the momentary insane conviction that Luca and Zia's father could only be one and the same man!

Oh, dear heaven, how could she have forgotten herself to that extent? And the answer came back. He kissed like Zia's father. Earthquake-force seduction. Smooth as glass. Going for the kill like a hitman, faster on his feet than a jump-jet. She was devastated by the completeness of her own surrender, and utterly dumbfounded by that weird sense of the familiar which afflicted her, that crazy paranoiac sense of *déjà vu...*

For her Venetian lover had known nothing about her and could never have discovered her identity. Her secrecy that night had been more than a game she'd played to tantalise. She had been honestly afraid that reality would destroy the magic. After all, he had been attracted by a woman who didn't really exist. And his uninterest in further contact had been more than adequately proven when he'd left her standing on the Ponte della Guerra the following day!

Yet only he and Luca had ever had such an effect on her, awakening a shameless brand of instant overpowering lust that sent every nerve-ending and hormone into overdrive and paid not the slightest heed to self-control or moral restraint. She breathed in deep to steady herself.

Maybe all Italian men learned to kiss like that in their teens, she told herself grimly. Maybe she was just a complete push-over for Italian men—at least those of the tall, dark, well-built and sensationally desirable variety. Maybe living like a nun and refusing to recognise that she might *have* physical needs had made her a degradingly easy mark for any male with the right sensual technique.

But what was technique without chemistry? she asked herself doggedly. It was pathetic for her to try and deny one minute longer that she was wildly, dangerously attracted to Luca Raffacani. For what pride had refused to face head-on, her own body had just proved with mortifying eagerness.

As Luca thanked her stepmother for the party, Margo gave Darcy's hot cheeks a frozen look while Nina surveyed her stepsister as if she had just witnessed a poor, defenceless man being brutally attacked by a sexually starved woman. Darcy's farewells were incoherent and brief.

The night air hit her like a rejuvenating bucket of cold water. 'We've played our part well enough to satisfy,' Luca had said, only minutes earlier. At that recollection Darcy now paled and stiffened, as if she had been slapped in the face.

Naturally that kiss had simply been part of the masquerade. He had been *acting*. Acting as if he was attracted to her, in love with her, on the very brink of marrying her. Oh, dear heaven, had he guessed? Did he for one moment suspect that *she* hadn't been acting? How much could a man tell from one kiss? As kisses went, her response had been downright encouraging. Her self-respect cowered at that acknowledgement.

'That went off OK,' Luca drawled with distinct satisfaction.

'Yes, you were marvellous,' Darcy agreed, struggling to sound breezy, approving and grateful, and instead sounding as if each individual word had been wrenched from her at gun-point. 'The kiss was a real bull's-eye clincher too. Strikes me you could make a fortune as a gigolo!'

With a forced laugh, she trod ahead of him, valiantly fighting to control her growing sense of writhing mortification.

'Say that again...'

Stalking rigid-backed down the pavement, Darcy slung another not very convincing laugh over her shoulder. 'Well, you've got everything going for you in that line,' she told him with determined humour. 'The look, the charm, the patter, the screen-kiss technique. If I was some fading lonely lady with nothing but my money to keep me warm, I would've been swept off my feet in there!'

Without warning, a shockingly powerful hand linked forcibly with hers and pulled her round to face him again. Startled, Darcy looked up and clashed with blazing golden eyes as enervating as a ten-ton truck bearing down on her shrinking length.

'*Porca miseria!*' Luca growled in outrage. 'You compare me to a gigolo?'

Genuinely taken aback by that reaction, Darcy gawped at him. And then the penny dropped. Considering the monetary aspect of their private arrangement, her lack of tact now left her stricken. 'Oh, no, I never thought... I mean, I really *didn't* mean—'

'That I am a man who would sell himself for money?' Luca incised in a raw tone that told her he took himself very seriously.

Darcy was so appalled by her own thoughtlessness that her hand fluttered up between them to pluck apologetically at his lapel and then smooth it down again. 'Luca...*honestly*, I was just trying to be funny—'

'Ha...ha,' Luca breathed crushingly. 'Give me the car keys.'

'The—?'

'You've had too much champagne.'

Darcy had had only a single glass. But out of guilt over her undiplomatic tongue, she handed over the keys. He swung into the driver's seat.

'You'll need directions.'

'I have total recall of our death-defying journey here.'

She let that comment on her driving ability go unchallenged. She did drive pretty fast. And in three days' time they needed to get married. There was now some source of relief in the awareness that the marriage would be a fake. He had no sense of humour and a filthy temper. Even worse, he brooded. She stole a covert glance at his hard, dark chiselled profile...but, gosh, he *still* looked spectacular!

In the moonlight, she averted her attention from him, torn with shame at that betraying response. Deep in the pit of her taut belly, she felt a surge of guilty heat, and was appalled by the immediacy of that reaction. He reminded her of Zia's father...was that the problem? She shook her head and studied her tightly linked hands, but although she tried to fight off those painful memories, they began flooding back...

When Richard had changed his mind about marrying her three years earlier, Darcy had ended up taking their honeymoon trip solo. Of course it had been dismal. Blind to the glorious sights, she had wandered round Venice as if she was homeless, while she struggled to cope with the pain of Richard's rejection. Then, one morning, she had witnessed a pair of youthful lovers having a stand-up row in the Piazza San Marco. The sultry brunette had flung something at her boyfriend. As the thick gilded card had fluttered to rest at Darcy's feet the fiery lovers had stalked off in opposite directions. And Darcy had found herself in unexpected possession of an invite to a masked ball at one of the wonderful palaces on the Grand Canal.

Two days later, she had finally rebelled against her boredom and her loneliness. She had purchased a mask and had donned that magical green evening dress. She had felt transformed, excitingly different and feminine. In those days she hadn't owned contact lenses, and since her spectacles combined with her long mane of hair had seemed to give her the dowdy look of an earnest swot she had taken them off, choosing to embrace myopia instead. She had had a cold too, so she had generously dosed herself up with a cold remedy. Unfortunately she hadn't read the warning on the packaging not to take any alcohol with the medication...

When she had seen the vast *palazzo* ablaze with golden light she had almost lost her nerve, but a crush of important guests had arrived at the same time, forcing her to move ahead of them and pass over her invitation. She had climbed the vast sweeping staircase of gilded brass and marble. By the time she'd entered the superb mirrored ballroom, filled with exquisitely dressed crowds of beautiful people awash with glittering jewels, her nerve had been failing fast. At any minute she had feared exposure as a gatecrasher, sneaking in where she had no right to be.

After hovering, trying desperately hard not to look conspicuous in her solitary state, she had slowly edged her path round to the fluttering curtains on the far side of the huge room and slid through them to find herself out on a big stone balcony. One secure step removed from the festivities, she had watched the glamorous guests mingle and dance—or at least she had watched them as closely as her shortsightedness allowed.

When an unmasked male figure in a white jacket had strolled out onto the balcony with a tray bearing a single glass, to address her in Italian, she'd quite naturally assumed he was a waiter.

'*Grazie,*' she said, striving to appear as if she was just taking the air after a dance or two, and draining the glass with appropriate thirsty fervour.

But he spoke again.

'I don't speak Italian—'

'That was Spanish,' he imparted gently in English. 'I thought you might be Spanish. That dress worn with such vibrant colouring as yours is dramatic.'

In the lingering silence of her disinterested shrug, he remarked, 'You appear to be alone.' Not easily disconcerted, he lounged lazily back against the stone balustrade, the tray abandoned.

'I *was,*' she pointed out thinly. 'And I like being alone.'

He inclined his dark head back, his features a complete blur at that distance, only his pale jacket clearly visible to her in the darkness as he stared at her. In a bolshy mood, she stared back, nose in the air, head imperiously high. All of a sudden she was sick to death of being pushed around by people and forced to fulfil *their* expectations. Her solo trip to Venice had been her first true rebellion, and so far she could not comfort herself with the belief that she had done much with the opportunity.

'You're prickly.'

'No, that was *rude,*' Darcy contradicted ruefully. 'Outright, bloody rudeness.'

'Is that an apology?' he enquired.

'No, I believe I was clarifying my point. And haven't you got any more drinks to ferry around?' she prompted hopefully.

He stilled, wide shoulders tautening, and then unexpectedly he laughed, a shiveringly sensual sound that sent a curious ripple down her taut spine. 'Not at present.'

His easy humour shamed her into a blush. 'I'm not in a very good mood.'

'I will change that.'

'Not could, but *will,*' she noted out loud. 'You're very sure of yourself.'

'Aren't you?'

In that instant, her own sheer lack of self-confidence flailed her with shamed bitterness, and she threw her head back with desperate pride and a tiny smile of wry amusement. 'Always,' she murmured steadily then. '*Always.*'

He moved forward, and as an arrow of light from the great chandeliers in the ballroom fell on him she saw an indistinct image of the hard, bitingly attractive angles of his strong bone structure, the gleam of his thick black hair, the brilliance of his dark eyes. And her heart skipped a startled beat.

'Dance with me,' he urged softly.

And Darcy laughed with undeniable appreciation. Only she could gatecrash a high society ball and end up being chatted up by one of the waiters. 'Aren't you scared that someone will see you and you'll lose your job?'

'Not if we remain out here...'

'Just one dance and then I'll leave.'

'The entertainment doesn't meet with your approval?' he probed as he slid her into his arms, his entire approach so subtle, so smooth that she was surprised to find herself there, and then flattered by the sensation of being held as if she were fashioned of the most fragile and delicate spun glass.

'It's suffocatingly formal, and tonight I feel like something different,' she mused with perfect truth. 'Indeed, tonight I feel just a little wild...'

'Please don't let me inhibit you,' he murmured.

And Darcy burst out laughing again.

'Who did you come here with tonight?' he queried.

'Nobody...I'm a gatecrasher,' she confided daringly.

'A *gatecrasher?*'

'You sound shocked...'

'Security is usually very tight at the Palazzo d'Oro.'

'Not if you enter just in front of a party who require a great deal of attentive bowing and scraping.'

'You must've had an invitation?'

'It landed at my feet in the Piazza San Marco. A beautiful brunette flung it at her boyfriend. I thought you asked me to dance,' she complained, since they had yet to move. 'Are you now planning to have me thrown out?'

'Not just at present,' he confided, folding her closer and staring down at her with narrowed eyes. 'You are a very unusual woman.'

'Very,' Darcy agreed, liking that tag, which hinted at a certain distinction.

'And your name?'

'No names, no pack drill,' she sighed. 'Ships that pass and all that—'

'I want to board...'

'No can do. I am not my name...my name wasn't even chosen with me in mind,' she admitted with repressed bitterness, for Darcy had always been a male name in her family. 'And I want to be someone else tonight.'

'Very unusual and *very* infuriating,' he breathed.

'I am a woman who is very, very sure of herself, and a woman of that stature is certain to infuriate,' she returned playfully, leaning in to his big powerful body and smiling up at him, set free by anonymity to be whatever she wanted to be.

And so they danced, high above the Grand Canal, all the lights glittering magically in her eyes until she closed them and just drifted in a wonderful dreamy haze...

CHAPTER FOUR

A BURST of forceful Italian dredged Darcy out of that sleepy, seductive flow of memory. Eyelids fluttering, she returned to the present and frowned to find the Land Rover at a standstill, headlights glaring on the high banks of a narrow lane.

'What...*where*—?' she began in complete confusion.

'We have a flat tyre,' Luca delivered in a murderous aside as he wrenched open the rattling driver's door.

Darcy scrambled out into the drizzling rain. 'But the spare's in for repair!' she exclaimed.

Across the bonnet, Luca surveyed her with what struck her as an overplay of all-male incredulity. 'You have *no* spare tyre?'

'No.' Darcy busied herself giving the offending flat tyre a kick. 'Pretty far gone, isn't it? That won't get us home.' She looked around herself. 'Where on earth *are* we?'

'It is possible that in the darkness I may have taken a wrong turn.'

Considering that they were in a lane that came to a dead end at a field twenty feet ahead, Darcy judged that a miracle of understatement. 'You got lost, didn't you?'

Luca dealt her a slaughtering, silencing glance.

Darcy sighed. 'We'd better start walking—'

'*Walking?*' He was aghast at the concept.

'What else? How long is it since you saw a main road?'

'Some time,' Luca gritted. 'But fortunately there is a farmhouse quite close.'

'Fat lot of use that's going to be,' Darcy muttered. 'At two in the morning, only an emergency would give us the excuse to knock people up out of their beds.'

'This *is* an emergency!'

Darcy drew herself up to her full five feet two inches. 'I am not rousing an entire family just so that we can ask to use their phone. In any case, who would you suggest I contact?'

'A motoring organisation,' Luca informed her with exaggerated patience.

'I don't belong to one.'

'A car breakdown recovery business?'

'Have you any idea what that would cost?' Darcy groaned in horror. 'It's not worth it for a flat tyre! The local garage can run out the spare in the morning. They'll only charge me for their time and petrol—'

'I am not spending the night in that filthy vehicle,' Luca asserted levelly.

'You figure cosying up to those cows would be more fun?' Darcy could not resist saying, surveying the curious beasts who, attracted by the light and the sound of their voices, had ambled up to gawk over the gate at them.

'I passed through a crossroads about a kilometre back. I saw an inn there.' With the decisive air of one taking command, Luca leant into the car. 'I presume you have a torch?'

''Fraid not,' Darcy admitted gruffly.

Not a male who took life's little slings and arrows with a stiff upper lip, Darcy registered by the stark exhalation of breath. Not remotely like the charming, tolerant male she had encountered in Venice three years ago. And how the heck she had contrived to imagine the faintest resemblance now quite escaped her. This was a male impatient of any mishap which injured his comfort—indeed, almost outraged by any set of circumstances which could strand him ignominiously on a horribly wet night in a muddy country lane.

So they walked.

'I should have paid some heed to where we were going,' Darcy remarked, proffering a generous olive branch.

'"If onlys" exasperate me,' Luca divulged.

Rain trickling down her bare arms, Darcy buttoned her lips. With a stifled imprecation, Luca removed his dinner jacket and held it out to her.

'Oh, don't be daft,' Darcy muttered in astonished embarrassment at such a gesture. 'I'm as tough as old boots.'

'I *insist*—'

'No…no, honestly.' Darcy started walking again in haste. 'You've just come from a hot climate…you're more at risk of a chill than I am.'

'*Per amor di Dio…*' Luca draped the jacket round her narrow shoulders, enfolding her in the smooth silk lining which still carried the pervasive heat and scent of his body. 'Just keep quiet and wear it!'

In the darkness, a spontaneous grin of appreciation lit Darcy's face. As she stumbled on the rough road surface Luca curved a steadying arm round her, and instead of withdrawing that support, kept it there. It was amazing how good that made her feel. He had tremendously good manners, she conceded. Not unnaturally, he was infuriated by the inefficiency that had led to the absence of a spare tyre, but at least he wasn't doggedly set on continually reminding her of her oversight.

The inn perched at the juncture of lanes was shrouded in darkness. Darcy hung back in the porch. 'Do we *have* to do this?'

Without a shade of hesitation, Luca strode forward to make use of the ornate door-knocker. 'I would knock up the dead for a brandy and a hot bath.'

An outside light went on. A bleary-eyed middle-aged man in a dressing gown eventually appeared. Darcy heard the rustle of money. The security chain was undone at speed. And suddenly mine host became positively convivial. Getting dragged out of his bed in the middle of the night might almost have been a pleasure to him. He showed them up a creaking, twisting staircase into a pleasant room and retreated to fetch the brandy.

'How much money did you give him, for heaven's sake?' Darcy demanded in fascination.

'Sufficient to cover the inconvenience.' Luca surveyed the room and the connecting bathroom with a frowning lack of appreciation.

'It's really quite cosy,' Darcy remarked, and it was when compared with her own rather barn-like and bare bedroom at the Folly. The floor had a carpet and the bed had a fat satin quilt.

The proprietor reappeared with an entire bottle of brandy and two glasses.

Darcy discarded the jacket, studying Luca, whose white shirt was plastered to an impressive torso which gleamed brown through the saturated fabric. Her attention fairly caught as she stood there, tousled hair dripping down her rainwashed face, she glimpsed the black whorls of hair hazing his muscular chest in a distinctive male triangle as he turned back to her. Her face burned.

'Give me a coin,' Darcy told him abruptly.

A curious brow quirking, Luca withdrew a coin from his pocket. 'What—?'

Darcy flipped it from his fingers. 'We'll toss for the bed.'

'I beg your pardon?'

But Darcy had already tossed. 'Heads or tails?' she proffered cheerfully.

'*Dio*—'

'Heads!' Darcy chose impatiently. She uncovered the coin and then sighed. 'You get the bed; I get the quilt. Do you mind if I have first shower? I'll be quick.'

Moving to the bathroom without awaiting a reply, Darcy closed the door with some satisfaction. The trick was to get over embarrassing ground fast. Had money not been in short supply, she would've asked for a second room, but why bother for the sake of a few hours? Luca was highly unlikely to succumb to an attack of overpowering lust and make a pass... I should be so lucky, she thought, and then squirmed with boiling guilt.

Stripping off, she stepped into the shower. In five minutes she was out again, smothering a yawn. After towel-drying her hair, she put her bra and pants back on, draped her sodden dress over one exact half of the shower curtain rail and opened the door a crack.

The room was empty. Darcy shot across the bedroom, snatched the quilt and a pillow off the divan, and in ten seconds flat had herself tucked in her makeshift bed on the carpet.

Ten minutes later, Luca reappeared. '*Accidenti*...this isn't a schoolgirl sleep-over!' he bit out, sounding as if he was climbing the walls with exasperation. 'We'll share the bed like grown-ups.'

'I'm perfectly happy where I am. I lost the toss.'

Luca growled something raw and impatient in Italian. 'I've slept in far less comfortable places than this. Do stop fussing,' she muttered, her voice muffled by the quilt. 'I'm a lot hardier than you are—'

'And what is *that* supposed to mean?'

Her wide, anxious gaze appeared over the edge of the satin quilt. She collided with heartstopping dark golden eyes glittering with suspicion below flaring ebony brows. Her stomach clenched, her breath shortening in her dry throat. 'Why don't you go and get your hot bath and your brandy?' she suggested tautly, and in so doing tactfully side-stepped the question.

Dear heaven, but he was gorgeous. She listened to him undress. She wanted to look. As the bathroom door closed on him she grimaced, feverishly hot and uneasy and thoroughly ashamed of herself. He was a decent guy and he had made a real effort on her behalf tonight. A Hollywood film star couldn't have been more impressive in his role. And here she was, acting all silly like the schoolgirl he had hinted she was, reacting to him as if he was a sex object and absolutely nothing else. Didn't she despise men who regarded women in that light?

Sure, Darcy, when was the last time a male treated *you* like a sex object? *Venice.* She shivered. Instantly she remembered that passionate kiss out on the balcony high above the Grand Canal, how that fierce sizzle of electric excitement in her veins had felt that very first time. Excitement as dangerously addictive as a narcotic drug. And tonight she had experienced that same wild hunger all over again...

A hot, liquid sensation assailing the very crux of her body, Darcy bit her lower lip and loathed her weak, wanton physical self. But no wonder she had been shaken up earlier. No wonder she had briefly imagined more than a superficial resemblance of looks and nationality between Luca and her daughter's father. But there *was* no mystery. Her own shatteringly powerful response to both men had been the sole source of similarity.

The bathroom door opened, heralding Luca's return.

'Darcy…get into the bed,' Luca instructed very drily.

Darcy ignored the invitation, terrified that he might sense her attraction to him if she got any closer. 'I never really thanked you properly for tonight,' she said instead, eager to change the subject. 'You were a class act.'

'*Grazie*…would you like a brandy?'

'No, thanks.'

After the chink of glass, she heard the blankets being trailed back, the creak as the divan gave under his weight. The light went out. 'You know, when I said you'd make a great gigolo, I was really trying to pay you a compliment,' she advanced warily.

'I'll bear that in mind.'

Emboldened by that apparent new tolerance, Darcy relaxed. 'I suppose I owe you an explanation about a few things…' In the darkness, she grimaced, but she felt that he had earned greater honesty. 'When I was a child, Fielding's Folly paid for itself. But Margo liked to live well and my father took out a mortgage rather than reduce their outgoings. I only found out about the mortgage a couple of years ago, when the Folly needed roof repairs and the estate couldn't afford to pay for them.'

'Wasn't your stepmother prepared to help?'

'No. In fact Margo tried to persuade my father to sell up. I was really scared she might wear him down,' she confided. 'That was when we had a bit of *good* luck for a change. I had a piece of antique jewellery valued and we ended up selling that instead—'

'A piece of jewellery?' Luca interposed with silken softness.

'A ring. My father had forgotten it even existed, but that ring fetched a really tidy sum,' Darcy shared with quiet pride.

'Fancy that,' Luca drawled, and the dark timbre of his deep-pitched accented voice slid down her spine in the most curiously enervating fashion. 'Did you sell it on the open market?'

In the darkness, Darcy turned over restively. 'No, it was a private sale. I assumed the estate was secure then. I didn't realise how serious things really were until my father died. He never confided in me. But you have to understand that there is nothing I wouldn't do to keep the Folly in the family.'

'I understand that perfectly.'

Darcy licked at her taut lower lip. 'So when my wealthy godmother died a few months ago, I was really hoping that she would leave me some money...'

'Nothing more natural,' Luca conceded encouragingly.

'There were three of us...three god-daughters. Myself, Maxie and Polly,' Darcy enumerated heavily. 'But when the will was read, we all got a shock. Nancy left us a share of her estate, but only on condition that we each marry within the year.'

'How extraordinary...'

'So that's why I needed you...to inherit.' The hardness of the floor was starting to make its presence felt through the layers of both carpet and quilt. Shifting from one slender unpadded hip to the other with increased discomfort, Darcy added uneasily, 'I suppose you think that's rather calculating and greedy of me…?'

'No, I think you are very brave to take me on trust,' Luca delivered gently.

Darcy smiled, relieved by the assurance and encouraged. 'This floor is kind of hard…' she admitted finally.

'And you're being such a jolly good sport about it,' Luca remarked slumberously from the comfort of the bed. 'I really admire that quality in a woman.'

'Do you?' Darcy whispered in surprise.

'But of course. You're so *delightfully* democratic! No feminine sulks or pleas for special treatment,' Luca pointed out approvingly. 'You lost the toss and you took it on the chin just like a man would.'

Darcy nodded slowly. 'I guess I did.'

It didn't seem quite the moment to suggest that he took the floor instead. But a helpless little kernel of inner warmth blossomed at his praise. He mightn't fancy her but he seemed to at least respect her.

'*Buona notte,* Darcy.'

'Goodnight, Luca.'

Darcy woke with a start to find Luca standing over her fully dressed. She blinked in confusion. He looked so impossibly tall, dark and handsome.

'The Land Rover's outside,' he imparted.

'Outside…*how?*' She sat up, hugging the quilt and striving not to wince as every aching muscle she possessed shrieked complaint.

'I called your local garage. They were keen to help. I'll see you downstairs for breakfast,' Luca concluded.

It was already after nine. Darcy hurried into the bathroom and looked in anguish at her reflection. Overnight her hair had exploded into dozens of babyish Titian curls. She ran her fingers through them and they all stood up on end. In despair, she tried to push them down again.

Ten minutes later, Darcy went downstairs, curls damped down, last night's dress crumpled, and the sensation of looking an absolute mess doing nothing for her confidence. She slunk over to the corner table where Luca was semi-concealed behind a newspaper, beautifully shaped dark imperious head bent, luxuriant black hair immaculate, not a single strand out of place.

Darcy sank down opposite, in no hurry to draw attention to herself. And then her attention fell on the photograph of the statuesque blonde adorning the front page of his newspaper. 'Give me that paper!' she gasped. *'Please!'*

Ebony brows knitting in incomprehension, Luca began lowering the paper, but Darcy reached over and snatched it from him without further ado, spreading the publication flat on the table to read the blurb that went with the picture.

'She's married already...*married!'* Darcy groaned in appalled disbelief. 'Page four...' she muttered, frantically leafing through the pages to reach the main story.

'Who has got married?'

'Maxie Kendall...one of Nancy's other goddaughters.'

'The lady has beaten you to the finishing line?' Luca enquired smoothly.

Darcy was too busy reading to reply. 'Angelos Petronides...oh, dear heaven would you look at that dirty great enormous mansion they're standing outside?' she demanded in stricken appeal. 'Not only has she got herself a husband, he looks *besotted,* and he *has* to be loaded—'

'Angelos Petronides…yes…loaded,' Luca confirmed very drily.

'I feel *ill!*' Darcy confessed truthfully, thrusting the offending newspaper away in disgust.

'Jealous…envious?'

Darcy turned shaken eyes of reproach on him. 'Oh, no…it's just…it's just everything always seems so *easy* for Maxie…she's incredibly beautiful! We were practically best friends until Richard fell in love with her. That's why we didn't get married,' she completed tightly.

After that dialogue, breakfast was a silent meal. Darcy was embarrassed by her outburst and insulted by his response. Jealous? Envious? She thought about that as she drove them back to the Folly. *No*…Luca had got her completely wrong.

As her chief bridesmaid, Maxie had stayed at the Folly the week running up to that misfired wedding three years earlier. The glamorous model had accepted the bridegroom's attention and admiration as her due, responding with flirtatious smiles and amusing repartee. Richard had been, quite simply, *dazzled*. And Darcy had been naively pleased that her friend and her fiancé appeared to be getting on so well.

But on their wedding day Richard had turned to look at Darcy at the altar, only to confess in despair, 'I *can't* go through with this…'

The wedding party had adjourned to the vestry.

'I've fallen in love with Maxie,' Richard had admitted baldly, his shame and distress at having to make that admission unconcealed.

'What the hell are you talking about?' Maxie had demanded furiously. 'I don't even *like* you!'

Fierce anger had filled Darcy then. She could have

borne that devastating change of heart better had Maxie returned Richard's feelings. Then, at least, there might have seemed some point to the whole ghastly mess. But Maxie's careless encouragement of male homage had done the damage. Both Darcy *and* Richard had been bitterly hurt and humiliated by the experience.

Darcy had long since forgiven Richard, indeed still regarded him as a dear friend. Yet she had not been half so generous to Maxie, she conceded now. She had awarded her former friend the lion's share of the blame. Only now did it occur to her that Maxie had been a thoughtless teenager at the time, she herself only a year older. Perhaps, she reflected grudgingly, she had been unjust...

Face still and strained over her troubling reflections, for Darcy never liked to think that she had been less than fair, she climbed out of the Land Rover outside the Folly.

'Do you realise that you have not spoken a single word since breakfast?' Luca enquired without any expression at all.

Darcy tautened defensively. 'I was thinking about Richard.'

Dark colour slowly rose to accentuate the hard angles of Luca's slashing cheekbones, his lean, strong face tightening. He surveyed her from beneath dense inky black lashes, eyes broodingly dark and icy cold. Colliding unexpectedly with that chilling scrutiny, Darcy felt her stomach clench as if she had hit black ice. 'What's wrong?'

'What could possibly be wrong?'

'I don't know, but...' Darcy continued with a frown of uncertainty. 'Gosh, I owe you some money for our overnight stay—'

'I will present you with a bill for all services rendered,' Luca asserted with sardonic cool.

'Thanks…a cheque might bounce if I wrote it today.' But Darcy's green eyes remained anxious. 'When are you planning to move in?' she asked abruptly.

'The day of our wedding,' Luca revealed.

'So what time will you be here, then?' she pressed.

'I'll be at the church in time for the ceremony.' An almost dangerous smile curved his wide, sensual mouth. 'You need cherish no fear that I might fail to show. After all, in this materialistic world, you get what you pay for.'

Disturbed at having her secret apprehensions so easily read, Darcy watched him stroll fluidly towards the Porsche. How did he do it? she wondered then in fierce frustration. How *did* he contrive to make her agonisingly aware of that dynamic masculinity and virile sexuality even as he walked away from her? The angle of his proud dark head, the strong set of his wide shoulders, the sleek twist of his lean hips and the indolent grace of those long, powerful legs as he moved all grabbed and held her attention.

As he opened the car door he glanced back at her.

Caught staring again, Darcy looked as guilty as she felt.

'By the way,' Luca murmured silkily, 'I forgot to mention how impressed I was by that pre-nuptial contract I signed. That we each leave the marriage with exactly what we brought into it is very fair.'

'Sexual equality,' Darcy muttered, unable to take her eyes off the way the sunlight glistened over black hair she already knew felt like luxurious silk beneath her fingertips. And she recalled with a little frisson of helpless pleasure how good it had felt in Margo and Nina's radius to have a man by her side she could trust.

'I'm *all* for it,' Luca informed her lazily, angling the most shatteringly sensual smile of approval at her.

Even at a distance that fascinating smile had the power to jolt and send a current of all too warm appreciation quivering through her. As he drove off, Darcy gave him a jerky, self-conscious wave.

'Do you realise how often you have mentioned Luca's name over the past two days?' Karen prompted tautly.

'Luca *is* rather central to my plans, and we are getting married tomorrow,' Darcy pointed out with some amusement as she straightened Zia's bed, Karen having arrived in the midst of the bedtime story ritual. 'Love you, sweetheart,' she whispered, dropping a kiss on her daughter's smooth brow.

The toddler mumbled a sleepy response and burrowed below the duvet until only a cluster of black curls showed. Darcy switched off the bedside light and walked out into the corridor, leaving the door ajar.

'I'm scared that you're developing a crush on the guy,' Karen delivered baldly, determined to send the message of her concern fully home.

'I think I'm a little too mature for a crush, Karen—'

'That's what's worrying me.' The brunette grimaced. 'You are *paying* Luca to put on a good act. He's hired help—whatever you want to call it… You can't afford to fall in love with him!'

Darcy looked pained. 'I'm not going to fall in love with him.'

'Then why do you keep on talking about how much he shone at Margo's party?'

'Because I give honour where it's due and he *did!*'

'Not to mention how wonderful his manners are and how many and varied are the subjects on which he can converse like Einstein!' Karen completed doggedly.

'So I was impressed...' Darcy shrugged, but her cheeks were flushed, her eyes evasive.

'Darcy...you've had a pretty rough time the last couple of years and you're vulnerable,' Karen spelt out uncomfortably. 'I'm sure Luca is a really terrific bloke, but you don't know him well enough to trust him yet. In fact, he could be thinking you'll be a darned good catch with this house behind you.'

'He knows I'm in debt up to my eyeballs,' Darcy contradicted.

Confronted with the full extent of her friend's unease, however, Darcy took some time to get to sleep that night. Was it so obvious that she was attracted to Luca? Was it obvious to *him?* She cringed at the suspicion. But, even so, Karen was mad to suggest that she was in danger of falling for Luca.

She had returned from Venice with a heart broken into so many pieces she had been torn apart by her own turmoil. Falling like a ton of bricks for a complete stranger in the space of one night had been a hard lesson indeed. Her battered pride, her pain and her despair had taken a very long time to fade. Darcy had not the slightest intention of allowing her undeniable attraction to Luca go one step further than appreciation from a safe distance.

In its day, it had been a costly designer dress. The ivory silk wedding gown hugged Darcy's shoulders, smoothly clung to her slender waist and hips and fanned out into beautifully embroidered panels between mid-thigh and ankle. It had belonged to her late mother, and, foolish and uneasy as she felt at using the dress for such a purpose, she thought it would look very odd if she didn't make some effort to put on a show of being a *real* bride.

And this afternoon Darcy also had an important appointment to keep with her bank manager. Hopefully a candid explanation of the terms of her godmother's will would persuade the older man that the Folly was a more secure investment than he had previously believed. With his agreement she would be able to re-employ the most vital estate workers, and very soon things would get back to normal around her home, she thought cheerfully.

'Pretty Mummy,' Zia enthused, liquid dark eyes huge as she took an excited twirl in the pink summer dress and frilly ankle socks which she loved. 'Pretty Zia?' she added.

'*Very* pretty,' Darcy agreed with a grin.

Karen drove them to the church in her car. Darcy was shaken to see quite a crowd waiting in the churchyard to see her arrive. She recognised every face. Former estate staff and tenants, people she had known all her life.

An older woman who had retired as the Folly's last housekeeper moved forward to press a beautiful bouquet into Darcy's empty hands. 'Everybody's so happy for you, Miss Fielding,' she said with embarrassing fervour. 'We all hope you have a *really* wonderful day!'

As other voices surged to offer the same sincere good wishes for her future happiness, Darcy's eyes stung and flooded with rare tears. She blinked rapidly, touched to the heart but also wrenched by guilt that her coming marriage would only be an empty pretence.

As she entered the small church, Luca turned his imperious head to stare down the aisle. His strong, dark face stilled in what might have been surprise at her appearance in the silk gown, dark golden eyes glittering. Darcy's tear-drenched gaze ran over him. Sheathed in an exquisitely tailored charcoal-grey suit, he exuded the most breathtaking aura of command and sophistication. He had such incredible impact that she forgot how to breathe and her knees wobbled. There was just *something* about him, she thought with dizzy discomfiture.

Unexpectedly, another, younger man stood beside Luca. Slim and dark, he looked tense, his eyes slewing away from Darcy as she gave him a friendly nod of acknowledgement.

The ceremony began. Only at the point where Luca took her hand to put on the ring did Darcy register that she had totally overlooked the necessity of supplying one. Relief filled her when Luca produced a narrow gold band and slid it onto her wedding finger. 'Thanks...' she muttered, only half under her breath, reddening at the vicar's look of surprise at that unusual bridal reaction.

When the brief marriage service was concluded, the register was signed. Karen and the other man, whom Luca addressed as Benito, performed their function as witnesses. All formalities dealt with, Darcy rubbed her still damp and stinging eyes, and accidentally dislodged one of her contact lenses. With an exclamation of dismay, she dropped to her knees. 'Don't move, anyone...I've lost one of my lenses!'

Luca reached down and flicked up the tiny item from where it glimmered on the stone floor. He slipped it into his pocket, evidently aware that without the aid of cleansing solution she could not immediately replace the lens. 'Relax, I have it...'

Amazed by the speed of his reactions, Darcy skimmed a glance up at him. At the same time he bent down to help her upright again. As she focused myopically on him through one eye, she closed the other in an involuntary attempt to see better. In that split second his features blurred, throwing his strong facial bones into a different kind of prominence that lent them a stark, haunting familiarity. Darcy froze in outright disbelief. Her Venetian lover!

In that instant of incredulous recognition shock seized her by the throat and almost strangled the life force from her. 'You…*y-you?*' she began, stammering wildly.

Darcy gaped at Luca in an uncomprehending stupor. Her head pounded sickly and he swam back out of focus again. As she blacked out, Luca caught her in his arms before she could fall.

CHAPTER FIVE

'TAKE a deep breath...' Luca's deep, dark drawl instructed with complete calm.

Whoosh. The air flooded back into Darcy's constricted lungs. Perspiration broke out on her clammy brow. Her eyes fluttered open again. She found herself seated on a hard wooden pew.

'*See...*' Karen was soothing Zia, several feet away. 'Mummy's all right.' And then, in a whispered aside to Luca, 'I bet Darcy fainted because she's exhausted—she works eighteen-hour days!'

As Darcy lifted her swimming head everything came hurtling back to her. She simply gawped at Luca, still doubting the stunning evidence provided by that one myopic glance. Shimmering dark eyes held her bemused gaze steadily, and all over again that frantically disorientating sense of frightening familiarity gripped her.

'You can't be...you *can't* be!' she gasped abruptly, impervious to the presence of the others.

'Take it easy, Darcy,' Karen advised, evidently unaware that anything was seriously wrong. 'You passed out and you're confused, that's all. Look, I'll keep Zia with me until you're feeling better. You should lie down for a while. I'll call over later and see how you are.'

Still in a world of her own, Darcy moved her muzzy head as if she was afraid it might fall off her neck. Luca Raffacani could not be the man with whom she had spent the night in Venice; he could not *possibly* be the same man! And yet, he *was!* It made no sense, it seemed beyond the bounds of even the wildest feat of imagination, but those strong promptings of familiarity which had troubled her apparently had their basis in solid fact.

'Can you stand?' Luca enquired.

'I'm fine...really,' Darcy whispered unconvincingly as she fought to focus her mind. She got up on legs that felt like cotton wool sticks. She shook hands with the vicar, who was anxiously hovering. Then she stared at Luca again with a kind of appalled fascination and knew she would never feel fine again, knew she felt, rather, as if she had lost her mind in that devastating moment of recognition.

'The car's outside, sir.' Benito spoke for the first time as he turned from the window.

Darcy's attention swivelled to the younger man. *Sir?* She encountered a fleeting look of pity in Benito's gaze. The sort of pity one experienced for someone sick when all hope had gone, Darcy labelled with a bemused shudder.

What on earth was going on? Who *was* Gianluca Fabrizio Raffacani? And whoever he was, whatever he was, she had just made him her husband!

'Calm yourself,' Luca urged before they walked back out of the church to face the crowd of well-wishers waiting to see them off.

'But I recognised you...' she told him shakily.

'You mean you *finally* shuffled the memory of one face out of the no doubt countless one-night stands you have enjoyed?' Luca murmured in a silken smooth stab, making her shrink in stricken disbelief at such a charge. 'Am I to feel honoured by that most belated distinction?'

His cool confirmation that he was who she believed

he was shook Darcy up even more. In the back of her mind she had still somehow expected and foolishly hoped that Luca would turn with a raised brow to tell her that he hadn't a clue what she was talking about.

'You don't understand,' she began, in an unsteady attempt to defend herself, so confused was she still. 'I could hardly see you that night, not in any detail…your face was a blur and out of focus—you looked different…'

'I guess one bird for the plucking looks much like another,' Luca responded with a sardonic bite that sizzled down her spine like a hurricane warning and made her turn even paler.

A bird for the plucking? She didn't understand that crack any more than she could understand anything else. As they left the churchyard her attention fell on the big silver limousine waiting by the kerb. Pressed into a vehicle which was the very last word in expensive luxury, she was even more bewildered. Benito swung into the front seat. The tinted glass barrier between the front and the back of the limo was partially open, denying them privacy.

Darcy snatched in a shuddering breath. Her brain ached, all at once throwing up a dozen even more confusing inconsistencies. In a daze, she struggled hopelessly to superimpose the image of the Luca she had thought she was getting to know over her memory of the male who had romanced her in Venice, the sleek, seductive rat who had torn her inside out with the pain of loss…

Involuntarily she focused on Luca again. There was a strikingly relaxed quality to the indolent sprawl of his strong, supple body. In the state Darcy was in, that supreme poise and cool was uniquely intimidating.

Within minutes the limo drew up outside the Folly. Darcy scrambled out in haste, her heartbeat banging in her eardrums. With damp, nerveless hands she unlocked and thrust open the heavy front door to walk into the echoing medieval hall with its aged flagstoned floor.

She spun round, then, to face Luca, where he had stilled by the giant smoke-blackened stone fireplace. Her oval face was stiff with strain as she attempted to match his aura of complete self-command.

'I can't believe that coincidence has anything to do with this...' Darcy admitted jaggedly.

'Very wise.' Luca surveyed her with a grim satisfaction that was chilling.

'How could you *possibly* have found out who I was...or where I lived?'

'With persistence, no problem is insuperable. It took time, but I had you traced.'

'You had me traced...dear heaven, *why?*' Darcy could not hide her incredulity. 'Why the heck would you even want to do such a thing?'

'Don't play dumb,' Luca advised with derision.

Darcy shook her head dizzily as she braced her hands on the back of a tapestry-covered chair to steady herself. 'You came to that interview in disguise...you have to be certifiably nuts to have gone to such outrageous lengths—'

'No...merely guilty of the inexpressibly vain assumption that I might be in some danger of being recognised.'

Darcy winced at that jibe and closed her eyes, but then she had to open them again, possessed as she was by a sick compulsion to keep on watching Luca. But his lean, hard features betrayed nothing. 'Why did you *do* this? What's in it for you? You can't be unemployed or b-broke.'

'No... What was that vulgar term you used about your fortunate friend, Maxie? I'm ''loaded'',' Luca conceded with a scornful twist of his lips. 'But you will not profit from that reality, I assure you.'

'I don't understand...' Her hand flew up to her pounding temples. 'I'm getting the most awful headache.'

'Retribution hurts,' Luca slotted in softly. 'And by the time I am finished with you, a headache will be the very least of your problems.'

'What's that supposed to mean? For heaven's sake...are you *threatening* me?' Darcy gasped, releasing her hold on the chair to take an angry step forward.

'No, I believe I am revelling in the extraordinary sense of power I'm experiencing. I've never felt like that around a woman before,' Luca mused thoughtfully. 'But then, where you are concerned, I have no pity.'

'You're trying to scare me...'

'How easily do you scare?' Luca enquired with appalling self-possession.

'You don't behave like the man I met in Venice!' Darcy condemned shakily.

'You're not the woman I met then either. But she'll emerge eventually... I have this wonderful conviction that over the next six months whatever I want, I will receive.' Brilliant dark eyes gleamed with cruel amusement below level black brows. 'My every wish will be your command. *Nothing* will be too much trouble. I will just snap my fingers and you will jump...'

Darcy tried and failed to swallow. The living nightmare of her own confusion was growing. While one small part of her stood back and believed that he was talking outrageous nonsense, all the rest of her was horribly impressed by the lethal edge of cool, collected threat in that rich, dark drawl and the deadly chill in his level gaze. 'What are you trying to say?'

'As a sobering taste of your near future, consider this...depending on my choice of timing, if I walk out on this marriage *you* will lose *everything* you possess.' Luca spelt out that reminder with an immovable cool that made what he was saying all the more shocking.

The silence, broken only by the steady tick of the grandfather clock, hung there between them as breakable as a thin sheet of glass.

'No...no...' Every scrap of remaining colour drained from Darcy's shaken face as she absorbed the full weight of that threat. 'You *can't* do that to me!'

'I think you'll find that I can do anything I want...' Strolling closer with fluid ease, Luca stretched out a seemingly idle hand and closed it over her clenched fingers. Slowly, relentlessly employing the pressure of his infinitely greater strength, he pulled her towards him.

'Stop it...let go of me!' Darcy cried, totally unprepared for this even more daunting development, heartbeat thundering in panic, breath snarling up in her convulsing throat.

'That is no way to talk to a new husband,' Luca censured indolently as he skimmed a confident hand down to the shallow indentation at the base of her spine and held her there, mere inches from him. He studied her with satisfaction. 'And particularly not one with such *high* expectations of your future behaviour. All that cutesy tossing of coins and sleeping on the floor like a naive little virgin...it's *wasted* on a male who has perfect recall of being pushed down on a bed and having his shirt ripped off within hours of meeting you!'

As that rich, dark-timbred voice flailed down her taut spine like a silken whip, Darcy's eyes grew huge and raw with stricken recollection of her own abandon that night in Venice. She trembled, her pallor now laced with hot ribbons of pink.

'You were *wild,*' Luca savoured huskily. 'It may be the most expensive one-night stand I ever had, but the sex was unforgettable.'

Expensive? But she still couldn't concentrate. She gazed up at him, as trapped as a butterfly speared by a cruel pin. Only in her case the pin was the stabbing thrust of intense humiliation piercing her to the heart. Raising one lean brown hand, he rubbed a blunt forefinger over the tremulous line of her full lower lip and she shivered, spooked by the blaze of those brilliant dark golden eyes so close, the shocking effect of that insolent caress on her tender mouth. With stunned disconcertion she felt a spark of heat flame into a smouldering tight little knot that scorched the pit of her tense stomach.

'You burned me alive,' Luca whispered mesmerically. 'And you're going to do that for me again...and again...and again until I don't want you any more...is that understood?'

No, nothing was understood. Too much had happened too fast, and at absolutely the wrong psychological moment. Darcy had stood at that altar, firmly and exultantly believing that she was in the very act of solving her every problem. Everything had fallen apart when she was least equipped to deal with it. Now she was simply reeling from moment to moment in the suffocating grip of deep, paralysing shock.

'Who *are* you...why are you doing this to me?' she demanded all over again, her incomprehension unconcealed as he released her.

'Isn't it strange how the passage of time operates?' Luca remarked with a philosophical air. 'What you once didn't want to know for your own protection, you are now desperate to discover—'

'You can't do this to me...you can't threaten me...I won't *let* you!' Darcy swore vehemently.

'Watch me,' Luca advised, consulting the rapier-thin gold watch on his wrist with tremendous poise. 'Now, I suggest you locate your passport and start packing.'

'Passport...*p-packing?*' Darcy parroted.

'My surprise, *cara.*' His mocking smile didn't add one iota of warmth to the cold brilliance of his dark eyes. 'In a couple of hours a helicopter will pick us up and take us to the airport. We're flying to Venice. I want to go home.'

Darcy backed away from him, green eyes burnished by angry bewilderment. 'Venice? Are you out of your mind? I'm not going to Italy with you!'

A fleeting smile of sardonic amusement curved his expressive mouth. 'Think that refusal through. If I leave this house without you, I will not return, and you will forfeit any hope of winning your inheritance in six months' time.'

'You bastard...' Darcy mumbled sickly as that message sank in. Evidently Luca knew far more than she had naively told him. He knew the *exact* conditions of her godmother's will. A marriage that lasted less than that six-month deadline would not count.

His stunning dark eyes narrowed to an icy splinter of gold. 'In the light of the circumstances of your child's birth, I'm astonished to hear you use that particular word.'

Slashed with guilty unease by that unwelcome reminder, Darcy's facial muscles locked tight. *Zia*...her mind screamed with equal suddenness, as she finally faced up to and acknowledged the connection between this particular male and her child. *Their* child. The furious colour in her cheeks receded to leave her pale as milk. Zia was Luca's daughter as well—not that he appeared to have even a suspicion of the fact, although he seemed to have a daunting grasp of every other confidential aspect of her life.

'And by the way,' Luca murmured *sotto voce*, 'when you collect your daughter from the lodge, try not to forget the confidentiality clause in the pre-nuptial contract we both signed. If you talk about this, I will talk to the executor of your godmother's will.'

Darcy closed her eyes tightly again. 'I can't believe this is happening to me...' she ground out unsteadily.

And it was true. She had played into his hands so completely that she had tied herself in knots. Her home, her security, both her future and her daughter's were entirely reliant on Luca maintaining his verbal agreement with her. If they parted company a day before that six months was up, she would indeed lose everything she had worked so hard to retain.

Luca lifted one of her hands and lazily uncurled her fingers to plant something into her palm. 'Your missing lens...perhaps if you replace it, your view of the world will be clarified.'

Her lashes flew up. 'You are one sarcastic—!'

'And when you have shed the equivalent of Miss Havisham's wedding gown, which strangely enough does more for you than anything I have recently seen you in, is it possible that you could dig very deep into your wardrobe and produce something even passably presentable in which to travel?' Luca enquired gently.

'I'm not going to Italy...I'm not leaving to go *any-where*...I have too many responsibilities here!' Darcy shot at him in a rising crescendo of desperation. 'This is my home...you cannot make me leave it!'

'I can't *make* you do anything,' Luca conceded softly. 'The choice is yours.'

Outrage gripped Darcy at that quip. Both her hands closed into fierce fists of frustration. 'You're black-mailing me...what choice do I have?'

Luca surveyed her with immovable cool and said nothing.

Unnerved by that lack of reaction, Darcy twisted away and raced upstairs to her bedroom.

Her mind was in a state of utter turmoil, stray thoughts hitting her like thrown knives thudding into a shrinking target. How would Luca feel if he found out that she had conceived his child that night in Venice? She was in no hurry to find out. Wouldn't that give him even more power over her? And why the heck had she had Zia christened Venezia? Or was that fanciful use of the Italian name of that great city too remote a connec-tion to occur to anyone but her own foolish and senti-mental self?

What the heck was Luca trying to do to her? Most of all, her brain screeched, *why* was he doing it? His behaviour made not the smallest sense. In fact her sheer inability to comprehend why Luca Raffacani should have employed diabolical cunning and deception to sneak into her life and threaten to blow it asunder was the most terrifying aspect of all. He knew so much about her, but as yet she knew next to nothing about him—and ignorance was not bliss!

Galvanised into action by that acknowledgement, Darcy reached for the phone by her bed and punched out the number of Richard's stud farm, praying he was in his office because he hated mobile phones and refused to carry one. 'Richard…it's Darcy—'

'How are you, old girl?' Richard cut in warmly. 'Odd you should ring. I was actually thinking of dropping down this—'

'Richard…do you remember telling me that it's possible to find almost any information you want on the Internet?' Darcy interrupted with scant ceremony. 'Could you do that for me as a favour and fax anything you get?'

'Sure. What kind of information are you after?'

'Anything you can get on an Italian called…Gianluca Raffacani.'

'There's something vaguely familiar about that surname,' Richard commented absently. 'I wonder if he's into horses…'

'I'll be grateful for anything you can send me, but don't tell anyone I've been enquiring,' she warned nervously.

'No problem. Anything wrong down there?' he enquired. 'You sound harassed. What's the connection? Who is this chap?'

'That's what I'm trying to find out. Talk to you soon…thanks, Richard.' Darcy replaced the receiver.

She studied the framed photo of Richard by her bed and gave his grinning cheerful image the thumbs-up sign. To fight Luca she had to find out who and what she was dealing with.

No way could she go to Italy! The Folly could not

be left empty. And who would feed the hens and Nero, her elderly horse, look after the dogs? Work that the wedding had so far prevented her from carrying out today, she recalled dully. Shedding her late mother's gown, she pulled on her work jeans and an old sweater. She could not *bear* the idea of leaving her home…

But if she didn't, she would lose the Folly for ever. *For ever.* Perspiration beaded her upper lip. Her shoulders dropped in defeat. In the short term, what choice did she have but to play along with Luca's demands? And that meant going to Italy with Zia. Before she could lose her nerve, she dug a couple of suitcases out of a box room further down the corridor. She packed them with a hastily chosen selection of her clothing and her daughter's, squeezing in toys until both cases bulged.

A quiet knock sounded on the bedroom door.

It was Benito. His face a study of careful solemnity, he passed her several sheets of neatly trimmed fax paper. 'This was on the machine in the library when I went to use it, *signora.*'

Her fair complexion awash with disconcerted pink as she glimpsed the topmost page, which bore a recognisable picture of Luca, she said stiffly, 'You work for Luca?'

'As his executive assistant, *signora.*'

Closing the door again, wondering in hot-cheeked chagrin if Luca had personally censored the information sent by Richard or if, indeed, he considered her efforts to learn about him a source of amusement rather then a worrying development, Darcy spread the results of her former fiancé's surf on the Internet across the bed.

Then she started reading. A piece entitled 'Billion Kill on Wall Street'. It was three months old. Luca was described as a finance magnate, brilliant at playing the world currency markets, born rich and getting even richer. His personal fortune was estimated in a string of noughts that needed counting and incredulous re-counting before she could suspend scepticism. And this is the guy who took a cheque from me when I was stony broke and he *knew* it…? Darcy thought in numbed dis-belief.

He was a louse—lower than a louse, even. He was microscopic bacteria! He had no honour, no decency, no shame, no scruples. She read on. Reference was made to Luca's reputation as a commitment-shy wom-aniser, his ruthless business practices, his implacable nature, his complete lack of sentiment. Darcy was chilled by the perusal of such accolades, and soon de-cided that it was better not to read any more because it was in all likelihood ninety per cent rubbish and gossip.

No Fielding had ever been guilty of running away from a fight, she reminded herself fiercely. But her problems with the estate were all financial, and Luca had probably been the sort of child who'd started in-vesting his pocket money and playing the stock market at the age of six. She was outmatched, and she felt quite sick at the memory of having confided in him about her overdraft.

Even allowing for exaggeration, Luca was evidently a strikingly effective financial strategist. He was rich, feared and envied, doubtless used to wielding enormous power and influence. A control freak? She glanced down at the grainy picture. So forbidding, so severe, so utterly and completely unlike the male she had fallen madly in love with in Venice. But so dauntingly, chill-ingly like the male she had married today…

Nothing she had read suggested that he was secretly

insane, or given to peculiar starts and fancies, but she was not one bit closer to solving the mystery of his motivation in seeking to punish her. What did he want to punish her *for?* What had she done? She had spent only one night with him, yet for some inexplicable reason he had gone to huge lengths to track her down and hog-tie her by deception into a marriage that had never been intended to be anything but a sham. In achieving that feat, Luca now had the ability to influence and ultimately control her every move over the next six months. The price of defiance would be the loss of everything she held dear.

And although she didn't want to do it, she made herself remember that night in Venice, when her explosive response to his first kiss had shocked her inside out. Within seconds, Darcy was plunging back into the past—indeed, suddenly stung into eagerly seeking out those memories, almost as if some part of her believed they might be a comfort...

'I said just one dance before I leave,' she reminded Luca stiffly, thoroughly unnerved by her own behaviour and pulling hurriedly back from him.

For Richard had never *once* made her feel like that. Only now did she understand why her relationship with the younger man had failed. Neither of them had made an effort to share a bed before their wedding. Richard had said he didn't mind waiting. Theirs had been a love without a spark of passion, an unsentimental fondness which they had both mistaken for something deeper.

'Why should you leave?' Luca demanded.

'I don't belong here—'

He vented a soft, amused laugh. 'Running scared all of a sudden?'

'I'm not scared. I—'

'Are you committed to someone else?'

Recalling Richard's betrayal, fiery pride made her eyes flash. 'I don't believe in commitment!'

'If only that was the truth,' Luca drawled, supremely unimpressed by that declaration. 'In my experience all women ultimately want and expect commitment, no matter what they say in the beginning.'

Darcy flashed him a look of supreme scorn. Having come within inches of the deepest commitment a man could make to a woman and lost out, she no longer had any faith in the worth and security of promises. 'But I don't follow the common herd...haven't you realised that yet?'

As she stepped back from him, he shot out a hand and linked his fingers firmly with hers to keep her close. 'Either you're bitter...or extremely clever.'

'No, frank...and easily bored.'

'Not when I kiss you—'

'You *stopped!*' she condemned.

An appreciative smile of intense amusement slashed his dark features. 'We were attracting attention. I'm not a fan of public displays.'

In the mood to fight with her own shadow, Darcy shrugged. 'Then you're too sedate, too cautious, too conventional for me...'

And, like Neanderthal man reacting with reckless spontaneity to a challenge, Luca hauled her back into his arms and crushed her mouth with fierce, hungry passion under his again. When she had emerged, her lips tingling, every sense leaping with vibrant excitement and delighted pride at this proof of her feminine powers to provoke, she had giggled. 'I liked that...I liked that very much. But I'm still going to leave.'

'You can't—'

'Watch me…' Sashaying her slim but curvaceous hips, she had spun in her low-heeled pumps and moved towards the doors that stood open on the ballroom, willing him to follow her with every fibre of her being.

'If you walk out of here, you will never see me again…'

'Cuts both ways,' she murmured playfully over one slight shoulder, and then she recalled that he was a waiter…or *was* he? Somehow that didn't seem quite as likely as it had earlier.

'*Are* you a waiter?' she paused to ask uncertainly. 'Because if you are, I'm not playing fair.'

'What would you like me to be?'

'Don't be facetious—'

'So that treatment *doesn't* cut both ways! Of course I am not a waiter,' he countered in impatient dismissal.

She smiled then. So he had lifted a tray and brought her a drink specifically to approach *her*. She was impressed, incredibly flattered as well. 'Then you're a guest, a legitimate one, yet you're not masked.'

'I'm—'

'You really are dying to introduce yourself, aren't you? I don't want to know… After tonight, I'll never see you again. What would be the point?'

'You might be surprised—'

'I don't think so…are you going to follow me out of here?'

'*No,*' he delivered with level cool.

'OK…fine. I felt like company, but I'm sure I can find that elsewhere…but then I sort of like you—the way you kiss anyway,' she admitted baldly.

'One moment you behave like a grown woman, the next you talk like a schoolgirl.'

Darcy's face burned with chagrin. As she attempted to stalk off he tugged her back to him and spoke in a lazy tone of indulgence. 'Tell me, what *would* you like to do tonight that you cannot do here?'

She put her head to one side and answered on impulse. 'Sail in a gondola in the moonlight...'

Luca flinched with almost comical immediacy. 'Not my style. Tourist territory.'

Darcy pulled her fingers free of his. 'I am a tourist. I *dare* you.'

'I'll arrange a trip for you tomorrow—'

'Too late.'

'Then sadly, we are at an impasse.'

'It's your loss.' With a careless jerk of one shapely shoulder, Darcy strolled back into the ballroom. She took her time strolling, but he didn't catch up with her as she had hoped. She wondered why she was playing such dangerous games. She wondered if, her whole life through, she would ever again meet a man who could turn her bones to water and her brain to mush with a single kiss...

On that thought, her stroll slowed to a complete crawl. She glanced back in the direction she had come and froze, suddenly horrified by the discovery that she couldn't pick him out from all the other guests milling about on the edge of the dance floor. Already he was lost.

'Blackmail leaves me cold,' a familiar and undeniably welcome drawl husked in her ear from behind, making her jump a split second before a huge surge of relief washed over her, leaving her weak. 'But that look of pure panic soothes my ego!'

Whirling round, she laughed a little uneasily. 'I wasn't—'

'It is rather frightening to feel like this, isn't it, *cara?*'

'I don't know what you mean—'

'Oh, yes, you do…stay frank, I prefer it.'

'How do you feel about one-night stands?' she asked daringly.

He stilled. A silence thick as fog sprang up.

'I don't do them,' he said drily. 'I was rather hoping you didn't either.'

'How do you feel about virgins?'

'Deeply unexcited.'

'OK, you don't ask me any questions, I won't tell you any lies…how's that for a ground rule?'

'You'll soon get bored with those limitations,' he stated with supreme confidence.

But she *knew* she would not. Honest answers would expose the reality she longed to escape. The young woman who had disappointed from birth by being a girl, who had been denied the opportunity even to continue her education, and who had finally crowned her inadequacies by being jilted at the altar, subjecting her family, to whom appearances were everything, to severe embarrassment and herself to bitter recriminations. She had no desire to pose as an object of pity.

Within minutes he led her down that grand staircase. Realising only then that she had won and that they were leaving the ball together, she stretched up on her toes to kiss him in the crowded hall, generous in victory. Hearing what sounded like a startled buzz of comment erupt around them, she drew back, stunned by her own audacity. She blushed, but he just laughed.

'You're so natural with me,' he breathed appreciatively. 'As if you've known me all your life…'

A magnificent beribboned gondola was moored outside, awaiting their command. A gondola with a cabin swathed in richly embroidered fabric and soft velvet cushions within. And what followed *was* magical. Luca didn't just point out the sights, he entertained her with stories that entranced her. The Palazzo Mocenigo, where Lord Byron had stayed and where one of his many distraught mistresses threw herself from a balcony. The debtor's prison cell from which Casanova contrived a daring escape. The Rialto where Shakespeare's Shylock walked.

His beautiful voice slowly turned husky with hoarseness, and captured in that haze of romantic imagery she smiled dreamily, sensing his deep love and pride in the city of his birth, reaching up to him to kiss him and meet those dark deep-set eyes with a bubbling assurance she had never experienced in male company before. At one point they glided to a halt in a quiet side canal to be served champagne and strawberries by a sleepy-eyed but smiling waiter.

'You're a fake, *cara mia*,' Luca breathed mockingly then. 'You say you don't want romance, but you revel in every slushy embellishment I can provide.'

'I'm not a fake. Why can't we have *one* perfect night? No strings, no ties, no regrets?'

'I'll make you a bet—a sure-fire certainty,' Luca murmured with silken assurance. 'Whatever happens tonight, I'll meet you tomorrow at three on the Ponte della Guerra. You *will* be there.'

'Tomorrow doesn't exist for us,' she returned dismissively, not even grasping at that point that he might understand her better than she understood herself, that almost the minute she was away from him she would want to be back with him, no matter what the risk. 'Take me home,' she told him then, impatient of the deeply inhibiting need to keep her hands off him in public.

'Where are you staying?'

'*Your* home…'

'We'll have breakfast together—'

'I'm not hungry.'

He had stared steadily down at her. 'You know nothing about me.'

'I know I want to be with you…I know you want to be with me…what *more* do I need to know?'

A spasm of stark pain infiltrated Darcy as she recalled that foolish question. It shot her right back to the present, where fearful uncertainty and frustration ruled. At that moment she could not bear to relive the final hours she had spent with Luca in Venice. And she was tormented by the awareness that her own behaviour that night had been far more reckless, provocative and capricious than she had ever been prepared to admit in the years since.

The door opened without warning. Taken by surprise, Darcy scrambled awkwardly off the bed. Thrusting the door closed again, Luca surveyed her, sensual mouth curling as he scanned the shabby shrunken jeans. 'I always used to believe that a woman without vanity would be an incredible find. Then fate served me with you,' he imparted grimly. 'Now I know better.'

'What's that supposed to mean?' Darcy snapped defensively.

'You'll find out. Sloth in the vanity department won't be a profitable proposition.'

His frowning attention falling on the large framed photo, Luca strode across the room to lift it from the cabinet. There was a stark little silence. He was very still, his chiselled profile clenched taut. 'You sleep with a picture of Richard Carlton by your bed?' he breathed a tinge unevenly, a slightly forced edge to the enquiry that thickened his accent.

'Why not…? We're still very close.' Darcy saw nothing strange in that admission, particularly when her mind was preoccupied with more pressing problems. She drew in a sharp breath. 'Luca…I don't know what's going on here. This whole situation is so crazy, I feel…I feel like Alice in Wonderland after she went through the looking glass!'

'You astonish me. In every depiction I have ever seen Alice sported fabulous long curly hair and a pretty dress. The resemblance is in *your* mind alone.'

Darcy groaned. 'Now you're being flippant. From my point of view you are acting like a man who has escaped from an asylum—'

'That is because you have an extremely prosaic outlook,' Luca delivered softly. 'You cannot grasp the concept of revenge because you yourself would consider revenge a waste of time and effort. I too am practical, but I warn you, I also have great imagination and a constitutional inability to live with being bested by anyone. Setting the police on your trail wouldn't have given me the slightest satisfaction—'

'The…the *police?*' Darcy stressed with a look of blank astonishment.

Luca flicked her a shrewd, narrow-eyed glance, eyes black and cold as a wintry night. 'You play the innocent so well. I can ever understand why. You were far from home. You felt secure in the belief that you would never be identified, never be traced, never be punished for your dishonesty—'

'I don't know what the blazes you're talking about!' Darcy spluttered. 'My…*dishonesty?*'

'But you miscalculated…the role of victim is not for me,' Luca declared. 'And now it's your turn to savour the same experience. A flare for the prosaic will be of no benefit whatsoever in the weeks to come.'

'I've got a lot more staying power than you think!' Darcy fired back, determined to stand up to him. 'So why don't you tell me why you're making crazy references to the police and my supposed dishonesty?'

Luca sent her a winging glance of derision. 'Why waste my breath? I prefer to wait until you get tired of pretending and decide to make a pathetic little confession about how temptation got the better of you!'

'I can hardly confess to something I haven't done!' Darcy objected in vehement frustration.

Ignoring that fierce protest, Luca lifted up a sheet of the fax paper, directing his attention to the business address of the stud farm at the top. 'Carlton's place,' he registered grimly. 'So it was Carlton you got in touch with.'

'I didn't tell Richard anything…I just wanted to know who you really were—*not* an unreasonable wish when I find myself married to a man who hasn't told me one single word of truth!' Darcy shot at him in ringing condemnation.

'But you couldn't wait to get married to me,' Luca reminded her with gentle irony. 'And, I, who have never felt the tiniest urge to give up my freedom, was equally eager in this instance to see the legal bond put in place.'

'Because now you think you've got me where you want me.'

Luca regarded her with hard intensity. His arrogant

dark head tipped back. Eyes hard as diamonds raked her defiant face. 'Carlton's still your lover, isn't he?'

'That's none of your business...in fact if I had a lover for every different day of the week, it would be none of your business!' Darcy slung back.

'No?' Luca said softly.

'No!' As her temper rode higher, Darcy was indifferent to the menace of that velvet-soft intonation.

Luca shifted a lean dark hand with fluid grace and eloquence. 'Even the suspicion that you could be contemplating infidelity will be grounds for separation. You see, although I have laid it all before you in very simple terms, you still fail to appreciate that I hold every card. You cannot afford to antagonise a husband you need to retain.'

Darcy shivered with anger, outraged by that, 'very simple terms', which suggested she was of less than average intelligence. 'The price could well be too high—'

'But it *has* to be high, and more than you want to pay...how could I enjoy this otherwise?' Luca countered, the dark planes of his strikingly handsome features bearing a look of calm enquiry.

As her green eyes flashed with sheer fury, Luca shot her a provocative smile.

In that instant, Darcy lost her head. Temper blazing, she stalked forward and lifted a hand with which to slap that hateful smile into eternity. With a throaty sound of infuriating amusement, Luca sidestepped her. Closing two strong hands round her narrow ribcage, he lifted her clean off her feet and tumbled her down onto the bed behind her.

CHAPTER SIX

BREATHLESS and stunned as Luca captured her furiously flailing hands in one of his, Darcy whispered in outrage, 'What do you think you're doing?'

'I'm not thinking right now,' Luca confided, luxuriant lashes low on liquid golden eyes of sensual appraisal as he scanned the riot of bright curls on her small head. 'I'm wondering how long your hair will get in six months... You'll grow it for me, just as you will do so many other things *just* for me—'

'*Dream on!*'

Confident eyes gleamed down into scorching green.

As Luca slowly lowered his lean, well-built body down onto hers, a jolt of sexual awareness as keen and sharp as an electric shock currented through Darcy. The sensation made her even more determined to break free.

Luca banded both arms more fully round her violently struggling figure. 'Calm down...you'll hurt yourself!' he urged impatiently.

'You are in the wrong position to tell me to do that!' Darcy warned breathlessly.

'Assault would be grounds for separation too,' Luca informed her indolently.

Darcy's knee tingled. She, who had never in her entire life hurt another human being, now longed to deliver a crippling blow. Luca contemplated her with almost scientific interest, making no attempt to protect himself. 'I want to hurt you!' she suddenly screeched at him in driven fury.

'But this crumbling pile of bricks and mortar stands between you and that desire,' Luca guessed with galling accuracy. 'It will be interesting to see how much you will tolerate before you snap and surrender.'

Darcy's blood ran cold at that unfeeling response.

'You'll play the whore in my bed for the sake of this house...but then what you've already done once should come even more easily a second time,' Luca surmised icily.

'You're talking rubbish, because I'll never sleep with you...I will *never* sleep with you again!' In a wild movement of repudiation, Darcy garnered the strength to tear herself free. But Luca had frighteningly fast reflexes. With a rueful sigh over her obstinacy, he snapped long fingers round her shoulder before she could move out of reach, and simply tipped her back into his arms.

'Of course you will,' he countered levelly then, brilliant dark eyes locked to her furiously flushed face.

'I *won't!*' Darcy swore.

As Luca slowly anchored her back to the mattress with his superior body weight, the all pervasive heat of his big, powerful frame engulfed her limbs in a drugging paralysis. Momentarily Darcy forgot to struggle. She also forgot to breathe.

Luca angled down his arrogant dark head and tasted her soft mouth with a devastatingly direct hunger that shot right down to her toes. Her lips burned; her thighs trembled. She looked up at him in complete shock, her mind wiped clean of thought. But her heart pounded as if she was fighting for her life, her pupils dilated, her breath coming in tiny frantic pants. She collided with the blaze of sexual challenge in his gaze and it was as if he had thrown the switch on her self-control. Dear heaven, she loved it when he looked at her like *that*...

Deep down inside, she melted with terrifying anticipation of the excitement to come. Her breasts stirred inside her cotton bra, nipples peaking with painful suddenness into taut, straining buds. Luca shifted and she felt the hard, masculine thrust of his erection against her pelvis. She quivered, her spine arching as her yielding body flooded with liquid heat and surrender. Neither one of them heard the soft rap on the bedroom door.

His dark eyes burned gold with fierce satisfaction. He rimmed her parted lips with the tip of his tongue, teasing, taunting, the warmth of his breath fanning her, locking her into breathless intimacy. Every atom of her being was desperate for his next move, the moist, sensitive interior of her mouth aching for his penetration.

'Fight me...' Luca instructed huskily. 'After all the fun of the chase, an easy victory would be a real disappointment.'

Almost simultaneously, a loud knock thudded on the sturdy door. Darcy flinched and jerked up her knee in fright, accidentally connecting with Luca's anatomy in an unfortunate place. As he wrenched back from her in stunned pain and incredulity Darcy cried, 'Oh, no...*gosh,* I'm sorry!' and she reeled off the bed like a drunk, frantically smoothing down her rumpled sweater and striving to walk in a straight line to the door.

'Is Luca with you, *signora?*' Benito enquired levelly. 'The helicopter has arrived early.'

Hearing a muffled groan from somewhere behind her, Darcy coughed noisily to conceal the sound, and with crimson cheeks she muttered defensively, 'I don't know where he is...and we can't leave yet anyway. I have hens to feed.'

'Hens…' Benito echoed, and nodded very slowly at that information.

Closing the door again, and tactfully not looking in Luca's direction, Darcy whispered in considerable embarrassment, 'Are you all right, Luca?'

Luca gritted something that didn't sound terribly reassuring in his own language.

'I'll get you a glass of water,' Darcy proffered, full of genuine remorse. 'It was an accident…honestly, it was—'

'Bitch…' Luca ground out with agonised effort.

Darcy withdrew a step. The silence thundered.

'I'll see you later,' she muttered curtly. 'Right now, I've got work to do.'

'We're flying to Venice!' Luca shot at her rawly.

Only then did Darcy also recall the appointment she had made at the bank. Checking her watch, she emitted a strangled groan and took flight.

Half an hour later, having mucked out Nero's stable, Darcy mustered the courage to enter the poultry coop. Henrietta the hen, who regarded every human invasion as a hostile act, gave her a mean look of anticipation.

'Please, Henrietta, *not* today,' Darcy pleaded as she hurriedly filled a bowl with eggs, her thoughts straying helplessly back to Luca and the excruciating awareness that he could still rip away her defences and make her agonisingly vulnerable.

She was so desperately confused by the emotions flailing her. She knew now that prior to the revelation of Luca's real identity she had grown to trust him, *like* him, even. She had revelled in his sophisticated cool at Margo's party, his seeming protectiveness, even the envious looks of other women. Dear God, how pathetic she had been, and now she felt gutted, absolutely gutted by the most savage sense of loss and bewilderment, and quite incapable of comprehending what was going on inside her own head.

And as for her wretched body…? Recalling that kiss on the bed, reliving the shameless and eager anticipation which had flamed through her, Darcy hated herself. Luca had been taunting her, humiliating her with her own weakness. The tables had been turned with a vengeance, she acknowledged painfully. For hadn't she foolishly believed for the space of one night three years ago that she, too, could treat sex as a casual experience for which pleasure would be the only price?

Hadn't she been bitterly conscious that night in Venice that she was still a virgin? Hadn't she been rebelling against her own image? Hadn't she longed to taste the power of being a sexually aware and sexually appealing woman? And hadn't the idea of throwing off her inhibitions far from home been tempting? And hadn't she known the same moment Luca melted her bones with one passionate kiss that she wanted to go to bed with him and forever banish the demeaning memory of her sterile, sexless relationship with Richard?

And, worse, hadn't she thrown herself at Luca at every opportunity, stubbornly evading his every attempt to slow the pace of their intimacy? All that champagne on top of her medication had left her bereft of every inhibition. For so long she had used the alcohol in her veins as an excuse. But the imagery that now assailed Darcy in split-second shattering Technicolor frames, the undeniably shocking memories of how she had treated Luca that night, now filled her with choking shame.

She had never once allowed herself to remember exactly what she had done to Luca in that bedroom. She had been in the grip of a wanton hunger, a hunger fanned to white-hot heat by the knowledge that this beautiful, gorgeous, sophisticated guy was weak with lust for *her*. She hadn't wanted him to suspect that he was her first lover...and she had gone to indecent lengths not to give him the smallest grounds for that suspicion.

As a pained moan of mortification escaped Darcy under the assault of those memories, Henrietta jabbed a vicious beak into her extended hand.

With a startled yelp of pain, Darcy exited backwards from the coop, her dogs barking frantically at her heels.

'Sta zitto!' That command slashed through the air like a whip.

Darcy twisted round in dismay. In the light of her recent thoughts she was truly appalled to see Luca poised on the path several feet away. Her face flamed. There he was, six feet four inches of staggeringly attractive, sleek and powerful masculinity, luxuriant black hair smooth, charcoal-grey suit shrieking class and expensive tailoring. But, disconcertingly, Darcy's defiant subconscious threw up a much more disturbing image of Luca. Luca sprawled gloriously naked across white sheets, a magnificent vision of golden-skinned male perfection, a life-sized fantasy toy entirely at her mercy.

Far, far too late had she learnt that Luca had inspired her with something infinitely more dangerous than desire. He would laugh longest and loudest if he ever realised that truth.

Suddenly sick with pain and regret at her own stupidity, Darcy twisted her bright head away under the onslaught of those fiercely intelligent dark eyes.

As Humpf and Bert grovelled ingratiatingly round his feet, Luca scanned Darcy's bedraggled appearance. Her jeans were streaked with dirt, her sweater liberally adorned with pieces of straw. Dawning disbelief in his grim appraisal, he breathed with admirable restraint, 'You have exactly ten minutes to change and board the helicopter.'

'I can't!' Darcy protested, her evasive eyes whipping back in his general direction. 'I have to go to the bank—'

'Why? Are you planning to rob it?' Luca enquired sardonically. 'If I was your bank manager, nothing short of an armed assault would persuade me to advance you any further credit!'

Darcy compressed her lips in a mutinous line.

'No bank,' said Luca. 'We have a take-off slot to make at the airport.'

'I *can't* miss this appointment—'

Luca caught her by the elbow as she attempted to stalk past him. 'You're bleeding…what have you done to yourself?' he demanded.

Darcy flicked an irritable glance down at the angry scratch oozing blood on the back of her hand. 'It's nothing. Henrietta's always attacking me.'

'Henrietta?'

'Queen of the coop—the hen with attitude. I ought to wring her manic neck, but she'd come back and haunt me. In a strange way, I'm sort of fond of her,' Darcy admitted grudgingly. 'She's got personality.'

Luca's intent dark eyes now held a slightly dazed aspect. He was no Einstein on the subject of hens, she registered.

Darcy took advantage of his abstraction to pull free. 'I'll be back before you know it…I promise!' she slung over her shoulder as she sped off.

It took her ten minutes to change into the tweed skirt and tailored blouse she always wore to the bank.

Studiously ignoring the helicopter sitting on the front lawn, and the pilot pacing up and down beside it, she jumped into the Land Rover and rattled off down the drive.

Two hours later, having been to the bank, and then arranged for a local farmer to pick up and stable Nero, Darcy walked into Karen's kitchen to ask her to look after the dogs, feed the hens from a safe distance and keep an eye on the Folly.

Zia bounced up into her mother's arms. Darcy studied her daughter's clear dark eyes, smooth golden skin and ebony curls. A sinking sensation curdled her stomach. From her classic little nose to her feathery but dead level brows, Zia looked so *like* her father. Darcy buried her face in her daughter's springy hair and breathed in the fresh, clean scent of her child while she fought to master emotions and fears that were dangerously near to the surface. In fact, all she wanted to do at that instant was collapse into floods of overwrought tears, and the knowledge appalled her.

'Benito's been down twice to see if you're here…talk about fussing!' Karen told her above the toddler's animated chatter. 'What's all this about you going to Italy?'

'Don't ask,' Darcy advised flatly. 'I've just been to the bank. My bank manager says he's not a betting man.'

'I could've told you that without seeing him. He's so miserable, he wouldn't bet on the sun rising tomorrow!'

'He said that in six months' time, when I actually inherit, it'll be different, but that it would be wrong to allow me to borrow more now on the strength of what are only expectations.' That Luca had made the same forecast right off the top of his superior head infuriated Darcy.

'I'm really sorry…' Karen's eyes, however, remained bright with curiosity. 'But if you've got five minutes could you possibly tell me where the swanky limo and the helicopter have come from?'

'They belong to Luca.'

'So he *was* a dark horse. How very strange! People usually pretend to be more than they are rather than *less* than they are. Was Nina right, after all? Has he married you to gain a British passport?' Karen pressed with a frown. 'Why all the heavy secrecy? He's not one of these high-flying international criminals, is he?'

If Luca *had* been a criminal, the police might just have been able to take him away, Darcy thought helplessly. But then that wouldn't have suited her either. No matter how obnoxious he was, she needed to hang onto her husband for the next six months. What shook her even more at that moment was the sudden shattering awareness that in spite of the manner in which Luca was behaving, the threat of him disappearing altogether made her feel positively sick and shaky.

'Darcy…?' Karen prompted.

She averted her attention from her friend. 'There was a confidentiality clause in our pre-nuptial contract. I'd like to tell you everything,' she lied, because there was no way she wanted to tell a living soul about how stupid she had been, 'but I can't… Will you look after the Folly while I'm away?'

'Of course I will. I'll move in. Don't look so glum, Darcy…six months won't be that long in going by.'

But the Folly might well be repossessed long before that six months was up. Karen's purchase of the gate lodge had bought some time, by paying off the most pressing debts against the estate, but Darcy was still a couple of months behind with the mortgage repayments.

She drove back up to the house and clambered out. Luca emerged from the entrance, strong, dark face rigid, dark eyes diamond-hard with exasperation.

'Have you any idea what time it is?' he launched at her.

Zia skipped forward. She was unconcerned by that greeting. She had grown up with a grandfather who bawled the length of the room at everybody, and volume bothered her not at all. She extended a foot with a carefully pointed toe for Luca's inspection. 'See... pretty,' she told Luca chirpily.

'*Accidenti...*' Luca began, reluctantly tearing his attention from Darcy to focus with a frown on the tiny child in front of him.

'If you want peace, admire her frilly socks.'

'I beg your pardon?' Luca breathed grittily.

'Zia...' Darcy urged, holding out her hand.

But her daughter was stubborn. Her bottom lip jutted out. She wasn't used to being ignored. In fact, Darcy reflected, if Zia had a fault, it was a pronounced *dislike* of being ignored.

'Has you dot pretty socks?' Zia demanded somewhat aggressively of Luca.

'No, I haven't!' Luca ground out in fierce exasperation.

There was no mistaking that tone of rejection. Zia's eyes grew huge and then flooded with tears. A noisy sob burst from her instantaneously.

Darcy swept up her daughter to comfort her. 'You really are a cruel swine,' she condemned feverishly. 'She's only a baby...and if you think I'm travelling to

Italy with someone who treats my child like that, you're insane!'

Discovering that even the loyal Benito, who had come to an uneasy halt some feet away, was regarding him in shocked surprise, Luca felt his blunt cheekbones drench with dark colour. He strode back into the house in Darcy's furious wake.

'I'm sorry…I'm not used to young children,' he admitted stiltedly.

'That's no excuse—'

'Bad man!' Zia sobbed accusingly from the security of her mother's arms.

'Never mind, darling.' Darcy smoothed her daughter's tumbled curls.

'You could *try* contradicting her—'

'She'd know I was lying.'

But, mollified by the apology and the certain awareness that Luca had just enjoyed an uncomfortable learning experience, Darcy went back outside and climbed into the helicopter.

'Is she asleep?' Luca skimmed a deeply cautious glance into the sleeping compartment of his private jet to survey the slight immobile bump on the built-in divan, his voice a positive whisper in which prayer and hope were blatant and unashamed.

Darcy tiptoed out into the main cabin, her face grey with fatigue. In all her life she had never endured a more nightmare journey.

Zia had been sick all the way to London in the helicopter. The long wait in the VIP lounge until the jet could get another take-off slot had done nothing to improve the spirits of a distressed, over-tired and still nauseous little girl. Zia had whinged, cried, thrown hysterical tantrums on the carpet beneath Luca's utterly stricken and appalled gaze, and generally conducted herself like the toddler from hell.

'She's never behaved like that before,' Darcy muttered wearily for about the twentieth time.

By now impervious to such statements, Luca sank down with a shell-shocked aspect into a comfortable seat. Then he sat forward abruptly, an aghast set to his lean, dark features. 'Will she wake up again when we land?'

'Heaven knows...' Darcy was afraid to make any more optimistic forecasts, but maternal protectiveness prompted her to speak up in further defence of her daughter. 'Zia's not used to being sick. She likes a secure routine, her own familiar things around her,' she explained. 'Everything's been strange to her, and then when she was hungry and we could only offer her foreign food—'

'That was definitely the last straw,' Luca recalled with a shudder. 'I can still hear those screams. *Per meraviglia*...what a temper she has! And so stubborn, so demanding! I had no idea that one small child could be that disruptive. As for the embarrassment she caused me—'

'All right...*all right!*' Darcy groaned in interruption as she collapsed down into the seat opposite.

'Let me tell you, it is no trivial matter to have to trail a child screaming that I am a *bad man* through a crowded airport!' Luca slammed back at her in wrathful recollection. 'And whose fault was that? Who allowed that phrase to implant in the poor child's head? What I have suffered this evening would have taxed the compassion of a saint!'

Darcy closed her aching eyes. A policeman, clearly

alerted by a concerned member of the public, had intervened to request that Luca identify himself. Then a man with a camera and a nasty raucous laugh had taken a photo of them.

The flash of the powerful camera had scared Zia. Darcy had been shaken, it not having previously occurred to her that Luca might be a target for such intrusive press attention. Bereft even of the slight protection that might have been offered by Benito, who had left the Folly in the limousine, Luca had seethed in controlled silence. A saint he was not, but he *had* made a sustained effort to assist her in comforting and calming Zia.

Luca released his breath in a stark hiss. 'However, the original fault was of my own making. When I demanded an immediate departure from your home, I took no account of the needs of so young a child. It was too late in the day to embark on such a journey.'

Kicking off her shoes, Darcy curled her legs wearily beneath her. Such a concession was of little comfort to her now. She was wrung out.

'But this *is* our wedding night,' Luca reminded her, as if that was some kind of excuse.

Darcy didn't even have enough energy left to expel a grizzly laugh at that announcement. She sagged into the luxurious comfort of the seat and rested her head back to survey him with shadowed green eyes.

The sight of Zia asleep and the sound of silence appeared to have revived Luca. His dark eyes glittered with restive energy. He looked neither tired nor under strain, but he was no longer quite so immaculate, she noted, desperate to find comfort in that minor show of human fallibility. He now had a definable five o'clock shadow on his hard jawline. He had also loosened his tie and undone the top button of his shirt to reveal the strong brown column of his throat. And, if anything, he looked even more devastatingly attractive than he had looked at the altar, she acknowledged, and instantly despised herself for noticing.

With great effort, Darcy mustered her thoughts and breathed in deep. 'I have the right to know *why* you're doing this to me, Luca,' she told him yet again.

'But what have I done?' An ebony brow elevated. 'I agreed to marry you and have I not done so?'

Darcy groaned in unconcealed despair. 'Luca... *please!* I hate games. If I'd had the time and the peace at the Folly...if I hadn't been in so much shock at your threats...I wouldn't have allowed you to browbeat and panic me into this trip at such short notice.'

'I planned it that way,' Luca admitted, with the kind of immovable calm that made her want to tear him to pieces.

As her temper flared, colour burnished her cheeks and her eyes sparked with the fire of her frustration. 'You still have to tell me *why* you're doing this to me!' Darcy reminded him with fierce emphasis. 'And if you don't, I will—'

'Yes...what *will* you do?' Luca interposed deflatingly. 'Fly back to the UK alone and accept the loss of that house on which you place such value?'

It was the same threat which had intimidated Darcy into acquiescence that afternoon. But she was now beyond being silenced. 'You insinuated that I had done something dishonest that night in Venice...and that is an outrageous untruth.'

'Theft is a crime. It is never acceptable. But when theft is linked to deliberate deception, it is doubly abhorrent and offensive.' Luca delivered that condemnation with unblemished gravity.

Darcy's temples were beginning to pound with tension again. Her strained eyes locked to his cold, dark gaze. 'Let me get this s-straight,' she whispered, her voice catching in her throat. '*You* are actually accusing *me* of having stolen something from you that night?'

'My overnight guests don't as a rule use a small rear window as an exit,' Luca responded very drily. 'I was downstairs within minutes of the alarm going off!'

Darcy's face flamed with chagrin at the reminder of the manner in which she had been forced to leave his apartment. She had crept out of his bed while he was still asleep. When that horrible shrieking alarm had sounded as she'd climbed out of the window, she had panicked. Dying a thousand deaths in her embarrassment, she had raced down the narrow alley beyond at supersonic speed. 'For heaven's sake, I just wanted to leave quietly…but I couldn't get your blasted front door open!'

'Not without the security code,' Luca conceded. 'It would only have opened without the code if there had been a fire or if I had shut down the system. I was surprised that a thief ingenious enough to beat every other security device in that apartment *and* break into my safe should make such a very clumsy departure.'

'Break into your safe,' Darcy repeated, wide-eyed, weakened further by the revelation that this insane man she had married believed she was not only guilty of having stolen from him but also equal to the challenge of cracking open a safe.

'As a morning-after-the-night-before experience, it was unparalleled,' Luca informed her sardonically.

'I've never stolen anything in my life…I *wouldn't*!'

It was a strangled plea of innocence, powered by strong distaste. 'As for breaking into a safe, I wouldn't even know where to *begin!*' Darcy emphasised, eyes dark with disbelief that he could credit otherwise.

Luca searched her shaken face with shrewd intensity and slowly moved his arrogant dark head in reluctant admiration. 'You're even more convincing than I expected you to be.'

In an abrupt movement, Darcy uncoiled her legs and sprang upright to stare down at him. 'You've got to believe me…for heaven's sake…if someone broke into that apartment and stole from you as that day was dawning, it certainly wasn't me!'

'No, I made the very great misjudgement of taking the thief home with me so that she could do an easier inside job,' Luca commented with icy exactitude, his strong jaw clenching. 'And in a sense you're right; it wasn't you. You wore a disguise—'

'Disguise?' Darcy broke in weakly.

'You made the effort to look like a million dollars that night. You had to look the part.'

'Luca—'

'You gatecrashed an élite social function attended by some very wealthy people and were careful not to draw too much attention to yourself,' Luca continued grimly, his expressive mouth hard as iron. 'You refused to identify yourself in any way and you ensured that I brought you home with me…after all, with the number of staff around your chances of contriving to steal anything from the Palazzo d'Oro were extremely slim.'

'I didn't do it…do you hear me?' Darcy almost shrieked at him. *'I didn't do it!'*

Luca dealt her a withering glance of savage amusement. 'But you've already confessed that you did steal *and* sell the ring. Or had you forgotten that reality?'

Darcy's lashes fluttered in bewilderment. Left bereft of breath by that staggering assurance, she pressed a weak hand to her damp brow and tottered backwards into her seat again.

CHAPTER SEVEN

'DON'T you recall that sleepy and foolish little confession at the inn?' Luca prompted with a scathing look of derision. 'You admitted that the sale of an antique ring financed roof repairs for your family home and indeed may well have staved off the enforced sale of that home.'

'It was a *ring* which was stolen from your safe?' Darcy breathed shakily, belatedly making that connection. 'But that's just a stupid coincidence. The ring that my father sold belonged to my family!'

'The Adorata ring is stolen and only a few months later the Fieldings contrive to rescue their dwindling fortunes by the judicious discovery and sale of *another* ring?' Luca jibed, unimpressed by her explanation. 'There *was* no other ring! And, since your family estate is still in financial hot water, you must've sold the Adorata for a tithe of its true worth!'

'I've never heard of this Ador-whatever ring that you're talking about, nor have I been involved in any way in either stealing or selling it!' Darcy's taut voice shook, her growing exhaustion biting deep.

'You were wise enough to wait a while before selling it and you ensured that it was a private sale. Now I hope you also have sufficient wit to know when your back is up against a brick wall,' Luca spelt out icily. 'I want the name of the buyer. And you had better hope and pray for your own sake that I am able to reclaim the Adorata without resorting to legal intervention!'

'It wasn't your wretched ring. I swear it wasn't!' Darcy protested sharply, appalled by his refusal even to stop and take proper account of her arguments in her own defence. 'I don't know who bought it because my father insisted on dealing with the sale. He was a very proud man. He didn't want *anybody* to know that he was so short of money that he had to sell an heirloom—'

'Why waste my time with these stupid stories?' Luca subjected her to a hard scrutiny, his contempt and his impatience with her protests palpable. 'I despise liars. Before I put you back out of my life, you will tell me where that ring is…or you will lose by it.'

It occurred to Darcy then that no matter what she did with Luca, he intended her to lose by it. He had hemmed her in with so many threats she felt trapped. And the shattering revelation that he believed her to be a thief equal to safe-cracking just seemed to stop her weary brain functioning altogether.

Only two thoughts stayed in her mind. Luca might still be walking around as if he was sane, but he couldn't be. And possibly he had been watching too many movies in which incredibly immoral calculating women seduced the hero and then turned on him with evil intent. Safe-cracking? A glazed look in her eyes, Darcy contemplated the fact that she couldn't even operate a washing machine without going step by painful step through the instructions…

'Do you still find it magical?' Luca demanded, above the roar of the motorboat which had collected them from Marco Polo Airport to waft them across the lagoon into the city.

A woman in a waking dream, Darcy gazed out on

the Grand Canal. The darkness was dispelled by the lights in the beautiful medieval buildings and on the other craft around them. The grand, sweeping waterway throbbed with life. It was like travelling inside a magnificent painting, she thought privately. She assumed that they were heading to his apartment, but as far as she was concerned they could happily spend the rest of the night getting there.

When the boatman chugged into a mooring at the Palazzo d'Oro, with its splendid Renaissance façade, Darcy was astonished. 'Why are we stopping here?'

'This is my home,' Luca informed her.

'But it c-can't be...' Darcy stammered.

Deftly detaching Zia's solid little body from her arms, Luca stepped out onto the covered walkway semi-screened from the canal by an elaborate run of pillars and arches. At the entrance to the *palazzo,* an older woman in an apron stood in readiness. She made clucking sounds and extended sturdy arms to receive the sleeping child.

Darcy snatched at Luca's hand and stepped out onto the walkway. 'Who's that?'

'My sister Ilaria's old nursemaid. She will put Zia to bed and stay with her.'

'But I—'

As Luca urged her into the spectacular entrance hall, with its glorious domed ceiling frescoes far above, Darcy stilled. 'You *can't* live here—'

'My ancestors *built* the Palazzo d'Oro.'

Just as Luca finished speaking, a startling interruption occurred. Two enormous shaggy dogs loped noisily down the fantastic gilded staircase pursued by a shouting middle-aged manservant.

'*Santo cieo!*' Luca rapped out a sharp command that

forestalled the threatening surge of boisterous animal greeting. The deerhounds fell back, tails drooping between their impossibly long legs, great narrow heads lowered, doggy brown eyes pathetic in their disappointment.

The manservant broke into a flood of anxious explanation. Luca turned back to Darcy, exasperation etched in his lean, strong features.

'What are they called?' Darcy prompted eagerly.

'Aristide and Zou Zou,' Luca divulged reluctantly, his nostrils flaring. 'They belong to my sister.'

'Aren't they gorgeous?' Darcy began to move forward to pet the two dogs.

As a pair of very long tails began to rise in response to that soft, encouraging intonation, Luca closed an arm round his bride to restrain her enthusiasm. 'No, they are *not*,' he stressed meaningfully. 'They are undisciplined, unbelievably stupid and wholly unsuited to city life. But every time Ilaria goes away, she dumps them here.'

As Luca's manservant gripped their jewel-studded collars to lead them away, the two dogs twisted their heads back to focus on Darcy with pleading eyes. She was touched to the heart.

'Are you hungry?' Luca asked then.

'I couldn't eat to save my life.'

'Then I will show you upstairs.'

'If this is really your home,' Darcy whispered numbly about halfway up the second flight. 'That means…that means that you were the *host* at the masked ball.'

'You wouldn't let me tell you who I was. And since the ball invariably lasts until dawn, I could scarcely bring you back here for the remainder of the night. At the time, I had been using the apartment regularly while renovations were being carried out here.'

'There's so much I don't know about you—'

'And now you have all the time in the world to discover everything you ever wanted to know,' Luca pointed out in a tone of bracing consolation.

'I don't think I want to find out any more.'

'This has not been the most propitious of wedding days,' Luca conceded smoothly. 'But I'm certain you have the resilience to rise above a somewhat difficult beginning. After all, *cara mia*…I'm prepared to be very generous.'

Darcy gawped at him. *'Generous?'*

'If you satisfy my demands, I *will* allow you to inherit that one million. I'm not a complete bastard. There are those who say that I am,' Luca admitted reflectively, 'and I would concede that I am no bleeding heart, but I am always scrupulously fair in my dealings.'

'Is that a fact?' Darcy passed no opinion because she didn't have the energy to argue with him.

Passing down a corridor lined with fine oil paintings, Luca flung open the door of a superb bedroom full of ornate gilded furniture. One stunned glance was sufficient to tell Darcy that in comparison Fielding's Folly offered all the comfort of a medieval barn in an advanced state of decay.

'Your luggage will be brought up.'

'I want to see Zia. Where is she?'

'In the nursery suite on the floor above. Most mothers would be grateful for a break from childcare on their wedding night.'

'What is with this "wedding night' bit you keep on mentioning?' Darcy enquired with stilted reluctance.

Luca treated her to a slow, sensual smile. Dark golden eyes of intent gleamed below luxuriant black lashes. 'You are not that naive. Whatever else you may be, you are still a Raffacani bride, and tonight in the time-honoured tradition of my ancestors we will share that bed together.'

Darcy thought about this nightmare day she had enjoyed at Luca's merciless hands. She studied him in honest disbelief.

'You should congratulate yourself.' His exquisitely expressive mouth quirked. 'Only the memory of that incredibly passionate night we once shared persuaded me to go to the extremity of marrying you. The prospect of six sexually self-indulgent months played a major part in that decision.'

'I can imagine,' Darcy mumbled weakly, and she *could*.

Luca saw life's every event in terms of profit and loss. Almost three years ago he had suffered a loss for which he had falsely blamed her. Now he planned to turn loss into vengeful profit between the bedsheets. It was novel, she conceded. But for a rogue male to whom everything probably came far too easily, anything that supplied a challenge would always be what he wanted most.

Dear heaven, had she been that exciting in bed? She had been imaginative, she was prepared to admit, but that night had been a one-off. Heady romance, bitter rebellion and fiery desire had combined with champagne to send her off the rails. She had lived out a never to be repeated kind of fantasy and lived on to regret every single second of her reckless misbehaviour.

'I'll give you an hour to rediscover your energies and ponder the reality that a marriage that is *not* consummated is worthless in the eyes of the law.'

'What are you talking about?'

'Aren't you aware that sex is an integral part of the

marriage contract? And the lack of it grounds for annulment?'

Darcy's jaw dropped.

'You see, I'm not a complete bastard,' Luca contended, smooth as glass. 'A complete bastard would
have left you to sleep in ignorance and gone for non-
consummation at the end of the six months.'

Leaving her to reflect on that revelation of astounding
generosity, Luca strolled back out of the room.

That is one happy man, Darcy thought helplessly. An
utterly ruthless male with the persistence of a jugger-
naut, punch-drunk on the belief that he had her exactly
where he wanted her. He was destined to discover that
he had a prolonged battle ahead of him. Although she
was currently at a very low ebb, Darcy was by nature
a fighter.

A thief. He thought she was a thief. He genuinely
believed that she had stolen that wretched ring with the
stupid name. And, truth to tell, if it had been stolen the
same night, he had some grounds for that suspicion.
Indeed, when that theft was combined with her flight at
dawn, her status as a gatecrasher and her flat refusal to
tell him who she was throughout the evening, she had
to concede that his conviction that she was the guilty
party *was* based on some pretty solid-looking facts.

However, those facts were simply misleading facts.
Obviously she had been in the wrong place at the wrong
time. But Luca wasn't the type of male likely to question his own judgement. In fact, unless she was very
much mistaken, Luca prided himself on his powers of
logic and reasoning. That being so, for almost three
years he had staunchly believed that she was the culprit.
By now, the real thief and the ring had to be long gone.
Luca's mistake, not hers.

In the meantime, only by finding some proof that the ring her father had sold had been a different ring entirely could she hope to defend herself. Had her father kept any record of that sale? And what the heck was the use of wondering that when she was stuck in Venice and unable to conduct any sort of search? Why, oh, why had she allowed Luca to steamroller her into flying straight to Italy?

And the answer came back loud and clear. If she had refused, Luca would have gone without her. Challenged at the very outset of their marriage, Luca would have carried through on that threat.

An hour later, Luca sauntered back into the marital bedroom and stopped dead only halfway towards the canopied bed.

Contented canine snores alerted him to the presence of at least one four-legged intruder. And there was no room for a bridegroom in the bed, vast as it was. Darcy lay dead centre, one arm curved protectively round her slumbering daughter, the other draped across two enormous shaggy backs.

Zou Zou was snoring like a train. Aristide opened his eyes, and in his efforts to conceal himself did a comic impression of a very large dog trying to shrink himself to the size of a chihuahua. Pushing his head bashfully between his paws, perfectly aware that he was not allowed on the bed, he surveyed Luca pleadingly, unaware that the child on the other side of the bed was his most powerful source of protection.

Luca drew in a slow, steadying breath and backed towards the door very quietly. He had learnt considerable respect for the consequences of *not* letting sleeping toddlers lie…

*   *   *

Darcy was nudged awake at half past six in the morning by the dogs.

After a brisk wash in her usual cold water in the *en suite* bathroom, she trudged downstairs in her checked pyjamas and old wool dressing gown, startling the dapper little manservant breakfasting in the sleek, ultra-modern kitchen on the ground floor. Beneath the older man's aghast gaze, she fed and watered the dogs and refused to allow him to interrupt his meal. She then insisted on charring two croissants and brewing some not very successful coffee for herself. She wrinkled her nose as she ate and drank. Cooking had never been her metier, but her digestion was robust.

Finding Zia still soundly asleep when she returned to the bedroom, she succumbed to the notion of returning to bed to give her daughter a cuddle, but while in the act of waiting for the toddler to awaken naturally she contrived to drift off to sleep again.

The second time she woke up, she stretched luxuriantly. Then, as she recalled rising earlier, she was seized by instant guilt and wondered with all the horror of someone who never, ever had a lie-in what time it was.

'It's a quarter past nine, *cara mia,*' a deep, dark drawl responded to the anxious question she had unwittingly said out loud.

That reply so alarmingly close to hand acted like a cattle prod on Darcy. Eyes flying wide in dismay, she flipped over to her side to confront her uninvited companion. 'Good heavens...a q-quarter past nine?' she stuttered. 'Where's Zia?'

'Breakfasting upstairs in the nursery suite.'

His clean-shaven jaw supported by an indolent hand, Luca gazed down at Darcy's startled face with a slow, mocking smile that made her pulses race. Her shocked appraisal absorbed the width of his bare brown shoulders above the sheet. Instantly she knew that he wasn't wearing a stitch.

'This bed was busier than the Rialto at high season last night,' Luca remarked.

'Zia needed the security of being with me. She was too cranky to settle somewhere strange on her own,' Darcy rushed to inform him, heart banging violently against her breastbone as she collided with flaring eyes as bright as shafts of golden sunlight in that lean, dark, devastating face.

'Were the dogs insecure too?'

'They cried at the door, Luca! They were really pathetic…'

'I wonder if I should have tried getting down on all fours and howling. I could have pretended to be a werewolf,' Luca suggested, taking advantage of her confusion to snake out an imprisoning arm and hold her where she was before she could go into sudden retreat. 'Then you would've had every excuse to tie me to the bed again.'

Darcy turned a slow hot crimson. Every inch of skin above the collar of her pyjama top was infiltrated by that sweeping tide of burning colour. *Again!* That single word was like a depth charge plunging into her memory banks to cause the maximum chaos. And, worst of all, he was exaggerating. With the aid of his bow tie, she had only got as far as anchoring one wrist before laughter had got the better of her dramatic intentions.

'Speaking as a male who until that night had never, ever relinquished control in the bedroom, I was delightfully surprised by your creativity—'

'I was *drunk!*' Darcy hissed in anguished self-defence.

'With a passionate desire to live out every fantasy you had ever had. Yes, you told me,' Luca reminded her without remorse as he leant over her and long fingers flicked loose the button at her throat without her noticing. 'You also told me that I was your dream lover...and you were undeniably mine. I don't have dream aspirations, but what I didn't know I was missing, I had in abundance that night, and since then no other woman has managed to satisfy me.'

'You're not serious,' Darcy mumbled shakily, mesmerised by the blaze of that golden gaze holding her own.

'So that is why you are here,' Luca confided with husky exactitude. 'I want to know *why* I find you so tormentingly attractive when my intelligence tells me that you are full of flaws.'

'Flaws?'

'You don't give a damn about your appearance. You're untidy, disorganised and blunt to the point of insanity. You hack wood like a lumberjack and you let dogs sleep on my bed. And, strange as it is, I have to confess that none of those habits or failings has the slightest cooling effect on my libido...' Lowering his imperious dark head on that admission, Luca skimmed aside the loose-cut pyjama top to press his mouth hotly to the tiny pulse flickering beneath the delicate skin of her throat.

'*Oh*...what are you doing?' Darcy yelped.

Involuntarily immobilised by the startling burst of warmth igniting low in her belly, she gazed up apprehensively at Luca as he lifted his head.

'Don't do that again,' she muttered weakly, her voice failing to rise to the command level required for the occasion. 'It makes me feel peculiar and we have to talk about things—'

'What sort of things?' Luca enquired thickly.

'That wretched ring for a start—'

'*No.*'

'I didn't steal it, Luca! And you should be trying to find out who *did!*' Darcy told him baldly.

His heated gaze cooled and hardened in the thumping silence.

Darcy gave him a weary, pleading look. 'I wouldn't *do* something like that…and as soon as I get home I'll be able to prove that the ring my father sold wasn't yours!'

'What do you hope to gain from these absurd lies and promises?' Luca demanded with raw impatience. 'I *know* that you took the Adorata! It is not remotely possible that anyone else could have carried out that theft. An idiot would confirm your guilt on less evidence than I have!'

'Circumstantial evidence, Luca…nothing more concrete.'

'While you refuse to admit the truth, there's nothing to discuss.' Luca studied her flushed and frustrated face with smouldering dark golden eyes. With cool deliberation, he smoothed the tumbled curls from her brow. 'All I want to do at this moment is make passionate love to you.'

'No!'

Luca let a teasing forefinger trail along the taut line of her mutinous lips, watched her shiver in shaken reaction to that contact. 'Even when you want to?'

'I don't want to!'

Suddenly alarmingly short of breath, Darcy looked back at him. Little prickles of tormenting awareness were filling her with tension. She was shamefully conscious of the raw, potent power of his abrasive masculinity, and of its devastating effect on her treacherous body. Already her breasts felt heavy and full, her nipples wantonly taut.

The silence pulsed.

'I *don't!* You think I'm a thief!' Darcy cried, as though he had argued with her.

Luca's smile was pure charisma unleashed. 'Possibly that's the most dangerous part of your attraction.'

Thoroughly disconcerted by that suggestion, Darcy frowned.

And, in a ruthless play on her bewilderment, Luca bent his well-shaped dark head and kissed her. He plundered her mouth like a warrior on the battlefield in a make-or-break encounter. She jerked as if fireworks were going off inside her. The hot, lustful thrust of his tongue electrified her. As she responded with all the answering hunger she could not suppress, nothing mattered to her but the continuance of that passionate assault.

In an indolent movement Luca sat up and carried her with him. He pushed the top down off her shoulders and trailed it free of her arms, freeing her hands to rise and sink into his luxuriant black hair. He released her reddened mouth, burnished golden eyes dropping lower to take in the tip-tilted curves of her small breasts and the bold thrust of her rosy nipples.

'You are so perfect,' he savoured huskily.

Perfect? *Never,* she thought, but in the pounding silence Darcy still found herself watching as he curved appreciative hands to her aching flesh. With a stifled moan, she shut her eyes tightly, but felt with every quivering fibre the shockwave of shatteringly intense sensation as expert fingers toyed with the tender peaks. She trembled, her heartbeat thundering in her eardrums.

'*Dio*...' Luca drew in an audible breath. 'You always do exactly what excites me most...'

With a distinct lack of cool, he pushed her back against the pillows and closed his mouth urgently to the source of his temptation. As he tugged at the shamelessly engorged buds with erotic thoroughness she flung her head back, every muscle tensing as a low, keening sound of excitement escaped her. With every carnal caress he sent an arrow of shooting fire to the tormenting ache between her trembling thighs.

Her fingers knotted tightly into the glossy thickness of his hair, holding him to her, desperately urging him on. A moan of impatience left her lips as he abandoned her breasts to tug up her knees and free her restive lower limbs from the pyjama bottoms.

'Kiss me,' she muttered feverishly then.

'Want me?' Shimmering golden eyes welded to her darkened gaze and the longing she couldn't hide from him. 'How much?'

'Luca...' she whispered pleadingly, shivering with need.

'I find you incredibly sexy, *cara mia.*'

Rising over her, he slid a lean, hair-roughened thigh between hers and crushed her mouth with passionate fervour under his. There was no room for thought in her head. Passion controlled her utterly. Her body writhed beneath his, a flood of hungry fire burning at the very heart of her. Feeling the bold promise of his manhood pulsing against her hip, she pushed against him in instinctive encouragement.

Luca pulled back from her, eyes smoky with desire. 'You're too impatient...the pleasure is all the keener when you wait for what you want. And didn't you make me wait that night?' A tantalising hand slowly smoothed over the tense muscles of her stomach. He listened to her suck in oxygen in noisy gasps of anticipation. 'In fact, you pushed me right over the edge when I was least expecting it.'

Instantly she was lost in that imagery. Luca, helpless in her thrall, driven to satisfaction against his own volition, disconcerted, reacting by suddenly reasserting his masculine dominance and driving her crazy with desire. She reached up to him, finding his sensual mouth again for herself, parting her lips to the stabbing invasion of his tongue. He shuddered violently against her, his control slipping as he kissed her back with raw, hungry force.

His hand skated through the damp auburn curls crowning the apex of her thighs and discovered the satin sensitivity of the moist flesh beneath. Mastered by a need that overwhelmed every restraint, she felt her spine arch, her body opening to him as the terrible ache for satisfaction blazed up, making her whimper and writhe, hungrily craving what he had taught her to crave in a torment of excitement.

'When you respond like that, all I can think about is plunging inside you,' Luca groaned, sliding between her thighs.

The hot, hard thrust of his powerful penetration took her breath away. Nothing had ever felt so good. Her whole being was centred on the feel of him inside her, boldly stretching and filling, and giving such intense pleasure she would have died had he stopped.

'You told me I was absolutely brilliant at this,' Luca reminded her, gazing down at her with a staggering mixture of lust laced with reluctant amusement as he plunged deeper still and watched her eyes close on a wave of electrified and utterly naked pleasure. "'Gosh, you're incredibly good at this too...'' you said, in such surprise. I wondered if you were going to score my technique on a questionnaire afterwards—'

'Shut up!' Darcy moaned with effort.

'You said that too.'

She stared up at him, at a peak of such extraordinary excitement she was ready to kill him if he didn't move.

And Luca vented a hoarse laugh. He *knew* how she felt. And his own struggle to maintain control was etched in his taut cheekbones, the sheen of sweat on his dark skin and the ragged edge to his voice. With a muffled groan of urgent satisfaction, he drove deeper into her yielding body. Her heart almost burst with the force of her own frantic response.

Mindless, she clung to him as he took her with a wild vigour that destroyed any semblance of control. Her release brought an electrifying explosion. As the paroxysms of uncontrollable pleasure overpowered her, her nails raked down his damp, muscular back. Luca cried out her name and shuddered over her, as lost in that world of physical sensation as she was.

The most unearthly silence reigned in the aftermath of that impassioned joining.

Luca disentangled himself and rolled over to a cooler part of the bed. Darcy stared fixedly at the footboard. Even before the last quakings of sated desire and intense pleasure faded, she felt rejected.

So you slept with him, a little voice said inside her blitzed brain. Did you do it to make this a real marriage that couldn't be annulled? Did you do it to hang onto the Folly? Or did you do it because you just couldn't summon up sufficient will-power to resist him? After all, you knew how fantastic he would be.

Darcy flipped her tousled head over to one side to anxiously scan Luca. He looked back at her, his strikingly handsome face taut but uninformative, expressive eyes screened. Darcy's throat closed over. At that moment she wanted very, very badly to believe that she had sacrificed her body for the sake of her home. It might have been a morally indefensible move, but her pride could have lived with such a cold-blooded decision...

It would be an infinitely greater challenge to co-exist with the ghastly knowledge that she had made love with Luca because she found him totally and absolutely irresistible, even when she ought to hate him...but, unhappily for her, that was the dreadful truth. And any denial of the fact would be complete cowardice.

It was equally craven to lie in the presence of the enemy behaving like a victim, drowning in defeat and loss of face. Darcy flinched from an image infinitely more shameful to her than any loss of control in Luca's arms. It was unthinkable to let Luca guess that making love with him could reduce her to such a turmoil of painful vulnerability.

'Right,' Darcy said flatly, galvanised into action by that awareness and abruptly sitting up with what she hoped was a cool, calm air of decision. 'Now that we've got *that* out of the way, perhaps we can talk business.'

'*Business?*' Luca stressed in sharp disconcertion, complete incredulity flaring in his brilliant dark eyes.

CHAPTER EIGHT

'BUSINESS,' Darcy confirmed steadily.

'We have no mutual business interests to discuss,' Luca delivered rather drily.

'That's where you're wrong.' Her eyes gleamed at that dismissive assurance. 'As you were so eager to point out yesterday, the Folly estate is still on the brink of bankruptcy.' She breathed in deep. 'I only married you because I assumed that my bank manager would increase my overdraft limit once I explained to him about my godmother's will. However…he refused.'

From beneath dense ebony lashes, Luca surveyed her with something akin to unholy fascination.

'So as things stand,' Darcy recounted tautly, 'not only am I in no position to re-employ the staff laid off after my father's death, but I am also likely to have my home repossessed before that six months is even up.'

'One small question,' Luca breathed in a slightly strained undertone. He was now engaged on a fixed surveillance of the elaborate plasterwork on the ceiling above. 'Did you happen to mention my name to your bank manager?'

'What would I have mentioned your name for?' Darcy countered impatiently. 'I told him that I'd got married but that my husband would be having nothing to do with the estate.'

'Honesty is wonderful, but not always wise,' Luca remarked reflectively. 'I doubt that you need worry about any imminent threat of repossession. If you're only a little behind on the mortgage repayments, it's unlikely.'

'I disagree. I've had some very nasty letters on the subject already. Heavens, I'm scared to open my post these days!' Darcy admitted ruefully, thrusting bright curls from her troubled brow.

'Tell me, in a roundabout, extremely clumsy way, is it possible that you are trying to work yourself up to asking *me* for a loan?' Luca enquired darkly.

'Where on earth did you get that idea? I wouldn't touch your money with a barge-pole!' Darcy told him in indignant rebuttal. 'But I *need* to go home to visit all the other financial institutions that might help. I have to find somewhere prepared to invest in the future of the Folly!'

Luca now surveyed her with thunderous disbelief. 'That's a joke...isn't it?'

'Of course it's not a joke!' Darcy grimaced at the idea. 'Why would I joke about something so serious?'

As Luca sat up in one sudden powerful movement the sheet fell away from his magnificent torso. Outrage blazed in his dark eyes, his lean features clenched taut. 'Are you out of your tiny mind?' he roared back at her, making her flinch in shock from such unexpected aggression. 'I'm an extremely wealthy man...and as *my wife,* you dare to tell me that you plan to drag the Raffacani name in the dirt by scuttling round the banking fraternity begging for a *loan?* Are you trying to make me a laughing-stock?'

Darcy gazed back at him in stunned immobility. That possibility hadn't occurred to her. Nor, at that instant, would the prospect have deprived her of sleep.

'*Accidenti...*' Luca swore rawly, thrusting back the sheet and springing lithely from the bed to appraise her with diamond-hard eyes of condemnation. 'I now see that I have found a foe worthy of my mettle! You are one cunning little vixen! And if you dare put one foot inside the door of *any* financial institution, I will throw you out of my life the same day!'

A foe worthy of his mettle? An unearned compliment, Darcy conceded abstractedly, her attention wholly entrapped by the glorious spectacle of Luca striding naked up and down the bedroom with clenched fists of fury. Gosh, he was gorgeous. Glossy black hair, fabulous bone structure, eyes of wonderful vibrance. Broad shoulders, powerful chest, slim hips, long, long legs. The whole encased in wonderful golden skin, adorned with muscles and intriguing patches of black curly hair. All male.

She looked away, cheeks hot, shame enfolding her. She was so physically infatuated with the man she couldn't even concentrate on arguing with him. It was utterly disgusting.

'OK,' Luca snarled, further provoked by that seemingly stony and defiant silence. 'This is the deal. *I* will take over temporary responsibility for all bills relating to the Folly estate!'

Shaken by so unexpected not to mention so unwelcome a suggestion, Darcy turned aghast eyes on him. '*No way*...why would you want to do that?'

'I don't want to...but that arrangement would be preferable to placing an open chequebook into those hot, greedy little hands of yours! *Porca miseria!*' Luca shot her an intimidating glower of angry derision. 'The bedsheets are not even cooled before you start trying to rip me off again!'

He had a mind as complex as a maze, Darcy conceded, lost in wonder at such involved logic. He was so incredibly suspicious of her motives. All she had tried to do was stress how very urgently she needed to return home to sort out those problems with the estate, but Luca had flown off on another tangent entirely. He honestly believed that she had just tried to blackmail him. Admittedly, it should have dawned on her that he might be sensitive to the idea of his wife seeking to borrow money when he himself was filthy rich, but the reason it hadn't dawned on her was that she didn't feel remotely married to him.

'I don't want your rotten money...I've already told you that.'

'*Dio mio*...you will not seek to borrow anywhere else!' Luca asserted fiercely.

'That's not fair,' Darcy protested.

'Who ever said that I would be fair?'

'You did....' Darcy said in a small voice.

Luca froze at the reminder.

An electrifying silence stretched.

'Suddenly I have a great need for the calm, ordered atmosphere of my office!' Luca bit out with scantily controlled savagery. He strode into the bathroom and sent the door crashing shut.

So that's the temper...*wow!*

The door flew open again. 'Even in bed, don't you ever think of anything but that bloody house?' Luca flung, in final sizzling attack.

The door closed again.

Wow...Darcy thought again helplessly. He's so passionate when he drops the cool front. He slams doors like I do. He's a suspicious toad, so used to wheeling and dealing he can't take anything at face value. But he also thought she had put one over on him, she registered. The beginnings of a rueful smile tugged at the tense, unhappy line of her mouth.

What was the matter with her? she questioned as she slid out of bed. Why was she thinking such crazy thoughts? Why did she feel sort of disappointed that Luca was planning to leave her? Why wasn't she feeling more cheerful at that prospect? She stared down at the empty chair where she had draped her clothes the night before. With a frown, she finally noticed that her open suitcase had disappeared as well. She wandered into the dressing room and tugged open the unit doors to be greeted by male apparel on one side and on the other unfamiliar female garments.

Pyjama-clad, she knocked on the bathroom door. No answer. She opened it. He was in the shower.

'Where are my clothes, Luca?' she called.

The water went off. He rammed back the doors of the shower cubicle.

'I got rid of them,' Luca announced, raking an impatient hand through his dripping black hair and snatching up a towel.

'*Rid* of them?'

'Rather drastic, I know, but surely not a sacrifice?' Luca gave her an expectant look. 'Since you need lessons on how to dress. *Porca miseria!*' He grimaced, watched her face pale and telegraph hurt disbelief. 'That was tactless. But I just thought it would be easiest if I simply presented you with a new wardrobe. The clothes are in the dressing room. You won't even need to go shopping now.'

Darcy's eyes prickled with hot, scratchy tears. She was appalled. Never had she felt more mortified. This was a member of the opposite sex telling her she looked absolutely awful in her own clothes, telling her that *he,* a man, knew more than she did about how she should be dressing. 'How could you do that to me?' she gasped strickenly, and fled.

'It's a gift…a *surprise*…most women would be over the moon!' Luca fired back accusingly.

'Insensitive pig!' A sob tearing at her throat, Darcy threw herself back on the bed.

The mattress beside her gave with his weight.

'You have a beautiful face and an exquisite slender shape…but your clothes are all wrong,' Luca breathed huskily.

Darcy was humiliated and outraged by such smooth bare-faced lying. *She* knew better than anyone that she wasn't remotely beautiful! Flipping over in a blind fury, she raised her hand and dealt him a stinging slap.

'*Not*…most…women,' Luca muttered half under his breath, like somebody learning a very difficult lesson. With a slightly dazed air, he pressed long, elegant fingers to the flaming imprint of her fingers etched across one hard cheekbone and blinked.

Instantly, Darcy crumbled with guilt. 'I'm sorry…I shouldn't have done that,' she muttered brokenly. 'But you asked for it…you provoked me…go away!'

'I don't understand you—'

'I *hate* you…do you understand that?'

Darcy coiled away from him. She hurt so much inside she wanted to scream to let the pain out. She hugged herself tight. When Luca put a hand on her shoulder, she twisted violently away. When he reached for one of her hands, she shook him off.

'I actually liked you before I realised who you were!' she suddenly slung at him in disgust. 'I actually *trusted* you! Gosh, I've got great taste in men!'

'Haven't you already got what you wanted from me?'

Luca raked back at her in cold anger. 'I have promised you my financial backing for the duration of our marriage. Your problems are over.'

Darcy regarded him with bitter outrage. 'I'm not something you can buy with your money.'

Luca shot her an icy unimpressed appraisal. 'If you're not...what are you doing in my bed?'

There was no answer to that question. She couldn't even explain that to her own satisfaction, never mind his. And that he should throw her sexual surrender in her face made her curl up and die deep down inside.

She listened to him dressing, and she was so quiet she barely breathed.

Luca forced himself under her notice again by coming to a halt two feet from the bed. Clad in a lightweight beautifully cut pearl-grey suit, he looked absolutely stupendous, but icily remote and intimidating...like someone who ate debtors five to a plate for breakfast. But now she knew that his black hair felt like silk when she smoothed her fingers through it, that his smile was like hot sunlight after the winter and that even his voice trickled down her spine like honey and made her melt, she thought in growing agony.

'This is not how I thought things would be with us. I'm civilised...I'm very civilised,' Luca informed her with unfeeling cool. 'We're supposed to be skimming along the surface of things and having a great time in bed. So tell me who bought the Adorata ring and we'll get that little complication out of the way. Then there is hope that peace will break out.'

'I've already told you that I did not take that ring,' Darcy whispered shakily.

'And repetition of that claim has an excessively aggravating effect on my normally even temper,' Luca drawled. 'We're at an impasse.'

Darcy studied him, cold fascination holding her tight but pain piercing her like cutting shards of glass—that same pain bright and unconcealed in her eyes. 'I can't believe that you're the same guy I met three years ago...I can't believe that we laughed and danced and you were just so romantic and warm and—'

'*Stupid?*' Luca slotted in glacially, deep-set dark eyes hard as diamonds but a feverish flush accentuating the taut slant of his high cheekbones. 'Absurd? Ridiculous? After all, outside my own élite circle, I wasn't streetwise enough to protect myself from a calculating little predator like you!'

Darcy was shaken by that response, dredged from her own self-preoccupation to finally think about how *he* must have felt when he'd believed he had been robbed by the woman he had spent the previous evening romancing in high style, the woman he had brought into his home, the woman he had made love to over and over again until they'd fallen asleep in each other's arms. And for the very first time she recognised the raw, angry bitterness he had until now contrived to conceal from her. He was very proud, hugely self-assured. The discovery that the ring had gone could scarcely have failed to dent his male ego squarely where it hurt most. Heavens, what an idiot he must have felt, she registered, with a belated flood of understanding sympathy.

'Luca...' she breathed awkwardly. 'I—'

Luca vented a harsh laugh. 'You were clever, but not clever enough,' he murmured with a grim twist of his mouth. 'I *was* a very conservative guy. I was twenty-eight and I had never felt anything very much for any woman. But with you I felt something special—'

'S-something special?' Darcy broke in helplessly.

Derision glittered in the look he cast her intent face. 'You could have got so much more out of me than one night if you'd stayed around.'

'I don't think so,' Darcy whispered unevenly, desperately wanting to be convinced to the contrary. 'I was playing Cinderella that night.'

'Cinderella left her slipper behind…she didn't crack open the Prince's safe.'

'But it wasn't *real*…those hours we spent together,' she continued shakily, still praying that he would tell her different, and all because he had said those two words 'something special'. 'You said all the right lines; I succumbed… Yes, well, maybe I more than succumbed. I guess I was a bit more active than that, but you had no intention of ever seeing me again…' She shrugged a slight shoulder jerkily, no longer able to meet his shrewd gaze, and plucked abstractedly at the sheet. 'I mean…I mean, *obviously* you never had the smallest intention of showing up on the Ponte della Guerra the next day.'

'You remember that?' Luca said, with the kind of surprise that suggested he was amazed that she should have recalled something so trivial.

Darcy remembered standing on that bridge for hours, and she could have wept at the memory. If there ever had been a chance that he would turn up, there had been none whatsoever after he had realised that he'd been robbed that same night. So it was all *his* fault. All her agonies could be laid at his door. And why was she thinking like this anyway? He couldn't possibly find her beautiful. Though he had behaved as if he did that night. True, she had looked really well, but surely his standards of female beauty had to be considerably higher?

'I have bright red hair,' Darcy remarked stiltedly.

'I could hardly miss the fact, but it's not mere red, it's Titian, and I'd prefer to see a lot more of it,' Luca proffered after some hesitation.

'But you must've noticed that I have a...a snub nose?'

'Retroussé is the word...it's unusual; it adds distinction to your face... Why am I having this weird conversation with you?' Luca demanded freezingly. He strode to the door, glanced grudgingly back over one broad shoulder. 'I'll see you later.'

Emptied of his enervating presence, the room seemed dim and dull.

But Darcy lay where she was. Luca liked her nose; he liked her hair. What everybody else called skinny, he called 'slender'. Strange taste, but she knew she wouldn't have the heart to tell him that. So Luca, who resembled her every fantasy of physical male perfection, could get the hots for a skinny redhead with a snub nose. That fact was a revelation to Darcy. No wonder he was annoyed with himself, but all of a sudden she wasn't annoyed with him at all.

He hadn't made love to her just out of a desire for revenge. No, he wasn't as self-denying as that. Luca had really *wanted* to make love to her. There was nothing false about his desire for her. Everything he had said in bed must have been the truth...even the part about no other woman being able to satisfy him since?

Something special? Why did she feel so forgiving all of a sudden? Why was her brain encased in a fog of confusing emotion? That wretched, hateful ring that had been stolen, she reflected grimly. Take that problem out of their relationship and how might Luca behave then? But even if she contrived that miracle, exactly how would he react to the news that the toddler from hell was *his* daughter?

It was early days yet, Darcy decided ruefully. A lot could happen in six months. Telling him that he had fathered a child the night of the ball might presently seem like an impressive counter-punch, but she didn't want to use Zia like a weapon in a battle which nobody could win. In fact, she conceded then, unless their marriage became a real marriage, she was pretty sure she would never tell Luca that Zia was his child. What would be the point?

Right now she had much more important things to consider: the Folly estate and how she planned to save it in the short-term. Borrowing money appeared to be out of the question. And accepting Luca's financial help would choke her. So was she going to have to steel herself to sell some of the Folly's glorious Tudor furniture at auction? If she did so, the pieces could never, ever be replaced. But what alternative way did she have of raising the cash to keep her home afloat over the next six months?

An hour later, garbed in a figure-hugging sapphire-blue dress and horrendously high stilettos, Darcy bent down with extreme caution to lift Zia up into her arms, and *bang*—inspiration hit her the same second that her attention fell on the glossy gossip magazine the middle-aged nursemaid had left lying on a nearby chair. Didn't people pay good money for an insight into the lives of the rich and famous? Wasn't Luca both rich and famous? And didn't she have a second cousin who was a secretary on one of those publications?

What would an interview and a few photos of Gianluca Raffacani's bride be worth?

Darcy blinked, cringing from the concept but hardening herself against a sensitivity she could no longer afford. Luca had said that infidelity or desertion would be grounds for ending their marital agreement. But he hadn't mentioned publicity...

CHAPTER NINE

HAVING heard the commotion, Darcy rose from her seat in the drawing room and walked to the door that opened onto the vast reception hall. She froze there, taken aback by the scene being enacted before her startled eyes.

On his return home, Luca was being engulfed by his sister's dogs. It was like a rugby scrum. But astonishingly informative. Aristide and Zou Zou adored him, Darcy registered in surprise. And there he was, fondling shaggy ears and valiantly bearing up to the exuberant welcome he was receiving. Failing to notice her, Luca then took the stairs two at a time, a gift-wrapped package clutched in one hand.

Since Darcy was a very slow mover in the unfamiliar high heels, she didn't catch up with him. And she was perplexed when he strode past their bedroom to turn up the flight of stairs that led to the nursery suite. She came to a halt in the doorway of the playroom. By the time she got there, Zia had already ripped the paper off a box which she was now regarding with enraptured bliss.

'Dolly!' she gasped, squeezing the box so tight in her excitement that it crunched. 'Pretty dolly!'

Peer pressure and television had a lot to answer for, Darcy decided uncomfortably. All the other little girls Zia knew at the playgroup already had that doll, but Darcy had ignored all pleas to make a similar purchase. Why? Because that particular doll had always reminded her of Maxie. Now that seemed so inadequate an excuse

157

when she saw Zia reacting like a deprived child suddenly shot into seventh heaven.

'Shall I take her out of the box?' Luca enquired helpfully.

While Zia pondered whether or not she could bear to part with her gift even briefly, Darcy studied Luca's hard, classic profile, which showed to even better advantage when he was smiling. She was frankly bewildered by what she was seeing.

Zia extended the box. Hunkering down on a level with the toddler, Luca removed the packaging and finally freed the soft-bodied version of the doll. 'See, Mummy!' her daughter carolled with pride.

As Luca's well-shaped dark head whipped round to finally note Darcy's silent presence, Darcy reddened with awful self-consciousness beneath his lengthy appraisal. While unnecessarily engaged in smoothing down the skirt of her dress with damp palms, she strove to act unconcerned and evaded his scrutiny. 'Did you say thank you, Zia?'

'Kiss?' Zia proffered instantly, moving forward to land a big splashy kiss on Luca's cheek and then give him an enthusiastic hug.

'Isn't cupboard love great?' Luca mocked his own calculation with an amused smile and vaulted upright again. 'We got off on the wrong foot yesterday. A peace offering was a necessity.'

'It was a kind thought,' Darcy conceded stiltedly.

'I can be very kind, *bella mia*,' Luca countered huskily.

Darcy collided with his scorching dark stare. And quite without knowing *how* she knew it, she knew he was thinking about sex. That sixth sense awareness spooked her and plunged her into confusion.

As her skin heated her breath caught in her throat, and her heart gave a violent lurch. She couldn't look away from those stunning dark golden eyes. The impact of that look was staggering. She felt dizzy, unsteady on her feet and far, far too hot. The tip of her tongue skimmed along her dry lower lip in a nervous motion. Luca's intent scrutiny homed in on the soft fullness of her mouth. Something drew tight and twisted, low in her stomach, a sexual response so powerful it terrified her. Mercifully, Zia broke the connection by holding out her new doll for her mother's admiration.

'You haven't much time to say goodnight to her. My sister is joining us for dinner,' Luca advanced as he strode out through the door. 'I need a shower and a change of clothes.'

'Night-night, Luca!' Zia called cheerfully.

Luca paused and glanced back with a raised ebony brow. 'In the right mood, she's really quite sweet, isn't she?' His eyes became shadowed and his wide mouth compressed. 'I had nothing to do with Ilaria when she was that age…I was at boarding school. She was only seven when I went to university. I lived to regret not having a closer bond with her.'

Twenty minutes later, having tucked Zia into bed and read her a story, Darcy walked into their bedroom. Only his jacket and tie removed, Luca was in the act of putting down his mobile phone.

'You look fantastic in that dress…you know why?' A wolfish grin slashed his lean, strong face. 'It *fits*. It isn't two sizes too large or a foot too long!'

'Margo always helped me to choose my clothes,' Darcy confided. 'She said that I had to dress to hide my deficiencies.'

'You have none. You're in perfect proportion for your size.'

But Darcy's diminutive curves and lack of height *had* been deficiencies to a stepmother who was both tall and lushly female in shape. Margo had loathed red hair as well, insisting that Darcy could only wear dull colours. Growing up with Margo's constant criticism, and Nina's pitying superiority, Darcy had learned only to measure her looks against theirs. That unwise comparison had wrecked her confidence in her own appearance.

But now she gazed back at Luca and could not fail to recognise his sincerity. He'd told her she looked fantastic. And sensual appreciation radiated from the lingering appraisal in those intent dark eyes. If she didn't yet quite credit that she *could* look fantastic, she certainly realised with a surge of gratified wonder that Luca genuinely *believed* she did.

Her softened gaze ran with abstracted admiration over his long, lean, powerful physique. She was shaken to note the earthy and defiantly male thrust of arousal that the close fit of his well-cut trousers couldn't conceal. She reddened hotly, but she also felt empowered and outrageously feminine.

'Luca...' she whispered shakily.

Later, she couldn't recall who had reached out first. She remembered the way his gaze narrowed, the blaze of golden intent between black spiky lashes, and then suddenly she was crushed in his arms and clinging to him to stay upright. He parted her lips to invade her tender mouth with his thrusting tongue, dipping, twirling, tasting her with fierce, impatient need. He cut right through her every defence with that blunt, honest admission of desire. She trembled violently beneath that devouring kiss. He made her feel possessed, dominated, and utterly weak with hunger.

'I should never have left you…I've been in a filthy temper all day,' Luca confided raggedly, slumberous eyes scanning her lovely face with very male satisfaction, a febrile flush on his taut cheekbones. 'I want you *so* much…'

'Yes…' Darcy acknowledged a truth too obvious to be denied. She felt the same. Her heart was pounding, her whole body throbbing with intense arousal. It was like being in pain; it made her crave him like a drug.

'I can't wait until later…I'm in agony,' Luca gritted roughly.

Hard fingers splayed across her spine to press her into direct contact with his hard thighs. He shuddered against her with a stifled groan, kissing her temples, the top of her head, running his fingers through her hair and then bringing her mouth back hungrily under his again. She couldn't get close enough to him. He slid one hand beneath her skirt, skimming up a slender thigh to the very heart of her. The damp swollen heat of her beneath the thin barrier of her panties betrayed her response. Excitement made her squirm and moan against that skilled touch.

'Luca…*please,*' she gasped urgently.

He backed her down on the side of the bed. He leant over her, hands braced on either side of her head, and plunged deep into her mouth again, eliciting a low cry of surrender from her. Tugging down the zip on her dress, he removed it, skimming off her remaining garments with deft, impatient hands. He stilled for a second, reverent eyes scanning the pouting curves of her breasts and the silky dark red hair at the apex of her slender thighs.

'You are gorgeous, *bella mia*...how can you ever have doubted that?' Luca demanded as he stood over her, peeling off his own clothing at speed.

He came down to her, gloriously aroused. Cupping her breasts, he caressed the sensitive buds with his lips and his tongue, and then he kissed a slow tantalising trail down over the flexing muscles of her stomach, pushing her quivering thighs apart to conduct a more intimate exploration. She was shocked, but too tormented by her own aching need for his caresses to stop him. He controlled her utterly, pushed her to such a pitch of writhing, desperate excitement she was helpless.

He rose over her again, his breathing fractured. He dipped his tongue between her reddened lips in a sexy flick as he tipped back her thighs with almost clumsy hands, his own excitement palpable. Burnished golden eyes assailed hers. He hesitated at the crucial moment when she was braced for the hot, hard invasion of his body into hers.

'Luca!'

'*Dio mio*...I don't know myself like this!' he groaned ruefully. 'I feel wild...but I don't want to hurt you.'

'You won't...'

'You're so much smaller than I am.'

'I like it when you're wild,' she whispered feverishly.

Above her, Luca closed his eyes and slammed into her hard, releasing such a flood of electrifying sensation that Darcy moaned his name like a benediction. He withdrew and entered her again, with a raw, forceful sense of timing that was soul-shatteringly effective. Her entire being was centred on the explosive pleasure building inside her. Heart pounding in concert with his,

she cried out in ecstasy as he drove her over the edge.
Then she just collapsed, totally drained.

They lay together in a sweaty huddle. Luca released
her from his weight but retained a possessive hold on
her, pressing his mouth softly to her throat, lingering to
lick the salt from her skin and smooth a soothing hand
down over her slender back.

'That was unbelievable…that was paradise, *cara
mia,*' Luca sighed in a tone of wondering satisfaction.
'I have never felt this good.'

'What time is your sister coming?' Darcy mumbled.

Luca tensed, relocated the wrist with a watch, and
suddenly wrenched himself free. '*Porca miseria*…Ilaria
will be here at any moment!'

Feeling totally brainless and lethargic, Darcy watched
him spring off the bed.

'Darcy…' he gritted then.

'What?' she whispered with a silly smile, surveying
him with a kind of bursting feeling inside her heart.

'You can share my shower.' Luca scooped her up
into his powerful arms and strode into the bathroom
with her.

'I'll never get my hair dry!' But still she watched
him, trying desperately hard to work out why she felt
so ecstatically happy.

'Your eyes are glowing like neon lights.' Studying
her with a curiously softened look in his dark, deep-set
gaze, Luca hooked her arms round his strong brown
throat and kissed her again, holding her plastered to
every inch of him beneath the gushing cascade of water.
He raised his head again, a slight frown drawing his
black brows together. 'I assume you're on the pill…'

'Nope.'

'I didn't use anything to protect you,' Luca told her

slowly as he lowered her back down to the floor of the cubicle. '*Santo cielo*…how could I be that careless?'

Darcy had stiffened. How could *she* be that careless *again?* Yet another time. The first occasion had resulted in Zia's conception. She had foolishly assumed that the course of contraceptive pills she had stopped taking the day she failed to marry Richard would still prevent a pregnancy. Naturally it hadn't. Her own ignorance had been her downfall.

'Very little risk,' she muttered awkwardly, avoiding his searching scrutiny.

'You would know that better than I.'

He was wrong there, Darcy conceded ruefully. Her monthly cycles caused her so little inconvenience that she never bothered to keep a note of dates. She hadn't a clue what part of her cycle she was in, but she had almost supernatural faith in the power of Luca's fertility. Suppose she did become pregnant again… Oddly enough, the prospect failed to rouse the slightest sense of alarm. Indeed, as Darcy looked up at Luca, mentally miles away while he washed her, she was picturing a small boyish version of those same features that distinguished Zia. A buoyant warm sensation instantly blossomed inside her. Only when she appreciated how she was reacting to that prospect of pregnancy was she shocked by herself.

'What's wrong?' Luca prompted.

In her haste to escape those frighteningly astute eyes, Darcy lurched out of the shower. Grabbing up a towel, she took refuge in the dressing room to dry herself. I can't be in love with him. I can't be, she told herself sickly. It was a kind of immature infatuation and it had its sad roots in the past. Karen had been right about her: she *had* spent too much time alone. Building romantic castles in the air around Luca Raffacani would be a very stupid move, and, having done it once and learnt her mistake, she was convinced she was too sensible to be so foolish again.

By one of those strange tricks of fate Luca found her attractive, and they were sexually compatible, but she would have to be an idiot to imagine that Luca might now develop some form of emotional attachment to her. He had said it himself only this morning, hadn't he? He had talked with outrageous unapologetic cool about how they should be 'skimming along the surface of things and having a great time in bed' rather than arguing. Suddenly Darcy was very glad she had slapped him so hard…

'Tell me about your sister,' Darcy invited Luca as they left the bedroom. Having donned an elegant black dress and fresh lingerie at speed, she had attempted to coax her damp curls into some semblance of a style, but she was out of breath and her cheeks were still pink with effort. 'It'll look strange if I know nothing about her.'

Luca, as sleek and cool and elegant as a male who had spent a leisurely hour showering, shaving and donning his superb dinner jacket and narrow black trousers, gave her a wry look. 'My parents died in a plane crash when Ilaria was eight. My aunt became her legal guardian. I was only nineteen. Emilia was a childless widow, eager to mother my sister, but she was very possessive. She made it difficult for me to maintain regular contact with Ilaria.'

'That was selfish of her.'

'She also refused to allow me to share in Ilaria's upbringing when I was in a position to offer her a more settled home life. And she was a very liberal guardian.

She spoilt Ilaria rotten. When my sister turned into a difficult teenager, Emilia saw her behaviour as rank ingratitude. Being a substitute mother had become a burden. She demanded that I take responsibility for Ilaria and within the same month she moved to New York.'

'Oh, dear...' Darcy grimaced.

'Ilaria was devastated by that rejection and she furiously resented me. We had some troubled times,' Luca conceded with a rueful shrug. 'She's twenty now, but I have little contact with her. As soon as she reached eighteen, she demanded an apartment of her own.'

'I'm sorry.' Seeing his dissatisfaction with this detached state of affairs, Darcy rested her hand on his sleeve in a sympathetic gesture. 'I always think the worst wounds are inflicted within the family circle. We're all much more vulnerable where our own flesh and blood is concerned.'

'You're thinking of your father?'

'It's hard not to. I spent my whole life wanting to be *somebody* in his eyes, struggling to win his respect,' Darcy admitted gruffly.

'Everyone's like that with parents.'

Tensing as she noticed his attention dropping to the hand still curved to his arm, she hurriedly removed it, thinking then with pain that the kind of physical closeness which he was at ease with *in* bed seemed a complete no-no *out* of bed.

'But I was reaching for something I could never have. I don't think my father ever looked at me without resenting the fact that I wasn't the son he wanted...but all that made me do was try harder,' she confided ruefully.

Luca reached for her hand and curled lean fingers tautly round hers. 'Was that why you took the Adorata?'

he demanded in a roughened undertone, shrewd dark eyes drawn to her startled face. 'Darcy impressively riding to the rescue of the family fortunes with a pretend lucky find?'

Caught unprepared, Darcy lost every scrap of colour in her cheeks, her green eyes darkening with hurt at that absurd suspicion. Once again she had forgotten what lay between them, and with too great a candour she had exposed herself to attack.

'You must've lied to your father. He may have been domineering and aggressive, but he had the reputation of being an honest, upright man. Did you tell him that you had found it in some dusty antique shop where you had bought it for a song?' Luca pressed with remorseless persistence.

A door opened off the ball. Both Darcy and Luca whipped round. A slim, stunning girl with shoulder-length dark hair and a sullen expression subjected them to a stony appraisal.

'I have no intention of wasting an entire evening waiting for you to show up at your own dinner table, Luca,' Ilaria said with brittle sarcasm. 'Just why did you bother to invite me?'

'I hoped that you might want to meet Darcy. I'm sorry that we've kept you waiting,' Luca murmured levelly.

Ilaria vented a thin laugh. 'Why didn't you give me the opportunity to meet her *before* you got married?'

'I left several messages on your answering machine. You never call back,' Luca countered calmly.

The combination of aggression and hurt emanating from Ilaria was powerful. But then her big brother had married a total stranger. In those circumstances, her hostility was natural, Darcy conceded. Tugging free of

Luca, she walked over to his sister, a rueful look of appeal in her eyes. 'You have every right to be furious. And I don't know how to explain why—'

'We got married in a hurry,' Luca slotted in with finality as he thrust open the door of the dining room. Atmospheric pools of candlelight illuminated the beautifully set table awaiting them. 'There's not much else to say.'

'I can't imagine you doing anything in a hurry without good reason, Luca,' Ilaria gibed. 'Have you got her pregnant?'

Darcy froze, and then forced herself down into the seat Luca had spun out for her occupation. While Luca shot a low-pitched sentence of icy Italian at his sister, Darcy drowned in guilty pink colour and glanced at neither combatant. The suggestion had been chosen to insult, but it was more apt than either of her companions could know. However, she recognised the position Luca had put himself in, and she wanted to help minimise the damage to his already strained relationship with his sister.

'We had a quiet wedding because my father died recently.' Darcy spoke up abruptly. 'I have to admit that we were rather impulsive—'

'Impulsive? *Luca?*' Ilaria derided, unimpressed. 'Who do you think you're kidding? He never makes a single move that he hasn't planned down to the last detail!'

'In this case, he did,' Darcy persisted quietly. 'But it was selfish of us to just rush off and get married without letting our families share in the event.'

'Your family wasn't there *either?*' The younger woman looked astonished, but was visibly soothed by the admission. 'So where did you meet…and when?'

'That's a long story—' Luca began.

Darcy rushed to interrupt him. Telling the truth, or as much of it as was reasonable, would be wisest in the circumstances, rather than that silly story of her having reversed into his car in London and shouted at him. This *was* his sister they were dealing with, and Ilaria had to know that Luca would have wiped the pavement with any female that stupid.

'I met your brother almost three years ago at a masked ball here,' Darcy admitted, an anxious smile on her lips.

The effect of that simple statement stunned Darcy. To her left, Luca released his breath in a stark hiss and shot her a look of outright exasperation. To her right, Ilaria's face locked tight. She gaped at Darcy in the most peculiar way, her mouth a shocked and rounded circle from which no sound emitted, her olive skin draining to a sick pallor which made her horrified dark eyes look huge.

'I seem to have—'

'Put a giant foot in your mouth,' Luca completed grimly.

And then everything went crazy. Just as Darcy realised with a sinking heart that naturally his sister had to be aware of the theft that had taken place that night, and that she had just foolishly exposed Luca and herself to the need for an explanation that would be wellnigh impossible to make, Ilaria flew upright. The focus of her stricken attention was surprisingly not Darcy, but her brother.

As Ilaria began ranting hysterically at Luca in Italian she backed away from the table. A look of astonished incomprehension on his taut features, Luca rose upright and strode towards his sister. '*Cosa c'e che non va*...what's wrong?' he demanded urgently, anxiously.

Crying now in earnest, Ilaria clumsily evaded her brother's attempt to place comforting hands on her shoulders. Tearing herself away, she gasped out something in her own language and fled.

Instead of following her, Luca froze there as if his sister had struck him. He raised his lean hands, spread them slightly in an odd, inarticulate movement, and then slowly dropped them again.

Darcy hurried over to his side. 'What's the matter with her?'

His clenched profile starkly delineated against the flickering pools of shadow and light, Luca drew in a deep, shuddering breath. He turned a strange, unfocused look on Darcy. 'She said...she *said*...' he began unevenly.

'She said...*what?*' Darcy prompted impatiently, listening to Ilaria having a rousing bout of hysterics in the hall.

'Ilaria said *she* stole the Adorata ring,' Luca finally got out, and he shook his glossy dark head in so much shock and lingering disbelief he had the aspect of a very large statue teetering dangerously on its base.

'Oh...*oh, dear,*' Darcy muttered, so shaken by that shattering revelation that she couldn't for the life of her manage to come up with anything more appropriate.

Ilaria was sobbing herself hoarse in the centre of the hall. Darcy tried to put her arms round the girl and got pushed away. Ilaria shot an accusing, gulping stream of Italian at her.

'I'm sorry, but I was absolutely lousy at languages at school.' Darcy curved a determined hand round the girl's elbow and urged her into the drawing room. 'I know you're very upset…but try hard to calm down just a *bit*,' she pleaded.

'How can I? Luca will never forgive me!' Ilaria wailed, and she flung herself face-down on a sofa to sob again.

Sitting down beside her, Darcy let her cry for a while. But as soon as Luca entered the room she got up and said awkwardly, 'Look…I'll leave you two alone—'

'No!' Ilaria suddenly reached out to grab at Darcy's hand. 'You stay…'

'Yes…because if you don't, Darcy,' Luca muttered in the strangest tone of eerie detachment from his sister's distress, 'I may just kill her.'

'You're nearly as bad as she is!' Darcy condemned roundly as Ilaria went off into another bout of tormented sobbing. 'You won't get any sense out of her talking like that.'

'I know very well how to get sense out of her!'

Luca rapped out a command in staccato Italian which sounded very much like a version of pull-yourself-together-or-*else*.

'I'm sorry…I'm really s-sorry!' Ilaria gulped brokenly then. 'I panicked when I realised that Darcy was the woman you met that night… Because you had *married* her I thought you had guessed…and that you had brought me over here to confront me with what I did!'

'Your brother wouldn't behave like that,' Darcy said quietly.

Luca shot her a curious, almost pained look, and then turned his attention back to his sister. 'How did you do it?'

'You shouldn't have been at the apartment at all that evening because it was the night of the ball.' Sitting bolt-upright now on the sofa, clutching the tissue that

Darcy had fetched for her use, Ilaria began to shred it with restive, trembling hands. 'I needed money and you'd cut off my allowance…refused to let me even see Pietro…I was so *angry* with you! I was going to run away with him, but we needed money to do that—'

'You were seventeen,' Luca cut in harshly. 'I did what I had to do to protect you from yourself. If you hadn't been an heiress that sleazy louse wouldn't have given you a second glance!'

'Let her tell her story,' Darcy murmured, watching Ilaria cringe at that blunt assessment.

'I h-had a key to the apartment. I knew all the security codes. One day when I had lunch there with you, you went into the safe and I watched you do it from the hall,' Ilaria mumbled shamefacedly. 'I thought there would be cash in the safe…'

'Your timing was unfortunate.'

'All there was…was the Adorata,' Ilaria continued shakily. 'I was furious, so I took it. I told myself I was entitled to it if I needed it, but when I took the Adorata to Pietro, he…he laughed in my face! He said he wasn't fool enough to try and sell a famous piece of stolen goods. He said he would have had Interpol chasing him across Europe in pursuit of it…so I planned to put the ring back the next morning.'

'That was a timely change of heart,' Darcy put in encouragingly, although one look at Luca's icily clenched and remote profile reduced her to silence again.

'But you see, you went back to the apartment that night and stayed there…you found the safe open and the Adorata gone…I was too *late!*' Ilaria wailed.

'What did you do with the ring?'

'It's safe,' his sister hastened to assure him. 'It's in my safety deposit box with Mamma's jewellery.'

Momentarily, Luca closed his eyes at that news. *'Porca miseria…'* he ground out unsteadily. 'All this time…'

'If you'd called in the police I would have had to tell you I had it,' his sister muttered, almost accusingly. 'But when I realised you believed that the woman you'd left the ball with had taken it…' She shot a severely embarrassed glance at Darcy, belatedly recalling that that woman and her brother's wife were now one and the same. 'I mean—'

'*Me*…it's all right,' Darcy cut in, but her cheeks were burning.

'You see…' Ilaria hesitated. 'You weren't like a real person to me, and it didn't seem to matter who Luca blamed as long as he didn't suspect me.'

Darcy studied the exquisite Aubusson carpet fixedly, mortification overpowering her. She could well imagine how low an opinion Ilaria must have had of her at seventeen: some tramp who had dived into bed with her brother the same night she had first met him.

Disconcertingly, Luca vented a flat, humourless laugh. 'Aren't you fortunate that Darcy disappeared into thin air?'

Darcy was more than willing to disappear into thin air all over again. She turned towards the door. 'I think you need to talk without a stranger around,' she said with a rather tremulous smile.

Distinctly shaky after the strain of the scene she had undergone, Darcy shook her head apologetically at Luca's manservant, who was now hovering uncomfortably in the dining room doorway, obviously wondering what was happening and whether or not any of them intended to sit down and eat dinner like civilised people. She had enjoyed a substantial lunch earlier in the day and now she felt pretty queasy.

Poor Luca. Poor Ilaria. Such a shaming secret must have been horrible for the girl to live with for so long. A moment's reckless bitter rebellion over the head of some boy she had clearly been hopelessly infatuated with. As Ilaria matured that secret would have weighed ever more heavily on her conscience, probably causing her to assume a defensive attitude to cover her unease in Luca's presence.

Guilt did that—it ate away at you. Little wonder that Ilaria had avoided Luca's company. She had been too afraid to face up to what she had done and confess. And the instant Ilaria had appreciated that her brother's wife was also the woman Luca had once believed to be a thief, she had jumped to the panic-stricken conclusion that Luca somehow knew that *she* was the culprit. After all, how could Ilaria ever have guessed that her lordly big brother might have married a woman he *still* believed to be a thief out of a powerful need to punish her?

And now Luca would finally get that wretched ring back. Could he really believe that any inanimate object, no matter how valuable, precious and rare, was worth so much grief? How did he feel now that he knew he had misjudged her? Gutted, Darcy decided without hesitation. He had looked absolutely gutted when comprehension rolled over him like a drowning tidal wave. His *own* sister.

Darcy heaved a sigh. Maybe, as Luca had said himself, peace would now break out. Naturally he would have to apologise…in fact a bit of crawling wouldn't come amiss, Darcy thought, beginning to feel rather surprisingly upbeat. Having checked on Zia, she wandered downstairs again and into the dining room.

She sat down at the table, appetite restored, and tucked into her elaborate starter. No, she didn't want Luca to crawl. He was having a tough enough time with Ilaria and his spectacular own goal of misjudgement. She had to be fair. The evidence had been very much stacked against her. And how could he ever have suspected his seventeen-year-old sister of pulling off such a feat?

She was halfway through the main course when Luca appeared. '*Santo cielo*…how can you eat at a time like this?' he breathed in a charged tone of incredulity.

'I felt hungry…sorry to be so prosaic,' Darcy muttered, wondering where that rather melodramatic opening was about to take him. 'How's Ilaria?'

'I persuaded her to stay the night. I'm sorry about that…'

'About what?' Conscious that the sight of the cutlery still in her grasp seemed to be an offence of no mean order in his eyes, she abandoned her meal. In fact, in the mix of shadow and dim light in which Luca stood poised, the dark, sombre planes of his unusually pale features lent him an almost lost, lonely sort of aspect.

'About what?' Luca echoed, frowning as if he was struggling to get a grip on himself. 'Aren't you furious with Ilaria?'

'Gosh, no…she was terribly distressed. She's rather young for her age—very…well, emotional,' Darcy selected, striving to be tactful for once in her life.

'Being emotional is not catching…is it? You must be outraged with me,' Luca breathed starkly.

'Well, yes, I was when all this nonsense started—'

'*Nonsense?*' Luca cut in with ragged stress.

Darcy rose to her feet, wishing she could just run over and put her arms round him, spring him out of this strange and unfamiliar mood he was in, but he looked so incredibly remote now. As if he had lost everything he possessed. But he would strangle the first person who had the bad taste to either mention it or show a single hint of pity or understanding.

'I *always* knew I didn't take the wretched thing,' she pointed out gently. 'I'm awfully glad it's all cleared up now. And I understand why you were so convinced I was the thief…after all, you didn't *know* me, did you?'

Luca flinched as if she had punched him in the stomach. He spun his dark head away. 'No…I didn't,' he framed almost hoarsely.

She watched him swallow convulsively.

Feeling utterly helpless, craving the confidence to bridge the frightening gap she could feel opening up between them, Darcy was gripped by a powerful wave of frustration. He was so at a loss; she wanted to hug him the way she hugged Zia when she fell over and hurt herself. But she thought she would crack their tenuous relationship right down the middle if she made such an approach. He was too proud.

'We'll talk later,' Luca imparted with what sounded like a really dogged effort to sound his usual collected self. 'You need to be alone for a while.'

He needed to be alone for a while, Darcy interpreted without difficulty. He's going to walk out on me…what did I do wrong? a voice screamed inside her bemused head. Here she was, being as fair, honest and reasonable as she knew how to be, and the wretched man was withdrawing more from her with every second.

'Tell me…would you have preferred a screaming row?'

'We have nothing to row about any more,' Luca countered, without a shade of his usual irony. In fact he sounded as if his only enjoyment in life had been wrenched from him by the cruellest of fates.

As the clock on the mantelpiece struck midnight, Darcy rose with a sigh. And that was when she heard the sound of footsteps in the hall. As the drawing room door opened, she tensed. For a split second Luca stilled at the sight of her, veiled eyes astutely reading the anxious, assessing look in hers.

'Would you like a drink?' he murmured quietly as he thrust the door closed.

'A brandy…' She watched him stride over to the ornate oriental drinks cabinet. Lithe, dark, strikingly good-looking, every movement fluid as poetry. He didn't look gutted any more—but then she hadn't expected him to. Luca was tough, a survivor, and survivors knew how to roll with the punches.

But *she* must have been born under an unlucky star. What savage fate had decreed that she should be involved up to her throat in the two biggest mistakes Luca had ever made? It was so cruel. He would judge himself harshly and he would never think of her without guilty unease again. She was like an albatross in his life, always a portent of doom. She hoved in to his radius and things went badly wrong. If he was like every other man she had ever known, he would very soon find the very sight of her an objectionable reminder of his own lowest moments.

Luca handed her the balloon glass of brandy, his lean, strong face sombre. 'I have come to some conclusions.'

Menaced by both expression and announcement, Darcy downed the brandy in one long, desperate gulp.

'You must have found the last few days very traumatic,' Luca breathed heavily, fabulous bone structure rigid. 'In retrospect, it is impossible to justify anything that I have done. I can make no excuse for myself; I can only admit that from the instant I found you gone from the apartment, the safe open, the Adorata gone, I nourished an obsessive need to run you to ground and even what I saw as the score between us—'

Predictably, Darcy cut to the heart of the matter. 'You thought I'd made a fool of you.'

'Yes…and that was a new experience for me. I must confess that there was nothing I was not prepared to do to achieve my objective,' Luca admitted with a grim edge to his dark, deep voice. 'If Ilaria hadn't confessed tonight, I'd still have believed you guilty, and since it would not have been possible for you to satisfy my demand that you help me to regain the Adorata…I would, ultimately, have dispossessed you of Fielding's Folly.'

Darcy was ashen pale now. 'No…you wouldn't have done that.'

Slowly, Luca shook his dark head, stunning dark eyes resting full on her disbelieving face. 'Darcy, you're a much nicer person than I have ever been…I *would* have done it. When I married you, I already held the future of the Folly in the palm of my hand.'

'What do you m-mean?' she stammered, moisture beading her short upper lip as she stared back at him.

From the inside pocket of his beautifully tailored dinner jacket, Luca withdrew a folded document. 'I bought the company which gave your father the mortgage on the Folly. This is the agreement. You're in default of the terms of that agreement now. I could have called in the loan and forced you out at any time over the next six months,' he spelt out very quietly. 'It would've been as easy as taking candy from a baby.'

Her shattered eyes huge dark smudges against her pallor, Darcy gazed back at him transfixed. 'You...you *bought* the company?' she gasped sickly.

As he absorbed the full extent of her horror at such calculated foreplanning, Luca seemed to pale too. 'I had to tell you. I had to be completely honest with you. You have the right to know it all now.'

Her lips bloodless, Darcy mumbled strickenly, 'I don't think I wanted to know that...how could anybody sink *that* low?'

'I wish I could say that I don't know what got into me...but I *do* know,' Luca murmured with bleak, dark eyes. 'My ego could not live with what I believed you had done to me that night. I had the power to take a terrible revenge and that was my intention when I replied to your advertisement.'

Darcy nodded like a little wooden marionette, too appalled to do anything but gaze back at him as if he had turned into a monster before her very eyes.

A faint sheen now glossed Luca's golden skin. 'Not a very pretty objective...when I think back to that now, I am very much ashamed. You have made such a valiant struggle to survive against all the odds.'

Darcy shook her pounding head with a little jerk. She felt as if she was dying inside, and now she knew what was really the matter with her—could no longer avoid knowing. She had fallen in love with him. How else could he be hurting her so much? She turned almost clumsily away from him, a mess of raw, agonised nerve-endings, and sank down onto a sofa. 'I *slept* with you,' she muttered, suddenly stricken.

'I definitely don't think we should touch on that issue

right now,' Luca contended without hesitation. 'I'm sinking faster than a rock in a swamp as it is. What I want to do now…what I *need* to do…is make amends to you in every way possible.'

'I hate you…' And she did. She hated him because he didn't love her, because he had made a fool of her, because she had made a fool of herself and, last but not least, because she could not bear the thought of having to struggle to get over him again.

'I can live with that.'

'I want to go home.'

'Of course. The jet is at your disposal. When were you thinking of leaving?'

'Now—'

'It wouldn't be a good idea to get Zia out of bed.' Since Darcy was still staring numbly at the rug beneath her feet, Luca hunkered down in front of her. 'Shout at me…hit me if it makes you feel better. I don't know what to do when you're quiet!' he murmured fiercely.

'I'll leave first thing in the morning,' Darcy swore.

Luca reached for her tightly coiled hands. 'When do you want me to fly over?'

Darcy focused on him for the first time in several minutes but said nothing, her incredulity unfeigned.

Brilliant dark eyes glittered. 'You're stuck with me for the next six months,' Luca reminded her gently. 'Surely you hadn't forgotten that…had you?'

Darcy *had*. Her brain felt as if it was spinning in tortured circles.

Luca contrived to ease up each small coiled finger during the interim, and gain a hold on both of her hands. 'I promise to fulfil our agreement. No matter what happens, I will not let you down.'

Darcy snatched her hands back in a raw motion of repudiation. 'I couldn't *stand* it!'

'I have tried to express my remorse—'

'I don't think you have it in you to *feel* remorse!' Darcy condemned abruptly, her oval face flushing with a return of healthier colour as she got her teeth into that conviction. 'You're sneaky, devious...and I can't abide sneakiness or dishonesty. The only two things in life that excite you are sex and money.'

A dark rise of blood had delineated the savagely taut slant of his cheekbones. 'Once there was a third thing that excited me, far more than either of those.'

'What?' she gibed with a jagged laugh as she sprang upright, no longer able to stand being so close to him, terrified her fevered emotions would betray her. 'The prospect of taking revenge? Gosh, I should be flattered! Was that stupid bloody ring really worth this much effort?'

Luca vaulted back to his full commanding height, but with something less than his habitual grace. 'No...' It was very quiet.

'And do you want the biggest laugh of all?' Darcy slung shakily at him, green eyes huge with pain, her slender body trembling with the force of her feelings. 'I fell like a ton of bricks for you that night, only I didn't realise until it was too late. I even tried to find my way back to your apartment but I couldn't! What a lucky miss! You'd have had me arrested for theft before I'd cleared the front door!'

Luca looked poleaxed, as well he might have done. Darcy hadn't meant to spill out such a private painful truth, but she flung her head back with defiant pride, meeting the sheer shock in his spectacular dark eyes without flinching.

'You went to the Ponte della Guerra,' he breathed with ragged abruptness, catching her by surprise. 'No...please tell me you *didn't!*'

'While you were ferreting like a great stupid prat round your empty safe!' Taking a bold stance, Darcy stalked to the door. 'Don't you dare show your face at the Folly for a few weeks!'

'As we are supposed to be a newly married couple that might arouse suspicion,' Luca pointed out flatly.

'Luca...you're not seeing the whole picture here!' Darcy informed him with vigour. 'A honeymoon that lasts less than three days has obviously been a wash-out! An absentee workaholic husband completes the right image for a marriage destined to fail. And when you do come to visit, and everyone sees how absolutely useless you are at being my strong right arm, nobody's going to be one bit surprised when I dump you six months down the line!'

CHAPTER TEN

DARCY closed the glossy magazine with a barely restrained shudder, undyingly grateful that Luca would
never read the interview she had given. At her request,
the magazine had faxed the questions to her. After carefully studying some old magazines to see how other
women had talked in similar interviews, Darcy had responded to those questions with a cringe-making
amount of slush and gush.

Anyway, Luca was in Italy, and men *didn't* read
those sort of publications, did they? The sizeable cheque
she had earned for that tissue of lies about her blissfully
happy marriage and her even more wonderful new husband was more than sufficient compensation for a little
embarrassment. With the proceeds she would be able to
bring the mortgage repayments up to date, settle some
other outstanding bills and put the Land Rover in for a
service.

It had been two weeks and three days since she had
seen Luca. Every day, every hour had crawled. She felt
haunted by Luca. Having him around to shout at or even
ignore would have been infinitely more bearable. She
ached for him. And she was angry and ashamed that
she could feel such an overpowering need and hunger
for a male who had entered her life only to harm her.

Impervious to all hints, and beautifully well-
mannered to the last, Luca had seen them off at the
airport. Zia had actually burst into tears when she realised that he wasn't coming with them. Lifting the little

girl for a farewell hug, Luca had looked strangely self-satisfied. But seeing those two dark heads so close together had had a very different effect on Darcy.

The physical resemblance between father and daughter was startling. The Raffacani straight nose and level brows, the black hair and dark eyes...Darcy was now confronting unwelcome realities. Zia had the right to know her father. And Luca had rights too—not that she thought he would have the slightest urge to exercise them.

But if she didn't tell Luca that he had a daughter, some day Zia would demand that her mother justify that decision. And the unhappy truth was that her own wounded pride, her craven desire to avoid a traumatic confession and her pessimistic suppositions about how Luca might react, were not in themselves sufficient excuse for her to remain silent.

Richard had phoned in the week to say that he would come down for a night over the weekend with his current girlfriend. Darcy had been looking forward to some fresh company, but unfortunately Richard arrived on Friday afternoon, just as she was on her way out with Zia. He was alone.

Tall, loose-limbed, and with a shock of dark hair and brown eyes, Richard immediately made himself at home on the sagging sofa by the kitchen range. 'If you're going out, I intend to drown my sorrows,' he warned, his mobile features radiating self-pity in waves. 'I've been dumped.'

Darcy almost said, Not *again*, which would have been very tactless. Managing to bite the words back, she gave his slumped shoulder a consoling pat. He was like the brother she had never had, and utterly clueless about women. He had a fatal weakness for long-legged glamorous blondes, and the looks and the money to attract them if not to hold them. He didn't like clubbing or parties. He lived for his horses. He was a man with a Porsche in search of a rare, horsy homebody hiding behind the façade of a long-legged glamorous blonde.

'Zia's been invited to a party and I offered to stay and help,' Darcy told him. 'I'll be a while, so you're on your own unless you care to ring Karen.'

'Pity *she's* not a blonde,' Richard lamented, stuck like a record in a groove. He pulled a whisky bottle out of a capacious pocket. 'None of the women I like are blonde...'

'Doesn't that tell you something?'

'I wish I'd done the decent thing and married you. I probably would've been quite happy.'

'Richard...' Darcy drew in a deep, restraining breath, reminded that she had yet to tell Richard that she was currently in possession of a husband. 'Why don't you put the booze away and go down to the lodge and keep Karen company?'

'I'm not telling *her* I've been dumped again...she'd *laugh!*'

Darcy called Karen before she went out. 'Richard's here,' she announced. 'He's been dumped.'

Karen howled with laughter.

'I thought I'd let you get that out of your system before you see him in the flesh.'

It was almost seven by the time Darcy arrived home. After all the excitement at the party, Zia was exhausted and ready only for bed. Richard was in a maudlin slump in the kitchen. Darcy surveyed the sunken level on the whisky bottle in dismay. 'You're feeling *that* bad?'

'Worsh,' Richard groaned, opening only one blood-shot eye.

Pity and irritation mingled inside Darcy. She, too, was miserable. Some decent conversation might have cheered her up, but Richard was drunk as a skunk. And, since he had never behaved like that before, she couldn't even reasonably shout at him.

She took Zia upstairs, gave her a quick bath, tucked her into bed and started to read her a story, but Zia fell asleep in the middle of it. Her eyes filled with guilt and love, Darcy smoothed her daughter's dark curls tenderly from her brow and sighed. She owed it to Zia to tell Luca the truth.

With a steely glint in her gaze, Darcy went back downstairs to sort out Richard. Since he'd chosen to get legless in her absence, he could jolly well go and sleep it off.

'Time for bed, Richard,' she announced loudly. 'Get up!'

He lumbered upright in slow and very shaky motion. 'Ish still light...' he muttered in bewilderment.

'*So?*' Darcy pushed him towards the stairs. 'You're lucky Karen's not here...you know how she feels about alcohol after her experiences with her ex.'

Richard looked terrified. 'Not coming, ish she?'

Reflecting on the awkwardness of having two close friends who occasionally mixed like oil and water, she guided him into the room beside her own, which she had once promised Luca. Richard lurched down onto the mattress like a falling tree.

'Met your hushband...when did you get a hushband?' Richard contrived to slur, with only academic interest.

In the act of throwing a blanket over his prone body

Darcy stilled, not crediting what she was hearing. 'My husband?' she queried sharply.

Grabbing her hand, Richard tugged her closer and whispered confidentially, '*Not* a friendly chap…tried to hit me…would've punched my lights out if I hadn't fallen over…'

He was rambling, out of his skull, hallucinating. He *had* to be.

'Now isn't this cosy?' A dark sardonic drawl breathed at that exact same moment from the doorway.

Darcy got such a shock she almost leapt a foot in the air. An incredulous look on her face, she wrenched herself free of Richard and whipped round. 'Where did you come from?' she gasped, totally appalled and showing it. 'I've been home over an hour!'

'Since you were out, I went for a drive,' Luca divulged grimly.

And she looked awful, she reflected in anguish. Before bathing Zia she had sensibly changed into a faded summer dress. Had she known Luca was coming, she would have dressed up—*not* because she wished to attract him, but because she didn't want him thinking, Gosh, what a mess she is. What did I ever see in her? She had her pride and now it was in the dust.

Luca, clad in yet another of his breathtakingly elegant suits, looked absolutely stupendous. Navy suit, white shirt with fine red stripes, red silk tie. Smart enough to stroll out in front of television cameras. Slowly, very slowly, she allowed her intimidated gaze to rise above his shirt collar. Jawline aggressive. Beautiful mouth grim. Spectacular cheekbones harshly prominent and flushed. Sensational eyes blazing like gold daggers locking into a target.

Her mouth ran dry, her heart skipping a beat.

The very image of masculine outrage, Luca continued to stare at her, the sheer force of his will beating down on her. 'Carlton is *not* staying the night here!'

Richard opened his eyes. 'Thash him,' he said helpfully. 'Speaksh Italian like a native…'

'Oh, do shut up and go to sleep, Richard,' Darcy muttered unevenly.

'He stays…*I go*,' Luca delivered in a charged undertone.

'Don't be daft…he's not doing you any harm!'

Luca spun on his heel. Darcy unfroze and flew through the door after him. 'Luca…where are you going?'

He shot her a scorching look of incredulous fury. 'I'm leaving. *Per amor di Dio*… I will not stay beneath the same roof as your lover!'

'Are you out of your mind?' Darcy demanded, wide-eyed. 'Richard is *not* my lover.'

His shimmering eyes murderous, Luca spread both hands in a slashing motion and shot something at her in wrathful Italian.

Darcy gulped, registering that she was dealing with a seethingly angry male, presently incapable of accepting reasoned argument or explanation and indeed at the very limit of his control. 'OK…OK, I'll get rid of him,' she promised in desperation, because she knew at that moment that if she didn't, it was the end of everything. Luca would depart never to return.

She lifted the phone by the bed and dialled the lodge. 'Karen…I need a very big favour from you…in fact, it's so big I don't quite know how to ask. Richard is drunk, Luca's here and he's got this ridiculous idea that Richard and I are lovers. He's really furious and he wants him out of the house, and I—'

'Richard, drunk...?' Karen interrupted that frantic flood. 'Helpless, is he?'

'Pretty much. Could you possibly give him a bed for the night?' Darcy felt awful making such a request.

'*Oh, yes...*' Karen coughed suddenly, evidently clearing her throat, and added very stiffly, 'Yes, I suppose I could.'

'Thanks.' Darcy sagged with relief.

'We're going to go for a little walk, Richard,' she said winsomely as she yanked the blanket off him again.

Running through his pockets, she extracted his car keys and, anchoring a long arm round her shoulder, tried to haul him off the bed. 'Richard...you weigh a ton!' she groaned in frustration.

'Allow me,' Luca breathed savagely from behind her.

In dismay, Darcy released her hold on Richard. In a display of far from reassuring strength, Luca accomplished the feat of getting Richard upright again.

'Where are you taking him?' Luca demanded roughly.

'Not far. Just get him down into his car. Don't... don't hurt him,' she muttered anxiously on the stairs, as Richard staggered and Luca anchored a hand as gentle as a meat hook into the back of his sweater.

Richard loaded up, Darcy swung into the driver's seat of the Porsche and ignited the engine.

'Where we goin'?' Richard mumbled.

'You'll see.' She didn't have the heart to tell him. He had found himself at the withering end of Karen's sharp and clever tongue too often. Handing him over drunk and incapable of self-defence was the equivalent of handing a baby to a cannibal.

Karen had heard the car. She walked out into the lane

and had the passenger door open before Darcy had even alighted.

'Karen…?' Richard was moaning in horror.

'Relax, Richard,' Karen purred, sounding all maternal and caring. 'I'm going to look after you.'

Darcy gaped at her friend over the car bonnet. 'Karen…what's going on?'

'Have you any idea how long I've waited for a chance like this?' Karen whispered back, her eyes gleaming as she reached up to smooth a soothing hand over Richard's tousled dark hair. 'Blondes are bad news for you, Richard,' she told him in a mesmeric tone of immense compassion.

'Yesh,' Darcy heard Richard agree slavishly as Karen guided him slowly towards the lodge.

Karen was either planning to lull Richard into a false sense of security before she turned a hose on him in the back garden to sober him up, or she was planning to persuade Richard that his dream woman had finally arrived in the unexpected shape of a small but very attractive brunette.

Darcy walked back up to the Folly. Luca was waiting in the hall for her. He didn't even stop to draw breath. 'What was that drunken idiot doing here tonight?' he demanded rawly.

'For goodness' sake, he often stays, and he doesn't normally drink like that. He brings his girlfriends here too,' Darcy proffered tautly. 'I don't know where you get the idea that we're lovers—'

'Three years ago, you almost married Carlton. *He jilted you!*' Luca reminded her savagely. '*Porca miseria*…do you expect me to believe that he's now only a platonic friend?'

'Yes, I do expect you to believe that.' Darcy met his burnished gaze levelly.

'Even though he's the father of your child?' Luca framed with driven ferocity.

Darcy turned pale as milk. 'I assure you that Zia is *not* Richard's child.'

The tense silence simmered, but she saw some of the tension ease in Luca's angry stance.

Desperate to know what Luca was thinking now that she had made that admission, Darcy murmured tautly, 'Until Richard and I both fell for other people, neither of us realised what was missing in our relationship. We stayed friends. He's a terrific guy, kind, caring…'

Luca's mouth twisted as he listened, hooded eyes hard as stones as he followed her into the drawing room. 'Mr Wonderful…Mr Perfect…'

'No…he does tend to tell the same horsy stories and jokes over and over again.'

Darcy was surprised that he had made no further comment on the subject of Zia's paternity. Heavens, did he still think there had been other men in her life, then?

'And he's thicker than a block of wood…don't forget that minor imperfection,' Luca slotted in drily. 'But why didn't you tell him that you're married? *Accidenti*…so close a friend and he didn't even know I existed!'

'Tonight was the first time I'd seen him since our wedding, but I didn't have time to talk to him because I had to go out. When did you arrive?'

'After six. I did not expect to arrive here and find another man in residence!'

Darcy blinked, and thought about the last enervating half-hour. Luca had behaved like a jealous, possessive husband and instinctively she had reacted like a foolish and insecure new wife, eager to placate him. Luca, jealous? It was a stunning concept.

'Were you jealous when you thought Richard was my lover?' Darcy asked baldly.

Luca stilled and sent her a gleaming glance from below inky black lashes. 'I am naturally jealous of my dignity.'

'Your dignity?' Her hopeful face had fallen by a mile.

'Is it unreasonable for me to expect you to behave like a normal wife?' Luca countered levelly. 'In the light of your previous relationship with him, inviting Carlton to stay here alone with you was most unwise—'

'Unwise,' Darcy parroted, thinking what a bloodless, passionless word that was.

'As my wife, you are now in the public eye, and a potential target for damaging gossip. Surely you can't want anyone to have cause to suspect at this early stage that there is anything seriously wrong with our marriage?'

Darcy slowly nodded. He wasn't jealous. He was just an arrogant, macho male, determined to preserve his own public image. People might laugh if they suspected his wife was being unfaithful, and he wouldn't like that.

'By the way, I settled your mortgage,' Luca remarked with stupendous casualness.

Darcy's lower lip parted company with her upper in shock.

Brilliant dark eyes intent on her aghast expression, Luca continued smoothly, 'As you're so independent, I imagine you'll wish to repay me once you inherit your godmother's money, but in the short term you are no longer burdened by those substantial monthly payments.'

Darcy stumbled into speech. 'But, Luca...what right—?'

'I haven't finished yet. I have also had a word with your bank manager. There is no longer a limit on your overdraft. Don't throw it all back in my face,' he urged almost roughly, openly assessing her shaken, troubled face. 'I had no *right* to interfere, but I had a very powerful *need* to offer you what help I could.'

Still reeling, Darcy swallowed hard. She understood, oh, yes, she understood. Luca felt guilty. This was his way of making amends. His intervention on such grounds filled her with pained discomfiture, but she was in no position to refuse his efforts on behalf of the estate. He was making it possible for her to survive and re-employ the staff.

'Thanks,' she said stiltedly.

'I would have liked to do a great deal more, *cara mia*,' Luca admitted steadily. 'But I knew you wouldn't have accepted that.'

At that respectful acknowledgement, a slow, uncertain smile drove the tension from her tense mouth. 'Did you park your wings outside?'

'My wings?'

'You'd make a really good guardian angel.'

'I was afraid you were about to say fairy godmother,' Luca confided.

'It did cross my mind.' Darcy wrinkled her nose and laughed for the first time in weeks. And then she remembered what she still had to tell him and her face shadowed. Tomorrow, she decided, she would tell him tomorrow...

It was half past eight when the Victorian bell on the massive front door shrieked and jangled.

Luca was in the library, having excused himself to make some calls, and Darcy had gone upstairs to slide into an outfit that magically accentuated her every slender curve. Green, with a fashionably short skirt and fitted jacket. She thought it looked kind of sexy on her. She slid her feet into high heels and fiddled anxiously with her hair in the mirror. And the whole time she was engaged on that transformation she refused to think about *why* she was doing it.

When Darcy opened the door, out of breath from rushing full tilt down the stairs, her sensitive stomach somersaulted when she saw Margo and Nina standing outside. Her stepmother elegant in black, and her stepsister dressed to kill in a sugar-pink dress so perilously short it made Darcy's skirt look like a maxi.

Both women did a rather exaggerated double take over her altered image.

'Is that a Galliano?' Nina demanded in an envious shriek.

'A...a what?' Darcy countered blankly.

'And those shoes are Prada! He got you out of your Barbour and your wellies fast enough!' Nina gibed thinly. 'It's such a dangerous sign when a man tries to change a woman into something she's not.'

On her lofty passage towards the drawing room, Margo winced. 'And green simply *screams* at your red hair, Darcy!'

'But Darcy doesn't have *red* hair,' a deep, dark drawl interceded across the depth of the hall from the library doorway. 'It's Titian, a shade defined by the dictionary as a bright, golden auburn.'

Darcy threw Luca the sort of look a drowning swimmer gives to a life jacket.

Margo and Nina weren't quite quick enough to conceal their dismay and surprise at Luca's appearance.

'I understood that you were still in Italy, Luca.' Her stepmother's smile of greeting was stiff.

'I thought that might be why you were here.' As Luca strolled over to the fireplace and took up a relaxed stance there, he let that statement hang a split-second, while their uninvited visitors tensed with uncertainty at his possible meaning before continuing smoothly, 'How very kind of you to think that Darcy might be in need of company.'

'I'm sure Richard Carlton's been dropping in too,' Nina said innocently.

'Yes, and what a very entertaining guy he is,' Luca countered, smiling without skipping a beat while Darcy's fascinated gaze darted back and forth between the combatants. Margo and Nina had definitely met their match.

'Nina and I were only saying yesterday what a coincidence it is that Darcy and Maxie Kendall should have got married within weeks of each other!' Margo exclaimed, watching Darcy stiffen with suspicious eyes. 'Now what was the name of Nancy Leeward's other godchild?'

'Polly,' Darcy muttered tightly. 'Why?'

'Naturally I'm curious. That old woman left such an extraordinary will! I expect we'll be hearing of Polly's marriage next...'

'I doubt it,' Darcy slotted in. 'When I last saw her, Polly had no plans to marry.'

Nina directed a brilliant smile at Luca and crossed her fabulous long legs, her abbreviated dress riding so high Darcy wouldn't have been surprised to see pantie elastic. 'I bet you haven't a clue what we're talking about, Luca.'

Margo chimed in, 'I'm afraid it did cross my mind that Darcy might—'

'Might marry me to inherit a measly one million?' Sardonic amusement gleamed in Luca's steady appraisal. 'Yes, of course I know about the will, but I can assure you that an eccentric godmother's wishes played no part whatsoever in *my* desire to marry your step-daughter.'

'Yes,' Darcy agreed, getting into the spirit of his game with dancing green eyes. 'I believe Luca would say that when he married me, he had his own private agenda.'

'Ouch,' Luca breathed for her ears alone, and her cheeks warmed.

But Margo was not so easily silenced. 'I don't know how to put this without seeming intrusive...but frankly I was concerned when I learnt from friends locally that Darcy had come home alone after spending only forty-eight hours with you in Venice—'

'Mummy...it's hardly likely to be her favourite place,' Nina said with a meaningful look.

'I love Venice,' Darcy returned squarely.

'I know you gave your poor child that silly name—Venezia—but I notice you soon gave up using it,' Margo reminded her drily.

'Venezia?' Luca queried abruptly.

Darcy's sensitive insides turned a sick somersault. She encountered a narrowed stare of bemusement from Luca and turned her head away abruptly.

'Such a silly name!' Nina giggled. 'But then Darcy never did have much taste or discretion.'

Darcy felt too sick to glance again in Luca's direction. Her nerves were shot to hell. She wanted to put a sack over Nina and suffocate her before she said too much.

'Your sense of humour must often cause deep offence,' Luca drawled with chilling bite, studying Nina with contempt. 'I have zero tolerance for anything that might distress my wife.'

Two rosy high spots of red embellished Nina's cheeks. Heavens, Darcy thought in equal shock, he sounded so incredibly protective. Her strain eased as she realised that Nina had abandoned her intent to make further snide comments about Zia.

'Yes, you were very thoughtless, Nina,' Margo agreed sharply. 'That's all in the past now. I actually came here today to express my very genuine concern over something Darcy has done.'

'Really, Margo?' Darcy was emboldened by the supportive hand Luca had settled in the shallow indentation of her spine.

'You brought Luca to the engagement party I held and not one word did you breathe about his exalted status,' Margo returned thinly.

Too enervated to be able to guess what her stepmother was leading up to, Darcy saw no relevance whatsoever to that statement.

'So what on earth persuaded you to do *this?*' Her stepmother drew a folded magazine from her capacious bag, her face stiff with distaste and disapproval. 'Is there *anything* you wouldn't do for money, Darcy? How could you embarrass your husband like that?'

Instant appalled paralysis afflicted Darcy. Her green eyes zoomed in on the magazine which contained that dreadful gushing interview, and in the same second she turned the colour of a ripe tomato, her stomach curdling with horror. Embarrassment choked her.

Margo shook her blonde head pityingly. 'I was horrified that Darcy should sell the story of your marriage to a lurid gossip magazine, Luca.'

'Whereas I shall treasure certain phrases spoken in that interview for ever,' Luca purred in a tone of rich complacency, extending his arm to ease Darcy's trembling, anxious length into the hard, muscular heat of his big frame. 'When I read about Darcy's "mystical sense of wonder' and her ''spiritual feeling of soul-deep recognition' on first meeting me, I envied her ability to verbalise sensations and sentiments which I myself could never find adequate words to describe.'

'Luca?' Darcy mumbled shakily, shattered that he had actually read that interview and absorbed sufficient of her mindless drivel to quote directly from it.

But Luca, it seemed, was in full appreciative flow. 'Indeed, I was overwhelmed by such a powerful need to be with Darcy again I flew straight here to her side. I shall *always* regard that interview as an open love letter from my wife.'

For the space of ten seconds Margo and Nina just sat there, apparently transfixed.

'Of course, I'm very relieved to hear that the interview hasn't caused any friction between you. I was *so* worried it would,' Margo responded unconvincingly.

'You surprise me.' Fabulous bone structure grim, eyes wintry, Luca studied their visitors. 'Only a fool could fail to see through your foolish attempts to diminish Darcy in my eyes. She is a woman of integrity, and how she contrived to hang onto that integrity growing up with two such vicious women is nothing short of a miracle!'

'How dare you talk to me like that?' Margo gasped, rising to her feet in sheer shock.

'You resent my wife's ownership of an estate which has been within her family for over four hundred years. You're furious that she has married a rich man who will help her to retain that home. You hoped she would be forced to sell up because you planned to demand a share of the proceeds,' Luca condemned with sizzling distaste. 'That is why I dare to talk to you as I have.'

'I'm not staying here to be insulted,' Margo snapped, stalking towards the door.

'I think that's very wise.'

Luca listened to the thud of the massive front door with complete calm.

Stunned at what had just transpired, Darcy breathed. 'I need to check on Zia…'

'Venezia,' Luca murmured softly, catching her taut fingers in his as she started up the stairs. 'Obviously you chose that name because it held a special significance for you. You were happy with me that night in Venice?'

'Y-yes,' Darcy stammered.

'But we met in what was clearly a troubled and transitional phase of your life.' His lean, strong features were taut, as if he was selecting his words with great care. 'I understand now why you so freely forgave Carlton for jilting you. Evidently he wasn't the only guilty party. You went to bed with someone other than him before that wedding.'

'No, I didn't!' Angry chagrined colour warmed Darcy's face as she stopped dead in the corridor.

'*Accidenti!* What's the point of denying it?' Luca demanded in exasperation. 'You may well not have been aware of the fact that night, but you *were* pregnant when you first met me!'

'No...I wasn't,' Darcy told him staunchly, pressing open the door of Zia's bedroom. 'You're still barking up the wrong tree!'

'You must've been pregnant,' Luca contradicted steadily, as if he was dealing with a child fearfully reluctant to own up to misbehaviour. 'Your daughter was born seven months later.'

'Zia was premature. She spent weeks in hospital before I could bring her home...' Darcy held her breath in the silence which followed, and then steeled herself to turn and face him.

Luca had a dazed, disconcerted look in his dark, deep-set eyes. He stared at her. 'She was premature?' he breathed, so low he had to clear his throat to be audible.

'So you see, now that you've been through the butcher, the baker and the candlestick-maker, as they say in the nursery rhyme, we're running out of possible culprits,' Darcy pointed out unsteadily, her throat tight, her mouth dry, her heart thumping like mad behind her breastbone. 'And to be honest, there only ever *was* one possibility, Luca.'

In the dim light, his eyes suddenly flashed pure gold. 'Are you trying to tell me that...that Zia is mine?' he whispered raggedly.

CHAPTER ELEVEN

DARCY'S voice let her down when she most needed it. As Luca asked that loaded question she gave a fierce, jerky nod, and she didn't take her strained gaze from him for a second.

Black spiky lashes screened his sensational eyes. He blinked. He was stunned.

Darcy swallowed and relocated her voice. 'And there's not any doubt about it because Richard and I never slept together. We had decided to wait until we were married.'

'*Never?*' Luca stressed with hoarse incredulity.

Darcy grimaced. 'And, since we didn't *get* married, we never actually made it to bed.'

'That means...but that means that I would've been your first...*impossible—!*' Luca broke off and compressed his lips, studying her with shaken dark eyes.

Darcy reddened. 'I didn't want you to guess that night. You said virgins were deeply unexciting,' she reminded him accusingly.

'We both said and did several foolish things that night...but fortunately making Zia was not one of them.' With a roughened laugh that betrayed the emotions he was struggling to contain, Luca closed his hands on hers to draw her closer while he gazed endlessly down at Zia, and then back at Darcy, as if he was being torn in two different directions. '*Per amor di Dio*...the truth has been staring me in the face from the start,' he groaned. 'The fact that nobody knew who the

201

father of your child was. You wouldn't say because you *couldn't* say…you didn't even know my name!'

Her anxious eyes were vulnerably wide.

Slowly Luca shook his glossy dark head. 'I saw that photo of Carlton, and he's dark as well. I assumed he was her father and that you still loved him enough to protect him. Then, when you said he wasn't, it *still* didn't occur to me that she could be my child!'

'You didn't know Zia was born prematurely. She arrived more than six weeks early.'

'I want to wake her up to look at her properly,' Luca confided a little breathlessly as he suddenly released Darcy to look down at his daughter. 'But that's the first lesson she taught me. Don't disturb her when she's asleep!'

'She sleeps like the dead, Luca.'

'Where were my *eyes?*' he whispered in unconcealed wonder. 'She has my nose—'

'She got just about everything from you.' As she hovered there Darcy was feeling slightly abandoned, and, pessimist that she had been, she was unprepared for Luca's obvious excitement at the discovery that he was a father.

Excitement? No, she certainly hadn't expected that. But then nothing had gone remotely like any of her vague imaginings of this scene. Luca had been shocked, but he had skipped the mortifying protest stage she had feared and gone straight into acceptance mode.

'She's really beautiful,' Luca commented with considerable pride.

'Yes, I think so too,' Darcy whispered rather forlornly.

'*Per meraviglia*…I'm a father. I'd better get on to my lawyer straight away—'

'I beg your pardon? Your lawyer?'

'If I was to drop dead tonight before I acknowledge her as my daughter, she could end up penniless!' Luca headed straight for the door. 'I'll call him right now.'

Drop dead, then, Luca. Darcy's eyes prickled and stung. She sniffed. Of course she didn't mean that. In fact just thinking of anything happening to Luca pierced her to the heart and terrified her, but it was hard to cope with feeling like the invisible woman.

'Aren't you coming?' Luca glanced back in at her again.

She sat in the library, watching him call his lawyer. Then he called his sister, and by the sound of the squeals of excitement Ilaria was delighted to receive such a stunning announcement.

'Zia is mine. Obviously it was meant to be,' Luca drawled, squaring his shoulders as he sank down into the armchair opposite her. 'Now I want to hear everything from the first minute you suspected you might be pregnant.'

'I was about five months gone before I worked that out.'

'Five *months?*' Luca exclaimed.

'I didn't put on much weight, didn't have any morning sickness or anything. I *was* eating a lot, and I got a bit of a tummy, and then I got this *really* weird sort of little fluttery feeling...that's what made me go to the doctor. When he told me it was the baby moving I was shocked rigid!'

'I imagine you were.' Luca's spectacular dark eyes were brimming with tender amusement. Rising lithely from his chair, he settled down on the sofa beside her and reached for her hand to close it between his long fingers. 'So you weren't ill?'

'Healthy as a horse.'

'And how did your family react?'

'My father was pretty decent about it, but I think that was because he was hoping I'd have a boy,' Darcy admitted ruefully. 'He didn't give two hoots about the gossip, but Margo was ready to kill me. She went round letting everyone believe the baby was Richard's because, of course, that sounded rather better.'

'What did you tell your family about Zia's father?'

'More or less the truth…ships that pass…said I'd *forgotten* your name,' Darcy admitted shamefacedly.

'How alone you must have felt,' Luca murmured heavily, his grip on her small hand tightening. 'But that night you gave me to understand that you were protected.'

'I honestly thought I was. I didn't realise that you had to take those wretched contraceptive pills continuously to be safe…and, of course, I'd tossed them in the bin the first morning I was in Venice!'

'If *only* you hadn't run away from the apartment—'

'You'd have stuck the police on me instead.'

'I wouldn't have. Had you stayed, your innocence would never have been in doubt. *Why?*' Luca emphasised, intent, dark golden eyes holding her more evasive gaze. 'Why did you run away?'

'It's pretty embarrassing waking up for the first time in a strange man's bed,' Darcy said bluntly. 'I felt like a real tart—'

'You don't know the first thing about being a tart, so don't use that word,' Luca censured with frowning reproof.

But a split second later he was smiling that utterly charismatic smile of his, sending her heartbeat bumpety-bumpety-bump as he asked all sorts of questions about

Zia, demonstrating a degree of interest that was ency-clopaedic in its detail. At the end of that session, he murmured with considerable assurance, 'Well...there'll be no divorce now, *cara mia*.'

Even though that development was what Darcy had hoped for from the instant she knew that she loved Luca, she didn't like the background against which he had formed that instant arrogant supposition. She tugged her hand free of his, her face frozen. 'Why? Do you know something I don't?'

Luca dealt her a startled, questioning look. 'We have a child. She needs both of us. I simply assumed—'

'I don't think you should be assuming anything in that line!' Darcy told him roundly. 'It may be important that Zia has a father, but I'm concerned about what *I* need too.'

'You need me,' Luca breathed a shade harshly, all relaxation now wiped from his taut features and not a hint of a smile left either.

Darcy flew upright. 'Don't look at me like that!'

'In what way am I looking at you?' Luca enquired forbiddingly.

'Like I'm a bad debtor or something, and you're...you're trying to work out my Achilles' heel!' Suddenly frightened by the awareness that she was heading for an argument with him and that she didn't want that, didn't trust her own overwrought and con-fused emotions, or her too often dangerously blunt tongue, she said tightly, 'Look, I'm very tired. I'm go-ing up to bed.'

From the foot of the stairs she glanced back into the library. Luca was standing by the window, ferocious tension screaming from his stillness. Her heart sank at the sight. Everything had gone wrong from the moment

she questioned his conviction that they should now view
their marriage as a real marriage. And why the heck had
she done that? Why, when she herself longed for that
stupid agreement they had made to be set aside and
totally wiped from both their memories? Why had she
refused the offer of her own most heartfelt wish?

And she saw into herself then, was forced to confront
her own insecurity. She feared that Luca only wanted
their marriage to continue for Zia's benefit. Hadn't she
felt threatened and excluded by his unashamed absorp-
tion and delight in Zia? How foolish and selfish that
had been, on the very night he first learned that he was
a father!

Feeling considerably less bolshie, Darcy made up her
bed with fresh sheets. She took the dogs down the service stairs to sleep in the kitchen. Then she donned a
strappy oyster-coloured satin nightie and slid between
the sheets to wait for Luca.

But an hour later, when she heard footsteps in the
corridor and tensed with a fast-beating heart, Luca
passed by her room. In the silence of the old house she
listened to him enter the room Richard had briefly occupied earlier and close the door.

She fell back against the pillows then, shaken, hurt
and scared…utterly out of her depth with this Luca who
was not even tempted to make love to her after an absence of three weeks.

'Fabulous apartment,' Karen sighed when she arrived
for lunch, scanning the fantastic view of London from
the penthouse. 'And Luca…he is *the* perfect man; I am
totally convinced of that. The guy that clears off without
a murmur so that you can have lunch with your best
friend is special, and when he takes the toddler with

him, he zooms up the scale of perfection and hits the bell at the top!'

'He's a very committed father.'

'I wouldn't say he was a slow starter in the husband stakes either. In one month, he has transformed your life. He even brings you flowers and cute little gifts... Richard's not into flowers, but he gave me a sweater covered with embroidered horseshoes for my birthday. It is the most *gross* garment you have ever seen, but he phones me about five times a day, and he's so scared I'm going to dump him, it's unbelievable,' Karen shared with a rather dreamy smile.

'I'm glad you're happy.'

'Well, you don't look glad enough to satisfy me,' Karen responded drily. 'I hope you're not turning into one of those spoilt little rich madams who can't appreciate what she's got!'

Darcy managed to laugh. 'Can you see the day?'

'No, but I know by your expression that there's something badly wrong, and that was an easy way to open the subject!'

Darcy thought back over the last four weeks. The Folly estate was now employing a full quota of staff, not to mention giving added employment to all the local firms engaged in the repairs and improvements which Luca had insisted the house required without further delay. While that work was going on they had set up temporary home in London at Luca's apartment, and when the summer was over they were shifting to Venice, where they would make their permanent home.

'Has he got another woman?'

'Of course he hasn't!' Darcy said, aghast.

'He's not violent or alcoholic or anything like that, is he?'

'*Karen!*' Darcy took a deep breath. 'He just doesn't love me.'

'*This* is the problem that has you moping about like a wet weekend?' Karen breathed incredulously. 'Luca arranges to fly me up here in a helicopter to have lunch with you as a surprise…he hangs on your every word, watches your every move…I mean, the guy's so besotted he's practically turning somersaults to impress!'

Darcy shrugged, unimpressed, gloom creeping over her again. They were sleeping in separate bedrooms. He hadn't made the slightest move to change that. It was as if sex didn't exist any more. And she couldn't forget that he had once admitted that possibly his belief that she was a thief had been the most dangerous part of her attraction. And it *was* as if her sex appeal had vanished overnight. Yet, aside from that, loads of really positive things were happening in their relationship…

Although she wasn't sure that being more hopelessly in love with Luca than ever was a positive thing. He was being caring, kind, supportive and considerate of her every need bar the one. He never lost his temper—no, not even when Zia had drawn all over a set of important business documents that had had to be replaced at supersonic speed before a big meeting. He took her out to dinner all the time. He took her to parties. He behaved as if he was very proud of her and paid her lots of compliments. He laughed, he smiled, he was a dirty great ray of constant sunshine, but when night fell he climbed into his *own* bed.

'Have you mentioned that you love *him* yet? I don't think it would be immediately obvious from your current demeanour,' Karen opined rather drily. 'Or maybe he's just not very good with the words.'

An hour after Karen's departure for home, Zia

bounced into her mother's bedroom to show off the latest pair of new frilly socks on display. They had three layers of handmade lace round the ankle. She was tickled pink with them. Zia was just one great big sunny smile these days. She had her mother, her adoring father and a devoted nanny, not to mention shelves groaning with toys. As she danced out again, a restive bundle of energy, Luca strolled in.

'Did you enjoy seeing Karen?' he enquired.

'Yes, it was great...I should've invited her up myself, but I knew she wouldn't want to be away for long, not with her romance with Richard hotting up the way it is.'

Just looking at him, she felt her mouth run dry and her pulses race. So she had learnt *not* to look at him directly. One quick, sneaky glance and then away again. If he didn't find her attractive any more, then the very last thing she needed was for him to guess that she was suffering withdrawal symptoms of the severest, cruellest kind. But that one sneaky glance she stole was enough to send her dizzy. Either Luca literally *did* get more gorgeous with every passing day, or she was more than usually susceptible.

In her mind's eye, she summoned him up. Casual silver-grey suit, superbly fitted to his wide shoulders, lithe hips and long powerful legs, worn with a cashmere sweater the colour of charcoal. He radiated sex appeal in waves she could *feel*. In much the same way that secret radar could feel the impact of those stunning dark eyes of his watching her.

'Darcy...I invited Karen here in the hope that you would relax with her,' Luca imparted tautly. 'But it doesn't seem to have done much good.'

'You can't put a plaster on something that isn't broken.'

'Is that one of those strange English nursery sayings?' Luca enquired.

Darcy didn't even know why she had said it, except to fill the tense silence, so she wasn't able to help him there. She twisted back to him but didn't meet his eyes.

'You know something, *cara mia?*' Luca breathed in a dangerous tone. 'I have decided that tact, patience and sensitivity do not work with you.'

'Probably not,' Darcy conceded, wondering why he had raised his voice slightly.

'In fact any man foolish enough to devote himself to the hopeless task of winning your trust would probably hit his deathbed before he got there.'

'Winning my trust?' Darcy repeated.

'What the hell do you think I've been doing for the past month?' Luca suddenly splintered at her in raw frustration.

And the strands of pain in that intonation made her look straight at him. She saw the same lonely ache there that she saw in her own face every time she stared in the mirror, and she stilled in shock.

Luca spread his hands in a familiar gesture that tugged at her heart. 'One minute you give me hope, the next you push me down,' he groaned. 'I don't need you to tell me that I made an appalling hash of our relationship, but I've been trying really hard to make up for that...only you seem to be getting further and further away from me, and I can't *bear* that when I love you so much!'

'You...you *love* me?' Darcy whispered shakily.

'You told me that you fell for me, too, that night in Venice, and that gave me hope.'

'If you love me why have you been sleeping in another room?' Darcy demanded accusingly. 'Why don't you touch me any more?'

Luca gave her a sincerely pained appraisal. 'I wanted you to appreciate that I *really* loved you.'

'Bloody funny way of showing it,' she mumbled helplessly, not knowing whether she was on her head or her heels. 'I've been so miserable.'

In one stride, Luca closed the distance between them. 'I was waiting for you to give me some sign that you still wanted me...I couldn't afford to take *anything* for granted about this marriage!'

'If you love me,' Darcy breathed headily, 'you can take me for granted all you like.'

With a muffled groan, Luca brought his mouth down hard on hers and set off a devastating chain reaction of lust through her entire quivering body. He crushed her so close she couldn't breathe, backed up towards the door to turn the lock and then lifted his dark head again. 'I've never been so frustrated in my life...I *ache* for you, *cara mia*.'

She let her hand travel up over one blunt cheekbone in a caress and framed his face, her eyes full of love. 'Me too... I've been pretty stupid, putting my pride ahead of everything, closing you out when I needed you instead of showing it. I love you loads...and loads...and loads,' she told him a little tearfully, because her emotions were running so high they were right up there with the clouds. 'You should've been able to tell that a mile off!'

'You wouldn't even look at me any more!'

She gave him a flirtatious scrutiny from below curling lashes as he drew her hand down from his face and planted a kiss in the centre of her palm. 'You're a minx,' he told her huskily.

'I like the guy to do all the running. You see, the one time I did it the other way round, I ended up climbing out of a window with a burglar alarm screaming—and I also ended up pregnant,' she pointed out in her own defence.

'Zia's so precious, she could never be a source of regret,' Luca countered. 'I really fell for you in a very big way that night three years ago.'

'I find that so hard to believe—'

'That's because you don't think enough of yourself,' he scolded. 'You knocked me for six. You were so different from every other woman I had ever met. I fell asleep that night with you in my arms, and I felt pretty damned smug and self-satisfied—'

'And then it all went horribly wrong.'

'And I spent three insanely frustrating years trying to track you down... Make no mistake, I *was* totally obsessed,' Luca confided ruefully. 'I never admitted to myself how I really felt about you, but I could hardly wait for our wedding...all I allowed myself to think about was getting you back into bed.'

'I noticed that was a fairly big issue straight off.'

Luca flushed. 'I just didn't know what was going on inside my own head, but I was incredibly happy I had you back in my bed, under my roof, *trapped*... Then Ilaria confessed, and it was like being plunged into a big black loser's hole.'

'I know,' she sighed, sympathetically.

'And that was when I finally realised I loved you,' he groaned. 'I'd blown it every way possible. All I had to hang onto was that stupid agreement we'd made for a platonic marriage...what else did you need me for?'

'Gosh, I never thought of that…'

'So I decided you could comfortably do without being reminded of what a bastard I'd been for a couple of weeks. But it was hell without you,' Luca confessed as he bent and swept her possessively up into his arms and carried her over to the bed. 'And then Benito handed me that magazine interview to read. I know you don't truly think that I'm *that* wonderful, but by the time I'd read it about ten times…'

Darcy kicked off her shoes. 'So that's why you knew it by heart.'

Luca unzipped her dress, spread the edges back and planted his mouth almost reverently on a smooth bare shoulder. 'I decided that if you really hated me, the odd sour note would've crept through. So, inspired by hope—'

'And a certain amount of ego…'

'I jumped straight on the jet,' he completed, tugging her round in his arms to give her a reproachful look. 'And when I realised that Zia was my child, I was ecstatic…it meant I had another hold on you.'

'But you jumped the gun, saying that because of Zia we should stay married. Much as I love my daughter, I need to feel wanted for myself.'

'I was clumsy. I pushed for too much too fast. I didn't dare tell you I loved you that soon because you would never, ever have believed me,' Luca informed her ruefully.

'I might've done…I'm more credulous and trusting than you are,' Darcy teased, her heart singing with love and happiness as she collided with his brilliant dark eyes and the open tenderness there.

From the inside pocket of his jacket, Luca withdrew a miniature gold box the shape of a casket. He snapped it open and removed the ornate gold ring within. The star-shaped ruby caught the light in its rich depths.

Darcy caught her breath and gasped, 'This is *it*, isn't it…that wretched ring you thought I'd nicked?'

With a wolfish grin, Luca lifted her hand and slid the medieval ring onto her wedding finger. 'The Adorata…'

'It really is gorgeous,' Darcy whispered.

'Tradition holds that the Adorata is given to a Raffacani wife on the birth of the son and heir,' Luca shared huskily. 'But this is the nineties, and I think it's time it was awarded simply for the birth of the *first* child.'

'Yes, I like that,' Darcy told him appreciatively. 'None of that sexist rubbish about sons being more important in *our* family.'

Luca pressed his lips tenderly to the corner of her smiling mouth. 'I didn't quite have the nerve to ask before now but…is there any chance you might be expecting another baby?'

'Not unless you've come up with some very kinky way of ravishing me mentally…no, not this time, but maybe some other time,' she conceded softly, tenderly, as she laced her fingers blissfully through his luxuriant black hair. 'Gosh, I love having the right to mess up your hair…it's so tidy all the rest of the time!'

'I didn't like it when you said bankers were boring,' Luca confided. 'And then in that interview you said I was the most passionate man you had ever met.'

'You *are*…about me, about Zia. You're so intense beneath that cool front.' Darcy gave a little feeling wriggle to stress how much she liked that.

'Has anybody ever told you how unbelievably sexy you look in wellington boots?'

She giggled, something she never did. 'I really, really believe that you love me now!'

Reaching up to claim his sensual mouth for herself again, Darcy gave herself up to the promise of a future full of blissful contentment and joy.

CONTRACT BABY

CHAPTER ONE

FROM the slim document case clasped in one strong brown hand, Raul Zaforteza withdrew a large glossy photograph. 'This is Polly Johnson. In six weeks' time she will give birth to my child. I *must* find her before then.'

Somehow primed to expect a gorgeous blonde with a supermodel face and figure, Digby was disconcerted to find himself looking at a small, slim girl with a mane of hair the colour of mahogany, soulful blue eyes and an incredibly sweet smile. She looked so outrageously young and wholesome he just could not imagine her in the role of surrogate mother.

As a lawyer with a highly respected London firm, Digby Carson had dealt with some very difficult cases. But a surrogacy arrangement gone wrong? The surrogate mother on the run and probably determined to keep the baby? He surveyed his most wealthy and influential client with a sinking heart.

Raul Zaforteza's fabled fortune was founded on gold and diamond mines. He was a brilliant business tycoon, a legendary polo player and, according to the gossip columns, a notorious womaniser. He was already prowling like a black panther ready to spring. Six feet two inches tall, with the sleek, supple build of a born athlete and the volatile temperament of his colourful heritage, he was an intimidating sight, even to a man who had known him from childhood.

'Digby...I understood that my lawyer in New York

219

had already briefed you on this situation,' Raul drawled with barely concealed impatience.

'He said the matter was far too confidential to discuss on the phone. And I hadn't the slightest suspicion that you were planning to become a father through surrogacy,' the older man admitted. 'Why on earth did you embark on such a risky venture?'

'*Por Dios*...you watched me grow up! How can you ask me that?' Raul countered.

Digby looked uncomfortable. As a former employee of Raul's late father, he was well aware that Raul had had a pretty ghastly childhood. He might be rich beyond avarice, but he had not been anything like as lucky in the parent lottery.

His bronzed features taut, Raul expelled his breath in a slow hiss. 'I decided a long time ago that I would never marry. I wouldn't give any woman that amount of power over me *or*, even more crucially, over any child we might have!' Fierce conviction roughened his rich, accented drawl. 'But I've always been very fond of children—'

'Yes...' An unspoken *but* hovered in the tense silence.

'Many marriages end in divorce, and usually the wife gets to keep the children,' Raul reminded the lawyer with biting cynicism. 'Surrogacy impressed me as the most practical way in which to father a child outside marriage. This wasn't an impulsive decision, Digby. When I decided to go ahead, I went to a lot of trouble to ensure that I would choose a suitable mother for my child.'

'Suitable?' Digby was keen to hear what Raul, with his famed love of fast, glitzy society blondes, had considered 'suitable' in the maternal stakes.

'When my New York legal team advertised for a surrogate mother, they received a flood of applications. I employed a doctor and a psychologist to put a shortlist of the more promising candidates through a battery of tests, but the responsibility for the final choice was naturally mine.'

The older man frowned down at the photograph of Polly Johnson. 'What age is she?'

'Twenty-one.'

Digby's frown remained. 'She was the *only* suitable candidate?'

Raul tautened. 'The psychologist did have some reservations but I decided to overlook them.'

Digby looked shaken.

'Everything that the psychologist saw in Polly I *wanted* in the mother of my child,' Raul stressed without a shade of regret. 'It was a gut feeling and I acted on it. Yes, she was young and idealistic, but she had the right moral values. She wasn't motivated by greed but by a desperate need to try and finance surgery which she hoped might extend her mother's life.'

'I wonder how that desperation affected her ability to make a rational decision about what she was getting involved in,' Digby remarked.

'Wondering is a pointless exercise now that she is pregnant with my child,' Raul countered very drily. 'But I *will* find her soon. Her background was exhaustively investigated. I now know that, just two months ago, she was at her godmother's home in Surrey. I don't yet know where she went from there. But before I do find her I need to know what my rights are in this country.'

Digby was in no hurry to break bad news before he had all the facts. British law frowned on surrogacy. If the mother wanted to keep the baby instead of handing it over, no contract was likely to persuade a British judge that taking that child from its mother was in the child's best interests.

'Tell me the rest of the story,' he advised.

While running through the bare facts for the older man's benefit, Raul stared unseeingly out of the window, grimly recalling his first sight of Polly Johnson through a two-way mirror in the New York legal office. She had reminded him of a tiny porcelain doll. Fragile, unusual and astonishingly pretty.

She had been brave and honest. And so impressively *nice*—not something Raul had ever sought in a woman before, but a trait he had found very appealing when he had considered all the positive qualities a mother might hand down to her child. Certainly Polly had been younger and less worldly wise than was desirable, but he had recognised her quiet inner strength as well as her essentially tranquil nature.

And the more Raul had watched Polly, the more he had learnt about Polly, the more he had wanted to *meet* Polly face to face, in the flesh, so that some day in the future he could comfortably answer his child's curious questions about her. But his New York lawyer had said absolutely not. Strict anonymity would be his only defence against any form of harassment in later years. But Raul had always been a ruthless rule-breaker, with immense faith in his own natural instincts, nor had he ever hesitated to satisfy his own wishes...

And acting on that essential arrogance, he conceded grudgingly now, was how everything had begun to fall apart. Worst of all, he who prided himself on his intelligence and his shrewd perceptive powers had somehow failed to notice the warning signs of trouble on the horizon.

'So once you knew that the girl had successfully conceived, you installed her in a house in Vermont with a trusted family servant to look after her,' Digby recapped, because Raul had fallen silent again. 'Where was her mother while all this was going on?'

'As soon as Polly signed the contract her mother went into a convalescent home to build up her strength for surgery. She was very ill. The woman knew nothing about the surrogacy agreement. When Polly was only a couple of weeks pregnant, her mother had the operation. Polly had been warned that her mother's chances of survival were at best only even. She died two days after surgery,' Raul revealed heavily.

'Unfortunate.'

Raul slung him a fulminating glance of scorn. *Unfortunate?* Polly had been devastated. And Raul had been uneasily conscious that her sole reason for becoming a surrogate had died that same day. Aware from the frustratingly brief reports made by the maid, Soledad, that Polly was deeply depressed, Raul had reached the point where he could no longer bear to stay at a supposedly sensible distance from the woman carrying his baby.

Understandably he had been concerned that she might miscarry. He had sincerely believed that it was his responsibility to offer her support. Isolated in a country that wasn't her own, only twenty-one-years old, pregnant with a stranger's baby and plunged deep into a grieving process that her optimistic outlook had not prepared her to face, the mother of his child had really *needed* a sympathetic shoulder.

'So I finally made contact with her,' Raul admitted

tautly. 'Since I could hardly admit that I was the father of her baby, I had to employ a certain amount of deception to make that contact.'

Unseen, Digby winced. Raul should have avoided any form of personal involvement. But then Raul Zaforteza was a disturbingly complex man. He was a merciless business opponent and a very dangerous enemy. More than one woman had come to grief on the rocks of his innate emotional detachment. But Raul was also a renowned philanthropist, the most genuine of friends to a chosen few and a male still capable of powerful emotional responses.

Raul compressed his firm lips. 'I took a weekend place near where she was staying and ensured that our paths crossed. I didn't conceal my identity; I didn't need to...the Zaforteza name meant nothing to her. Over the following months, I flew up there regularly and called on her. I never stayed long...she just needed someone to talk to.' Radiating tension now, in spite of that studiously nonchalant explanation, Raul shrugged, his accented drawl petering out into another brooding silence.

'*And?*'

'And nothing!' As he swung round from the window, Raul's hard, dark eyes were sardonic in their comprehension. 'I treated her like a little sister. I was a casual visitor, nothing more.'

Digby restrained himself from pointing out that since Raul was an only child he could only have the vaguest notion of how one treated a little sister. And Digby had three daughters, every one of whom swooned at the mere mention of Raul's name. Indeed, the last time he had taken Raul home for dinner it had been a downright embarrassing experience, with all three daughters dressed to kill and competing for Raul's attention. Even his wife said that Raul Zaforteza might well have been packaged by the devil specifically to tempt the female sex.

He pictured a lonely young woman who might only have faced up to what surrogacy really *meant* in the aftermath of her mother's death. When that nice, naive young woman had suddenly found herself entertaining a member of the international jet set as self-assured, sophisticated and charismatic as Raul, what effect had it had on her?

'When did she go missing?' Digby prompted.

'Three months ago. She disappeared one day... Soledad went out shopping and left her alone,' Raul confided grimly. 'Do you realize that in three months I have hardly slept a night through? Day *and* night I have been worried sick—'

'I suppose there *is* a strong possibility that she may have gone for a termination—'

'Por Dios...' Raul dealt the older man a smouldering look of reproof. 'Polly wouldn't abort my child!'

Content to have issued that warning, Digby didn't argue.

'Polly's very soft, very feminine, very caring...she would *never* choose that option!' Raul continued to argue fiercely.

'You asked about your rights.' Digby breathed in deep, straightening his shoulders to brace himself for the blow he was about to deliver. 'I'm afraid unmarried fathers don't have any under British law.'

Raul stared back at him with rampant incredulity. 'That isn't possible.'

'You couldn't argue that the girl would make a bad mother either. After all, you *chose* her,' the older man pointed out ruefully. 'You described a respectable girl, drawn into a surrogacy agreement only because she was trying to help her mother. As the rich foreigner who used his wealth to tempt her into making a decision which she later regretted, you wouldn't look good in court—'

'But she has reneged on a legal contract,' Raul spelt out harshly. '*Dios mio!* All I want is the right to take my own child back to Venezuela. I haven't the slightest desire to take this into a courtroom! There has to be some other way in which I can get custody.'

Digby grimaced. 'You *could* marry her...'

Raul gave him a forbidding look. 'If that was a joke, Digby...it was in the worst possible taste.'

Henry pulled out a chair for Polly to sit down to her evening meal. His mother, Janice Grey, frowned at the young woman's shadowed blue eyes and too prominent cheekbones. At eight months pregnant, Polly looked drawn and ill.

'You should be resting at this stage of your pregnancy,' Janice reproved. 'If you married Henry now, you could give up work. You could take things easy while he helped you get your godmother's will sorted out.'

'It would be the best move you could make.' Solid and bespectacled, with thinning fair hair, Henry nodded in pompous agreement. 'You'll have to be careful that the Inland Revenue doesn't take too large a slice of your inheritance.'

'I really don't want to marry anybody.' Beneath her wealth of rich, reddish brown hair, Polly's delicate features were becoming stiff and her smile strained.

An awkward silence fell while mother and son exchanged meaningful glances.

Polly focused on her nicely cooked meal with a guilty lack of appetite. It had been a mistake to take a room in Janice's comfortable terraced home. But how could she ever have guessed that her late godmother's trusted housekeeper had had an ulterior motive for offering her somewhere to stay?

Janice and her son *knew* the strange terms of Nancy Leeward's will. They *knew* that Polly would inherit a million pounds if she found a husband within the year and stayed married for at least six months. Janice was determined to persuade Polly that marrying her son would magically solve her every problem.

And, to be fair to Janice, calculating she might be, but she saw such a marriage as a fair exchange. After all, Polly was an unmarried mum-to-be and couldn't claim her godmother's money without a husband. Henry was single, and in a job he loathed. Even a small share of a million pounds would enable Henry to set up as a tax consultant in a smart office of his own. Janice would do just about anything to further Henry's prospects, and Henry wasn't just attached to his widowed mother's apron strings, he was welded to them.

'Babies can be very demanding,' Janice pointed out when her son had left the room. 'And, talking as someone who has done it, raising a child alone isn't easy.'

'I know.' But at the mere mention of the word 'baby' a vague and dreamy smile had formed on Polly's face. There was nothing practical or sensible about the warm feeling of anticipation which welled up inside her.

Janice sighed. 'I'm only trying to advise you, Polly. You're not in love with Henry, but where did falling in love get you?'

Polly's blissful abstraction was cruelly punctured by that reminder. 'Nowhere,' she conceded tightly.

'I've never liked to pry, but it's obvious that the father of your child took off the minute you got pregnant. Unreliable and irresponsible,' the older woman opined thinly. 'You certainly couldn't call my Henry either of those things.'

Polly considered Henry's joyless and stolid outlook on life and suppressed a sigh.

'People don't always marry for love. People get married for all sorts of other reasons,' Janice persisted. 'Security, companionship, a nice home.'

'I'm afraid I would need more.' Polly got up slowly and heavily. 'I think I'll lie down for a while before I go to work.'

Breathless from climbing the stairs, Polly lay down on her bed in the prettily furnished spare room. She grimaced. Never in a million years would she marry Henry just to satisfy the terms of Nancy Leeward's will and inherit that money.

She was too shamefully conscious that a craving for money had reduced her to her present predicament. Her late father, a strongly religious man, had been fond of saying that money was the root of all evil. And, looking back to the twisted, reckless decision she had made months earlier, Polly knew that in her case that pronouncement had proved all too true.

Her mother had been dying. But Polly had refused to accept the reality that the mother she had grown up without and had barely had time to get to know again *could* be dying: she hadn't believed the hand of fate could be that cruel. Armed by that stubborn belief, Polly had gone that extra mile that people talked about, but she had gone that extra mile in entirely the wrong direction, she acknowledged wretchedly.

How could she *ever* have believed that she would find

it possible to give her baby up to strangers? How could she *ever* have imagined that she could surrender all rights, hand over her own flesh and blood and agree never, ever to try and see her own child again? She had been incredibly stupid and immature. So she had run away from a situation which had become untenable, knowing even then that she would be followed and eventually *traced*...

As the ever-present threat of being found and called to account for her behaviour assailed Polly, her skin turned clammy with fear. In her own mind she was no better than a criminal. She had signed a contract in which she had promised to give up her baby. She had sat back while an unbelievably huge amount of money was expended on her mother's medical care and then she had fled. She had broken the law, yet she had been wickedly and savagely deceived into signing that contract...but what proof did she have of that fact?

Sometimes she woke from nightmares about being extradited to the USA and put on trial, her baby taken from her and parcelled off to a life of luxury with his immoral and utterly unscrupulous father in Venezuela. Even when she didn't have bad dreams, it was becoming increasingly hard to sleep. She was at that point in pregnancy when she couldn't get comfortable even in bed, and she was often wakened by the strong, energetic movements of her baby.

And in her mind's eye then, when she was at her weakest, she would see Raul. Raul Zaforteza, dark, devastating and dangerous. What a trusting and pathetic victim she had been! For she had fallen in love with him, hopelessly, helplessly, blindly in love for the first time in her life. She had lived only from one meeting to the next, frantically counting the days in between,

agonised if he didn't turn up and always tormented by
the secret she had believed she was still contriving to
keep from him. A jagged laugh was torn from her lips
now. And all the time Raul had known she was pregnant. After all, he was the father of her baby…

An hour later, Polly headed to work. It was a cool, wet
summer evening. She walked past the bus stop. She was
presently struggling to save every penny she could.
Soon she wouldn't be able to work any more, and once
she had the baby she would need her savings for all
sorts of things.

The supermarket where she worked shifts was a
bright beacon of light and activity in the city street. As
Polly disposed of her coat and her bag in the rest room,
the manageress popped her head round the door and
frowned. 'You look very tired, Polly. I hope that doctor
of yours knows what he's doing when he tells you that
it's all right for you to be still working.'

Polly flushed as the older woman withdrew again.
She hadn't actually seen a doctor in two months, but at
her last visit she had been advised to rest. How could
she rest when she had to keep herself? And if she approached the social services for assistance they would
ask too many awkward questions. So she lived in a state
of permanent exhaustion, back aching, ankles swollen,
and if she pushed herself too hard she got blinding
headaches and dizzy spells.

By the end of her shift on one of the checkouts Polly
was very tired, and really grateful that she was off the
next day. Tomorrow, she decided, she would pamper
herself. Shouldering her bag, she left the shop. The rain
had stopped. The street lights gleamed off the wet pavements and cars swished by splashing the kerbs.

Polly didn't even try to close her coat. Only a tent would have closed round her swollen stomach, and the weight of her own body contributed to her fatigue. Not long now, she consoled herself. She felt as if she had been pregnant for ever, but soon she would be getting to know her baby as a separate little person.

Engaged in her thoughts of the near future, head downbent, Polly didn't register the existence of a large obstacle in her path. Only at the last possible moment, when she almost cannoned into the impossibly tall and solidly built male blocking her passage, did she notice the presence of another human being and seek to side-step him.

As she teetered dangerously off balance, a cry of dismay escaping her, a pair of strong hands shot out to catch her by the shoulders and steady her. Heart pounding with fright, she reeled as he held her there, her head tipping back from a view of her rescuer's silver-grey silk tie to look up.

Raul Zaforteza gazed down at her from his great height, his facial muscles locking his staggeringly handsome features into a bronze mask of impassivity that was uniquely chilling.

In severe shock, Polly trembled, soft mouth opening and closing again without sound, a look of pure panic in her gaze as she collided with eyes that had the topaz golden brilliance of a tiger ready to claw the unwary to the bone.

'There is no place in this whole wide world where you could hope to stay hidden from me,' Raul spelt out in a controlled tone of immense finality, his rich, accented vowel sounds tingling in her sensitive ears, throwing up a myriad of despoilt memories that could only torment her. 'The chase is over.'

CHAPTER TWO

'LET me go, Raul!' Polly gasped convulsively, her heart thudding like a trapped animal's behind her breastbone, nervous perspiration beading her short upper lip.

'How can I do that?' Raul countered with level emphasis. 'You're expecting my baby. What sort of a man *could* walk away?'

Without warning, pain flashed in a scorching burst across Polly's temples, provoking a startled moan from her parted lips. Her hand flew up to press against her throbbing brow. Nausea stirred nastily in her stomach as the overpowering dizziness washed over her.

'*Por Dios*...what is the matter with you?' Raul tightened his hold on her as she swayed like a drunk, straining with every sinew to stay upright and in control.

In another moment he bent and swept her up into his arms, cradling her easily into the strength and heat of his big, powerful frame. As the street light shone on the greyish pallor of her upturned face, Raul emitted a groan and said something hoarse in Spanish.

'Put me down...' Polly was not too ill to appreciate the cruel irony of Raul getting that physically close to her for the very first time.

Ignoring her, chiselled profile aggressively clenched, Raul jerked his imperious dark head and the limousine parked across the street filtered over to the kerb. The chauffeur jumped out and hurried to open the passenger door. Raul settled her down on the squashy leather back seat, but before he could climb in beside her Polly took him by surprise and lurched half out again, to be violently sick in the gutter. Then she sagged back on the seat, pressing a tissue to her tremulous lips and utterly drained.

As she lay slumped on her side, a stunned silence greeted her. Momentarily, a dull gleam of amusement touched her. Raul Zaforteza had probably got to the age of thirty-one without ever having witnessed such a distasteful event. And she hated him for being there to witness her inability to control her own body. Although she was the kind of person who automatically said sorry when other people bumped into *her*, a polite apology would have choked her.

'Do you feel strong enough to sit up?'

As she braced a slender hand on the seat beneath her, Raul took over, raising her and propping her up like a rag doll. Involuntarily she breathed in the elusive scent of him. Clean, warm male overlaid with a hint of something more exotic.

'So you finally ran me to earth,' Polly acknowledged curtly, refusing to look at him, staring into space with almost blank blue eyes.

'It was only a matter of time. I went first to the house where you're staying. Janice Grey wasn't helpful. Fortunately I was already aware of where you worked,' Raul imparted flatly.

She could feel the barrier between them, high and impenetrable as toughened frosted glass, the highwire tension splintering through the atmosphere, the restive, brooding edge of powerful energy that Raul always emanated. But *she* felt numb, like an accident victim. He had found her. She had made every possible effort to remain undetected—moved to London, even lied to friends so that nobody had a contact address or phone number for her. And all those endeavours had been in vain.

As a spasm of pain afflicted her, she squeezed her eyes tight shut.

'What *is* it?' Raul demanded fiercely.

'Feel like my head's splitting open,' she mumbled sickly, forcing her eyes open again.

Raul was now studying the pronounced swell of her stomach with a shaken fascination that felt deeply, offensively intrusive.

In turn, Polly now studied him, pain like a poisonous dart piercing her bruised heart. His hair—black as midnight now, but blue-black in sunlight—the strong, flaring ebony brows, the lean, arrogant nose, the magnificent high cheekbones and hollows, the wide, perfectly modelled mouth so eloquent of the raw sensuality that laced his every movement. A devastatingly attractive male, so staggeringly good-looking he had to turn heads wherever he went, and yet only the most audacious woman would risk cornering him. There was reinforced steel in those hard bones, inflexible control in that strong jawline.

The baby kicked, blanking out her mind, making her wince.

His incongruously long and lush black lashes swept up, and she was pinned to the spot by glinting gold eyes full of enquiry.

'May I?' he murmured almost roughly.

And then she saw his half-extended hand, those lean brown fingers full of such tensile strength, and only after a split second did she register in shock the source of his interest. His entire attention was on the giant mound of her stomach, a strangely softened expression driving the tension from his firm lips.

'May I feel my child move?' he clarified boldly.

Polly gave him a stricken look of condemnation, and with shaking, frantic hands tried somewhat pointlessly to try and yank her coat over herself. 'Don't you *dare* try to touch me!'

'Perhaps you are wise. Perhaps touching is not a good idea.' Nostrils flaring, Raul flung himself back in the corner of the seat, hooded eyes betraying only a chilling glint of intent gold, his bronzed face cold as a guillotine, impassive now in icy self-restraint.

And yet Polly was reminded of nothing so much as a wild animal driven into ferocious retreat. He had never looked at her like that in Vermont, but she had always sensed the primal passion of the temperament he restrained. Then, as now, it had exercised the most terrifying fascination for her—a male her complete opposite in nature, an outwardly civilised sophisticate in mannerism, speech and behaviour, but at heart never, ever cool, predictable or tranquil.

'Take me home,' she muttered tightly. 'I'll meet you tomorrow to talk.'

He lifted the phone and spoke in fluid Spanish to his driver. Polly turned away.

She remembered him in Vermont, addressing Soledad in Spanish. She remembered the maid's nervous unease, her undeniable servility. When Raul had been around, Soledad had tried to melt into the woodwork, too unsophisticated a woman to handle the cruel complexity of the situation he had unthinkingly put her in. In his eyes she had only been a servant after all. Raul Zaforteza was not a male accustomed to taking account of the needs or the feelings of lesser beings...and in Soledad's case he had paid a higher price than he would ever know for that arrogance.

The powerful car drew away from the kerb and shot Polly's flailing and confused thoughts back to the present. While Raul employed the car phone to make a lengthy call in Spanish, she watched him helplessly from below her lashes. She scanned the width of his shoulders under the superb fit of his charcoal-grey suit, the powerful chest, lean hips and long muscular thighs that not the most exquisite tailoring in the world could conceal.

'*I* can't touch *you* but every look you give me is a visual assault,' Raul derided in a whiplash aside as he replaced the phone. 'I'd eat you for breakfast, little girl!'

Her temples throbbed and she closed her eyes, shaken that he could speak to her like that. So many memories washed over her that she was cast into turmoil. Raul, tender, laughing, amber eyes warm as the kiss of sunlight, without a shade of coldness. And every bit of that caring concern aimed at the ultimate well-being of the baby in her womb, at the physical body cocooning his child *not* at Polly personally. She had never existed for him on any level except as a human incubator to be kept calm, content and healthy. But how could she ever have guessed that shattering truth?

'You look terrible,' Raul informed her tautly. 'You've lost a lot of weight and you were very slim to begin with—'

'Nobody could ever accuse me of that now.'

'Your ankles are swollen.'

Polly rested her pounding head back wearily, beyond caring about what she must look like to him now. It scarcely mattered. She had been ten times more presentable in Vermont and he had not been remotely attracted to her, although she had only recognised that humiliating reality in retrospect. 'You're not getting my baby,' she warned him doggedly. 'Not under any circumstances.'

'Calm yourself,' Raul commanded deflatingly. 'Anxiety won't improve your health.'

'*It* always comes first, right?' Polly could not resist sniping.

'*Desde luego*…of course,' Raul confirmed without hesitation.

She winced as another dull flash of pain made her very brain ache. She heard him open a compartment, the hiss of a bottle cap released, liquid tinkling into a glass, and finally another unrecognisable sound. And then she jerked in astonishment when an ice-cold cloth was pressed against her pulsing brow.

'I will take care of you now. Did I not do so before? And look at you now, like a living corpse…' Raul condemned, his dark drawl alive with fierce undertones as he bent over her. 'I wanted to shout at you. I wanted to make you tremble. But how can I do *that* when you are like this?'

Her curling lashes lifted. Defenceless in pain, she stared up into frustrated and furious golden eyes so nakedly at variance with the compassionate gesture of that cool, soothing cloth he had drenched for her benefit. Being kind to her was killing him. She understood that. Suffering that grudging kindness was killing *her*.

'You taught me to *hate*,' she whispered, with a sudden ferocity alien to her gentle nature until that moment.

The stunning eyes veiled to a slumberous gleam. 'There is nothing between us but my baby. *No* other connection, *nada más*…nothing more,' he stressed with gritty exactitude. 'Only when you can detach yourself from your emotional mindset and recall that contract will we talk.'

Hatred flamed like a shooting star through Polly. She needed it. She needed hatred to race like adrenalin through her veins. Only hatred could swallow up and ease the agonizing pain Raul could inflict.

'You bastard,' Polly muttered shakily. 'You lying, cheating, devious bastard…'

At that precise moment the limo came to a smooth halt. As the chauffeur climbed out, Polly gaped at the well-lit modern building with its beautifully landscaped frontage outside which the car had drawn up. 'Where are we?' she demanded apprehensively.

A uniformed nurse emerged from the entrance with a wheelchair.

In silence Raul swung out of the limo and strode round the bonnet to wave away the hovering chauffeur. He opened the door beside her himself.

'You need medical attention,' he delivered.

Her shaken eyes widened, filling with instantaneous fear. Not for nothing had she visited the library to learn all she could from newspapers about Raul Zaforteza's ruthless reputation. 'You're not banging me up in some lunatic asylum!' she flung in complete panic.

'Curb your wild imagination, *chica*. I would do nothing to harm the mother of my child. And don't you *dare* try to cause a scene when my only concern is for your well-being!' Raul warned with ferocious bite as he leant in and scooped her still resisting body out of the luxurious car as if she weighed no more than a feather.

'The wheelchair, sir,' the nurse proffered.

'She weighs nothing. I'll carry her.' Raul strode through the automatic doors, clutching her with the tense concern of someone handling a particular fragile

parcel. *The mother of his child.* Cue for reverent restraint, she reflected bitterly. Restraint and concern that
the human incubator should be proving less than efficient. But, weak and sick from pain, even her vision
blurring, she rested her head down against a broad
shoulder.

'Hate you,' she muttered nonetheless, and would
have told him that with her last dying breath because it
was her only defence.

'You're not tough enough to hate,' Raul dismissed as
a grey-haired older man in a white coat moved towards
them.

Raul addressed him in a flood of Spanish. Scanning
her with frowning eyes, the doctor led the way into a
plush consulting room on the ground floor.

'Why does nobody speak English? We're in London,'
Polly moaned.

'I'm sorry. Rodney Bevan is a consultant who
worked for many years in a clinic of mine in Venezuela.
I can talk faster in my own language.' Raul laid her
down carefully on a comfortable treatment couch.

'Go away now,' Polly urged him feverishly.

Raul stayed put. The consultant said something quiet
in Spanish. Raul's blunt cheekbones were accentuated
by a faint line of dark colour. He swung on his heel and
strode out to the waiting area, closing the door behind
him.

'What did you say?' Polly was impressed to death.

As the waiting nurse moved forward to help Polly
out of her coat, the older man smiled. 'You're the star
here, not him.'

The nurse took her blood pressure. Why were their
faces so solemn? Was there something wrong with her

blood pressure? Her body felt like a great weight pulling her down.

'You need to relax and keep calm, Polly,' the doctor murmured. 'I want to give you a mild sedative and then I would like to scan you. Is that all right with you?'

'No, I want to go home,' she mumbled fearfully, knowing she sounded like a child and not caring, because she didn't feel she could trust anybody so friendly with Raul.

The voices went away. Raul's rich, dark drawl broke into her frantic barely half-formed thoughts. 'Polly...*please* let the medics do what they need to do,' he urged.

She forced her eyes open, focusing on him with difficulty, seeing those lean bronzed features through a blur. 'I can't trust you...or them...you *know* him!'

And even in the state she was in she saw him react in shock to that frightened accusation. Raul turned pale, the fabulous bone structure clenching hard. He gripped her hand, brilliant eyes shimmering. 'You *must* trust him. He's a very fine obstetrician—'

'He's a friend of yours.'

'*Sí, pero*...yes, but he is also a *doctor*,' Raul stressed with highly emotive urgency.

'I don't want to go to sleep and wake up in Venezuela... Do you think I don't know what you're capable of when you're crossed?' Polly managed to frame with the last of her energy.

'I've never broken the law!'

'You *would* to get this baby,' Polly told him.

The silence smouldered, fireworks blazing under the surface.

Raul stared down at her, expressive eyes veiled, but she knew she had drawn blood.

'You're not well, Polly. If you will not believe my assurances that you can trust the staff here, then at least think of the baby's needs and put those needs first,' he breathed, not quite levelly.

A pained look of withdrawal crossed her exhausted face. She gave a jerky nod of assent, but turned her head to the wall. A minute later she felt a slight prick in her arm and she let herself float, and would have done anything to escape that relentless pounding inside her skull and forget that unjust look of cruel reproach she had seen in Raul's gaze.

As she drifted like a drowning swimmer, all the worst moments of her life seemed to flash up before her.

Her earliest memory was of her father shouting at her mother and her mother crying. She had got up one morning at the age of seven to find her mother gone. Her father had flown into a rage when she'd innocently tried to question him. Soon after that she had been sent to stay with her godmother. Nancy Leeward had carefully explained. Her mother, Leah, had done a very silly thing: she had gone away with another man. Her parents were getting a divorce, but some time, hopefully soon, when her father gave permission, her mother might come to visit her.

Only Leah never had. Polly had got her mothering from her godmother. And she had had to wait until she was twenty years old and clearing out her father's desk, days after his funeral, to discover the pitiful wad of pleading letters written by the distraught mother who had to all intents and purposes abandoned her.

Leah had gone to New York and eventually married her lover. She had flown over to England half a dozen times, at an expense she could ill afford, in repeated attempts to see her daughter, but her embittered ex-husband had blocked her every time—not least by putting Polly into boarding school and refusing to say where she was. Polly had been shattered by what she'd uncovered, but also overjoyed to realise that her mother had really loved her, in spite of all her father's assertions to the contrary.

In New York, she had had a tearful, wonderful reunion with Leah, whose second husband had died the previous year. Her mother had been weak, breathless, and aged far beyond her years. The gravity of her heart condition had been painfully obvious. She had been living on welfare, what health insurance she had had exhausted. The harassed doctor at the local clinic had reluctantly told Polly under pressure that there *was* an operation performed by a world-famous surgeon which might give her mother some hope, but that it would take a lottery win to privately finance such major surgery.

Up, down—too much down in her life recently, and not enough up, she thought painfully as she wandered through her own memories.

And then she saw Raul, strolling through the glorious Vermont woods where she had walked every day, escaping from Soledad's kind but fussing attentions to cry in peace for the mother she had lost. Raul, garbed in faultlessly cut casual clothes, smart enough to take Rodeo Drive by storm and so smooth, so impressively natural in his surprise at stumbling on her that it was a wonder he hadn't cut himself with his own clever tongue.

And she had met those extraordinary eyes of amber and bang...crash...*pow*. She had been heading for a down that would take her all the way to hell, even

though she had naively felt she was on an up the instant
he angled that first smouldering smile at her.

Polly woke up the following morning wearing a hideous
billowing hospital gown. She had a room to herself with
a private bathroom. Her head no longer hurt, but tiredness still filled her with lethargy.

The nurse who came in response to the bell cheerfully
ran through routine checks, efficiently helped her to
freshen up and neatly side-stepped most of her anxious
questions. She consulted her chart and informed Polly
that she was to have complete bedrest. Mr. Bevan would
be in around lunchtime, she confided, just as breakfast
was delivered.

A couple of hours later Raul's chauffeur arrived, like
an advance party before him. He settled down a suitcase
that Polly recognised because it was her own. The case
bulged with what struck her as very probably every possession she had last seen in her room at the Greys'. A
maid in an overall came in and helped her change into
one of her own nighties. Polly then retrieved a creased
brown envelope from the jumble of items in the foot of
her case. It was time to confront Raul with the worst of
the deceptions practised on her.

By the time mid-morning arrived, Polly was sitting
bolt upright with wide, angrily impatient eyes and, had
she but known it, the first healthy colour in her cheeks
for weeks. She raked restive fingers through the silky
mahogany hair tumbling round her shoulders and focused on the door expectantly, like someone not only
preparing to face Armageddon but overwhelmingly eager to meet it.

The ajar door finally spread wide, framing Raul.

Her breath caught in her throat.

Sleek and powerful, in a summerweight double-breasted beige business suit, he looked sensationally attractive, supremely poised and shockingly self-assured. Polly lost her animated colour, ashamed of that helpless flare of physical response to those dark good looks and that lithe, lean, muscular physique. He was a ruthless and unashamed manipulator.

Black eyes raked over her, black eyes without any shade of warm gold. Emotionless, businesslike, not even a comforting hint of uncertainty about his stance. 'You look better already,' he remarked levelly.

'I feel better,' Polly was generous enough to admit. 'But I can't stay here—'

'Of course you can. Where else could you be so well cared for?'

'I've got something here I want you to explain,' Polly delivered tautly.

His attention dropped to the envelope clutched between her tense fingers. 'What is it?'

A shaky little laugh escaped Polly. 'Oh, it's not real proof of the manipulative lies I was fed…you needn't worry about that! Your lawyer was far too clever to allow me to retain any original documents, but I took photocopies—'

Raul frowned at her. '*Dios mio*, cut to the base line and tell me what you're talking about,' he incised impatiently. 'You were told no lies at any time!'

'Off the record lies,' Polly extended tightly. 'It was very clever to give me the impression that I was being allowed a reassuring glimpse at highly confidential information.'

Raul angled back his imperious dark head. 'Explain yourself.'

Polly tossed the envelope to the foot of the bed. 'How

you can look me in the face and say that I will never know.'

Raul swept up the envelope with an undaunted flourish.

'And don't try to pretend you didn't know about it. When I was asked to sign that contract, I said I couldn't sign until I was given some assurances about the couple who wanted me to act as surrogate for them.'

'The...*couple*?' Raul queried flatly, ebony brows drawing together as he extracted the folded pages from the envelope.

'Your lawyer said that wasn't possible. His clients wanted complete anonymity. So I left. Forty-eight hours later, I got a phone call. I met up in a café with a young bright spark from your lawyer's office. He said he was a clerk,' Polly related jerkily, her resentment and distaste blatant in her strained face as she recalled how easily she had been fooled. 'He said he *understood* my concern about the people who would be adopting my child, and that he was risking his job in allowing me even a glance at such confidential documents—'

'Which confidential documents?' Raul cut in grittily.

'He handed me a profile of that *supposed* couple from an accredited adoption agency. There were no names, no details which might have identified them...' Tears stung Polly's eyes then, her voice beginning to shake with the strength of her feelings. 'And I was really moved by what I read, by their own personal statements, their complete honesty, their deep longing to have a family. They struck me as wonderful people, and they'd had a h-heartbreaking time struggling to have a child of their own...'

'*Madre mía...*' Raul ground out, half under his

breath, scorching golden eyes pinned to her distraught face with mesmeric force.

'And you see,' Polly framed jaggedly, 'I really *liked* that couple. I felt for them, thought they would make terrific parents, would give any child a really loving home…' As a strangled sob swallowed her voice, she crammed a mortified hand against her wobbling mouth and stared in tormented accusation at Raul through swimming blue eyes. 'How *could* you sink that low?' she condemned strickenly.

Raul gazed back at her, strikingly pale now below his olive skin, so still he might have been a stone statue, a stunned light in his piercing dark eyes.

With the greatest difficulty, Polly cleared her throat and breathed unevenly. 'I asked the clerk to let me have an hour reading over that profile and I photocopied it without telling him. That afternoon, I went in and signed the contract. I thought I was doing a really good thing. I thought I would make that couple so happy… I was inexcusably dumb and shortsighted!'

The heavy silence stretched like a rubber band pulled too taut. And then Raul unfroze. In an almost violent gesture, he shook open the pages he still held. He strode over to the window, his broad back turned to her, his tension so pronounced it hummed like a force field in a room that now felt suffocatingly airless.

Polly sank wearily back against the pillows and fought to get a grip on the tears still clogging her aching throat.

Timeless minutes later, Raul swung back, his darkly handsome features grim and forbidding. 'This abhorrent deception was not instigated by me,' he declared, visibly struggling to contain the outrage blazing in his eyes, the revealing rawness to that harshened plea in his own defence. 'I had no knowledge of your request for further information *or* of your initial reluctance to sign that contract.'

'How am I supposed to believe anything you say?'

'Because the guilty party will be called to account,' Raul asserted with wrathful bite. 'At no stage did I give any instruction which might have implied that I would countenance such a deception. There was no need for me to stoop to lies and manipulation. There were other far less scrupulous applicants available—'

'Were there?' Polly breathed, not best pleased to realise that she had featured as one of many.

He was shocked and furious, so furious there was a slight tremor in his fingers as he refolded the pages she had given him. His sincerity was fiercely convincing.

'So now I know why you have no faith in my word. It wasn't only my decision to conceal my identity as the father of your child in Vermont that made you change your mind about fulfilling the contract.'

It was an unfortunate reminder. He only had to mention that cruel masquerade to fill Polly with savage pain and resentment. She surveyed him with angry, bitter eyes. 'I would never, ever have agreed to a single male parent for my child, and when I found out who you really were, I was genuinely appalled—'

Raul skimmed a startled glance at her. '*Dios mio*...''appalled'? What an exaggeration—'

'No exaggeration. I wouldn't give a man with your reputation a pet rabbit to keep, never mind an innocent, helpless baby!' Polly fired back at him.

Raul gazed back at her with complete incredulity. 'What is wrong with my reputation?'

'Read your own publicity,' Polly advised with unconcealed distaste, thinking about the endless string of glamorous women who had been associated with him. There was nothing stable or respectable about Raul's lifestyle.

Outrage sizzled round Raul Zaforteza like an intimidating aura. He snatched in a deep shuddering breath of restraint. 'What right do you have to stand in judgement over me? So subterfuge was employed to persuade you into conceiving my child—I deeply regret that reality, but nothing will alter the situation we're in now. That child you carry is *still* my child!'

Polly turned her head away. 'And mine.'

'The Judgement of Solomon. Are you about to suggest that we divide him or her into two equal halves? Let me tell you now that I will fight to the end to prevent that obnoxious little nerd I met last night raising my child!' Raul delivered with sudden explosive aggression.

Polly blinked. 'What little nerd?'

'Henry Grey informed me that you're engaged to him,' Raul imparted with a feral flash of white teeth. 'And you may believe that that is your business, but *anything* that affects my child's welfare is also very much *my* business now!'

Stunned to realise that Henry should have claimed to be engaged to her, Polly surveyed the volatile male striding up and down the room, like a prowling tiger lashing his tail at the confines of a cage. Why did she want to hold Raul in her arms and soothe him? she asked herself with a sinking heart.

'I think you should leave, Raul.' As that dry voice of reproof cut through the electric atmosphere, Polly tore her mesmerised attention from Raul. In turn, Raul swung round. They both focused in astonishment on the consultant lodged in the doorway.

'*Leave?*' Raul stressed in unconcealed disbelief.

'Only quiet visitors are welcome here,' Rodney Bevan spelt out gravely.

Dressed in an Indian cotton dress the same rich blue as her eyes, Polly turned her face up into the sun and basked, welded to the comfy cushioning on the lounger. The courtyard garden at the centre of the clinic was an enchanting spot on a summer day. Even Henry's unwelcome visit couldn't detract from her pleasure at being surrounded by greenery again.

Henry gave her an accusing look. 'Anybody would think you were enjoying yourself here!'

'It's very restful.'

Until Polly had escaped Henry and his mother for three days, she hadn't appreciated just how wearing their constant badgering had become. She was tired of being pressurised and pushed in a direction she didn't want to go. Now that Raul had found her, she was no longer in hiding. After she had sorted out things with Raul, she would be able to take control of her own life again.

'Mother thinks you should come home,' Henry told her with stiff disapproval.

'You still haven't explained *why* you told Raul we were engaged.'

Henry frowned. 'I should've thought that was obvious. I hoped he'd go away and leave us alone. What's the point of him showing up now? He's just complicating things, swanning up in his flash car and acting like he owns you!'

Strange how even a male as insensitive as Henry had recognised that Raul behaved as if he owned her. Only it wasn't her, it was the baby he believed he owned.

Dear heaven, what a mess she was in, Polly conceded worriedly. There was no going back, no way of changing anything. Her baby was also Raul's baby and always would be.

'It was kind of you to call in, Henry,' she murmured quietly. 'Tell your mother that I really appreciate all her kindness, but that I won't be coming back to stay with you—'

'What on earth are you talking about?' Henry had gone all red in the face.

'I just don't want to marry you…I'm sorry.'

'I'll visit later in the week, when you're feeling more yourself.'

As Henry departed, Polly reflected that she was actually feeling more herself than she had in many weeks. Stepping off the treadmill of exhaustion had given her space to think.

As she slowly, awkwardly raised herself, Raul appeared through a door on the far side of the courtyard. He angled a slashing, searching glance over the little clusters of patients taking the fresh air nearby. Screened by the shrubbery, Polly made no attempt to attract his attention.

His suit was palest grey. He exuded designer chic. In the sunlight, his luxuriant hair gleamed blue-black. His lean, strong face possessed such breathtaking sexy symmetry that her breathing quickened and her sluggish pulses raced. Raul radiated raw sexuality in virile waves. The media said that men thought about sex at least once a minute. One look at Raul was enough to convince her.

But a feeling of stark inadequacy and rejection now threatened her in Raul's radius. How the heck had she ever believed that a male that gorgeous was interested in her? How wilfully blind she had been in Vermont! If a woman excited Raul, he probably pounced on the first date, or maybe he got pounced on, but he had never made a pass at *her*, or even tried to kiss her. At first he had made her as nervous as a cat on hot bricks. But before very long his exquisite manners and flattering interest in her had soothed her inexperienced squirmings in his presence and given her entirely the wrong impression.

Incredibly, she had believed that one of the world's most notorious womanisers was actually a cautious and decent guy, mature enough to want to get to know a woman as a friend before trying to take the relationship any further. Remembering that fact now made Polly feel positively queasy. She had thought Raul was perfect; she had thought he was wonderful; she had thought he was really attracted to her because he continued to seek out her company...

Far from impervious to Raul's cool exasperation when he finally espied her, lurking behind the shrubbery, Polly dropped her head, her shining fall of mahogany hair concealing her taut profile.

'What are you doing out of bed?' Raul demanded the instant he got within hailing distance. 'I'll take you back up to your room.'

'I'm allowed out for fresh air as long as I don't overdo it,' Polly said thinly.

'We'll go inside,' Raul decreed. 'We can't discuss confidential business here.'

Polly swung her legs off the lounger and got up. 'Business? I've learnt the hard way that my baby is not a piece of merchandise.'

'Do you really think I feel any different?' Raul breathed with a raw, bitter edge to his rich, dark drawl.

'Do you really think you're the only one of us to have learnt from this mess?'

She couldn't avoid looking at him in the lift. He stood opposite her, supremely indifferent to the two nurses in the corner studying him with keen female appreciation. He stared at Polly without apology, intense dark eyes welded broodingly to her heart-shaped face and the heated colour steadily building in her cheeks.

She had one question she desperately wanted to ask him. Why did a drop-dead gorgeous heterosexual male of only thirty-one feel the need to hire a surrogate mother to have his child? Why hadn't he just got married? Or, alternatively, why hadn't he simply persuaded one of his innumerable blonde bimbo babes into motherhood? Why surrogacy?

The minute Polly settled herself down on the sofa in her room, Raul breathed with a twist of his expressive mouth, 'You're still angry with me about Vermont. We should deal with that and get it out of the way…it's clouding the real issues at stake here.'

At that statement of intent, Polly stiffened, and her skin prickled with shrinking apprehension. 'Naturally I'm still angry, but I see no point in talking about it. That's in the past now.'

Raul strolled over to the window. He dug a lean brown hand into the pocket of his well-cut trousers, tightening the fit of the fine fabric over his narrow hips and long, muscular thighs. Polly found herself abstractedly studying a part of the male anatomy she had never in her life before studied, the distinctively manly bulge of his manhood. Flushing to the roots of her hair, she hurriedly looked away.

But it was so peculiar, she thought bitterly. So peculiar to be pregnant by a man she had never slept with, never been intimate with in any way. And Raul Zaforteza was *all* male, like a walking advertisement for high testosterone levels and virility. Why on earth had he chosen to have his child conceived by an anonymous insemination in a doctor's surgery?

'If I'm really honest, I wanted to meet you and talk to you right from the moment you signed the contract,' Raul drawled tautly, interrupting her seething thoughts.

'Why, for heaven's sake?'

'I knew my child would want to know what you were really like.'

A cold chill of repulsion trickled down Polly's spine. So impersonal, so practical, so utterly unfeeling a motivation.

'After your mother died, I was aware that you were in considerable distress,' Raul continued levelly. 'You needed support…who *else* was there to provide that support? If you hadn't discovered that I was the baby's father, you wouldn't have been so upset. And isn't it time you told me how you *did* penetrate that secret?'

In her mind's eye, Polly pictured Soledad and all the numerous members of her equally dependent family being flung off the ancestral ranch the older woman had described in Venezuela. She gulped. 'You gave yourself away. Your behaviour…well, it made me suspicious. I worked the truth out for myself,' she lied stiltedly.

'You're a liar…Soledad told you,' Raul traded without skipping a beat, shrewd dark eyes grimly amused by her startled reaction. 'A major oversight on my part. Two women stuck all those weeks in the same house? The barriers came down and you became friendly—'

'Soledad would never have betrayed you if you hadn't come into my life without admitting who you were!' Polly interrupted defensively. 'She couldn't cope with being forced to pretend that she didn't know you.'

'I was at fault there,' Raul acknowledged openly, honestly, taking her by surprise. 'I'm aware of that now. Vermont *was* a mistake…it personalised what should have remained impersonal and compromised my sense of honour.'

A mistake? A gracious admission of fault, an apology underwritten. Gulping back a spurt of angry revealing words, Polly swallowed hard. He was so smooth, so reasonable and controlled. She wanted to scratch her nails down the starkly handsome planes of those high cheekbones to make him feel for even one *second* something of what she had suffered!

'So, now that you know how I found out, are Soledad and her family still working for you?' Polly enquired stiffly.

Raul dealt her a wry smile. 'Her family is, but Soledad has moved to Caracas to look after her grandchildren while her daughter's at work.'

A light knock at the door announced the entry of a maid, bearing Polly's afternoon tea. Raul asked for black coffee, it not occurring to him for one moment that as a visitor he might not be entitled to refreshment. Blushing furiously, the maid literally rushed to satisfy his request.

Cradling the coffee elegantly in one lean hand, Raul sank down lithely into the armchair opposite her. 'Are you comfortable here?'

'Very.'

'But obviously it's a challenge to fill the empty hours. I'll get a video recorder sent in, some tapes, books…I know what you like,' Raul asserted with complete confidence. 'I should've thought of it before.'

'I'm not happy with what this place must be costing you,' Polly told him in a sudden rush. 'Especially as I am not going to honour that contract.'

Raul scanned her anxious blue eyes. A slight smile momentarily curved his wide, sensual mouth. 'You need some time and space to consider that decision. Right now, I have no intention of putting pressure on you—'

'Just having you in the same room is pressure,' Polly countered uncomfortably. 'Having you pay my bills makes it even worse.'

'Whatever happens, I'm still the father of your baby. That makes you my responsibility.'

'The softly, softly, catchee monkey routine won't work with me... I'm so fed up with people telling me that I don't know what I want, or that I don't know what I'm doing.' Polly raised her small head high and valiantly clashed with brilliant black eyes as sharp as paint. 'The truth is that I've grown up a lot in the last few months...'

Raul held up a fluid and silencing hand in a gesture that came so naturally to him that she instinctively closed her lips. 'In swift succession over the past year or so you have lost the three people you cared about most in this world. Your father, your mother and your godmother. That is bound to be affecting your judgement *and* your view of the future. All I want to do is give you another possible view.'

Setting aside his empty coffee cup, he rose gracefully upright again. Polly watched him nervously, the tip of her tongue stealing out to moisten the dry curve of her lower lip.

Raul's attention dropped to the soft, generous pink curve of her mouth and lingered, and she felt the oddest buzzing current in the air, her slight frame automatically tensing in reaction. Raul stiffened, the dark rise of blood emphasising the slashing line of his hard cheekbones. Swinging on his heel, he strode over to the window and pushed it wider.

'It's stuffy in here… As I was saying, an alternative view of the future,' he continued flatly. 'You can't possibly *want* to marry that little jerk Henry Grey—'

Taken aback, Polly sat up straighter. 'How do you know?'

His chiselled profile clenched into aggressive lines. 'He's just being greedy…he wouldn't look twice at a woman expecting another man's child *unless* she was an heiress!'

Polly flinched at that revealing assertion. 'So you found out about my godmother's will…'

'Naturally…' Raul skimmed an assured glance in her direction. 'And the good news is that you don't have to marry Henry to inherit that money and make a new start. You're only twenty-one; you have your whole life in front of you. Why clog it up with Henry? He's a pompous bore. I'm prepared to *give* you that million pounds to dump him!'

In sheer shock, Polly's lips fell open. She began to rise off the sofa. 'I b-beg your pardon?' she stammered shakily, convinced he couldn't possibly have said what she thought he had said.

Raul swung fluidly round to face her again. 'You heard me. Forget that stupid will, and for the present forget the baby too…just ditch that loser!'

Her blue eyes opened very wide. She gaped at him, and then she took a step forward, fierce anger leaping up inside her. 'How dare you try to bribe me into doing what *you* want me to do? How *dare* you do that?'

Raul's cool façade cracked to reveal the cold anger

beneath. He sent her a sizzling look of derision. '*Caramba!* Surely you'd prefer to stay rich and single when Henry's the only option on offer?'

Without an instant of hesitation, Polly snatched up the water jug by the bed with a feverish hand and slung the contents at him. '*That's* what I think of your filthy offer! I'm not for sale this time and I never will be again!'

Soaked by that sizeable flood, and astonished by both her attack and that outburst, Raul stood there dripping and downright incredulous. As his lean fingers raked his wet hair off his brow, his dark eyes flamed to a savage golden blaze.

'I'm not sorry,' Polly admitted starkly.

Raul slung her a searing look of scantily leashed fury. '*Por Dios*...I am leaving before I say or do something I might regret!' he bit out rawly.

The door snapped shut in his imperious wake. Polly snatched in a slow steadying breath and realised that even her hands were shaking. She had never met with a temper that hot before.

CHAPTER THREE

A VIDEO recorder arrived, complete with a whole collection of tapes, and was installed in Polly's room by lunchtime the following day.

As a gesture, it was calculated to make her feel guilty. That evening, Polly sat in floods of tears just picking through titles like *The Quiet Man* and *Pretty Woman* and *Sabrina*. All escapist romantic movies, picked by a male who knew her tastes far too well for comfort. She grabbed up another tissue in despair.

Raul Zaforteza unleashed a temper she hadn't known she had. He filled her to overflowing with violent, resentful and distressingly confused emotions. She hated him, she told herself fiercely. He was tearing her apart. She hated him even more when she felt herself react to the humiliating pull of his magnetic sexual attraction.

Worse, Raul understood her so much better than she understood him. In Vermont, she had trustingly revealed too many private thoughts and feelings, while he had been coolly evaluating her, like a scientist studying something curious under a microscope. Why? He had answered that straight off the top of his head and without hesitation.

So that he could answer her child's questions about her in the future.

Polly shivered at the memory of that admission, chilled to the marrow and hurt beyond belief. It wasn't possible to get more detached than that from another human being. But how many times had Raul already

emphasised that there was nothing but that hateful surrogate contract between them? And why was she still
torturing herself with that reality?

He had coolly, contemptuously offered her a million
pounds to dump Henry and stay single. And why had
he done that? Simply because he felt threatened by the
idea of her marrying. Why hadn't she grasped that fact
sooner? If she married, Raul would be forced, whether
he liked it or not, to stand back while another man
raised his child. So why hadn't she told him she wasn't
planning to marry Henry?

Polly was honest with herself on that point. She
hadn't seen *why* she should tell him the truth. What
business was it of his? And she had been prepared to
hide behind a pretend engagement to Henry, a face-
saving pretence that suggested her life had moved on
since Vermont. Only Raul had destroyed that pretence.
Acquainted as he was with the intricacies of her godmother's will, he had realised that that inheritance was
the only reason Henry was willing to marry her. It mortified Polly that Raul should have guessed even that. In
his presence, she was beginning to feel as if she was
being speedily stripped of every defence.

But then what did she know about men? It was laughable to be so close to the birth of her own child and
still be so ignorant. But her father had been a strict,
puritanical man, whose rules and restrictions had made
it impossible for her to enjoy a normal social life. It had
even been difficult to hang onto female friends with a
father who invariably offended them by criticising their
clothing or their behaviour.

She had had a crush on a boy in her teens, but he
had quickly lost interest when her father refused to allow her to go out with him. When she had started the

university degree course that she'd never got to finish, she had lived so close to the campus she had had to continue living at home. She had kept house for her father, assisted in his many church activities and, when his stationery business began to fail, helped with his office work.

She had sneaked out to the occasional party. Riven with guilt at having lied to get out, she had endured a few over-enthusiastic clinches, wondering what all the fuss was about while she pushed away groping, over-familiar hands, unable to comprehend why any sane female would want to respond to such crude demands.

She had met another boy while studying. Like his predecessors, he had been unwilling to come to the house and meet her father just to get permission to take her out at night. At first he had thought it was a bit of laugh to see her only during the day. Then one lunch-time he had taken her back to his flat and tried to get her to go to bed with him. She had said no. He had ditched her there and then, called her 'a pathetic, boring little virgin' and soon replaced her with a more available girl who didn't expect love and commitment in return for sex.

It had taken Raul Zaforteza to teach Polly what she had never felt before...a deep, dark craving for physical contact as tormenting to endure as a desperate thirst...

Polly was restless that evening. Aware that she wasn't asleep, one of the nurses brought her in a cup of tea at ten, and thoughtfully lent her a magazine to read.

As always, during the night, her door was kept ajar to allow the staff to check easily and quietly on her. So when, out of the corner of her eye, Polly saw the door open wider, she turned with a smile for the nurse she was expecting to see and then froze in surprise when she saw Raul instead. Visiting time finished at nine, and it was now after eleven.

'How did you get in?' Polly asked in a startled whisper.

Raul leant lithely back against the door until it snapped softly shut. In a black dinner jacket and narrow black trousers, a bow tie at his throat, he exuded sophisticated cool. 'Talked my way past the security guard and chatted up the night sister.'

Strolling forward, he set a tub of ice cream in front of her. 'Peppermint—your favourite...my peace offering,' he murmured with a lazy smile.

That charismatic smile hit Polly like a shot of adrenalin in her veins. Every trace of drowsiness evaporated. Her heart jumped, her mouth ran dry and burning colour started to creep up her throat. He lifted the teaspoon from the cup and saucer on the bed-table she had pushed away and settled it down helpfully on top of the tub.

'Eat it before it melts,' he advised, settling down on the end of the bed in an indolent sprawl.

It shook her that Raul should recall that peppermint was her favorite flavour. It shook her even more that he should take the trouble to call in with ice cream at this hour of the night when he had obviously been out somewhere.

With a not quite steady hand, Polly removed the lid on the tub. 'Henry lied,' she confided abruptly. 'We're not engaged. I'm not going to marry him.'

In the intimate pool of light shed by the Anglepoise lamp by the bed, a wolfish grin slashed Raul's darkly handsome features. Polly was so mesmerised by it, she dug her teaspoon into empty air instead of the tub and only discovered the ice cream by touch.

'You could do a lot better than him, *cielita*,' he responded softly.

Polly's natural sense of fairness prompted her to add, 'Henry isn't that bad. He was honest. It wasn't like he pretended to fancy me or anything like that…'

Slumberous dark eyes semi-screened by lush ebony lashes, Raul emitted a low-pitched laugh that sent an odd little tremor down her sensitive spine. 'Henry has no taste.'

The silence that fell seemed to hum in her eardrums.

Feeling that languorous heaviness in her breasts, the surge of physical awareness she dreaded, Polly shifted uneasily and leapt straight back into speech. 'Why did you decide to hire a surrogate?' she asked baldly. 'It doesn't make sense to me.'

His strong face tensed. 'I wanted to have a child while I was still young enough to play with a child…'

'And the right woman just didn't come along?' Polly assumed as the silence stretched.

'Perhaps I should say that I like women but I like my freedom better. Let's leave it at that,' Raul suggested smoothly.

'I'm so sorry I signed that contract.' Troubled eyes blue as violets rested on him, her heart-shaped face strained. 'I don't know how I thought I could actually go through with it…but at the time I suppose I couldn't think of anything but how sick my mother was.'

'I should never have picked you. The psychologist said that he wasn't convinced you understood how hard it would be to surrender your child—'

'Did he?'

'He said you were too intense, too idealistic.'

Polly frowned. 'So why was I chosen?'

Raul lifted a broad shoulder in a slight fatalistic shrug that was very Latin. 'I *liked* you. I didn't want to have a baby with a woman I couldn't even like.'

'I was a really bad choice,' Polly muttered ruefully. 'Now I wish you'd listened to the psychologist.'

Raul vented a rather grim laugh. 'I never listen to what I don't want to hear. People who work for me know that, and they like to please me. That's why you were fed lies to persuade you into signing the contract. A very junior lawyer got smart and set you up. He didn't tell his boss what he'd done until *after* you'd signed. He expected an accolade for his ingenuity but instead he got fired.'

'Did he?' Polly showed her surprise.

'*Sí…*' Raul's mouth tightened. 'But my lawyer saw no reason to tell me what had happened. He had no idea that either of us would ever be in a position to find out.'

Polly ate the ice cream, lashes lowering as she savoured each cool, delicious spoonful. The seconds ticked by. Raul watched her. She was aware of his intent scrutiny, curiously satisfied by the attention, but extremely nervous of it too, as if she was a mouse with a hawk circling overhead. It was so quiet, so very quiet at that hour of the night, no distant buzzing bells, no quick-moving feet in the corridor outside.

And then Polly stiffened, a muffled little sound of discomfort escaping her as the baby chose that moment to give her an athletic kick.

Raul leant forward. '*Que*…what is it?' he demanded anxiously.

'The baby. It's always liveliest at night.' She met the question in his eyes and flushed, reaching a sudden decision. Setting down the ice cream, she pushed the bedding back the few necessary inches, knowing that she was perfectly decently covered in her cotton nightie but still feeling horrendously shy.

Raul drew closer and rested his palm very lightly on her stomach. As he felt the movement beneath his fingers, a look of wonder filled his dark, shimmering gaze and he smiled with sudden quick brilliance. 'That's amazing,' he breathed. 'Do you know if it's a boy or a girl yet?'

'Mr Bevan offered to tell me but I didn't want to know,' Polly admitted unevenly, deeply unsettled by that instant of intimate sharing but undeniably touched by his fascination. 'I like surprises better.'

Raul slowly removed his palm and tugged the sheet back into place. His hands weren't quite steady. Noting that, she wondered why. She could still feel the cool touch of his hand like a burning imprint on her own flesh. He was so close she could hardly breathe, her own awareness of him so pronounced it was impossible to fight. At best, she knew she could only hope to conceal her reaction, but though she was desperate to think of something to say to distract him her mind was suddenly a blank.

'You can be incredibly sweet...' Raul remarked, half under his breath.

Her intent gaze roamed over him, lingering helplessly on the glossy luxuriance of his black hair, the hard, clean line of his high cheekbones and the dark roughening of his jawline that suggested a need to shave twice a day. Reaching the wide, passionate curve of his mouth, she wondered as she had wondered so often before what he tasted like. Then, wildly flustered by that disturbing thought, her eyes lifted, full of confusion, and the dark golden lure of his gaze entrapped and held her in thrall.

'And incredibly tempting,' Raul confided huskily as he brought his sensual mouth very slowly down on hers.

She could have pulled back with ease; he gave her every opportunity. But at the first touch of his lips on hers she dissolved into a hot, melting pool of acquiescence. With a muffled groan, he closed his hand into the tumbling fall of her hair to steady himself and let his tongue stab deep into the tender interior of her mouth. And the whole tenor of the kiss changed.

Excitement so intense it burned flamed instantly through her, bringing her alive with a sudden shocking vitality that made her screamingly aware of every inch of her own humming body. And as soon as it began she ached for more, lacing desperate fingers into the silky thickness of his hair, palms sliding down then to curve over to his cheekbones. Only at some dim, distant, uncaring level was she conscious of the buzzing, irritating sound somewhere close by.

Raul released her with a stifled expletive in Spanish and sprang off the bed. With dazed eyes, Polly watched him pull out a mobile phone. And in the deep silence she heard the high-pitched vibration of a woman's voice before he put the phone to his ear.

'*Dios*…I'll be down in a moment,' Raul murmured curtly, and, switching the phone off, he dug it back into his pocket.

'I'm sorry but I have to go. I have someone waiting in the car.' He raked restive fingers through his now thoroughly tousled black hair, glittering golden eyes screened from her searching scrutiny, mouth compressed into a ferocious line. 'I'll see you soon. *Buenas noches.*'

The instant he left the room, Polly thrust back the bedding and scrambled awkwardly out of bed. She flew over to the window which overlooked the front entrance and pulled back the curtain. She saw the limo…and she saw the beautiful blonde in her sleek, short crimson dress pacing beside it. Then she watched the blonde arrange herself in a studied pose against the side of the luxury car so that she looked like a glamorous model at an automobile show.

Polly rushed back across the room to douse the lamp and then returned to the window. Raul emerged from the clinic. The blonde threw herself exuberantly into his arms. Polly's nerveless fingers dropped from the curtain. She reeled back against the cold wall and closed her arms round her trembling body, feeling sick and dizzy and utterly disgusted with herself.

Oh, dear heaven, why hadn't she slapped his face for him? Why, oh, why had she allowed him to kiss her? Feeling horribly humiliated and raw, she got back into bed with none of the adrenalin-charged speed with which she had vacated it. Tonight Raul had been out with his latest blonde. Now they were either moving on to some nightclub or heading for a far more intimate setting. She could barely credit that Raul had called in to see her in the middle of a date with another woman, as relaxed and unhurried as if he'd had all the time in the world to spend with her.

Polly felt murderous. She could still see the ice cream tub glimmering in the darkness. Gosh, weren't you a push-over? a sarcastic little inner voice gibed. Easily impressed, pitifully vulnerable. Her defences hadn't stood a chance with Raul in a more approachable mood. And he hadn't even kissed her because he was attracted to her—oh, no. Nothing so simple and nothing less flattering than the true explanation she suspected.

He had felt the baby move. That had been a disturbingly intimate and emotional experience for them both. For the first time they had crossed the barriers of that contract and actually *shared* something that related to the baby. And Raul was a very physical male who had, in the heat of the moment, reacted in an inappropriately physical way. The constraint of his abrupt departure had revealed his unease with that development. She was convinced he wouldn't ever let anything like that happen between them again.

Yet for so long Polly had ached for Raul to kiss her, and that passionate kiss had outmatched her every naive expectation. Without ever touching her, Raul had taught her to crave him like a dangerous drug. Now she despised herself and felt all the shame of her own wantonly eager response. She did hate him now, she told herself vehemently. Technically she might still be a virgin, but she wasn't such an idiot that she didn't know that sexual feelings could both tempt and confuse. Her response had had nothing to do with love or intelligence.

She had stopped loving Raul the same day that she'd discovered how he had been deceiving her in Vermont. But the complexity of their current relationship was plunging her into increasing turmoil. For what relationship *did* they have? She wasn't his lover but she was expecting his baby, and she couldn't even claim that they were friends, could she...?

A magnificent floral arrangement arrived from Raul the next day. Polly asked the maid to pass it on to one of the other patients. She didn't want to be reminded of Raul every time she looked across the room.

He phoned in the afternoon. 'How are you?'

'Turning somersaults,' Polly said brittly. 'Leafing through my frantically crammed social diary to see what I'll be doing today. Do I really need to stay here much longer?'

'Rod thinks so,' Raul reminded her. 'Look, I'll be away on business for the next week. I wanted to leave a contact number with you so that you can get in touch if you need to.'

'I can't imagine there being any need when I'm surrounded by medical staff and being waited on hand and foot.'

'OK. I'll phone *you*—'

Polly breathed in deep. 'Would you mind if I asked you not to?'

'I don't like having this type of conversation on the phone. It's a very female method of warfare,' Raul drawled grimly.

'I was just asking for a little space,' Polly countered tightly. 'In the circumstances, I don't think that's unreasonable. You may be the father of my child, but we don't have a personal relationship.'

'I'll see you when I get back from Paris, Polly.'

The line went dead. But Polly continued to grip the receiver frantically tight. She didn't want to see him; she didn't want to hear from him. Her eyes smarted. But the tears were nothing to do with him. Late on in pregnancy women were often more emotional and tearful, she reminded herself staunchly.

Mid-morning, late in the following week, Polly had just put on a loose red jersey dress with a V-neckline and short sleeves when Raul arrived to visit her. Hearing the knock on the door of her room, she emerged from the bathroom, still struggling to brush her long hair. She fell still in an awkward pose when she realised who it was.

Her heart skipped a complete beat. Raul was wearing a navy pinstriped business suit so sharply tailored it fitted his magnificent physique like a glove. Worn with a dark blue shirt and red silk tie, it made him look sensationally attractive and dynamic. Her throat closed over. It felt like a hundred years since she had last seen him. She wanted to move closer, had to forcefully still her feet where she stood.

Raul strolled forward and casually reached up to pluck the brush from her loosened hold. Gently turning her round by her shoulders, he teased loose the tangle she had been fighting with before returning the brush to her hand. 'I owe you an apology for my behaviour on my last visit,' he murmured with conviction.

Polly tensed. There was a mirror on the back of the bathroom door. She could see his reflection, the cool gravity of his expression, the dark brilliance of his assessing gaze.

Colour stained Polly's cheeks but she managed to laugh. 'For goodness' sake,' she said with determined lightness, 'there's no need for an apology. It was just a kiss...no big deal!'

Something bright flared in his dark eyes and then they were veiled, his sensual mouth curling slightly. '*Bueno.* I wondered if you would like to have lunch out today?'

In surprise, Polly swivelled round, all constraint put to flight by that unexpected but very welcome suggestion that she might return to the outside world for a few hours. 'I'd love to!'

In the foyer they ran into Janice Grey.

'Oh, dear, were you coming to visit me?' Polly muttered with a dismay made all the more pungent by a guilty sense of relief. 'I'm so sorry. I'm afraid we're going out for lunch.'

'That does surprise me.' Janice raised an enquiring brow. 'I understood you were here to rest.'

'I'm under the strictest instructions to see that she doesn't overtire herself, Mrs Grey,' Raul interposed with a coolly pleasant smile. 'I'm also grateful to have the opportunity to thank you for all the support you have given Polly in recent weeks.'

The middle-aged blonde gave him a thin smile and turned to Polly. 'Henry said that you weren't coming back to stay with us.' She then shot Raul an arch look that didn't conceal her hostility. 'Do I hear wedding bells in the air?'

Polly paled, and then hot, mortified colour flooded her cheeks. The silence simmered.

Raul stepped calmly into the breach. 'I'm sure Polly will keep you in touch with events, Mrs Grey.

'A tough cookie,' Raul remarked of the older woman as he settled Polly into the limousine a few minutes later. 'I'm relieved that you didn't choose to confide in her about our legal agreement. But why the hell did you look so uncomfortable?'

Polly thought of those crazy weeks in Vermont, when she had foolishly allowed herself to be wildly, recklessly in love with Raul. Her imagination had known no limits when every moment she could she'd tried to forget the fact that she was pregnant. Those stupid girlish daydreams about marrying Raul were now a severe embarrassment to recall. She had to think fast to come up with another explanation for her discomfiture.

'Janice *was* kind to me...but she'd never have offered me a room if she hadn't known about my inheritance. She couldn't understand why I wasn't prepared to marry Henry for the sake of that money. She thought I was being very foolish and shortsighted.'

'You don't need to make a choice like that now. In any case, *gatita*...you're far too young to be thinking about marriage.'

An awkward little silence fell. Polly was very tense. She was already scolding herself for having reacted to Raul's invitation as if his only aim was to give her a pleasant outing. Raul did nothing without good reason. Over lunch, Raul was undoubtedly planning to open a serious discussion about their baby's future. The subject could not be avoided any longer, and this time she would try to be as calm and rational as possible.

'Waiting to hear what you're going to say makes me very nervous,' she nonetheless heard herself confide abruptly. 'I may be pregnant, but I'm not likely to pop off at the first piece of bad news. Do you think you could just tell me right now up front whether or not you're planning to take me to court after the baby's born?'

Raul sent her a shimmering glance, his mouth curling. 'Much good it would do me if I did have such plans. Although it seems very wrong to me, in this country I have no legal rights as the father of your child.'

'*Honestly?*' Polly surveyed him through very wide and surprised blue eyes. 'But what about the contract?'

'Forget the contract. It might as well not exist now. Do you seriously think that I would even want to take such a personal and private matter into a courtroom?'

'I never thought of that,' Polly admitted, suddenly

feeling quite weak with the strength of her relief. 'I just had nightmares about being extradited to the USA.'

An involuntary smile briefly curved Raul's lips. 'Force wouldn't work in a situation like this.'

Did he think that persuasion would? Polly worried about that idea. She knew that her own convictions ran so deep and strong he had no hope of changing her mind; she was determined to keep her baby. But she was burdened by the increasingly guilty awareness that that wasn't very fair to Raul, and that some way, somehow, they had to find a compromise that would be bearable for them both.

Yet where could they possibly find that compromise? Raul had chosen surrogacy because he wanted a child, but not a child he had to share in a conventional relationship. Raul had opted for a detached, businesslike arrangement without strings. But no matter what happened now he had no hope of acquiring sole custody of his own child. How could she not feel guilty about that?

Raul took her back to a luxury apartment in Mayfair. Polly felt intimidated by the grandeur of her surroundings. A light and exquisitely cooked lunch was served by a quiet and unobtrusive manservant. Throughout the meal, Raul chatted about his business trip to Paris. He was very entertaining, a sophisticated and amusing raconteur. But, while she laughed and smiled in response, all she could really think about was how easily he had fooled her with that charismatic polish in Vermont.

It meant nothing. It just meant he had terrific social skills. She had learned to read Raul well enough to recognise that essential detachment just beneath the surface, not to mention his smooth ability to avoid giving personal information. All those visits in Vermont and what had she picked up about him? That he had no close family alive, that he was a businessman who travelled a lot, and that he had been born in Venezuela. Precious little.

Raul ran hooded dark eyes over her abstracted face. 'I feel like you're not with me.'

'Perhaps I'm tired,' she said uncomfortably.

Instantly Raul thrust back his chair and rose lithely upright. 'Then you should lie down in one of the guest rooms for a while.'

'No…we need to talk,' Polly acknowledged tautly. 'I want to get that over with.'

Leaving the table, she settled down into a comfortable armchair. The coffee was served. Raul paced restively over to the window and then gazed across the room at her. 'Don't look so anxious…it makes me feel like a bully,' he admitted grimly.

Polly clutched her cup. 'You're not that,' she acknowledged fairly. 'You've been very patient and more understanding than I could ever have expected.'

Raul spread lean brown hands with an eloquence that never failed to engage her attention. 'I have a possible solution to this situation. Please hear me out,' he urged.

Tense as a bowstring, Polly sat very still.

'The biggest difference between us is that I planned to be a parent from the very outset of our association,' Raul delineated with measured clarity. 'But *you* did not. When you became pregnant you did not expect to take on permanent responsibility for that child.'

Polly nodded in wary, reluctant agreement.

'I think you're too young to handle becoming a single parent. I understand that you have become attached to the baby, and that you are naturally very concerned about its future well-being. But if you choose to keep the baby you will have to sacrifice the freedom that most young women of your age take for granted.'

Polly gave him a stubborn look. 'I know that. I'm not stupid. And I'm hardly likely to miss what I've never had—'

'But you *could* have that freedom now. You should be making plans to return to university to complete your degree,' Raul told her steadily. 'If you let me take my child back to Venezuela, I will allow you access visits, regular reports, photographs. I will agree to any reasonable request. My child will know you as his mother but you will not be the primary carer.'

Raul had taken her very much by surprise. Polly hadn't expected such a willingness to compromise from a male to whom she sensed 'compromise' was an unfamiliar word. On his terms, she guessed it was a very generous offer. He was offering to share their child to some extent, and that was a lot more than she had anticipated.

'I believe every child deserves two parents,' she responded awkwardly. 'Two parents on the spot.'

'That's impossible.'

'I was brought up by my father, and there wasn't a day I didn't long for my mother.'

'This child may be a boy.'

'I don't think that makes any difference. Because of my own experiences, I couldn't face being parted from my child. Whatever it takes, I need to *be* there for my baby and do the very best I can to be a good mother.' Polly was very tense as she struggled to verbalise her own deepest feelings. 'And, yes, it is a very great pity that I didn't work that out before I signed that contract...but my only excuse is that I honestly didn't even begin to understand how I would feel once I was actually pregnant.'

'That's in the past now. We need to concentrate on the present.' With that rather deflating assurance, Raul flung back his darkly handsome head, his dark eyes formidable in their penetration. 'If you really mean what you say when you protest that you intend to be the very best mother you can be...then you must move to Venezuela.'

'Venezuela?' Polly exclaimed, wildly disconcerted at having that stunning suggestion flung at her in cool challenge.

'I will set you up in a house there. You will have every comfort and convenience, and your child as well.'

Polly blinked, still attempting to absorb a staggering proposition that entailed moving to the other side of the world. 'I *couldn't*—'

'Por Dios...ask yourself if you are being fair. If the child needs his mother, then he also needs his father. And that child will inherit everything I possess.' Raul spelt out that reminder with imperious pride and impatience.

'Money isn't everything, Raul—'

'Don't be facile. I'm talking about a way of life that you have not the slightest conception of,' Raul returned very drily, watching her flush. 'At least be practical, Polly. My child needs to know that Venezuelan heritage, the language, the people, the culture. If you won't come to Venezuela, what am I to do? With the claims on my time, I can't possibly visit the UK often enough to form a close relationship with my child.'

Polly tried to picture living in Venezuela, with Raul picking up all her bills, walking in and out of her life with one blonde babe girlfriend after another and eventually taking a wife. No matter how he might feel now, she was convinced that he would succumb to matrimony sooner or later. In such a situation she would always be an outsider, an interloper, neither family nor friend, and a lot of people would simply assume that she was his discarded mistress. She knew she would never be able to cope with such a dependent, humiliating existence on the fringe of Raul's world. She needed to get on with her own life. It was time to be honest about that reality.

'Raul...I want to stay in the UK with my baby. I don't want to live in Venezuela, having you oversee every move I make,' Polly admitted, watching him bridle in apparent disbelief at that statement. 'You have the right to be involved in your child's future...but what you seem to forget is that that future is *my* life as well! Anyway, you may not think it now, but some day you'll get married, have other children—'

Raul released his breath in a charged hiss of frustration. 'I would sooner be dead than married!'

'But you see...I *don't* feel the same way,' Polly shared with rueful honesty. 'I would like to think that even as an unmarried mum I will get married eventually.'

'Saying that to me is the equivalent of blackmail, Polly,' Raul condemned, pale with anger beneath his golden skin, eyes hot as sunlight in that lean, dark, devastating face. 'I do not want *any* other man involved in my child's upbringing!'

Temper stirred in Polly, and the more she thought about that blunt and unashamed declaration the angrier she became. Did Raul really believe that he had the right to demand that she live like a nun for the next twenty years? Lonely, unloved, celibate. She stared at him. Yes, that was what he believed and what he wanted, if he was not to have sole custody of their child.

Raising herself out of the armchair, Polly straightened her slight shoulders and stood up. 'You are so *incredibly* selfish and spoilt!' she accused fiercely.

Astonished by that sudden indictment, Raul strode across the room, closing the distance between them. 'I can't believe that you can dare to say that to me—'

'I expect not…as you've already told me, you're accustomed to people who want to please you, who are eager to tell you only what you want to hear!' Polly shot back with unconcealed scorn. 'Well, I'm *not* one of those people!'

His eyes blazed. 'I have bent over backwards to be fair—'

'At what *personal* sacrifice and inconvenience?' Polly slung back, trembling with rage. 'You are a playboy with a reputation as a womaniser. You enjoy your freedom, don't you?'

'Why shouldn't I?' Raul was unmoved by that angle of attack. 'I don't lie to the women who pass through my life. I don't promise true love or permanency—'

'Because you've never *had* to, have you? You know, listening to you, Raul…I despise my own sex. But I despise you most of all,' Polly confessed, with hands knotting into furious fists by her side. 'It's one rule for you and another for me—a hypocritical sexist double standard the belongs in the Prehistoric ages with Neanderthals like you! You say you want this child, but you didn't want a child badly enough to make a commitment like other men, did you? And what do you offer me—?'

'The only two possible remedies to the mess we're now in. I'm not about to apologise because you do not like the imperfect sound of reality,' Raul delivered with slashing bite.

'Reality? You call it "reality' to offer me a choice between giving up my child almost completely...and living like a *nun* in Venezuela?'

Raul flicked her a grimly amused glance. 'You want the licence to sleep around?'

'You know very well that's not what I'm trying to say!'

'But you wouldn't want me to share your bed without all that idealistic love, commitment and permanency jazz...would you, *querida*?' Raul breathed with sizzling golden eyes, watching her freeze in shock at that plunge into the more intimate and personal. 'You see, what you want and what I want we can't have, because we both want something different!'

Every scrap of colour drained from Polly's face. 'I *don't* want you...like that,' she framed jerkily.

Raul cast her a glittering appraisal that was all male and all-knowing. 'Oh, yes, you do...that sexual hunger has been there between us from the moment we met.'

Polly backed away from him. She could not cope with having his knowledge of her attraction to him thrown in her teeth. 'No—'

'I didn't take advantage of you because I knew it would end in your tears.'

'Don't kid yourself...I might've ditched you first!' Polly told him with very real loathing, her pride so wounded she wanted to kill him. 'And let me tell you something else too, I put a much higher price on myself than your interchangeable blonde babes do.'

'I admire that...I really do,' Raul incised with complete cool, his temper back under wraps again at disorientating, galling speed. 'You have such rigid moral values, *gatita*. Well, warned in advance, I was careful to keep my distance in Vermont.'

Polly shuddered with a rage that was out of control, a rage that had its roots in pain and violent resentment. She was shattered by the sudden ripping down of the careful barriers that had made it possible for them to skim along the surface of their complex relationship. Without those barriers, and shorn by Raul of all face-saving defences, she was flailing wildly.

A look of positive loathing written in her furious eyes, she snapped, 'Then you'll have no problem understanding that the only way you'll ever get me to Venezuela…the only way you'll *ever* achieve full custody of your child…is to marry me, Raul!'

A silence fell between them like a giant black hole, waiting to entrap the unwary.

Raul was now formidably still, brilliant dark eyes icy with incredulity. 'That's not funny, Polly. Take it back.'

'Why? Do you want me to lie to you? Say I didn't mean it?' Polly demanded rawly as she tipped her head back, mahogany hair rippling back from her furiously flushed face. 'I'm being honest with you. If I stay here in the UK, I will get on with my life and you will *not* interfere with that life! I am not prepared to go to Venezuela as anything *other* than a wife!'

Raul sent her a derisive look that said he was unimpressed. 'You are not serious.'

Polly studied him with so much bitterness inside her she marvelled she didn't explode like a destructive weapon. 'I am. Let's see how good you are at making sacrifices when you expect *me* to sacrifice everything! Why? Because I'm not rich and powerful like you? Or because I'm going to be the mother of your child and you have this weird idea that a decent mother has no entitlement to any life of her own?'

Raul jerked as if she had struck him, a feverish flush slowly darkening his hard cheekbones.

This time the silence that fell screamed with menace.

A tiny pulse flickered at the whitened edge of his fiercely compressed mouth. His hands had closed into fists, betraying his struggle for self-command. But, most frightening of all for Polly, for the very first time Raul stared back at her with very real hatred. Cold, hard, deadly loathing. And, in shock, Polly fell silent, mind turning blank, all the fight and anger draining from her, leaving only fear in their place.

'I'll take you back to the clinic,' Raul drawled with raw finality. 'There is no point in allowing this offensive dialogue to continue.'

CHAPTER FOUR

Two days later, Polly was still recovering from the effects of that catastrophic lunch out.

But her mind was briefly removed from her own problems when she picked up a magazine dated from the previous month and learnt that her childhood friend, Maxie Kendall, had got married, indeed had already been married for several weeks. Maxie and her husband, Angelos Petronides, had kept their marriage a secret until they were ready to make a public announcement. Polly read the article and scrutinised the photos with great interest, and a pleased smile on Maxie's behalf.

She had last met Maxie at the reading of Nancy Leeward's will. Her godmother had actually had three god-daughters, Polly and Maxie and Darcy. Although the girls had been close friends well into their teens, their adult lives had taken them in very different directions.

Maxie had become a famous model, with a tangled love life in London. Darcy had been a single parent, who rarely left her home in Cornwall. Polly had tried to keep in touch with both women but regular contact had gradually lapsed, not least because Darcy and Maxie were no longer friends.

'Isn't she gorgeous?' one of the nurses groaned in admiration, looking over her shoulder at the main picture of Maxie on the catwalk. 'I would give my eye teeth to look like that!'

'Who wouldn't?' Polly's smile of amused agreement

slid away as she found herself reflecting that Maxie closely resembled what appeared to be Raul's ideal of a sexually attractive woman. Tall, blonde and stunning. And here she was, a five-foot-one-inch-tall, slightly built brunette, who had never looked glamorous in her life.

She grimaced, still angry and bitter about the options Raul had laid before her with a cruel air of understanding generosity. If she lived until she was ninety she would not forget her crushing sense of humiliation when Raul had dragged her attraction to him out into the open and squashed her already battered pride.

In Vermont, Raul had evidently seen her susceptibility and quite deliberately steered clear of encouraging her. That awareness now made her feel about a foot high. She had honestly believed that she hadn't betrayed herself, had fondly imagined that she had managed to match his cool and casual manner. She had deliberately avoided every temptation to do otherwise, biting her tongue many, many times in his presence.

She had always left it to him to say when or if he was coming again, had never once complained when he didn't show up, had never attempted to pry into his private life. And, boy, had she been wasting her time in trying to play it cool, she thought now in severe mortification. Raul had been ahead of her. 'Sexual hunger', he had called it! How gallant of him to pretend that he had been tempted too, because she didn't believe that—indeed, not for one second *could* she believe that!

And now she blamed Raul even more bitterly for her own painful misconceptions during that time. Why hadn't he mentioned the existence of other women in his life? Even the most casual reference to another relationship would have put her on her guard. But, no,

Raul had been content to allow her to imagine whatever she liked. That had been safer than an honesty that might have made her question his true motive for seeking out her company.

So Raul needn't think that she was going to apologise for telling him that a wedding ring was the only thing likely to persuade her to move to Venezuela. It had been the honest truth. She hadn't expected him to like that truth, or even pause for a second to consider marriage as a possible option to their problem, but she *had* wanted to shock him just as he had shocked her, she conceded uncomfortably.

Yet the raw hostility and dislike she had aroused had not been a welcome result. In fact, his reaction had terrified her, and in retrospect even that annoyed her and filled her with shame. She had to learn to deal with Raul on an impersonal basis.

Raul arrived that evening while she was lying on the sofa watching the film *Pretty Woman*. He strode in at the bit where the heroine was fanning out a selection of condoms for the hero's benefit. Shooting the screen a darkling glance, he said with icy derision, 'I've never understood how a whore could figure as a romantic lead!'

Polly almost fell on the coffee table in her eagerness to grab up the remote control and switch the television off. Hot-cheeked, she looked at him then. He had never seemed more remote: fabulous bone structure taut, lean features cool, his dark and formal business suit somehow increasing his aspect of chilling detachment.

Eyes as black and wintry as a stormy night assailed hers. 'I've applied for a special licence. We'll get married here in forty-eight hours.'

In the act of lifting herself from the sofa, Polly's arms

lost their strength and crumpled at the elbows. She top-
pled back onto the sofa again, a look of complete astonishment fixed to her startled face. 'Say that again—'

'You have made it clear that you will not accept any
other option,' Raul drawled flatly.

'But I never expected.... I mean, f-for goodness'
sake, Raul,' Polly stammered in severe shock. 'We
can't just—'

'Can't we? Are you about to change your mind? Are
you now prepared to consider allowing me to take my
child back home with me?' Raul shot at her.

'No!' she gasped.

'Are you willing to try living in Venezuela on any
other terms?'

'No, but—'

'Then don't waste my time with empty protests. You
have, after all, just got exactly what you wanted,' Raul
informed her icily.

'Not if you feel like this about it,' Polly protested
unevenly. 'And it isn't what I precisely wanted—'

'Isn't it? Are you now telling me that you *don't* want
me?'

Polly flushed to the roots of her hair, still very sensitive on that subject. 'I... I—'

'If I were you, I wouldn't argue on that point,' Raul
warned, a current of threatening steel in his rich, accented drawl. 'In the space of one minute, I could make
you eat your words!'

Already in shock, as she was, that level of blunt assurance reduced Polly to writhing discomfiture, but she
still said, 'When I mentioned marriage, I didn't mean it
as a serious possibility—'

'No, you laid it out as the ultimate price, the ultimate
sacrifice.' Raul's hard sensual mouth twisted. 'And I'll

get used to the idea. It will be a marriage of convenience, nothing more. I won't allow my child to grow up without me. I also hope I'm not so prejudiced that I can't concede that having both a mother and a father may well be better for the child.'

In a daze of conflicting feelings, Polly muttered, 'But what about...*us*?'

'That baby is the only thing that should matter to either of us. Why should he or she pay the price for this fiasco?'

That was a telling point for Polly. She bowed her head, guilty conscience now in full sway. Only she still couldn't prevent herself from muttering, 'I expected to marry someone who loved me—'

'I didn't expect to marry at all,' Raul traded, without an ounce of sympathy.

'I'll have to think this over—'

'No, you won't. You'll give me your answer now. I'm not in the mood for prima donna tactics!'

Polly experienced a powerful urge to tell him to get lost. And then she thought about being married to Raul, and other, infinitely stronger emotions swamped her. Over time they could work at building up a reasonable relationship, she told herself. They would have the baby to share. Surely their child would help to bring them together? And, all false pride laid aside, Polly was suddenly agonisingly conscious that she would do just about anything to at least have that chance with Raul. If she didn't make that leap of faith now, there would be no second opportunity.

'I'll marry you,' she murmured tautly.

'*Muy bien.*' Raul consulted his watch with disturbing cool. 'I'm afraid I can't stay. I have a dinner engagement.'

'Raul…?'

He turned back from the door.

Polly swallowed hard. 'You can *live* with this option?' she prompted anxiously.

His sudden blazing smile took her completely by surprise, and yet inexplicably left her feeling more chilled than reassured. 'Of course.… I only hope you're equally adaptable.'

Two days later, Polly, clad in a simple white cotton dress, waited in her room for Raul to arrive.

Rod Bevan had told her that he had suggested the courtyard garden for the wedding ceremony, but Raul had apparently wanted a more private setting. Something quick that wouldn't interfere with his busy schedule too much or attract the attention of others, Polly had gathered rather sourly. It was hard to believe that this was her wedding day. No flowers, no guests, nothing that might be construed as an attempt to celebrate the event. Had she been out of her mind to agree to marry Raul?

She had tossed and turned half the night, worrying about that. Absently she rubbed at the nagging ache in the small of her back. It had begun annoying her around dawn, presumably because she'd been lying in an awkward position. She felt like a water melon, huge and ungainly. She felt sorry for herself. She felt tearful. She felt that she might well be on the brink of making the biggest mistake of her life.

But Raul himself had put it in a nutshell for her. They were putting the baby first, and this way their baby would have two parents. That was very important to Polly, and she had with constant piety reminded herself of that crucial fact. There was just one cloud on the

horizon…a cloud that got bigger and blacker every time
her conscience stole an uneasy glance at it.

Raul didn't *want* to marry her. He had made no attempt to pretend otherwise. The occasional flash of san-
ity told Polly that that was all wrong, totally unacceptable as a basis even for a marriage of convenience. But
what was the alternative? Polly couldn't see *any* alternative. Only marriage could give them both an equal
share of their child.

She stretched awkwardly, and used her fingers to
massage the base of her spine. At that moment, Raul
strode in.

'*Dios*…let's get this over with as quickly as possible,' Raul urged impatiently as he reached down a
strong hand to enclose hers and help her up off the sofa.

Thirty seconds later Rod Bevan arrived, accompanied
by two other men. One was the registrar who would
perform the ceremony, the other Raul introduced as his
lawyer, Digby Carson. The service was very brief.
When it was over, everybody shook hands and everybody smiled—with the exception of Raul. His cool impassivity didn't yield or melt for a second.

In the midst of an increasingly awkward conversation, a sharp, tightening sensation formed around
Polly's abdomen. A stifled gasp was wrenched from her.

'What's wrong?' Raul demanded, anxiety flaring in
his stunning dark eyes.

'I think we'd better forget the coffee and the scones,'
Rod Bevan concluded with a rueful smile as he showed
the other two men out.

While he was doing that, Raul scooped Polly up in
his arms and laid her down gently on the bed. The impassive look had vanished. His lean, proud face was full

of concern. 'The baby's not due for another two weeks,' he told her tautly.

'Babies have their own schedule, Raul. I'd say this one has a pretty good sense of timing,' Rod asserted cheerfully.

'I'll stay with you, Polly,' Raul swore.

'No, you will not!' Polly exclaimed in instantaneous rejection. 'I don't want you with me!'

'I'd like to see my baby born,' Raul murmured intently, staring down at her with all the expectancy his powerful personality could command.

Dumbly she shook her head, tears of embarrassment pricking her eyes. She could not imagine sharing anything that intimate with a man she hadn't even shared a bedroom with.

As he rang the bell for a nurse, she heard the consultant say something in Spanish. Raul's response was quiet, but perceptibly edged by harshness. The door thudded shut on his departure.

'He's furious!' Polly suddenly sobbed, torn by both resentment and an odd, stabbing sense of sharp regret.

'No...he's *hurt*,' the older man contradicted, patting her clenched fingers soothingly. 'For a male as squeamish as Raul, that was one hell of a generous offer!'

Polly gazed down in drowsy fascination at her baby and fell head-over-heels in love for the second time in her life. He was gorgeous. He had fine, silky black hair and big dark eyes, and a cry that seemed to be attached by some invisible string to her heart. He looked so small to her, but the midwife had said he was big—a whole ten pounds one ounce worth of bouncing, healthy baby.

As the nurse settled him into the crib, Raul appeared with Rod Bevan. Although medication had left Polly feeling sleepily afloat, and incapable of much in the way of thought or speech, she stared at Raul in surprise. His darkly handsome features were strained, his expressive mouth taut, his eyes shadowed. His tie was missing, the jacket of his suit crumpled and his white shirt open at his strong brown throat.

'What's wrong?' Polly asked worriedly.

Broodingly, Raul surveyed his sleeping son and thrust a not quite steady hand through his already rumpled black hair. 'He's wonderful,' he breathed with ragged appreciation. 'But supremely indifferent to the danger he put you in!'

The consultant absorbed Polly's frown of incomprehension. 'Raul equates a Caesarean section with a near death experience,' he explained with gentle satire as he took his leave in the nurse's wake.

Faint colour overlaid Raul's blunt cheekbones. He studied Polly's weary face and frowned darkly. He reached for her hand and coiled long fingers warmly round hers. 'I wasn't prepared for surgical intervention…why didn't you warn me?'

Polly slowly shook her head.

'Rod tells me you've known for months that the baby would probably have to be delivered that way,' Raul persisted.

'It's quite common,' Polly managed to slur, her eyelids feeling as if they had weights driving them downward.

'You're so tiny,' Raul muttered almost fiercely. 'I should've thought—'

'Bit late now,' Polly incised with drowsy wit.

'My son is beautiful,' Raul murmured. 'At least we got something right.'

'*Our*…son,' she mumbled.

'We'll call him Rodrigo—'

She winced.

'Jorge?'

She pulled a face.

'Emilio?'

She sighed.

'Luis?'

A faint, drowsy smile curved her lips.

'Luis...Zaforteza,' Raul sounded thoughtfully.

Polly went to sleep.

Polly studied the four confining walls of her room and smiled. Tomorrow she was leaving the clinic. Her smile faded, her eyes apprehensive. They were to spend a couple of days in Raul's apartment and then fly to Venezuela. Pulling on a luxurious thin silk wrap, she left her room. Every day Luis went to the nursery for a while to allow her to rest. Repossessing her son had become the highlight of her afternoon.

A slight frown line drew her brows together. The day Luis was born, Raul had seemed so concerned for her, so approachable, she reflected ruefully. But over the past five days the barriers had gone up again.

Raul's fascination with his son was undeniable. Yet what she had believed might bring them closer together seemed instead to have pushed them further apart. Why was it that when Raul visited she often felt like a superfluous but extremely well-paid extra? Was it the fact that Raul never came through the door without some outrageously extravagant gift, which he carelessly bestowed on her in the manner of a rather superior customer bestowing a tip?

Day one, a diamond bracelet. Day two, a half-dozen sets of luxurious nightwear. Day three, a watch from

Cartier. Day four, a magnificent diamond ring. It had become embarrassing. Raul was rich. Raul was now her husband. But it felt very strange to be receiving such lavish presents from a male so cool and distant he never touched her in even the smallest way.

As she turned the corner into the corridor where the nursery was, Polly was dismayed to see Raul talking with Digby Carson outside the viewing window. Neither man having heard her slippered approach, she ducked into an alcove out of sight. She was too self-conscious to join them when she was so lightly clad, and was thoroughly irritated that vanity had made her set aside her more sedate but shabby dressing gown.

'So how do you feel about this…er…development?' the older man was saying quietly, only yards away from her ignominious hiding place.

'Deliriously happy, Digby.'

'Seriously, Raul—'

'That was sarcasm, not humour, Digby. My little bride is much smarter than the average gold-digger,' Raul breathed with stinging bitterness. 'She used my son as a bargaining chip to blackmail me into marriage!'

Rigid with shock at that condemnation, Polly pushed her shoulders back against the cool wall to keep herself upright.

'But whatever happens now I will keep my son,' Raul completed with harsh conviction.

There was a buzzing sound in Polly's ears. She heard the older man say something but she couldn't pick out the words. Dizzily, she shook her head as the voices seemed to recede. When she finally peered out, the corridor was empty again.

Without even thinking about what she was doing, she fled back to the privacy of her room. A gold-digger…a blackmailer. Trembling with stricken disbelief at having heard herself described in such terms, Polly folded down on the bed, no longer sure her wobbly knees would support her.

The pain went deep and then deeper still. Raul despised her. *'Whatever happens now I will keep my son.'* A cold, clammy sensation crawled down Polly's spine. What had he meant by that? And this was the husband she was hoping to make a new life with in Venezuela? A husband who obviously loathed and resented her? In her turmoil, only one fact seemed clear. She could no longer trust Raul…and she couldn't possibly risk taking her son to Venezuela without that trust.

Minutes later, a nurse wheeled in Luis's crib. Seeing Polly already wearing her wrap and slippers, she smiled. 'I see you were just about to come and collect him. Your husband said you were still asleep when he looked in on you earlier, but I know you like to feed Luis yourself.'

Alone with her child again, Polly drew in a shivering, steadying breath. Fear still etched in her shaken eyes, she gazed down at her son's innocent little face, and then she got up in sudden decision.

From the cabinet by the bed she extracted her address book. Leafing frantically through it, she found the phone number her friend Maxie had insisted on giving her when they had parted after the reading of Nancy Leeward's will. 'Liz always knows where I am,' she had promised.

Using the phone by the bed, Polly rang Liz Blake. As soon as the older woman had established who she was, she passed on Maxie's number. When she heard Maxie's familiar husky voice answering her call, Polly felt weak with relief.

'It's Polly…' she muttered urgently. 'Maxie, I need somewhere to stay…'

An hour after that conversation, having left a note of explanation addressed to Raul, Polly walked out of the clinic with Luis in her arms and climbed into the taxi waiting outside. The receptionist was too busy checking in new patients to notice her quiet exit.

CHAPTER FIVE

POLLY wheeled the stroller in from the roof garden. Threading back her spectacular mane of blonde hair with a manicured hand, Maxie Petronides bent to look in at a warmly-clothed Luis and exclaimed, 'He's so cute I could steal him!'

Polly surveyed her sleeping son with loving eyes. He was four weeks old and he got more precious with every passing day. Remorsefully aware that Raul was being deprived of their son, she had twice sent brief letters containing photos of Luis to Rod Bevan at the clinic, knowing he would pass them on.

The fabulous penthouse flat which she was looking after belonged to Maxie and her husband, Angelos, who used an even more spacious central London apartment. Polly was acting as caretaker for the property while the floors below were transformed into similar luxury dwellings. When the work was complete, Angelos Petronides would put the building on the market with the penthouse as a show home.

'So how are *you* feeling?' Maxie prompted over the coffee that Polly had made.

'Guilty,' Polly confessed ruefully, but she forced a smile, determined not to reveal the real extent of her unhappiness. Every time Raul came into her mind, she forced him out again. He had no business being there. He had *never* had any business being there. Learning to think of Raul only in relation to Luis was a priority.

'You shouldn't be feeling like that,' Maxie reproved.

'You needed this time alone to sort yourself out. This last year, you've been through an awful lot.'

'And made some even more *awful* mistakes,' Polly stressed with a helpless grimace. 'I shouldn't have married Raul. It was incredibly selfish and unfair. I *still* don't know what got into me!'

'Love has a lot to answer for. Sometimes you get so bitter and furious, you want to hit back hard,' Maxie proffered, disconcerting Polly with the depth of her understanding. 'And that just creates more strife. It's only when it all gets too much that you suddenly simmer down and come to your senses.'

'I wish I'd hit that point *before* I married Raul,' Polly muttered wretchedly.

'But Raul has made mistakes too,' Maxie contended firmly. 'He's also sent out some very confusing messages about exactly what he wants from you. But if you're honest with him when you contact him again, it should take some of the heat out of the situation.'

Polly tried to imagine telling Raul that she loved him and just cringed. Some excuse to give a man for forcing him into marrying her! That *was* what she had done, she acknowledged now. And admitting that even to herself still appalled her. But, whether she liked it or not, Raul had had grounds to accuse her of using their son to blackmail him into marriage. That wasn't what she had intended, but that, in his eyes, had been the end result.

In the clinic she had brooded over the hurt and humiliation Raul had carelessly inflicted in Vermont. If she had never seen Raul again she would have got over him eventually, but being forced into such regular contact with him again had plunged her right back into emotional turmoil. She'd been too proud to face up to her continuing feelings for him…a woman scorned? She shuddered at that demeaning label. Whatever, she had been stubbornly blind to what was going on inside her own head.

She had still been so bitterly angry with Raul. Instead of putting those dangerous emotions behind her, before trying to seriously consider their son's future, she had let herself glory in them that day at his apartment. Admittedly, Raul had provoked her with his refusal to even allow that she might be entitled to a life of her own. But marriage would only have been a viable alternative if Raul had been a willing bridegroom.

On their wedding day she had also become a new mother. That in itself would have been quite enough to cope with, but Raul's subsequent behaviour had increased her anxiety about what their future together might hold. That overheard conversation had pushed the misgivings she had been trying to repress and ignore out into the open.

'Initially Angelos wasn't that fussed about getting married either,' Maxie confessed, taking Polly by surprise.

'Did he ever say he would sooner be dead than married?'

'Well, no…'

Of course not. Angelos was besotted with his wife. And Maxie was besotted with her husband. But then Maxie was gorgeous, Polly reflected wryly, and naturally physical attraction had initially brought the couple together. Angelos hadn't looked at Maxie and thought, I *like* her…she'd make a good surrogate mother. So why on earth had she tried to make a comparison?

After Maxie's visit, Polly spent the rest of the day being extremely conscious of the presence of every phone in the apartment. She knew it was time to get in touch with Raul direct. It was now over three weeks since she had left the clinic on a surging tide of rage, pain and fear after hearing Raul's opinion of her. But as that anger had subsided she had gradually come to appreciate that Raul had more right to be bitter than she had initially been prepared to admit.

And at least she now knew what had to be done about the situation, she reflected while she showered in the palatial *en suite* bathroom off the master bedroom. She was ready to humbly acknowledge her mistake, ready to talk to Raul about having their ill-judged marriage annulled. That would put them right back where they had started, but surely it would at least eradicate Raul's hostility? Fearful of the response she was likely to receive, it was after nine that evening when she finally dialled the number Raul had given her weeks earlier in the clinic.

'It's Polly…'

Silence buzzed on the line, and then she heard some background noise she couldn't identify. 'Raul?' she queried uncertainly.

'I heard you,' Raul finally responded, the dark, rich timbre of his accented drawl washing over her with a familiarity that almost hurt. 'Where are you?'

'I thought we should clear the air on the phone first,' Polly admitted tautly. 'Did you get my note?'

'Three pages isn't exactly a "note".'

'I was very upset when I heard you talking about me like that,' Polly admitted tightly.

'I did get that message. But I was letting off steam that day. It never occurred to me that I'd be overheard.'

Polly relaxed slightly.

'Tell me about my son,' Raul urged.

'Could you...could you just once manage to say *our* son?'

'That would be difficult.'

'Why?' Polly pressed.

'"Our" suggests sharing...and right at this minute you are not sharing anything with me,' Raul traded.

Polly paled, but she still coiled round the phone as if it was a fire on an icy night. 'I didn't mean...I didn't *plan* to push you into a marriage you didn't want,' she told him unsteadily.

'You just accidentally fell into that wedding ring, *gatita*?'

Polly turned pink, scrutinising the narrow gold band where it sat in prominent isolation on the coffee table, removed the same day she'd faced up to the fact that it was the symbol of a farce. 'Where are you?'

'In my car...you were saying?' Raul prompted.

'We don't have to stay married!' Polly rushed to make that point and redeem herself without touching on anything more intimate.

Silence greeted that leading statement.

Polly cleared her throat awkwardly in that interim. 'I suppose you're still very annoyed that I left the clinic...?' Her voice rose involuntarily, turning that sentence into a nervous question.

'It's possible...'

'All of a sudden I didn't feel I could trust you, and I felt trapped...I didn't think I had any alternative—but it was an impulsive decision—'

'You're distressingly prone to impulses, *gatita*,' Raul incised with sudden bite. 'And this dialogue is just irritating the hell out of me!'

The line went dead. With a frown, Polly shook the silent phone. Nothing. Taken aback that Raul should have cut off her call, Polly blinked and slowly straightened. The silence of the apartment enclosed her. Only one soft pool of lamplight illuminated the corner of the big lounge.

Rising, she smoothed down her satin and lace nightgown and went to check on Luis. He was sound asleep, but he was due for a feed soon. In the elegant kitchen she tidied up the remains of her supper and prepared a bottle for Luis. All the time she was doing that, she agonised over that conversation with Raul. He had sounded so strange. Strained, wary, then bitingly angry.

The doorbell went, making her jump and then as quickly relax again. Maxie was her only visitor, and Maxie had called in one other evening, when Angelos had had a business dinner. Polly hurried across the octagonal hall. Without bothering to use the intercom, she hit the release button on the security lock which barred access to the private lift in the underground car park.

Then she stilled with a frown. Why would Maxie come to see her twice in one day? Only if there was something wrong! Running an apprehensive hand through the fall of her mahogany hair, Polly waited impatiently. It seemed ages before she heard the low, distant hum of the approaching lift, then the soft ping as it reached the top floor. The doors purred back.

But it was *not* Maxie; it was Raul who strode out of the lift.

Polly went into startled retreat, aghast eyes pinned to his intimidatingly tall and powerfully male physique.

Scathing dark-as-night eyes flashed into hers. '*Dios mio*...you deserve a bloody good fright!' Raul informed her wrathfully. 'All that high tec security and you don't even *check* who your visitor is before you invite him up?'

In shock, Polly felt her teeth chatter together. 'I...I just assumed it was Maxie—'

'Don't you have any sense? I could've been a rapist, or a robber, and I bet you're alone in this apartment!'

Swallowing hard, Polly gave a jerky nod, her attention fully locked to him. He looked spectacular in a fabulous silver-grey suit, cut to enhance every sleek, muscular angle of his wide-shouldered, lean-hipped and long-legged frame. As her shaken gaze ran over him, her stomach flipped and her mouth ran dry. His magnetic dark good looks were like a visual assault on senses starved of him.

'How...how did you find out where I was?' Her bewilderment was unconcealed.

Raul's wide mouth curled with impatience. 'Once I had your phone number, it was a piece of cake to get the address. Why do you think I kept you on the line for so long?'

Since Polly hadn't been conscious until the end of that call that anyone but her had been controlling anything, she gulped.

'Angelos Petronides will answer to me for this,' Raul breathed with sudden chilling conviction, lean, strong face forbidding.

'Angelos... Maxie's husband? You *know* him?' Polly exclaimed in surprise.

'Of course I know him, and he owns this building. Here you are on Petronides ground. I thought better of Angelos. I didn't think he'd get involved in hiding my wife from me, but now that he *has*—'

'No, he hasn't!' Polly protested vehemently. 'I've never even met Maxie's husband! I asked her to help me find somewhere to stay and she brought me here— said they needed someone to look after the place.

Maxie's certainly not aware that you know Angelos. And, as I asked her to be discreet, she's only told Angelos that she has an old friend staying here for a while…'

As her voice faltered to a halt, she experienced the feeling that she had already lost Raul's full attention. As his dark golden gaze roamed over her scantily clad figure, Polly suddenly became intensely conscious of the revealing nature of her nightgown, the delicate straps which exposed her bare shoulders, the sheer lace covering her breasts, the light, clinging fabric which outlined her once-again-slim hips and slender thighs for his appraisal.

As the silence which had seemed to come out of nowhere pulsed, Polly felt her breasts swell with languorous heaviness. Her nipples pinched tight, as if a current of fire had touched them. As she folded her arms over herself in mortified discomfiture, she snapped, 'Has anybody ever told you that it's very rude to stare?'

The silence lay still and impenetrable as glass.

And then Raul flung his darkly handsome head back and laughed with a rich spontaneity that shook Polly. Laughter put to flight his gravity, throwing his innate charisma to the fore. Her heart lurched. She tried to give him a reproving look, needing him to show her a mood she recognised and stay in it long enough for her to respond accordingly. But at that moment she was like a novice actress without a script and unable to improvise.

'You've gone from voluptuously ripe and enticing to sinfully, sexily slender,' Raul murmured with husky amusement. 'And you think it's *rude* that I should stare at my own wife?'

A deep flush lit Polly's fair skin. She didn't know

where to look, but was pretty sure she was not going to look back at him while he was saying things like that. *Sinfully, sexily slender?* Now she knew what Maxie had meant when she had criticised Raul for giving her conflicting messages. An impersonal and detached relationship had to have firm boundaries. Raul had been both impersonal and detached after their wedding, politely concerned that she should be comfortable and content, but nothing more. He had made no attempt to behave like a normal husband who had a relationship with the mother of his child.

And then Polly called herself an idiot. Here she was, wondering why Raul was behaving so strangely! But wouldn't most men react differently to a woman standing around half-naked in front of them? Hot colour flooded her cheeks at that obvious explanation.

'I'll go and put something on and then we can talk,' Polly muttered in a rush.

'Let me see Luis first,' Raul countered, moving closer to catch her hand and check her before she could move.

'You're not still annoyed with Maxie's husband, are you?' Polly asked anxiously as she took him down the corridor.

'I have a certain tolerance for a man plunged unsuspecting into an embarrassing situation by his bride,' Raul imparted wryly. 'Angelos is Greek, traditional as they come. He'd come down on his wife like a ton of bricks if he realised that she'd been helping to hide *my* wife and child from me!'

'It wasn't like that—'

'Only violence or abuse on my part would justify such interference between a man and his wife.'

Was that the third or the fourth time that Raul had referred to her as *his wife* in as many minutes? Polly thought abstractedly. After three weeks of telling herself that their marriage was a pathetic charade, it seemed so odd to have Raul referring to her in such terms.

'Raul...I really needed some time and space to think,' she murmured tautly.

Raul released her hand. 'You've had months to think without me around.'

But their relationship had changed radically in recent weeks, Polly wanted to protest in frustration as she watched him fluidly cross the elegant guest room to where Luis lay in his cradle. Their marriage had been one of reckless haste, entered into without proper consideration or adequate discussion.

She hadn't simply taken umbrage and run away; she had known that ultimately she would have to face Raul again and deal with the situation.

But in her distress and turmoil she had been in no fit state to confront a male who had a naturally domineering and powerful personality—and, worst of all, a male who had everything to gain from putting pressure on her to still accompany him to Venezuela. She had known she had to have time to think away from Raul before she decided what to do next.

Raul sent her a cool, assessing glance. 'I've known Digby all my life. What you heard was a private conversation with a friend. I imagine you and your friend Maxie have been less than charitable about me on at least *one* recent occasion...'

Unprepared for that embarrassingly accurate stab, Polly was betrayed by the burning wave of colour which swept up her throat.

'*Exactly,*' Raul purred with rich satisfaction, removing his attention from her to study his infant son, who was squirming into wakefulness. 'Do you see me get-

ting all worked up about a fact of life? Could you see
me writing three vitriolic pages and vanishing into thin
air on such slender proof of intent as the mood of a
moment?'

'No, but—'

'There is no "but",' Raul broke in with derision.
'Only women behave like that. Rod thought it might be
the baby blues, or some such thing! I knew better.'

'I was in the wrong...I should've confronted you,'
Polly conceded tightly, heart-shaped face fixed in a mutinous expression, revealing the struggle it was to voice
those words of contrition.

'Instead of throwing a tantrum on paper,' Raul
emphasised, subjecting her to a hard, steady appraisal.
'Because I warn you now, I will never, ever allow you
to be in a position again where you can use our son as
a weapon against me.'

At that opportune moment, Luis mustered his lungs
into a cross little cry for attention. Pale and taut now,
in receipt of that menacing warning, Polly was grateful
for the opportunity to turn away. But Raul reached his
son first, sweeping him up with complete confidence.
Smiling down at Luis, he talked to him in soft, soothing
Spanish.

In the blink of an eye Raul had gone from that chilling threat to an unashamed display of tenderness with
their son, Polly registered. That was the most intimidating thing to watch—the speed and ease with which
he could switch emotional channels. Although there had
been nothing emotional about his determination to tell
her how he felt about her flight from the clinic. Cool,
scornful, cutting.

'I'll get his bottle,' Polly muttered.

She skidded down to the bedroom to pull on a fluttering silk wrap first. When she returned to the dimly lit bedroom, Raul rose from the armchair to let her take a seat. He settled Luis into her arms and then hunkered lithely down to watch his son greedily satisfy his hunger.

'*Dios mío!* No wonder he's grown so much!'

Polly cleared her throat awkwardly. 'I want you to know that I would never use Luis as a weapon—'

'You already have,' Raul told her without hesitation, smoothing an astonishingly gentle hand over Luis's little head before vaulting upright again. 'In disputes between couples, the child is often a weapon. You should understand that as well as I do. When your parents' marriage broke up, your father kept you and your mother apart. Why? He was punishing her for leaving him for another man.'

Polly was astonished that he should still recall that much information about her background. 'I suppose he was,' she conceded as she got up to change Luis.

'Love turns to hatred so easily. It never lasts,' Raul murmured with supreme cynicism.

'It lasts for a lot of people,' Polly argued abstractedly, down on her knees and busily engaged in dealing with her son's needs. But she gathered courage from not being forced to meet Raul's often unsettling gaze. 'You know what I said on the phone earlier…about us not having to stay married?'

Having expected an immediate response to that reminder, Polly looked up in the resounding silence which followed.

Raul was staring back at her with penetrating and grim eyes. 'I do.'

'Look, why don't you wait in the lounge while I settle Luis?' Polly suggested uncomfortably.

A few minutes later, Luis was back in the cradle, snug and comfy and sleepy.

'I love you, you precious baby,' Polly whispered feelingly, not looking forward to the discussion she was about to open but convinced that Raul would be extremely relieved when she suggested that they have their marriage annulled.

As she entered the lounge, Raul swung round from the fireplace. 'I don't like this room. It's claustrophobic with that conservatory built over the windows,' he said with flat distaste. 'It's insane to close out such magnificent views!'

'Maxie's terrified of heights. That's why it's like that...' Polly hovered awkwardly. 'Raul—?'

'I'm not giving you a divorce,' Raul delivered before she could say another word.

Was he thinking angrily about the prospect of having to offer a divorce settlement? Did he imagine she was planning to make some greedy, gold-digging claim on his legendary wealth?

Polly reddened with annoyance at that suspicion. 'We don't need to go for a divorce. We can apply for an annulment and everything will be put right. It will be like this wretched marriage of ours never happened.'

Raul had gone very still, dark eyes narrowing into watchful and wary arrows of light in his dark, devastating face. 'An annulment?' he breathed, very low, that possibility evidently not having occurred to him.

'Well, why not?' Polly asked him tautly. 'It's the easiest way out.'

'Let me get this straight...' Raul spread two lean brown hands with silent fluency to express apparent astonishment. 'Just one short month ago you married me, and now, without living a *single* day with me, you have changed your mind?'

'You're making me sound really weird,' Polly muttered in reproach. 'I was wrong to let you marry me, knowing that you didn't want that option. Now I'm admitting it—'

'But too late…you're admitting it too late,' Raul declared.

'But it's not too late…' Polly's brow furrowed with confusion, because the discussion was not going in the direction she had expected. 'It's not as if we've lived together…or anything like that. Why are you looking at me like I'm crazy? You don't *want* to be married to me.'

As he listened to that stumbling reminder, dark colour flared over Raul's slashing cheekbones and his stunning dark eyes suddenly blazed gold. 'But I have come to terms with the fact that I *am* married to you!'

'I think we both deserve a bit more than that out of marriage,' Polly opined in growing discomfiture. 'We rushed into it—'

'*I* didn't rush,' Raul interrupted. 'I just wanted to get it over with!'

'Yes, well…doesn't it strike you that that isn't a promising basis for *any* marriage?' Polly framed carefully, alarmingly awake to the angry tension emanating from his tall, commanding figure. 'I thought you'd be pleased at the idea of having your freedom back.'

'Freedom is a state of mind. I now see no reason why marriage should make the slightest difference to my life,' Raul returned with grating assurance.

Polly was momentarily silenced by that sweeping statement.

'You're my wife, and the mother of my son. I suggest

you get used to those facts of life,' Raul completed, studying her in angry, intimidating challenge.

A bemused look now sat on Polly's face. Her lashes fluttered. The tip of her tongue crept out to nervously moisten the taut fullness of her lower lip. 'I don't understand…'

Hooded eyes of gleaming gold dropped to linger on the ripe pink contours of her mouth. 'Sometimes you talk too much, *gatita*…'

'What does that mean…that word you keep on using?' Polly whispered, because the very atmosphere seemed to sizzle, warning her of the rise in tension. Suddenly she was finding it very difficult to breathe.

'*Gatita?*' Raul laughed as he closed the distance between them in one easy stride. 'It means "kitten". The shape of your face, those big blue eyes…you remind me of a little fluffy cat, cute and soft with unexpected claws.'

Having spent a lifetime fighting the downside of being smaller than most other people, Polly was not best pleased to be linked with any image described by words like 'little', 'fluffy' or 'cute'.

'What do you think I am? Some kind of novelty?' she demanded, fighting not to be intimidated by his proximity and towering height.

'If I knew what it was that attracts me to you, the attraction probably would have died by now,' Raul said cynically.

Polly stilled, feathery brows drawing together. 'But you're *not* attracted to me…'

Raul dealt her a rampantly amused appraisal. 'I may have controlled my baser urges, but I've lost count of the times I almost succumbed to the temptation of hauling you into my arms in Vermont,' he admitted frankly.

'Then I believed your appeal was related to the simple fact that I knew you were carrying *my* child…'

'Yes?' Polly conceded breathlessly, with the aspect of a woman struggling to take a serious academic interest in a confession that had flung her brain into wild confusion. Her heart was now thumping like a manic hammer below her breastbone.

'But now I've finally worked out what got us into this in the first place,' Raul confided, and, without giving her a hint of his intentions, he lifted his hands and slowly tipped the wrap from her taut shoulders. 'Subconsciously I picked you to be Luis's mother because you appealed to my hormones… Once I'd reached that conclusion, suddenly everything that's gone wrong between us started making sense!'

In her complete bemusement at that declaration, Polly was standing so still the garment simply slid down her arms and pooled on the carpet. 'What…*what*?' she began with a nervous start.

Bending, Raul closed his strong arms round her and almost casually swept her up off her feet.

'What are you doing?' Polly shrieked in sheer shock.

Raul dealt her a slashing smile of unashamed satisfaction. 'Husbands don't need to control their baser urges.'

'Put me down—'

But Raul silenced that angry command by bringing his hungry mouth crashing down on hers without further ado.

Polly saw stars. Stars inside her head, stars exploding like hot sunbursts in all sorts of embarrassing places inside her. It wasn't like the only other kiss they had shared—a slow burner, cut off before it reached its height. Raul's devouring demand had an instant urgency this time, intensifying her own shaken response. He probed her mouth with tiny little darting stabs of his tongue. The raw sexuality of that intimate assault was shockingly effective. It set up a chain reaction right through her whole body, filling her with a wild, wanton need for more.

Polly uttered a strangled moan low in her throat, hands sweeping up to dig possessively into his luxuriant black hair and hold him to her. Without warning, Raul broke free to raise his head, dark golden eyes intent on her hectically flushed face as he strode out into the hall and started down the corridor. '*Dios*...I could make love to you all night, but I know you're not ready for that yet,' he groaned in frank frustration.

Surfacing in turmoil from that predatory kiss, Polly gasped, 'Where on earth do you think you're taking me?'

Unerringly finding the master bedroom, opposite the guest room in which Luis slept, Raul shouldered wide the door, strode across the carpet and deposited her with almost exaggerated gentleness on the vast divan bed. He hit the light switch by the bed, dimly illuminating the room. Then he straightened with an indolent smile.

Polly reared up, bracing herself on her hands, her hair tumbling round her pink cheeks, her eyes very blue as she studied him in shaken disbelief. 'Do you honestly think I'm about to go to bed with you?'

It didn't take Raul two seconds to respond to that question. Surveying her steadily, he jerked loose his silk tie. '*Sí*...you're my wife.'

'This is not a normal marriage!' Polly argued, still gazing at him with very wide and incredulous eyes.

'That's been our biggest problem. The sooner this marriage becomes ''normal' the better,' Raul delivered, discarding his tie and sliding fluidly out of his jacket to pitch it on a nearby chair. 'It's time to forget how we started out—'

'But we didn't start *anything*!' Polly slung back, watching him unbutton his tailored silk shirt with the transfixed aspect of a woman unable to credit that he was actually undressing in front of her. 'I was pregnant before we even met!'

'Stop complicating things. You were pregnant with my baby. That created a special intimacy from the outset. Naturally that made a difference to how I reacted to you—'

'In Vermont?' Polly threw in helplessly. 'When you dropped in out of the blue whenever it suited you?'

'It's difficult to be casual any other way.'

'I bet you *always* suit yourself!' Polly condemned thinly.

Raul gave her a wondering and decidedly amused appraisal. 'Five-foot-nothing tall and you're nagging at me like a little shrew!' he marvelled.

Polly could feel her temper rising like a rocket desperate to go into orbit. 'I want you to treat me seriously, Raul.'

'Then say something relevant to the present,' he advised rather drily. 'Vermont was months ago. Vermont was when I still believed I was going to collect my child and walk away. We've moved on a lot since then.'

He peeled off his shirt.

Polly stared, throat closing, tongue cleaving to the roof of her dry mouth. He was incredibly beautifully built. All sleek bronzed skin and muscles, a hazy triangle of dark curls sprinkling his impressive torso. She blushed and averted her eyes. 'I'm not ready to share a bedroom with you yet,' she informed him tautly.

'I'm ready enough for both of us,' Raul said with amused assurance.

Without looking at him, Polly sat forward and linked her hands round her upraised knees. 'But I wasn't prepared for this... Before you came here tonight, I thought we'd be applying for an annulment to *end* our marriage,' she reminded him tensely. 'And sex isn't something I can treat casually—'

'*Bueno*...I'm delighted to hear it.'

'And...I haven't done this before,' Polly completed jerkily.

The silence spread for endless seconds that clawed cruelly at her nerves.

'*Como?*' Raul breathed in a near whisper.

Polly snatched in a shaky breath and simply squeezed her eyes tight shut. 'I've never had a lover.'

'That's not possible,' Raul informed her.

'Yes it is!' Polly said, almost fiercely in her embarrassment, desperate to drop the subject but registering by his audibly shattered responses that there was no current prospect of an easy escape.

'Look at me!' Raul commanded.

Her hot face a study of mingled chagrin and resentment, Polly glanced up and collided with incredulous dark golden eyes. 'Some women *don't* sleep around!' she snapped.

Raul moved closer to the bed, his frowning bemusement doing nothing to reduce her suspicion that he now saw her as some kind of freak. 'But you were at university...you must've had at least *one* relationship.'

'Not a physical one. I don't believe in intimacy without commitment,' Polly admitted stiffly, doggedly fighting her own discomfiture. 'And ''commitment' is a dirty word to a lot of men these days. I may be out of step with the times, but I'm not ashamed of my views.'

'Technically still a virgin,' Raul murmured sibilantly, letting his glittering golden gaze roam over her with hungry intent. 'I'm very surprised—but, since I shall be your first lover, I think I can handle the situation. And, as my wife, you can hardly question the level of *my* commitment.'

That proud and confident assurance hovered there for a split second. Polly lost colour and dragged her troubled eyes from him to focus on the bare pink toes which protruded from below the hem of her nightgown. 'But you didn't *want* that commitment,' she reminded him in a strained tone.

'I'll get used to it.'

Polly swallowed hard and took her courage in both hands, determined to go to the heart of her misgivings and be frank. 'But if we share a bed, Raul...I expect you to be faithful.'

The silence thickened and lay heavily.

'No woman tells me what to do,' Raul countered with ferocious bite. 'And that includes you!'

Polly froze, and then stared at the fancy silk bedspread until it blurred below her shaken eyes. Then she angled her head back and forced herself to meet the onslaught of his chilling dark eyes. 'I think fidelity is the least commitment you could make.'

'*Dios*...' Raul growled, reaching for his discarded shirt in an abrupt movement and pulling it back on. 'So you have found another weapon. Off the top of my head I could name a dozen married men and women cheating on their spouses...do you think *they* didn't make promises?'

Polly's heart was beating so fast it felt as if it was sitting at the foot of her throat. 'But that's not—'

'This marriage is on trial, as every new relationship is. Do you think living together like brother and sister is a fair test of any relationship between a man and a woman?' Raul derided with lancing scorn, black eyes raking mercilessly over her disconcerted face. 'Do you fondly imagine that I will be a good little celibate boy while you sit back and smugly weigh up whether or not you can trust me enough to reward me with the right to share your bed?'

'I didn't mean it like that, Raul!' Polly argued strickenly as she sprang off the bed.

'So far you have had everything your way, but here it stops,' Raul delivered, his cold rage unconcealed. 'If you refuse to behave like a normal wife, *don't* expect me to behave like a husband!'

Shocked and distressed by the savage anger she had provoked, Polly clutched at his arm as he reached for his jacket, 'Raul, I—'

He swung back and closed a powerful arm round her slight body, imprisoning her. He meshed long fingers into her hair, forcing her eyes to meet his. 'First you bargain with my son, then you bargain with sex.'

Breathless and trembling, she gazed up at him, lost herself in the brilliance of his shimmering dark eyes. '*No!*' she protested painfully.

Bending, Raul slid his arm below her slim hips and lifted her unceremoniously up to his level, crushing her swelling breasts into the muscular wall of his chest. Her nostrils flared on the enervating, hot, husky male scent of him. Hard black eyes assailed hers and held them by pure force of personality. 'You will not dictate terms to me. You will not demand empty and meaningless guarantees. A proper wife doesn't put a price on her body!'

'I...I wasn't doing that—'

'The marriage is on trial...*I am not*!' Raul stressed forcefully. 'I will not be judged on the basis of my past!'

Polly couldn't get breath into her lungs. Soft lips parting, she snatched in tiny little pants, drowning against her volition in the power of those compelling dark eyes.

'You're such a little hypocrite,' Raul delivered in a contemptuous undertone, scanning her dilated pupils and flushed cheeks. A sensually intent glitter flared in his assessing gaze, giving him the look of a tiger about to spring as he cupped her chin, lean fingers lingering to smoothly stroke the smooth curve of her jaw. 'This close to me, you're like a stick of dynamite hoping for a match!'

'I don't know what you're talking about—'

Striding over to the bed, Raul lowered her and followed her down onto the divan in one smooth, lithe motion. 'Then let me *show* you...'

Before she could even guess his intention, he had anchored her in place with one long, powerful thigh and brought his hard, mobile mouth crashing down on hers. With his tongue he plundered the sensitive interior with raw, erotic thoroughness. She groaned, plunged helplessly into the grip of mindless pleasure. He slid a hand beneath her, arching her up into contact with the aggressive thrust of his arousal, sending a cascade of fire trickling through her veins to accelerate every pulse.

Raul lifted his head. Her eyes were dazed, her ripe mouth reddened and swollen. Looking up at that lean, strong face, she trembled, caught up in a spell she was too weak to fight. With a slumberous smile, Raul flicked loose the tiny pearl buttons on the lace bodice of her nightie. And all the time Polly was involuntarily watching *him*, studying the black density and length of the lashes fanning his high cheekbones—the sole feminising influence in those hard-boned features—the luxuriant ebony hair tumbled by her fingers on to his brow, the blue-black shadow already roughening his strong jawline. All male, stunningly sexy.

'You have beautiful breasts,' Raul sighed.

Disconcerted, she followed the direction of his gaze. Thunderstruck, she stiffened and flushed at the sight of her own breasts, rising bare and shameless for his appraisal, her nipples already distended into wanton pink buds. 'Raul...?' she mumbled unevenly, lying there, wanting to cover herself, wanting to move, and yet inexplicably powerless to attempt to do either.

He allowed his thumb to delicately rub over one prominent peak, and her whole body jerked on the wave of sudden sensation that made her teeth grit in sensual shock and fired an insistent throb between her thighs.

'And you are *so* responsive,' he husked, angling back from her and then, without any warning whatsoever, smoothly sliding off the bed to spring upright again.

She suddenly found herself lying there alone and exposed, and a muffled cry of dismay escaped Polly. She rolled over onto her stomach, shaken, bewildered eyes pinned to Raul. Hooking his jacket on one forefinger, he glanced back at her from the door, bronzed face saturnine, black eyes several degrees below freezing.

'I could take you any time I wanted...and I *will*,' he swore, soft and low.

'You can't make me do anything I don't want to do!'

'Oh, yes, I can, *gatita*. Haven't the last five minutes

taught you anything?' Raul skimmed back with merciless cool. 'You have an amazing capacity to lose yourself in passion. By the time I'm finished with you, you will be begging me to share the marital bed!'

Polly was already so devastated by what he had just done to her that she just gaped at him, heart sinking like a stone, stomach clenching sickly. A cruelly humiliating and deliberate demonstration of sexual power from a male who had homed in like a predator on her one weakness. *Him.* She was appalled by a depth of diabolic calculation alien to her own more open nature.

'A car will pick you up tomorrow evening. We're flying home,' Raul drawled indolently as he sauntered out through the door. '*Buenas noches*, Señora Zaforteza.'

She listened to him walk down the corridor, her hands bunched into fists. She wanted to scream with angry frustration and pain. She hated him, but she hated herself more. He had kissed her and nothing else had mattered. Now her body ached with guilty, unfulfilled passion, the enemy of every fine principle she had ever believed in. She was finally finding out how hard it was to withstand physical temptation.

And Raul? she thought furiously. Raul had simply walked away, content to have made his point in the most ego-crushing manner available.

CHAPTER SIX

POLLY sat in a comfortable seat in the spacious cabin of Raul's private jet and suppressed a sigh. Luis was asleep in his skycot and Raul had still to arrive. He had been delayed.

She glanced curiously at Irena, the young and pretty stewardess watching out for Raul's arrival. A sultry brunette, she looked like a model in her smart uniform, but in spite of the long wait she had coolly avoided any real contact with her employer's wife. A man's woman, uninterested in her own sex, Polly had decided.

Hearing the sound of feet on the metal steps outside, seeing Irena's face blossom into surprising warmth as she moved out of view to greet Raul, Polly was annoyed to recognise her own powerful sense of anticipation—and, mortifyingly, her childish stab of envy that the brunette should get to see him first. Swallowing hard on that lowering awareness, she studied the carpet, fighting to contain her own dangerously volatile emotions.

'Sorry, I'm late...' Raul drawled with infuriating cool, crossing the cabin to peruse his slumbering son and comment, in a tone of satisfaction and pride, 'Luis is always so peaceful.'

'You've never seen him any other way. Actually, your son kept me up half the night!' Polly complained thinly, before she could think better of it.

Disorientatingly, Raul laughed as he sank lithely down opposite her, forcing her to look at him for the first time. And his sheer stunning impact simply slaugh-

318

tered her carefully prepared outer shield of tranquillity.
Last night he had finally ripped away her defences and
made her betray herself in his arms. Now she discovered
there could be no pretense of indifference or detachment, not when her nails were already digging painfully
into her palms, her skin dampening, her breathing
quickening, her eyes unable to rest any place but on
him.

Those bronzed features, already as familiar to her as
her own yet still possessed of the most intense charismatic appeal. The lean, arrogant nose, the spectacular
dark, deep-set eyes, the wide, hard mouth, the aggressive jawline. Drop-dead gorgeous, and yet every angle
of that darkly handsome face was stamped with immense strength and character.

'At the *hato*...the ranch, the whole household will
revolve round our son,' Raul promised with quiet
amusement. 'He will be spoiled by so many willing
helpers that your nights should be undisturbed from
now on.'

Polly could see no reflection of her own highwire
tension in him. He talked briefly, lightly about their des-
tination. The isolated ranch where his ancestors had
lived for generations was on the cattle plains he called
the *llanos*. It would be very hot, possibly quite wet as
the rainy season wasn't quite over yet, Raul warned in
the sort of bracing, healthy, dismissive tone she suspected the hardy might use to refer to a hellhole they
loved and honoured as home, regardless of its deficiencies.

Soon after the jet had taken off, Raul released his
belt and leant forward to unsnap Polly's. Rising, he
curved strong hands over her taut shoulders to urge her
up into the circle of his arms.

'What are you—?'

'Lesson one on being a proper wife,' Raul murmured with amused dark eyes as he scanned her bewildered face. 'Even when you're really mad at me, you should always look glad to see me when we've been apart.'

That close to that lithe, lean body, Polly trembled. 'You are so changeable,' she condemned shakily. 'You were furious with me last night—'

'I'm just not used to a negative response in the bedroom,' Raul countered with velvet-soft satire. 'And when I've been forced to ride roughshod over my every reservation to become a legally wedded husband, that negative response took some swallowing.'

'But I tried to explain how I felt—'

'Not with an explanation I can take seriously, Polly,' Raul interrupted with conviction. 'You want me. I want you. You have a wedding ring to satisfy your principles. Sex is only a physical hunger, an appetite…not something important enough to become a divisive issue between us.'

Polly blinked, striving to think that through and shrinking from the feelings she experienced in response. *Not important?* An appetite, something to be casually, even carelessly satisfied as and when the need took him? Such terminology ensured that there was little danger of her overestimating the extent of her own attractions, she conceded in fierce pain.

A firm hand caught her chin, tipping up her face, making her meet the passionate gold of his intent gaze. 'If you expect too much from me, I am certain to disappoint you. Don't do that to us. Be satisfied with what we have,' Raul warned almost roughly.

Polly flung her head back. 'And what *do* we have?'

In answer, he attacked on her weakest flank. He lifted

GET 2 BOOKS FREE!

To get your 2 free books, affix this peel-off sticker to the reply card and mail it today!

MIRA® Books, The Brightest Stars in Fiction, presents

Superb collector's editions of the very best books by some of today's best-known authors!

★ **FREE BOOKS!** To introduce you to "The Best of the Best" we'll send you 2 books ABSOLUTELY FREE!

★ **FREE GIFT!** Get an exciting surprise gift FREE!

★ **BEST BOOKS!** "The Best of the Best" brings you the best books by some of today's most popular authors!

GET 2

HOW TO GET YOUR 2 FREE BOOKS AND FREE GIFT!

1. Peel off the MIRA® sticker on the front cover. Place it in the space provided at right. This automatically entitles you to receive two free books and an exciting surprise gift.

2. Send back this card and you'll get 2 "The Best of the Best™" books. These books have a combined cover price of $11.98 or more in the U.S. and $13.98 or more in Canada, but they are yours to keep absolutely FREE!

3. There's no catch. You're under no obligation to buy anything. We charge nothing – ZERO – for your first shipment. And you don't have to make any minimum number of purchases – not even one!

4. We call this line "The Best of the Best" because each month you'll receive the best books by some of today's most popular authors. These authors show up time and time again on all the major bestseller lists and their books sell out as soon as they hit the stores. You'll like the convenience of getting them delivered to your home at our special discount prices . . . and you'll love your *Heart to Heart* subscriber newsletter featuring author news, horoscopes, recipes, book reviews and much more!

5. We hope that after receiving your free books you'll want to remain a subscriber. But the choice is yours – to continue or cancel, anytime at all! So why not take us up on our invitation, with no risk of any kind. You'll be glad you did!

6. And remember...we'll send you a surprise gift ABSOLUTELY FREE just for giving THE BEST OF THE BEST a try.

SPECIAL FREE GIFT!

We'll send you a fabulous surprise gift, absolutely FREE, simply for accepting our no-risk offer!

Visit us online at
www.mirabooks.com

® and TM are registered trademarks of Harlequin Enterprises Limited.

BOOKS FREE!

Hurry!

Return this card promptly to GET 2 FREE BOOKS & A FREE GIFT!

Affix peel-off MIRA sticker here

YES! Please send me the 2 FREE "The Best of the Best" books and FREE gift for which I qualify. I understand that I am under no obligation to purchase anything further, as explained on the back and on the opposite page.

385 MDL DRTA   185 MDL DR59

FIRST NAME	LAST NAME

ADDRESS

APT.#   CITY

STATE/PROV.   ZIP/POSTAL CODE

▼ DETACH AND MAIL CARD TODAY! ▼

(P-BB3-03) ©1998 MIRA BOOKS

THE BEST OF THE BEST™ — Here's How it Works:

Accepting your 2 free books and gift places you under no obligation to buy anything. You may keep the books and gift and return the shipping statement marked "cancel." If you do not cancel, about a month later we will send you 4 additional books and bill you just $4.74 each in the U.S., or $5.24 each in Canada, plus 25¢ shipping & handling per book and applicable taxes if any.* That's the complete price and — compared to cover prices starting from $5.99 each in the U.S. and $6.99 each in Canada — it's quite a bargain! You may cancel at any time, but if you choose to continue, every month we'll send you 4 more books, which you may either purchase at the discount price or return to us and cancel your subscription.

*Terms and prices subject to change without notice. Sales tax applicable in N.Y. Canadian residents will be charged applicable provincial taxes and GST. Credit or Debit balances in a customer's account(s) may be offset by any other outstanding balance owed by or to the customer.

her up into his powerful arms, his sensual mouth took hers and she was lost, filled with the mindless pleasure of simply being there. All she was capable of at that moment was feeling—feeling what *he* could make her feel. The wild, sweet excitement as seductive as a drug, the shivering sensitivity of her own body crushed into the wonderfully masculine strength of his, heady sensation born at every point where they touched.

He released her lips and she discovered she was sprawled across his lap like a wanton, without any memory of how she had got there. Struggling to catch her breath, she stared into the stunning eyes level with her own. Long brown fingers framed her flushed cheekbones and eased her back from him.

'At least we have a starting point, *gatita*. It will be enough,' Raul swore with silken satisfaction. 'Now I think you should get some rest.'

'Rest?' she repeated unevenly.

'You look exhausted, and this is a very long flight.'

'Luis…?' she mumbled.

'I can manage him for a few hours,' Raul asserted with cool confidence.

Polly scrambled clumsily upright again, face burning under the onslaught of a wave of hot colour. Her legs were so wobbly she wasn't sure she could walk, and she felt dizzy, disorientated.

Raul watched her retreat to the sleeping compartment every step of the way, a slightly amused smile beginning to curve his expressive mouth. Polly shut the door and sagged, furious with him, furious with herself. First he treated her like a toy to be played with, then he dismissed her like a child after a goodnight kiss! It made her feel controlled and horribly vulnerable, because she literally didn't know at any given time what Raul was planning to do next. Just because he was experienced...and she wasn't!

Oh, dear heaven, no, she reflected, not wanting to even think about how and where he had gained all that cool sexual assurance. She curled up in a tight ball on the built-in bed. Until Raul had said it, she hadn't realised just how very tired she was. Hopefully she would be better equipped to deal with him when she felt a little more buoyant.

Polly woke up slowly, eyes opening blankly on her surroundings until she finally registered that she was still on the Zaforteza jet. Glancing at her watch, she groaned in disbelief. She had just enjoyed the equivalent of a full night's sleep for the first time since Luis had been born...*Luis!* Pushing her wildly tumbled hair off her brow, Polly rolled off the bed and opened the door back into the main cabin.

A cosy and unexpected little scene met her startled eyes. Chattering in soft, intimate Spanish, Irena was leaning over Raul while he cradled Luis. She was as close to Raul as a lover. Her big brown eyes swept Polly's sleep-flushed face and crumpled clothing in a hostile look at the interruption.

'Why didn't you wake me up sooner?' Polly demanded curtly of Raul.

'You were exhausted, and Irena was happy to help out.' As Raul ran his stunning dark eyes over her tousled appearance, his ebony brows drew together in a slight but highly effective frown. 'You should get changed. We'll be landing at Maiquetia in an hour.'

The stewardess still had one possessive hand resting on Raul's shoulder. Polly was appalled to register that the source of her own ferocious tension was undeniably a hot nasty jealousy which fuelled instantly suspicious thoughts. What had they been doing all those hours while she was asleep and safely out of the way? Was that why Raul had been so keen to send her off to rest? Why did Irena look like a cat that had got the cream?

As Polly studied Raul with a highly combustible mix of suspicion, distrust and embittered shameful longing, he stood up and calmly settled their son into his neat little cot. 'I need a shave.'

'Did you get *any* sleep?' Polly muttered tautly.

'Enough. I don't need much.' Raul strode past her.

'Your husband is a real dynamo, *señora*. He has worked for most of the flight,' the young stewardess shared with a coy look of admiration, tossing her head with a husky little laugh. 'But don't worry, I ensured that he ate and took time out to relax.'

At that news, Polly paled and went back into the sleeping compartment, but Raul had already disappeared into the compact bathroom next door. She lifted the white lightweight dress she had laid out earlier and smoothed abstractedly at the remaining creases while she waited for Raul to emerge. Finally the door opened. She felt absolutely sick by then, suspicion and jealousy making mincemeat of all rational thought.

'Do you sleep with Irena?' That blunt question just erupted from Polly. It was inside her head, but she could not for the life of her work out how the question had got from her brain onto her tongue.

Raul studied her without any expression at all. 'Tell me you didn't ask me that.'

That eerie lack of reaction completely spooked Polly. She crimsoned, pinned her lips together and then opened them again, driven by an overwhelming need for reassurance. 'After what you said the night before last about not behaving like a husband…not to mention the way *she's* behaving around you…naturally I'm suspicious!'

'If I answer that insanely stupid question, I will lose my temper with you,' Raul warned, very soft and low, narrowed dark eyes flaming gold between lush black lashes.

'I don't trust you—'

'I will not live with jealous scenes. In fact nothing would disgust me more or alienate me faster. I do not sleep with my employees. The only woman in my life at present is you,' Raul stated with a feral flash of even white teeth which suggested that even making that admission went severely against the grain.

Polly relaxed ever so slightly. 'I want to believe that, but—'

'The truth is that *you* are jealous of Irena,' Raul condemned with whiplash cool. 'Could that be because she makes the effort to look like an attractive adult woman while you're still dressing like an adolescent who doesn't want to grow up?'

Utterly unprepared for that counter-attack, Polly felt her soft mouth fall wide.

Raul flicked the white sundress off the bed. 'A three-year-old could wear this! Embroidered flowers at the neckline, ruched, shapeless—'

'It *was* bought in a children's department. Ordinary shops don't cater for women my height and size!' Polly shot at him shakily. 'And, since I don't want to dress like a precocious teenybopper, I have to choose the plain outfits.'

Raul shrugged. 'OK…I'll remedy that.'

'I am not jealous of *that woman*…and you needn't think you can change the subject—'

'Oh, I'm not changing it, Polly…I'm just refusing to talk about it,' Raul incised with sudden grimness, shooting her a coldly derisive look. 'Use your brain. Irena is Venezuelan. Venezuelan women are naturally glamorous, confident and flirtatious—'

'My goodness, I can hardly wait to meet the Venezuelan men! What a fun time I'm going to have in your country!' Polly forecast furiously.

In a sudden movement that shook Polly inside out, Raul strode forward and closed a lean and powerful hand round her slender forearm, dwarfing her with his intimidating height and breadth. With his other hand, he pushed up her chin, subjecting her to a splintering look of burning outrage that made her stomach turn an abrupt somersault and her knees go weak and wobbly.

'What is mine is *mine*,' Raul stressed with barely suppressed savagery. 'I'd break you into little pieces for the jaguar to feed on before I would let any other man near you!'

Plunged willy-nilly into an atmosphere suddenly raw with scorching lightning currents of threat, Polly simply gazed up at him like a stupefied rabbit.

With equal abruptness, Raul released her again, a betraying rise of blood delineating his proud cheekbones as he absorbed her bewilderment. 'I'm not a jealous man,' he asserted in a roughened undertone. 'But I am very conscious of my honour, and of my son's need for stability in his life.'

Polly nodded like a little wooden marionette, afraid to move too close to the hungry flickering flames of a bonfire.

Raul was pale now beneath his golden skin, his superb bone structure harshly prominent. 'I'm sorry if I overreacted…'

If, Polly reflected dizzily. Such a civilized term after so violent a loss of temper, brief though it had been. And she had discovered another double standard. The man who would be owned by no woman fully believed he owned his wife like a possession. But, ironically, what troubled her most at that instant was the stark awareness that she had really upset Raul. Yet she hadn't a clue why her silly sarcastic comments should have exploded his cool, controlled façade into a shocking blaze of primitive fury.

'Put it down to jet lag,' Raul added almost jerkily, pushing long brown fingers restively through his glossy blue-black hair. 'You are not *that* kind of woman. If you had been, I would never have agreed to marry you.'

What kind of woman? The unfaithful type? What a peculiar thought for a male like Raul to harbour! For, on the face of it, Raul Zaforteza was a real heartbreaker, possessed of every quality most likely to hold a woman's attention. Personality, looks, sex-appeal, wealth, power. How many women would risk losing Raul by betraying him in another man's bed?

'I will join you at the ranch in a couple of days,' Raul murmured flatly as he moved past her—suddenly, she registered, keen to abandon the dialogue…and *her*? The suspicion hurt.

'Join me?' Polly echoed uncertainly. 'What are you talking about? Where are you going?'

'Tonight I'm afraid I'll have to stay in Caracas. Tomorrow I'll be in Maracaibo, and possibly the next day as well. I have several urgent business matters to deal with. I've been abroad for many weeks,' he reminded her drily.

Alone again, Polly freshened up and slid with a distinct lack of enthusiasm into the simple white cotton

dress. When she returned to the main cabin she could
not avoid noticing Irena's frequent starstruck glances in
Raul's direction, and her pronounced need to hover at
his elbow as eager as a harem slave to satisfy his every
wish. No longer did she marvel at her own suspicions
earlier. The brunette had a real giant-sized crush on
Raul. And possibly Raul was so accustomed to inviting
female flattery and exaggerated attention that he genuinely hadn't noticed.

'OK, so there *is* a problem,' Raul breathed, disconcerting Polly with a dark satiric glance of acknowledgement in Irena's direction while she was gathering
up Luis's scattered possessions at the far end of the
cabin. 'We were both fifty per cent wrong, but, believe
me, I have never given her the slightest encouragement.'

Polly nodded in embarrassed silence, feeling like an
idiot over the fuss she had made but fearful of re-
opening the subject lest she make things even worse.

Raul parted from her at the airport as coolly and politely as a distant acquaintance, a shuttered look in his
brilliant dark eyes. Irena escorted Polly onto the light
plane which would whisk her and her son out to the
Zaforteza ranch. Polly's heart was already sinking.

Would it always be like this with Raul? Would she
never *know* Raul? Would she never understand what
went on inside that complex and clever head of his?
And was it possible that that 'urgent business' he had
mentioned had merely been a convenient excuse to
leave her? How humiliating it was to suspect that Raul
had actually intended to accompany her to his home
until she'd treated him to that foolish scene! After all,
hadn't he told her up front that jealousy disgusted him,
and that nothing would drive him away quicker?

*   *   *

It was lashing with rain when Polly clambered off the plane, protected by a giant umbrella extended over her and Luis by the pilot. He helped her into the waiting four-wheel drive. Neither he nor the driver appeared to have a word of English. Polly was now feeling less guilty and more angry with Raul. How did she think it felt for her to arrive at the *estancia* alone, where nobody knew her and where very possibly nobody would even be able to speak to her?

Through the streaming windows she caught glimpses of a large spreading collection of buildings. Palm trees were being battered in the torrential downpour. And yet the heat was intense, the humidity high. A hellhole, Polly decided, in the right mood to make that snap judgement. Raul had posted them out to the boonies to live in a hellhole and just gone on his own sweet way, just as he was used to doing, just as he no doubt expected to *continue* doing...

A huge colonial-style house adorned by fancy verandahs and an upper balcony wreathed with climbers loomed out of the rain. Clutching Luis like a parcel, Polly made a dive through the torrent when the car door opened, fled up the steps and surged indoors into the mercifully air-conditioned cool without a single sidewise glance or pause.

She had a split second to catch her breath on the magnificence of the vast reception hall she stood in before she focused on the huddle of female servants sheltering behind the front door, all staring at her and the baby she held wide-eyed. Silence hung for the space of twenty seconds.

A tall and stunningly beautiful blonde strolled into view. Frowning regally at Polly, she shot something at her in Spanish.

'I'm sorry, I don't speak—'

'I am the Condesa Melina D'Agnolo. Where is Raul?' the woman demanded in accented but perfect English.

'Still in Caracas.' Conscious of the staff now sidling out of a door to the left as fast as mice escaping a cat, Polly gazed enquiringly at the other woman. Sheathed in a superb cerise suit, glittering jewellery adding to her imperious air of well-bred exclusivity, the lady exuded angry impatience.

'*Caracas?*' It was an infuriated shriek of disappointment.

As the shrill sound echoed off the high ceiling, Luis jerked in fright and let out a loud, fretful wail.

Melina D'Agnolo stalked forward and surveyed him with unconcealed distaste. 'So this is the child I have heard rumours about. It *does* exist. Well, what are you waiting for? Stop it making that horrible noise!'

'He's just hungry—'

'When will Raul arrive?'

'In a couple of days.'

'Then I shall wait for him,' Melina announced, eyes hardening as Luis continued to cry noisily in spite of Polly's efforts to console him. 'But you will keep that child upstairs, out of my sight and hearing.'

'I'm afraid I have no intention—' Polly began angrily.

'I will not tolerate impertinence. You will do as you are told or you will very soon find yourself out of a job!' Melina informed her. 'In Raul's absence, I am in charge here.'

Realising that she had been mistaken for an employee, Polly raised her head high, intending to explain that she was Raul's wife. But the other woman had already walked away to utter a sharp command in Spanish. A middle-aged woman in a black dress appeared so quickly she must have been waiting somewhere nearby. Melina issued what sounded like a staccato stream of instructions.

The older woman glanced in open dismay at Polly.

'The housekeeper will take you upstairs to the nursery. You can eat up there. I don't want to be bothered by the child...is that understood?'

'Why do you say you're in charge here? Are you related to Raul?' Polly enquired stiffly, and stood her ground.

Melina's green eyes narrowed with suggestive languor, full lips pouting into a coolly amused smile. 'I've never been asked to identify myself in this house before. Raul and I have been intimate friends for a very long time.'

Every scrap of colour drained from Polly's face. There was no mistaking the meaning of that proud declaration. Her stomach curdled. It was a judgement on her, Polly thought sickly. She had foolishly made that scene over the infatuated Irena and now fate had served up her punishment: she was being confronted by the real thing. A genuine rival...

'Why are you looking at me like that?' Melina D'Agnolo enquired haughtily.

'I think this is going to be embarrassing,' Polly muttered.

Melina dealt her an impatient frown of incomprehension.

'Raul and I got married a month ago.'

The thunderous silence seemed to reverberate in Polly's ears, and then Luis started crying again.

The svelte blonde stared at Polly with raised brows,

her incredulity unfeigned. 'It isn't possible that you are *married* to Raul—'

'I'm afraid it is…' Polly cut in, and switched her attention ruefully to the housekeeper still waiting for her.

The older woman murmured gently, 'Let me take the little one upstairs and feed him for you, *señora*.'

Grateful for the chance to remove Luis from the hostile atmosphere, Polly laid her son in the housekeeper's arms with a strained smile.

'*Señora?*' Melina D'Agnolo echoed the designation with stinging scorn. 'I think we need to talk.'

Raul, where are you when I need you? Polly thought in furious discomfiture. This was his department, not hers! How could Raul possibly have overlooked the necessity of telling his mistress that he had acquired a wife? Polly turned reluctantly back to face the angry blonde. 'I don't think that would be a good idea.'

'If you prefer it, we can talk out here, where all the staff can hear us.'

Rigid with tension, Polly followed Melina into a gracious reception room filled with superb antique furniture. 'I don't see that we *have* anything to say to each other—'

'Obviously Raul married you because of the child. The oldest ploy of all. I expect you think you've been very clever.' Melina loosed a grim little laugh. 'Yes, I'm shocked, and I don't mind admitting it. Ten years ago Raul loved me, but he *still* wouldn't marry me, so I married someone else to teach him a lesson!'

Wanting no share of such confidences, Polly hovered, stiff with strain.

'So you needn't tell me that Raul loves you because I wouldn't believe it! I am the *only* woman Raul has ever loved,' Melina informed her with blistering confidence. 'I have never been concerned by his other little flirtations.'

'That's your business, not mine.'

'Your marriage won't last six months,' Melina said with dismissive certainty. 'Raul cherishes his freedom. When my husband died, I chose to be patient. I have never interfered with Raul's life—'

'Then don't do it now,' Polly slotted in tightly.

'If you think that is a possibility, you're even more of a child than you look!' Melina threw her a scornful look of superiority. 'And next month you'll be expected to deal with two hundred guests over the fiesta weekend. There'll be a rodeo, a friendly polo match and a non-stop party. Are you used to mixing with the wealthy élite? How good are you on a horse? I'm usually Raul's hostess, but now the job's yours…and if it doesn't go like clockwork, he'll be furious.'

Polly had paled. 'I'm sure I'll manage—'

'Raul will come back to me…of course he will. It's only a matter of time,' Melina asserted with contemptuous green eyes. 'If you're out of your depth with me, how much more out of your depth are you with him? I almost feel sorry for you. When Raul's bored, he is cruel and critical and callous—'

'I think it's time you left,' Polly interrupted flatly.

'If I were you, I wouldn't mention this meeting,' the blonde murmured sweetly as she strolled to the door. 'Raul detests jealous scenes. It would be much wiser for you to pretend that this meeting never took place.'

'Why should you be kind enough to give me that warning?'

Melina laughed unpleasantly. 'You already have all

the problems you can handle. I shall enjoy watching you struggle to fill my shoes!'

Polly watched the blonde stalk across the hall and up the imposing staircase. She released her breath very slowly but she still felt utterly stunned. Melina D'Agnolo had been a severe shock. Raul's mistress—proud and unashamed of her position in his life and in no hurry to vacate his bed.

And one look at Melina had been sufficient to tell Polly that her misapprehension about the pretty stewardess on board the jet had been laughable. Melina was much more convincing in the role of mistress. Melina with her exquisite face, fabulous figure and tremendous elegance and poise. Mature, classy and sophisticated. Raul's kind of woman. And what even the greatest optimist would acknowledge as *seriously* challenging competition...

No, Polly scolded herself fiercely. She wasn't going to allow herself to start thinking that way. Raul had said that she was the only woman in his life now, and he had given her no cause to doubt his sincerity. OK, she had just suffered through a horribly embarrassing encounter and been forced to endure the other woman's spiteful attacks, but Melina would pack and depart and she would never have to see her again. She would put Melina right back out of her mind. Raul's past was none of her business, she reminded herself staunchly.

Upstairs, Polly wandered across a huge landing and picked a passageway. Finally, after a couple of wrong choices, she peered into a nursery as exquisitely furnished as a room in a glossy magazine. A crowd of smiling, whispering female staff surrounded the imposing antique four-poster cot. Freshly clothed and clearly content, Luis nestled within the cot's hand-embroidered bedding like a little king, giving an audience and basking in all the attention.

'It has been so long since there was a child here,' the housekeeper confided.

'Was this Raul's cot?' Polly asked, smiling.

The older woman looked away uncomfortably. 'No, *señora*...but it was his father's.'

Briefly wondering what she had said to disconcert the woman, Polly was led down a corridor lined with fabulous oil paintings and into a magnificent big bedroom. Realising that it had stopped raining, Polly opened the French windows and stepped out onto the sun-drenched balcony to gaze out appreciatively on the beautifully landscaped gardens. Lush lawns and colourful vegetation were shaded by clumps of graceful mature trees. In the distance an architectural extravaganza of a small building complete with turrets caught her attention.

'What's that used for?' she asked her companion.

The older woman stiffened. 'It is not used for anything, *señora*.'

'What a waste...it's so pretty.'

'It is full of ghosts, not a good place.' The housekeeper retreated back indoors, seemingly unaware that she had said anything that might cause Polly to stare after her in wide-eyed surprise and curiosity. 'I will fix you some breakfast, *señora*. You must be hungry.'

That evening, Polly rested back in the huge sunken bath in the *en suite* bathroom and felt like a queen lying in solitary state. She poked a set of pink toes up through the bubbles covering the surface of the water and sighed.

Melina D'Agnolo had vanished like the bad fairy. Only when she had disappeared had it occurred to Polly to wonder *how* she had gone, and to where. By car, by plane? The Zaforteza ranch was set in miles and miles of cattle country.

In the afternoon Polly had walked out to the furthest edge of the gardens and seen the plains stretching as far as the eye could reach in every direction, their monotony broken up by occasional clumps of trees, stretches of flood water that glinted in the hot sun and ground that seemed to sweep up and merge with the endless blue sky.

She closed her eyes and let herself think about Raul. Would he phone? Once she had told him not to bother and he hadn't given her a chance to say no a second time. But how the heck could she possibly measure up to a woman as gorgeous as Melina? The fear crept in and she tried to squash the thought and the feeling simultaneously.

'Lesson two on being a proper wife...' a silken drawl imparted lazily from the door. 'If you have to be in the bath when I come home, make it one I can share. Omit the heavily scented bubbles.'

CHAPTER SEVEN

POLLY'S mouth fell open at the same instant as her eyes shot wide. Raul stood in the doorway, a sizzling smile of amusement slashing his mouth as he absorbed her astonishment.

'But you look kind of cute…' Raul conceded, brilliant dark eyes roaming with unconcealed interest over the rose-tipped breasts pertly breaking through the bubbles for his scrutiny.

Wrenching free of her paralysed stillness, Polly sat up in a frantic rush and hugged her knees to her chest. Raul gave an extravagant wince. 'Sometimes you act like a ten-year-old, *gatita.*'

'Couldn't you have knocked on the door?' Polly demanded defensively.

'The door wasn't even closed,' he reminded her drily, and he leant back against the door, slowly pushing it shut, as if he was making some kind of statement.

Sooner than ask him what he was doing, and already having discarded as too dangerously provocative the idea of asking him to step outside while she vacated the bath and covered herself, Polly studied him anxiously from below her dark lashes.

A tide of terrifying longing swept over her in a stormy wave. Her own heartbeat thundered inside her ears, and all the time her eyes were roaming all over him in hungry, helpless little darts. He was so incredibly tall in his light grey suit, his white shirt throwing his bronzed skin into exotic prominence, his luxuriant black hair gleaming under the recessed lights above, eyes glinting wicked gold in that lean, dark, devastating face.

'You missed me,' Raul purred, like a jungle cat basking in sunlight, his husky accent thickening and sending a trail of reaction down her taut spinal cord.

'For heaven's sake, how could I have missed you? I last saw you in the early hours of this morning!' Polly snapped, but it was a challenge to snap when it was so outrageously difficult to even breathe normally in his radius.

'You don't just need lessons on how to be a proper wife...you need a bloody intensive training course!' Raul shot back at her with shocking abruptness. 'What does it take to get a pleasant response from you? Thumbscrews?'

Jolted by that sudden blaze of temper, Polly gazed up at him strickenly. She felt the most awful stinging surge of tears threatening at the back of her eyes. Hurriedly she bent her head. Maybe meeting your gorgeous mistress spoilt my day, she almost slung accusingly, but caution restrained her.

'Maybe I'm not used to sharing a bathroom,' she muttered ruefully.

'Then this is where we will start,' Raul delivered.

Start what, where? Polly wondered in complete confusion.

'*Dios*...I can hardly believe I flew back here just to *be* with you!'

'Did you? I thought your urgent business took precedence.'

'Possibly the prospect of getting my bride horizontal on the marital bed had greater appeal.'

'Oh...' Polly said after a startled pause. 'Do you have to be so crude?'

Without the slightest warning, strong hands curved under her arms and a split second later she was airborne. Raul straightened and held her ruthlessly imprisoned in mid-air as she dripped water and bubbles everywhere, her shaken face aghast. 'Not so shrewish now, are you?' he murmured with unconcealed amusement.

'Please put me back in the water,' Polly mumbled pleadingly.

Raul gazed into her shrinking blue eyes and slowly lowered her back into the bath with careful hands. 'You're such a baby sometimes...I wasn't going to hurt you!' he breathed in stark reproach.

Still trembling, Polly hugged the far side of the bath. 'I don't know why I'm so nasty with you,' she lied—because she knew very well. 'I'm not usually like this with anybody.'

'You were so sweet in Vermont. I didn't even know you had a temper, never mind that viper's tongue,' Raul admitted wryly. 'What went wrong?'

You did. At that stupid question Polly was tempted to throw something at him. She had fallen hopelessly in love, more deeply in love than she had ever believed possible, and nothing had ever been the same since. He didn't love her, he didn't believe in love, and she couldn't risk letting him find out how she really felt about him. Given an ounce of such ego-boosting encouragement, he would walk all over her and take her for granted the way he had in Vermont.

The female sex had spoilt Raul. For minimum input he had always received maximum benefit—everything on his terms, everything the way *he* wanted it. And their marriage still felt like a deadweight threatening ball and chain to him. He didn't have to tell her that. She *knew* it. She marvelled that he should believe that taking her to bed would miraculously change anything, particularly when he had already spelt out the fact that he didn't rate sex any higher than an 'appetite'.

And where did that leave her? The virginal bride with novelty value? A fresh body for his enjoyment?

Raul discarded his jacket on a chair and tossed his tie on top of it. Emerging from her insecure reverie, Polly gaped. Shoes and socks were summarily discarded.

'What are you doing?'

Raul sent her a gleaming glance of intent. 'Losing your virginity is not akin to a visit to a sadistic dentist.'

'What would you know about it?'

A wolfish grin slashed his mobile mouth. 'I'll fill you in on my impressions tomorrow morning.'

Off came his shirt, to be carelessly discarded in a heap. Polly's throat clogged up at sight of that magnificent brown torso and the triangle of all male dark curling hair outlining his powerful pectoral muscles. 'Is this my anatomy lesson?' she whispered shakily.

'You need one?' As free of inhibition as she was repressed, Raul flicked loose his belt and slid out of his well-cut trousers.

Although Polly wanted to look away, she couldn't. Her throat thickened, her mouth running dry. Her mesmerised attention locked on to the silky furrow of hair running down over his flat, taut stomach to disappear tantalisingly beneath the band of a pair of black briefs.

'You're beginning to embarrass *me*,' Raul censured mockingly.

Caught staring, Polly twisted her head away, cheeks flaming. 'I don't think anything embarrasses you!' she condemned unevenly.

'You really *are* shy...I thought it was an act in

Vermont,' Raul confessed without warning. 'You were so open and forthright in every other way—'

'I don't put on acts,' Polly protested feverishly. 'I can't help the way I was brought up any more than you can.'

'What's that supposed to mean?' Raul breathed with sudden brooding darkness.

Involuntarily she shivered, catching the warning nuances in his accented drawl and spooked by what she could not understand. 'My father believed girls should be modest and quiet and strait-laced, and my godmother agreed with him—'

'Whatever happened to the "quiet"?' Raul cut in with unhesitating humour.

Her momentary ripple of foreboding ebbed, only to be replaced by a more pressing urge to leap out of the bath as Raul stepped in. Arms wrapped tightly round her knees, Polly twisted her head back round and slung him an accusing glance as he settled fluidly down on the other side of the bath and rested his burnished dark head back against the inset cushioning.

'Look, why can't we just do it in bed like other people?' she suddenly launched at him in mortified condemnation. 'I think you're going out of your way to make this more difficult for me!'

Dealing her a briefly bemused appraisal, Raul suddenly flung his head back and burst out laughing without restraint. '*Caramba, cielito*—'

'That is *it*...that is *finally* it!' Polly raked at him, chagrin tipping over into a sudden empowering rage that enabled her to begin rising without any constraining fear of exposing her own body.

Raul leant forward and caught her hand, tipping her sufficiently off-balance to ensure that she was powerless to resist the ease with which he reached up his other hand and tumbled her down on top of him, water splashing everywhere.

Panting furiously for breath, Polly pulled herself back from him. 'Let go of me!'

Raul regarded her with deceptive languor. 'I wasn't actually planning to consummate our marriage here...I just wanted to talk...'

'T-talk?' Polly parroted weakly as she subsided back beneath the water to conceal herself, carefully avoiding the slightest contact with his long extended limbs.

'No need to panic...at least...not yet,' Raul drawled smoothly, the golden gleam deep in his shimmering dark eyes increasing the colour in her hot face. 'In my innocence I believed that this was a comparatively mild first step towards greater intimacy.'

'Do you normally just *talk* in the bath with your women?' Polly practically snarled in her discomfiture, knowing that any plea of innocence was not to be trusted in this instance, perfectly well aware that Raul was highly amused by her enervated state.

The golden gleam vanished, leaving her gazing in sudden fear into wintry cool dark eyes. '*Infierno!* You're obsessed. Jealousy is a very destructive thing. Do you want to destroy us before we even begin with these constant attacks?'

Pale now, Polly just closed her eyes. In the space of a moment she saw a dozen beautiful female faces skim cruelly through her mind's eye. Only then did she grasp the source of her jealousy, the day when it had been born to increase the bitterness she had experienced after leaving Vermont. To satisfy her driving need to know more about the father of her child, she had gone to the library and scanned through newspaper gossip pages and glossy society magazines...

Time after time she had come on photos of Raul with some gorgeous blonde babe on his arm. And that was the day when she had finally accepted how pitiful her love was, how hopelessly without foundation or any prospect of reciprocation.

Then, months on, to have that impression of Raul as a heartless womaniser reinforced all over again—to watch Raul leave that London clinic to walk into another woman's arms, to live through that mortifying misunderstanding about the stewardess and then the very same day to be confronted with the horrendous real shock of Melina D'Agnolo. Was it any wonder that she was desperately insecure, afraid to trust Raul and lashing out in an attempt to protect herself from further pain?

'I won't live like this with any woman,' Raul breathed with terrifying quietness. 'It's like trying to fight an invisible enemy... Whatever I do you'll always be suspicious!'

As he pulled himself upright, her lashes lifted. Stepping out of the bath, Raul snatched a fleecy towel from the rail and strode back into the bedroom without a backward glance.

And, just as suddenly, Polly's defensive attitude fell away. She saw a marriage which hadn't even begun now going down the drain without fanfare. She saw the chance she had been given thrown away out of proud defiance and a refusal to face her own insecurities and faults.

Raul hadn't made love to her in Vermont. *She* had been the one who had misinterpreted *his* intentions. He had had the right to pursue other relationships. His free-

dom had been his own and she had had no claim on
him. That was the reality which she had failed to accept
all these months because *she* had fallen in love. And
what was she doing now but driving Raul away from
her, in spite of the fact that he had given her no cause
to distrust him?

In a panic, now that she had seen herself at fault,
Polly climbed out of the bath, tugged a black towelling
robe off a wall hook and hurriedly dug her arms into
the too long sleeves.

'Raul…I'm sorry!' she called in advance, afraid he
might already have left the bedroom beyond.

'Forget it…I need some fresh air.'

Rolling up the sleeves of what she now realised had
to be his robe, Polly edged apprehensively round the
door and peered out. Damp black wildly tousled hair
flopping over his bronzed brow, Raul was zipping up a
pair of skintight cream jodhpurs.

In silence, she watched him yank highly polished
leather boots out of a cupboard and sink down on the
chaise longue at the foot of the bed to pull them on.
'You're going riding?' she muttered uncertainly. 'But
it's getting dark.'

'Get back in your bath with your bubbles,' Raul advised with brooding satire. 'Immerse that little body you
protect so assiduously…and leave me alone.'

'Look…I said I was sorry.' Polly lifted her chin. 'Do
I have to crawl?'

Raul lifted his dark head and regarded her directly
for the first time since she had entered the room. She
was shaken by the black brooding distance etched with
clarity in his spectacular dark eyes. 'How are you on
disappearing?' he drawled in a tone like a silken whip-

lash. 'Because right now, I just don't want to be around you.'

Polly flinched from that brutal candour, the flush of pink in her cheeks receding to leave her paper-pale. Without warning, Raul was like a dark, intimidating stranger.

'So go back in the bathroom before I say anything else to hurt your sensitive feelings,' Raul told her harshly. 'I'm not in the mood to control my tongue!'

'I'm not afraid of what you have to say.'

'Then why the hell are you goading me like this?' Raul splintered back at her in frustration. 'I don't like being needled. I especially don't like snide comments. If you have something to say to me, have the guts to say it loud and clear, because I have no time for anything else!'

Melina loomed like the bad fairy in her mind's eye. Polly wanted to defend herself. She wanted to explain how upsetting and threatening she had found that encounter. But she had a greater fear that the mention of her own feelings in relation to yet another woman and him would be a dangerously provocative act that would simply send him through the roof. As he gazed expectantly back at her, Raul's eyes burned as gold as the flames in the heart of a fire.

'I haven't anything to say,' she stated, in what she hoped was a soothing tone likely to defuse the situation.

But, disconcertingly, that tone had the same effect as throwing paraffin on a bonfire. Raul sprang up, throwing her a blistering glance of derision. 'You have the backbone of a jellyfish! I'm ashamed to be married to such a spiritless excuse for a woman!'

'Maybe...m-maybe I have more control over my

temper than you have,' Polly stammered through teeth clenched with restraint.

Raul slashed an imperious hand through the air in savage dismissal. 'This morning I left you at the airport. I walked away from conflict. I've spent the last ten years doing that quite happily. I watched my father do that all his life with women,' he grated in a raw, hostile undertone. 'And then it dawned on me that I was married to you, and that if I start closing you out when you anger me, what future can this marriage have?'

'Raul, I—'

'*Cállate!* I am talking,' Raul broke in with supreme contempt as he yanked a garment out of a drawer. 'I find your continuing jealousy irrational and disturbing. And for someone so repressed she shrinks from even sharing a bath with her own husband, I find it even stranger that you should want to know what I might or might not have done with other women when I was answerable to nobody!'

Lips bloodlessly compressed to prevent them from trembling like the rest of her shivering, woefully weak body, Polly watched him pull on a white polo shirt and whispered shamefacedly. 'I don't want to know…' She was stumbling wretchedly. 'I *mean*—'

'Never again will I make the smallest sacrifice to make this marriage work!' Raul swore with hard emphasis. 'I have my son…what else do I need? Certainly not a silly little girl who cowers at the idea of making love with me!'

'Raul, please…' Polly muttered strickenly as he strode towards the door and flung it wide.

All volatile energy and movement now, he yelled something down the corridor. On cottonwool legs, Polly followed him to the threshold and watched one of the maids coming at an anxious run.

Raul rapped out instructions in Spanish. The maid bobbed her head in instant acquiescence and then sped off down the corridor again.

Raul sent Polly a smouldering look of derision. 'You need no longer fear my unwelcome approaches, *mi esposa*. The maid will convey your possessions to another room!'

CHAPTER EIGHT

POLLY paced the floor in the beautiful guest room the housekeeper had allotted to her without once meeting her eyes. The shame of so new a bride being ejected from the marital bedroom had been fully felt on Polly's behalf.

Over the next couple of hours, Polly ran the gamut of fiercer emotions than she had ever known. She had never come across anyone with a temper as volatile as Raul's. She had never dreamt that Raul might speak to her like that—even worse, *look* at her as he had. As if she was nothing to him, less than nothing, even, nothing but a pain and a nuisance, beneath his notice and utterly unworthy of any further attention.

She went from rage at his having made such a public spectacle of their differences to sudden all-engulfing pain at the sheer strength of that rejection. They had been together perhaps twenty-four hours, yet everything had fallen apart. A voice in her mind just screamed that she couldn't cope, couldn't handle the situation. She wanted to take Luis and run...run and make Raul *sorry*, she registered. The tears flowed then, in shame at the manner in which her thoughts went round and round in circles but never lost the need to keep Raul at the very centre.

Calmer, if no more happy once she had cried, she took a good, hard look at her own behaviour and didn't like what she saw. And when she exerted herself to try and see things from Raul's point of view, she just groaned and squirmed at her own foolish prickly resentment and insecurity.

Gorgeous, woman-killing, much sought-after and fêted guy becomes unwilling husband but makes decent effort to paper over the cracks. What with? Sex. What else? He doesn't *know* anything else. Every other woman can't wait to get him between the sheets to check out that fabled reputation, but his bride is inexplicably and therefore offensively reluctant. Not only reluctant but also sarcastic, jealous, and seemingly incapable of behaving like a mature adult committed to getting their marriage of convenience up and running.

And why had she behaved like an idiot?

Because she loved him, Polly conceded painfully, and she wanted, needed to be so much more than a convenient body in Raul's bed. And, worst of all, a sexually ignorant partner when he had to be accustomed to lovers with a considerable degree of sophistication and expertise, not to mention lithe and perfect bodies. So, out of stubborn pride and resentment over her own sense of inadequacy, she had driven him away.

If she had told him straight off about that clash with Melina D'Agnolo, at least he would have understood why she was in such a prickly mood. But she had missed her opportunity and knew that it would be an act of insanity to risk opening such a subject with Raul now. In fact even the thumbscrews he had mentioned wouldn't dredge Melina's name from her lips...not when he already saw her as an obsessively jealous woman.

And all his self-preserving male antennae were in perfect working order, Polly acknowledged at the lowest ebb of self-honesty. She was and had been jealous, and no doubt would be jealous again, because jealousy

thrived on insecurity. And she *did* want to own Raul,
body and soul.

Seeing how swollen her eyes were in the mirror, she
splashed her face over and over again with cold water.
Then she washed her hair, put on a little light make-up,
some perfume and slid into one of the silk nighties he
had given her. Creeping down the corridor like a burglar
sneaking under the cover of darkness, she walked back
into the marital bedroom and clambered into the big
wide bed to watch the moonlight slant across the ceiling
through the undrawn curtains.

She must have fallen asleep, because she woke with
a start later, hearing running feet and then raised anxious voices in the corridor outside. Thrusting her tumbled hair off her sleepy face, she switched on the light
and lurched out of bed. Opening the bedroom door, she
peered out.

A clutch of gesticulating staff surrounded Raul.
Liberally daubed in mud, and far from his usual immaculate self, he looked frantic, shooting out questions
at volume, expressive hands moving at volatile speed
to indicate his level of angry concern.

'Raul...?' Polly called worriedly as he paused for
breath. 'What's wrong?'

The staff huddle twisted round with a general look
of astonishment.

'Where the hell have you been?' Raul thundered at
her accusingly.

'In bed...sleeping,' Polly mumbled in bewilderment.
'Why?'

'*Why?*' Raul roared back in apparent disbelief.

The staff were now all slowly rolling back like a quiet
tide in the direction of the stairs. Raul strode past her

into the bedroom, shooting the rumpled bed a speaking glance of seeming amazement.

'Lesson three on being a proper wife.' Polly whispered her prepared opening sentence before she could lose her nerve. 'Never let the sun go down on a row.'

'It's rising…the sun,' Raul informed her half under his breath and, bending down, he scooped her unresisting body up into his arms, crossed the room and settled her back on the bed.

Frowning, not following that oddly strained if true remark, as the dawn light was indeed already burnishing the night sky, Polly gazed uncertainly up at him. 'What was going on out there?'

Dark colour flared over his superb cheekbones and his wide, sensual mouth hardened. 'You weren't where you were supposed to be. I thought you'd bolted again.'

'B-bolted where?' Polly asked, with some difficulty squashing the incautious giggle trying to break free of her taut throat.

'How do I know? There's two helicopters out there, a whole collection of cars, a stable full of horses! If you wanted to bolt, it wouldn't be much of a challenge to find the means,' Raul informed her grimly as he stood over her, six foot plus of dark, menacing authority. 'My bed was the last place I expected to find you!'

So he hadn't even looked. He had jumped to conclusions. He had checked the bedroom she should have been in and immediately raised the alarm. Although she was deeply embarrassed by that candid admission that he hadn't dreamt she would have the nerve to take up residence in his bed, she was also rather relieved to register that Raul was not omnipotent. He could not yet forecast her every move. But she turned her head away from the light, fearful that he would see too much in her expressive face.

'Do you want me to go?' she asked with studied casualness.

'No…I can recognise an olive tree when I'm handed one.'

'You mean an olive *branch*,' she contradicted gently.

'No, when you put on silk, scent, mascara and lipstick for my benefit, and arrange yourself like a little bridal sacrifice in my bed…' Raul murmured almost roughly as he stared down at her, brilliant eyes reflecting only the light in his darkly handsome features '…it's definitely not just a branch, it's a whole tree…in fact, it might well be the equivalent of an orchard.' He thrust impatient fingers through his disordered hair and shook his head ruefully. '*Dios mío*…what am I talking about?'

Standing there, talking like that, he seemed disturbingly different. He was still regarding her with a piercing, narrow-eyed intensity that didn't seem to be making him any more comfortable than it was making her. In fact, he looked pretty pale beneath his healthy bronze skin. As Polly was already achingly self-conscious about lying there in his bed, his reactions were increasing her anxiety level. Here she was, offering an invitation to the best of her ability, but maybe he no longer even *wanted* that invitation!

The tense silence seemed to scream in her ears.

'You must've been out riding for a long time…' she commented, desperate to break that nerve-straining quiet.

'I went some distance. I called in with…with a neighbour.' His stubborn jawline clenched, handsome mouth compressing, strong face suddenly shadowing as he strode towards the bathroom. 'I'm filthy. I need a shower.'

Pink-cheeked now, Polly studied him the same way a crossword addict without talent studies the *crème de la crème* of challenges, desperate for a hint of true inspiration. He stepped out of view, and she listened then to the strangely intimate sounds of a man undressing: the thud of his boots hitting the tiled floor, the snap as he presumably undid the waistband of his jodhpurs...

Oh, dear heaven, if Raul no longer even wanted her to share his bed, how did she get out of this situation without losing face?

'Maybe I should go back to my room,' Polly practically whispered.

Sudden silence fell.

Bare-chested and barefoot, Raul appeared in the doorway, all rampant virility with rumpled hair and the jodhpurs which had an indecently faithful fit to his long, lean thighs undone at his waist. 'Whatever you feel most comfortable doing.'

On receipt of that refusal to state an opinion either way—which from a male of Raul's domineering temperament was particularly hard to take—Polly blinked in bemused chagrin.

'But you can sleep here just as easily,' Raul pointed out with a careless shrug.

'Fine...' Polly managed to splutter, turning over on her side to glower with stinging eyes at the dawn filling the sky with such vibrant colour. The unfeeling louse didn't *want* an orchard of olive branches. Her so sophisticated, sexy and immensely self-assured husband was trying to let her down gently. And now she was stuck, because if she jumped out of bed and fled she was going to look really stupid and pathetic! And, furthermore, Raul would then work out for himself that her olive branch had been rather more emotionally motivated than she'd chosen to admit.

She listened to the shower switching off and grimaced. The lights went out. The mattress gave at the other side of the bed.

'If you sleep any closer to the edge, you might fall out,' Raul remarked lazily.

'I don't want to get in your way!' Polly snapped childishly.

Raul released his breath in an audible hiss. 'You don't have anything to fear, *gatita*. I realise that I've been...inconsiderate,' he selected after an uncharacteristic hesitation.

Stiff as a board, Polly strove to work out the intent of that unexpected admission.

'Naturally I want you to be happy,' Raul informed her out of the blue.

'Do you?'

'Of course. Why so amazed?' Raul queried. 'What else would I want?'

'You want the best for Luis,' Polly breathed, not quite levelly. 'I understand that—'

'*Dios*...when I thought you'd gone I never even thought to check on our son!' His slightly dazed tone was that of a male belatedly making that connection and not best pleased by it.

Good heavens, Polly thought in shock over that astonishing admission. Raul had actually thought of *her* first, put *her* first? Instantly it was as if a tight little knot of resentment was jerked loose inside her. She no longer felt like an unwanted wife, to be tolerated only because their son needed his mother. And she wondered when Raul's single-minded focus on Luis had stretched to include her as a person of some import in his own life. But she really didn't care *when* that minor miracle had taken place, she was just so very grateful that it had.

'I wouldn't bolt again…as you put it,' she shared awkwardly.

'I can forgive you for Vermont. That was understandable. The clinic too…you panicked. That's all in the past now.'

Polly turned over. 'But coming here was still a big thing for me…'

'No less a challenge for me, *querida*.' Raul reached for her clenched fingers where they lay above the sheet, and calmly tugged her across the divide between them.

Her breath caught in her throat as he eased her into his arms. Gazing up at him, she drank in the hard bones forming that lean, strong face, her stomach fluttering, her heartbeat racing, every fibre of her body pitched in anticipation of his next move.

Raul rubbed a blunt forefinger gently over the ripe fullness of her parted lips and looked down at her. A sigh feathered in her throat, her eyes widening, dark blue pools of unconscious invitation. 'I…I was just nervous earlier,' she confided.

'You have beautiful eyes. That was the first thing I ever noticed about you.'

'In Vermont?'

'I saw you long before then.'

Her brow furrowed. 'But *how*?'

'Your photograph, then your initial interview with my lawyer. Trick mirror. I was in the office next door,' he confided without apology.

'Devious,' she said breathlessly, her heart hammering as she stared up into mesmeric golden eyes.

'Cautious,' Raul contradicted.

The hard heat of his lean, virile body was seeping into her by pervasive degrees. She was so outrageously conscious of his proximity that she was keeping her lungs going on tiny little pants. 'Kiss me,' she muttered, before she could lose her nerve.

'I'm burning up to possess you,' Raul breathed thickly. 'I won't stop at kissing.'

She trembled and, closing her eyes, reached up to press her lips against his. Teasingly he circled her mouth with his own, refusing to deepen the pressure, and in sudden driving impatience Polly sank her fingers into the depths of his luxuriant black hair to pull him down to her.

Vibrant amusement shimmered in his eyes as he held himself above her. 'Is that a yes?'

Shaken then by her own boldness, she met the reckless golden glitter of sensual threat in his gaze and started melting down deep inside, the weighted languor of anticipation sentencing her to stillness. Helplessly she nodded.

With a slashing smile that turned her heart over, Raul lowered his imperious dark head. 'You have to understand that this is a first for me too,' he shared silkily. 'I've never had a virgin in my bed. It makes you very special.'

'I never know whether you're being ironic or sincere,' Polly muttered tautly.

'Only a very stupid man would be ironic on his wedding night,' Raul asserted as he brought his hard, mobile mouth passionately down on hers.

He kissed her with innate eroticism, parting her lips, letting his tongue plunge deep into the honeyed warmth within, seeking out and finding every tender spot. Clutching at him, she was madly conscious of every slight movement he made, and wholly at the mercy of the wild, sweet, seductive feelings sweeping through her quivering body. It was a passionate, urgent exploration that betrayed his very masculine hunger, a growl of satisfaction escaping his throat before he lifted his head again, surveying her with shameless satisfaction.

'I told you that you would come to me, *mi esposa*.'

Her lashes fluttered up. She gave him a dazed look of reproach, too shaken by the effect he was having on her to muster a tart response. He came back to her again, tasting her, delving deep and then skimming the tender roof of her mouth in a flickering, provocative caress until she was gasping for breath but still hanging onto him.

Leaning back from her then, an unashamedly predatory smile on his sensual mouth, Raul trailed the ribbon straps of her nightgown slowly down over her slight shoulders, brushing them down her arms and then carefully slipping her hands free at the wrists.

'I want to look at all of you,' he breathed huskily. 'Touch all of you. Taste every smooth, silken inch of that pale, perfect skin and then sink so deep into you, you won't know where I end and you begin.'

Transfixed, and hectically flushed, Polly stared up at him, utterly overpowered by the tiny little tremors already racking her taut length, the tormenting throb of heat she could feel between her slender thighs. Torn between fascination and shyness, she watched him smoothly tug down the bodice of her nightgown so that her small, firm breasts sprang free, her nipples already wantonly distended rosy buds.

'Raul, please...' she moaned, hot with a debilitating and confusing mix of embarrassment and excitement.

'*Dios*...but you are exquisite.' His dark golden eyes

blazed over her bare breasts with urgent appreciation and made her tremble.

With deft but impatient hands, Raul eased the night-gown tangled round her waist down over her slim hips, raising her knees to slide the garment finally free and discard it.

Smoothing a soothing hand over her shifting hips, he ran intent eyes over the slender length of her, her tiny waist, delicately rounded stomach, the cluster of dark curls crowning the juncture of her trembling thighs. As she made a sudden impulsive snatch at the sheet, he forestalled her, and gazed down at her with a wicked smile. 'I've waited a long time to see you like this.' Long brown fingers closed round her wrist and lingered. 'Your pulse is going crazy. Admit it…it's exciting to be looked at, appreciated and lusted over. What did you expect, *querida*? That I would fall on you like a clumsy, selfish boy and it would all be over in minutes? That is not how I make love…'

'No…' Polly conceded shakily, scarcely able to swallow, so constricted was her throat.

A dark line of colour lay over his superb cheekbones. 'I want this to be good for you…I want you to spend all day aching for the moment when I take you in my arms again…'

Trembling like a leaf, with the heat surging through her in waves, Polly mumbled, 'Ambitious…'

'Always…in everything. It's in my blood,' Raul husked in agreement, running an exploring hand lightly over her outrageously sensitive breasts and forcing a gasp of startled reaction from her.

Helplessly she strained up to him, and with the tip of his tongue he provocatively traced the already reddened curve of her lips, so that she tipped her head back, openly inviting the hot, hard pressure of his mouth which every sense craved.

With a roughened laugh he tasted her again, sliding a hand beneath her hips and pressing her into contact with the aggressive thrust of his own arousal, and excitement drenched her in a blinding, burning wave. She moaned beneath that devastating mouth of his, need rising like a greedy fire as he let his fingers finally stroke and tug her achingly sensitive nipples. Freeing her swollen lips, he slid down the bed and employed that expert mouth on her tender breasts instead.

Pushing up against him, she twisted wildly, unprepared for the raw tide of sensation engulfing her now. Every intimate caress felt so unbearably good, yet all the time she strained and yearned helplessly for more, intoxicated by physical feelings she had never experienced before and ruled by their demands.

'Easy, *gatita*,' Raul muttered softly, pulling her to him, stilling her helpless squirmings with the momentary weight of one long, powerful thigh. 'We're not running a race...'

Polly snatched in a long, shuddering breath, focusing on him in a dazed kind of wonderment. 'I didn't know it would be like this...'

'Like a raging fire in which two can burn up with pleasure?' Raul bent over her and let his lips brush tenderly over hers.

She jerked as he eased her thighs apart and embarked on a more intimate invasion, touching her where she had never been touched before, discovering the damp silken ache at the centre of her. And he caressed her with such shrewd comprehension of what would excite her most that she was overwhelmed by the uncontrollable pleasure, sobbing against his broad shoulder, al-

ways longing and needing and finally begging for more
as the desperate need for greater fulfilment rose to
screaming proportions inside her.

And then Raul came smoothly over her, and surged
into her before she could even get the chance to fear
the unknown. As he thrust deeper there was a short,
sharp pain that made her cry out, and then, a split second later, the most extraordinary and intense feeling of
physical pleasure as he abruptly stilled to gaze with
rather touching anxiety down at her.

'I hoped it wouldn't hurt,' Raul confessed raggedly.

And Polly smiled a little dizzily up at him, at that
moment loving him so much for caring that she was
weak with the strength of the emotion shrilling through
her.

'Doesn't matter,' she swore unsteadily.

And then he moved within her again, and her eyes
slid shut on the rush of sensation which was so inde-
scribably seductive and controlling. If he had stopped
she would have died, and she wrapped herself round
him, utterly lost within the surging domination of his
possession. He drove her up to the heights and she
splintered there in ecstasy, glorying in his groan of intense physical pleasure as he slammed into her one last
time with compulsive driving force.

Eyes welling with tears from the sheer raw intensity
of her emotions, Polly held him tight within the circle
of her arms, revelling in the sweetness of her new right
to do that, openly and unashamedly, without fear of
revealing too much. And she marvelled at how much
closer she felt to Raul now. She wanted those timeless,
tranquil moments to last for ever. He was an absolutely
fantastic lover, she decided. Lying in that gloriously intimate embrace and knowing that she had satisfied him,

in spite of her inexperience, filled her with new pride and confidence.

In that same instant of heady contentment Raul pulled away from her and sprawled back against the pillows again. He flipped his tousled dark head over and surveyed her with deceptively indolent dark golden eyes that gleamed with satisfaction. 'You see, love isn't necessary to sexual gratification.'

Already hurt by the speed of his withdrawal from physical proximity, Polly gazed back at him with a sinking sensation in her stomach. 'Is there a point to that comment?' she asked tautly.

'I think you get the point.'

'It's a re-run of the ''don't expect too much from me,'' escape hatch for the commitment-shy male, is it?' Polly condemned on a rush of bitter pain that filled her with a furious need to strike back. 'You are just so terrified of emotion I actually feel sorry for you, but why should you worry about disappointing me? After all, you've been disappointing me one way or another ever since the first day we met!'

Stunned by that ringing and unexpected indictment, any pretense of indolence now abandoned, Raul stared at her, eyes dangerous as black ice. 'Is that a fact?' he breathed unevenly—only so thick was his accent it sounded much more like, 'Ees-zat-a-fat?', so she knew she had hit home very hard.

Polly snatched up her nightie and pulled it over her head with trembling hands. 'Yes...but it hardly matters,' she assured him with a skimming look of scorn. 'I have nothing to lose and I'm not lowering my needs to the level of yours. You're on probation, Raul.'

So incensed was he by that patronising little speech, he threw back the sheet and sprang out of bed. 'I...Raul

Zaforteza…on *probation*?' he gritted in savage disbelief.

Squaring her slight shoulders, Polly was unrepentant. 'And so far you are not doing very well. You seem to think you've done me one very big favour marrying me…but ask me how *I* feel five months from now—'

'*Por qué?* What the hell is going to happen in five months?' Raul raked at her across the depth of the bedroom.

'I will inherit my godmother's money, and if I'm not happy with you, I'm not spending the rest of my life in misery.'

'*Misery?*' Raul ground out in outrage.

'I'm not,' Polly told him, and meant it. 'You needn't think you can toss diamond jewellery at me to keep me happy. Diamonds are quite pretty, but not something I feel I have to have.'

'*Pretty?*' Raul echoed in rampant disbelief.

'Other things mean much more to me…respect, affection, caring. I do appreciate that you have probably spent the entirety of your adult life giving extravagant gifts to women because you can't cope with emotional demands, but—'

'How dare you say I cannot cope?' Volatile golden eyes slammed into hers in a look as hostile as a physical assault.

'You said it yourself. You said you walk away when things get difficult.' Polly made that incendiary reminder with reluctance.

Raul studied her with a seething, wordless incomprehension that twisted her heart inside out. Then he spun away, presenting her with the long golden sweep of his flawless back to wrench open a drawer and start to haul on a pair of black jeans. She knew he didn't even trust himself to speak. She knew he was infuriated by the sudden struggle speaking English had become because he was in such an ungovernable rage.

'I realize I'm far from perfect, and that a lot of things I do and say must irritate you…but I don't think I deserve to feel that you only came home tonight to have sex with me,' Polly told him, her eyes stinging so hard she had to open her eyes very wide to hold the tears back. 'Like I'm some sort of novelty act…and then, right after it, regardless of my feelings, you have to gloat—'

On that charge, Raul swung back. 'All I said was that love was not necessary to—'

Polly drew in a deep, shuddering breath. 'And why did you say that?' she whispered painfully, suddenly sick and tired of pretending. 'You knew it wasn't true. You *must* know how I feel about you. I think you've *always* known…'

Raul went very still. Dense black lashes dropped low, spectacular eyes betraying only a glint of gold, ferocious tension tightening his bronzed skin over his fabulous bone structure. 'You're going to regret this…'

'No, I won't. I'm past caring,' Polly muttered with perfect truth. 'I love you to death, and you probably knew it before I did! If you'd had a single shred of decency you would've backed off in Vermont. In the same way you knew exactly why I wanted to marry you…yet you told Digby I was a gold-digger and a blackmailer. It's like a big black secret you won't acknowledge, but I won't live a lie, Raul.'

Utterly drained by that stark baring of her own tormented emotions, Polly slid out of the bed and walked towards the door.

'*Dios*…I can't give you love!' Raul launched at her with positive savagery.

'But with a little effort you could make a reasonable stab at respect, if not anything else. Because if you don't,' Polly whispered jaggedly, torn in two with pain and the regret he had so accurately forecast she would feel, 'I'll stop loving you, and love is all you have to hold me. I won't be a doormat…I won't be walked on.'

Without looking back, she flipped the door shut behind her. She was in a complete daze, shock at what she had done and said hitting her all at once. She was shaking all over, moving towards the sanctuary of the guest room she had abandoned earlier on jellied knees. But somehow she didn't feel like crying any more. What had passed between her and Raul had been too devastating. A shame something she had found so wonderful, so beautiful, had had to end in such emotional agony.

Raul simply couldn't have allowed it to stay that good. He had had to open that smart mouth of his and blow everything apart. Make her feel like a one-night stand instead of a wife who loved him—and who he knew damned well loved him! In the clear dawn light she lay down on the bed, a giant, aching hole where her heart had been. She didn't want a heart that hurt her so much.

When the door opened again, she sat up with a start. Raul thrust the door shut behind him and studied her, brilliant black eyes incisive.

'I too have faults,' Raul murmured. 'But, unlike you, I acknowledge them.'

'What are you saying?' Feeling worn and drained, Polly simply bowed her head defensively over her raised knees.

'Yes, I disappointed you in Vermont…but then you disappointed me too.'

Disconcerted by that assurance, Polly lifted her head. Raul held her questioning look with unflinching cool.

'If you had been the truly honest woman you like to believe you are, you would have told me that you were pregnant then. But, when it suited your purposes to remain silent, you were as neglectful of the truth as I was about my real identity. I think we're about equal on the score of disappointing each other,' Raul completed drily.

A slow, painful pink had surged into Polly's cheeks. It shook her to be faced with the fact that she had also made mistakes—not least by ignoring reality when it seemed to be within her own interests to do so. She had never come close to telling Raul that she was a surrogate mum-to-be, had been too frightened he would reject her in disgust. How ironic it was that he had known all along, and even judged her on that cowardly silence!

'I suppose you're right,' she contrived to force out rather hoarsely.

'As for last night, and your conviction that I only returned to have sex with you—do you really think I am so immature *or* so desperate for sexual release?' At that searing demand, Polly twisted her head away, no longer caring how he translated such a reaction. 'I'm here now because I accepted that I shouldn't have left you in the first place, and that such behaviour would only reinforce your fears about our future.'

Polly linked her fingers fiercely tight together. All rage put behind him, Raul's ice-cool and rational rebuttal of her angry accusations was a cruelly effective weapon of humiliation. 'OK,' she got out, when she couldn't bear his expectant silence any longer.

'And do you really think that threatening to leave me in five months' time is likely to add to the stability of our marriage?'

Polly flinched as if he had cracked a whip over her. She felt like a child being told off for bad behaviour.

'Now I think you're going to sulk,' Raul forecast, with an even more lowering air of adult restraint.

Polly struggled, and finally managed to swallow the enormous lump in her throat. 'I think you're probably right.'

CHAPTER NINE

RAUL'S equestrian centre was a vastly impressive installation set about a mile from the ranch. Polly settled Luis into his stroller and wandered down the asphalt lane in the sweltering heat, striving not to look like a woman out in search of her husband. But the truth was she was getting desperate, for she had seen virtually nothing of Raul over the past few days.

Indeed, after those twin earth-shattering scenes at dawn, she had initially expected to find Raul a good thousand miles away on business by the time he appeared the following day. Why? Because he was thoroughly fed up with her! Fed up with the virtual minefield she had already made of their marriage of convenience and fed up with her over-emotional reactions. What had happened to patience? Calm? Reasoned restraint?

But in the cruellest possible way she had Raul trapped. He might not be able to respond to emotional demands, but, challenged with an accusation of cowardice, sheer horror that she might be right would keep him on the spot. Only 'on the spot' at the ranch unfortunately seemed to mean that he could avoid her just as effectively.

He had a suite of rooms he used as offices on the ground floor, and staff who flew in and out as if helicopters were buses. He rose at dawn and went riding every morning and never returned to the ranch for breakfast. Either he was engaged in business the rest of the day or down at the equestrian centre. But every evening they dined together in the stifling formality of the dining room.

And, terrifyingly, it was as if that confrontation several days earlier had never happened—only now there was a divide the width of the Atlantic ocean between them. Raul didn't need to walk away to hold her at a distance. He could make civil conversation, express a courteous desire to know what she had done with her day, discuss Luis and generally treat her like an honoured house guest with whom, regrettably, he didn't have very much time to spend. Oh, yes, and leave her to sleep in a guest room bed without a visible ounce of regret.

So now, when Polly espied Raul chatting to a fair-haired man in front of the state-of-the-art stables, she attempted to appear slightly surprised to run into him. She wanted to behave normally, but without giving him the impression she had deliberately sought him out.

Embarrassingly sexual butterflies erupted in her tummy as she watched him lithely straighten from his elegant lounging position against the rail. As always, he looked stupendous, black hair flopping over his bronzed brow, dark, deep-set eyes narrowed, wide shoulders outlined by a black polo shirt, lean hips and long powerful thighs sheathed in skintight jodhpurs, polished boots gleaming in the sunshine.

'Fancy seeing you here' might well be interpreted as sarcasm, so she gave Raul a purposely casual smile. Her heartbeat thundered with suppressed excitement against her breastbone, ensuring that she swiftly removed her attention from him again. 'Luis and I are just out for a walk,' she announced, and then wanted to bite her tongue out because she sounded positively fatuous.

'This is Patrick Gorman, Polly.' Raul introduced the slim, fair-haired younger man already extending his hand to her. 'He runs the breeding programme for the polo ponies.'

'Delighted to meet you, Mrs Zaforteza.'

'You're English!' Polly registered with surprise and pleasure. 'And I think I recognise that accent. Newcastle?'

'Spot on!'

Polly laughed. 'I was born in Blyth, but my parents moved south when I was six.'

'That's why you don't have a hint of a Geordie accent.' Giving her an appreciative grin, Patrick bent over the stroller. 'I'm crazy about babies!' he exclaimed, squatting down to get a closer look at Luis, where he was contentedly drowsing under the parasol. 'He's incredibly little, isn't he?'

'He's actually quite big for his age,' Polly asserted proudly, thinking how wonderfully well this supposedly accidental meeting with Raul was going, because Patrick was the chatty type which naturally helped to break the ice.

'My niece is a year old, and quite a handful last time I saw her,' Patrick told her cheerfully.

'Luis doesn't do much more than eat and sleep at the minute.'

'You have a lot of fun ahead of you,' Patrick Gorman smiled. 'Since Raul has some calls to make, would you like me to show you around this operation?'

'The calls will wait. I'll do the guided tour,' Raul slotted in smoothly, his attention darkly fixed to his animated and chattering companions.

Polly risked a glance at Raul. Brooding tension had hardened his lean, dark face. In receipt of a smouldering look, she flushed. 'Are you sure you can spare the time?' she pressed anxiously.

Disconcertingly, Raul dropped a casual arm round her taut shoulders. 'Why not?'

'Did I say something wrong back there?' Polly asked as he walked her away from the younger man.

'You talked more in two minutes to a complete stranger than you have talked to me in three entire days,' Raul delivered silkily. 'However, I would advise you to maintain a certain formal distance with Patrick.'

'Why?'

'Don't be misled by all that boyish charm. Patrick is a serial womaniser.'

Polly blinked. 'He seemed very nice. He was so interested in Luis.'

'It was just a light word of warning,' Raul drawled dismissively, his blunt cheekbones accentuated by a slight darkening of colour as she frowned at him in patent confusion over why he should have found it necessary to give that warning.

He changed the subject. 'Actually, I thought you would've been down to the stables long before now. Country-bred Englishwomen are always mad about horses. They even take their ponies to boarding school with them!' He laughed with husky appreciation. 'I expect you ride pretty well yourself.'

Conscious of the approving satisfaction he didn't attempt to conceal in his assumption that she was used to being around horses, Polly muttered, 'Er…well—'

'I've never met an Englishwoman who didn't,' Raul confided, making her tense even more. 'And, as horses are a major part of my life, that's one interest we can share.'

'I'm probably a bit rusty…riding,' Polly heard herself

say, when she had *never* been on a horse in her entire life. But any wish Raul might express to share anything other than a bed deserved the maximum encouragement.

A split second later, she realised that she had just told a very stupid lie which would be easily exposed, but she had been so delighted at his talk of wanting to share his love of horses with her that she hadn't been able to bring herself to disappoint him. She would teach herself to ride, just enough to pass herself. It couldn't be that difficult, could it? In the meantime, all she had to do was make excuses.

He showed her round the stables. She copied every move he made with the horses poking their heads out over the doors. Mirroring worked a treat. Just about everything he told her went right over her head, because her knowledge of horseflesh began and ended with a childhood love of reading *Black Beauty*.

'It's all so fascinating,' she commented with a mesmerised smile while he talked about polo—an incomprehensible commentary on chukkas, throw-ins and ride-offs. His lean brown hands sketched vivid impressions to stress the fast and furious action. It occurred to her that even if he had been talking in Spanish she would still have been utterly hooked. His sheer enthusiasm had a hypnotic effect on her.

Registering the glow in her dark blue eyes as she listened to him, Raul smiled. 'You look happier today, *querida*.'

The silence that fell as he uttered the endearment seemed to thump in time with Polly's hopelessly impressionable heart. The tip of her tongue snaked out to dampen her dry lower lip. His stunning dark golden eyes homed in on the tiny movement and her tummy simply flipped. In the hot, still air, a storm of such powerful desire engulfed Polly that she quivered with embarrassment.

A slow smile curved Raul's beautiful mouth. Striding forward with confidence, he reached for her, a sudden burning brilliance blazing in his gorgeous eyes. 'You're trembling...'

And he knew why. He radiated an answering sexual heat that overwhelmed her every attempt to conceal her own reactions. And when he hauled her close with hungry hands, and plunged his mouth down passionately hard on hers, she felt as if the top of her head was flying off with excitement, and she simply went limp, eyes sliding shut, struggling to breathe, heart pounding like a manic trip-hammer.

'Oh, boy...' she gasped, as Raul lifted his imperious dark head again, pressing her shaken face against his shoulder. Feverishly she drank in his hot, clean scent, torn by a devouring need for him that was shatteringly intense.

But it was balanced by an awareness of *his* hunger, the jerky little shudder racking him as he snatched in a fractured breath. The barriers had come down, she sensed. He was touching her again. She was no longer off limits, like an ornament sheltering under a glass bell jar. And he wanted her, oh, yes, he wanted her, and this time that was going to be enough, she told herself urgently.

As he set her back from him, brilliant eyes veiled, Raul murmured lazily, 'I'll pick you up for a picnic lunch around three. Leave Luis at home.'

A little fretful squalling cry erupted like a comical complaint from the stroller. Raul burst out laughing. Surveying his wakening son's cross little face with a luminous pride he could not conceal, he sighed, 'We made a wonderful son together...I just wish we had made him between the sheets.'

Polly blushed, but she was touched that he should think along the same lines as she had done. 'Not much we can do about that.'

'But we'll do it the normal way the next time,' Raul asserted with amusement, and before she could even blossom at that reassuring implication that they would have another child some day, he added with deflating practicality, 'One of the grooms will run you back to the ranch. You shouldn't be out in this heat without a hat. Sunstroke is not a very pleasant experience.'

When she walked into her bedroom, two of the maids were hanging a rail of unfamiliar new garments in the wardrobe. Polly hovered, fingering rich fabrics, recognising wildly expensive designer tailoring. Dear heaven, Raul had bought her clothes. No asking, What do you like? No suggestion that she go and choose for herself. She eased a sleek dress in a smoky shade of blue from a padded hanger and held it against herself. Lordy, she'd never worn anything that short in her life!

But she was smiling, because she was already walking on air. *Next time.* Two little words that told her that Raul regarded their marriage as a lasting development. She put on the blue dress and then tracked down the housekeeper and asked for the keys of the curious little turreted building on the south boundary of the gardens. She had a couple of hours to kill, and yesterday had peered in through the shrouded windows and found the doors securely locked.

'No one goes there now, *señora*.' The older woman muttered something anxious in Spanish about *el patrón*, her kindly face strained as she finally passed over the keys with marked reluctance.

The staff might be superstitious about the place, but Polly was unconcerned by that troubled reference to *'el patrón'*. Raul wouldn't give two hoots if she went and explored. This was supposed to be her home now, and that picturesque building intrigued her.

She opened the Gothic front door and walked into a split-level, surprisingly spacious room with dust-covered furniture. The walls were faded and stained, the curtains in an advanced state of disintegration. She wandered through silent rooms, coming on a dated kitchen layered with dust before she walked up the cast-iron staircase.

There was a large bedroom, a bathroom, and then one other bedroom. She stopped in the doorway of the third room. It was a child's room, with little rusty cars still sitting on shelves, yellowing photos curling up on a noticeboard, as if the little boy had just gone away and never come back. It was eerie.

She peered at the photos. One she recognised as Raul's father. There were two portraits at the ranch that she had assumed were of Raul's parents. Eduardo, who bore a marked resemblance to Raul, and Yolanda, a regal blue-eyed blonde, who resembled him not at all. She didn't recognise the laughing brunette with the exotic tigerish eyes, although those eyes reminded her of…Raul's eyes?

The sounds of steps on the metal stairs sent Polly hurrying back out onto the landing. It was Raul, still dressed in his riding gear, breathing shallowly as if he had been hurrying.

'What are you doing poking around in here?' he demanded rawly, a savage glitter in his golden eyes, harsh lines of strain bracketing his sensual mouth.

Polly was thoroughly disconcerted by his reaction. 'I

wasn't "poking around'…I was just curious. Who lived here? I didn't realise anyone had actually lived here until I came inside.'

Raul studied her fiercely and then finally lifted a wide shoulder in a jerky shrug of grudging acceptance. 'I thought you knew. Everyone knows… My family background has been exhaustively dug up and raked over by the media.'

A sense of foreboding touched Polly then, her stomach muscles clenching tight. Raul was reacting like someone in shock, his eyes flickering uneasily over their surroundings and then skimming away again, a faraway look of grim vulnerability in his eyes until he shielded them, his facial bones ferociously prominent beneath his bronzed skin.

'I lived here with my mother until I was nine,' Raúl told her flatly.

'Your parents separated?' she asked in bewilderment.

Raul vented a hollow laugh. 'My mother was my father's mistress, Polly, *not* his wife!'

Floundering in shock, Polly stammered, 'B-but the blonde woman in the picture in the hall—?'

'My father's wife, Yolanda. Our lifestyle was somewhat dysfunctional.'

With a mistress in a flamboyant little house at the foot of the garden? He wasn't joking.

Raul explained in a very few words. His mother, Pilar, had been the daughter of a *llanero*, who'd worked on a neighbouring tenant's ranch. Pilar had already been pregnant with Raul when Eduardo Zaforteza married his beautiful oil heiress bride.

'When Yolanda found out about my mother, she locked the bedroom door, and my father used that as his excuse to bring us here to live,' Raul shared tautly.

'After my mother's death, he gave Yolanda half of everything he possessed to agree to my adoption.'

'What age were you when your mother died?' Polly muttered.

'Nine. There used to be a swimming pool out there. She drowned in it when she was drunk. She was frequently drunk,' Raul admitted flatly. 'What my father called "love' destroyed her...in fact it destroyed all our lives.'

'Yolanda never had any children?'

'Frequent miscarriages...*sí*, the bedroom door was unlocked eventually.' Raul grimaced. 'I think my father enjoyed having two women fighting over him. When it became a hassle, he just took off and left them to it for a while. He and Yolanda died in a plane crash almost ten years ago.'

Nausea was stirring in Polly's sensitive stomach. All of a sudden she was seeing and understanding so much, but recoiling from a vision of the distressing scenes which Raul must have witnessed as he grew up. An unhappy mother with a drink problem. No normal family life, no secure childhood, nothing but tangled adult relationships and constant strife.

She was imagining how much the wronged wife must have loathed Raul and his mother, and didn't even want to consider what it had been like for Raul to live in the same house with Yolanda from the tender age of nine. An embittered woman, who had forced her husband to pay for the right to adopt his illegitimate son. Little wonder Raul found it a challenge to believe in love or the deeper bonds of marriage.

'You should have this place cleared out.' Polly strove for a brisk tone.

'I haven't set foot here in years. It was my father

who insisted it stay as it was. He liked to come here when he felt sentimental,' Raul said with lethal derision.

Polly was frankly appalled by what he had told her, but working hard to hide it. She was annoyed that she had blundered in to rouse such unpleasant memories, and exasperated that she hadn't had more interest that long-ago day at the library in learning about Raul's background rather than about the women in his life. She started down the curving staircase, eager to be out in the fresh air again.

'I'll have this place emptied, then…OK?' Polly pressed, seeking agreement for what she saw as a necessary act.

Raul shrugged with comforting unconcern. The distant look had gone from his eyes as he scrutinised her appearance and his mouth quirked. 'So the clothes have arrived…I chose them when I was in Caracas. At least you've got something decent to wear until you do your own shopping,' he pointed out, for all the world as if she had been walking around in rags.

Half an hour later, they got into a four-wheel drive to head out for the picnic he had promised. They left the asphalt lanes that criss-crossed the vast spread of the ranch buildings to hurtle down a dusty trail and then out across the grassy plains. All sign of modern civilisation was left behind within minutes. Yellow poplars, gum trees and the ubiquitous palm grew in thickets on higher ground, where the floodwater hadn't reached. Great flocks of exotic multi-coloured birds rose from the trees with shrill cries as they passed.

The sky was a clear, cloudless turquoise over the sun-drenched savannah. It was a strange and unfamiliar terrain to Polly, yet the *llanos*, teaming with wildlife in their isolation, had a haunting, fascinating beauty.

'Where are we going?' she finally asked.

'Wait and see,' Raul advised lazily.

He brought the car to a halt and sprang out. As she followed, all she could see was a dense line of trees. Raul pulled a hamper out of the back seat. They walked under the trees, and then she caught her breath. In a gently sloping hidden valley below them, a waterfall tumbled down over ancient weathered rocks into a reed-edged lagoon.

'Once a tributary of the Orinoco river ran through here...this is all that remains.' Raul set the hamper down on the lush grass in the shade of the coconut palms.

Polly was enchanted. 'It's so peaceful.'

'My mother brought me here as a child. This place was special to her,' Raul confided. 'I suspect I might have been conceived here.'

'Don't you have any family left alive?' Polly asked as she sat down.

Raul swung round to look at her, his fabulous bone structure tensing, dark eyes sombre in the sunlight. 'My grandfather, Fidelio.' Raul shrugged. 'He disowned my mother. He's a very proud old man, and still refuses to acknowledge our relationship, but I told him about Luis last week.'

'I'm sorry I've been so prickly and awkward,' Polly said abruptly.

Raul gave her a slanting smile as he sank down beside her. 'I've been awkward too. This...you and I...it's all new to me.'

That rueful smile touched something deep inside her. Rising up on her knees, Polly took her courage in both hands. Planting her palms against his chest, she pushed him flat.

Startled, Raul gazed up at her, and then a wolfish grin slashed his face. 'And I was going to be a gentleman, *gatita*. I was planning to wait until you'd eaten! But, since we are both of one mind...' Raul murmured, taking pity on her as she hovered above him, uncertain of what to do next, and reaching up to slowly draw her down to him.

He sent his hands skimming down to her slim hips and eased her into the cradle of his long, muscular thighs with an erotic suggestiveness that was as bold as it was unashamed. Melded to every virile line of his powerful body, Polly turned boneless. He undid the zip on her dress and tipped it down off her shoulders.

Her firm breasts rose and fell inside the delicate cups of her lace bra. He unclipped the bra and curved appreciative hands over the pale, pouting curves that tumbled out. She gave a muffled gasp as he tugged at her straining nipples and arched her back, excitement seizing her in its hold.

Raul flipped her over gently onto her back. Vaulting upright, he proceeded to remove his clothes with a lack of cool that only excited her more. She lifted her hips, tugged down the dress, sat up to shyly dispose of her remaining garments—but all the time she was covertly watching him. As that superb bronze body emerged she was enthralled, mouth bone-dry, pulses accelerating.

A delicious little quiver of anticipation made her ache. Just looking at him, seeing the potent evidence of his desire for her, stole her breath away. He was so aroused she could feel herself melting into a liquid pool of submission. And when he returned to her she was already on fire, the swollen pink buds of her breasts begging for his attention, a sensation of damp heat throbbing almost painfully between her thighs.

His stunning eyes read the message in hers. He came down to her and kissed her breathless with a force of hunger that overwhelmed her own. 'I feel wild...' he groaned with a ragged laugh. 'One more night watching you across the dining table and I would've pulled you under it!'

'It didn't show.'

'*Infierno*...I get as hard as a rock just being in the same room with you,' Raul growled rawly. 'I don't think I have ever been so frustrated in my life! I was tempted to take you into the stables earlier and...' As her dark blue eyes widened in open shock at that series of blunt revelations, he compressed his lips, a dark rise of blood emphasising his cheekbones. 'I just want you so much I can't think of anything else right now.'

Polly was dazed by that almost apologetic conclusion. She had never once dreamt that Raul might come to desire her to such an extent. Colliding with devouring golden eyes, she shivered. He meshed a not quite steady hand into her hair.

'That's all right,' she mumbled, mesmerised by his intensity but even weaker now with wanton longing. 'I want you too.'

Heat flooded her as he kneed her legs apart. He had said he felt wild, and what he did to her *was* wild. Nothing could have prepared her for the storm of powerful need he released. He took her hard and fast, and then so slowly and so agonisingly sweetly that she was plunged into a mindless glory of acute pleasure, afterwards savouring every precious moment of satiated contentment in his arms, certain that they had turned a corner to forge deeper bonds.

She slept for a while then. She wakened, feeling ridiculously shy, to focus on Raul, where he lay fully dressed again in a careless sprawl, an unusually peaceful aspect to his stillness. Assuming he was asleep, she sat up. His lashes were as lush as black silk fans, his sensual mouth relaxed in repose, dark stubble already outlining his stubborn jawline. She could not resist running a loving finger down gently over one proud cheekbone.

He opened his eyes and she froze, like a thief caught in the act.

Whipping up a hand, he closed his fingers round her wrist and planted a kiss to the damp centre of her palm. 'You make me feel good,' he confided softly.

And the rush of love that surged through her in response left her dizzy.

Raul sat up, still retaining a light hold on her hand, and dealt her a wry look. 'How do you feel about having another baby in about nine months?'

'I...I b-beg your pardon?'

'I didn't take any precautions...' Raul raised two expressive hands, clearly primed for a furious outburst. 'I just didn't think...I was very excited.'

Hugging the dress he must have tossed over her while she slept, Polly reflected that he had gone from never having taken that risk to repeating it over and over again with a devastating lack of inhibition. But then she was his wife—once a chosen baby machine, she conceded rather sourly. No doubt he imagined it would be no big deal for her to find herself pregnant again so soon. But right at that moment Polly cringed at the prospect of her freshly slender and now apparently sexually attractive shape vanishing again. Raul wouldn't find her remotely attractive any more and he might stray, she thought fearfully.

'I'm sorry...' Raul breathed tightly as the silence stretched and stretched.

'It's all right for you...you're not going to get all fat and clumsy, are you?'

Instantly Raul closed an arm round her. 'You were not fat and clumsy...you were gorgeous.'

'You like babies. You're not likely to tell me the truth—and I've never been gorgeous in my life!' Polly added for good measure.

'Why did I find you so tempting while you were in the clinic, then?'

Polly stilled. 'Did you?'

'I thought you were incredibly sexy...like a lush, ripe peach.'

She supposed peaches were at least round. But she looked at him, saw his sincerity and swallowed hard on another tart retort. 'My body hasn't settled down yet,' she shared, striving not to be prim about discussing such a thing with him. 'So I don't know how much of a risk there is.'

As Polly shimmied back into her dress, Raul glanced at his watch and swore succinctly in Spanish. 'Caramba...look at the time—and we have guests coming to dinner!'

As she stood up, Raul zipped her dress for her. She was conscious of her body's decided tenderness, the result of their frantic lovemaking. He was oversexed, as well as careless, but she still loved him to death. Otherwise she probably would have killed him at that moment for simply dropping on her this late in the day the fact that they were entertaining guests.

'Who's coming?' she asked, balancing to slide into her second shoe.

'Melina D'Agnolo and—' A firm hand snaked out

swiftly to steady her as she staggered on one leg and nearly went headlong down the slope. '*Dios mío, mi esposa*...take care!' Raul urged.

'You were saying?' Her head bent to conceal her shock, Polly breathed in very shakily.

'Melina, our closest neighbour,' Raul shared, with what Polly considered to be megawatt cool. 'She grew up on the ranch she's currently renting from the estate. She's bringing the Drydons—mutual friends. Patrick will join us. He used to work for Rob Drydon.'

'I'll enjoy meeting them.' Polly sneaked a glance at Raul to see if he looked even slightly self-conscious. He didn't.

Raul swept up the hamper and even joked about the fact that they had eaten nothing. They strolled back to the car. Raul helped her into the passenger seat.

'I'm a brute,' he murmured, scanning the bluish shadows of tiredness under her eyes. 'But it was fantastic, *es verdad*?'

Melina was a neighbour. The *llanos* looked empty for miles and miles, but they harboured the poisonous Melina somewhere close by. It was ghastly news. Worse, Raul expected her to entertain his ex-mistress. He was cooler than an ice cube. But then he wasn't aware that she knew about that former relationship. *Former*, she emphasised to herself with determination.

Raul was a sophisticated male and she was being naive. His intimate relationship with Melina D'Agnolo might be over, but that didn't mean he would cut her out of his life altogether. She had to taken an adult view of this social encounter.

CHAPTER TEN

'I AM so very pleased for you both,' Melina murmured, with a look of deep sincerity in her green eyes as she reached for Polly's hand in an open and friendly manner.

Dear heaven, she could act me off the stage, Polly registered in dismay, not having been prepared for quite so impressive a pretence. Stunning, in a black lace dress which clung to her superb figure like a second skin, Melina curved a light hand over Raul's sleeve and recounted a witty little story which made him laugh.

Polly had been feeling really good in her scarlet off-the-shoulder dress—until just before she came downstairs. Now her head was aching. She hoped Melina's pleasantries were more than surface-deep.

Rob Drydon and his wife, Susie, were from Texas, and eagerly talking horses with Patrick Gorman. As they transferred to the dining room Melina was in full flow of conversation with Raul, and Polly was left to trail behind them. Patrick caught up with her.

'The *condesa* will walk all over you if you let her,' he whispered in her ear.

Polly's eyes widened. She glanced up at him.

Patrick gave her a rueful look. 'The scene she threw on your arrival was too good a story for the staff to keep quiet. I heard the grooms talking about it,' he confided. 'And as Raul needs the least protection of any male I know, why is he the only person around here

383

who *doesn't* know about the warm welcome you received?'

Polly tensed. 'There wasn't any need to involve him.'

'If you'd involved Raul, she wouldn't be here now, spoiling your evening,' Patrick dropped gently.

As Patrick tucked Polly into her chair at the foot of the table she encountered Raul's level scrutiny, and found herself flushing without knowing why. Picking up her wine glass, she drank.

'Raul told me to pick out a decent mount for you,' Patrick shared chattily.

Polly's wine went down the wrong way. She spluttered, cleared her throat, and gave her companion a pleading look. 'Can you keep a secret, Patrick?'

He nodded.

Leaning her head guiltily close to his, Polly whispered, 'I'm afraid I wasn't entirely honest about my riding ability.'

Patrick frowned. 'In what way?'

'I've never been on a horse in my life.'

After a startled pause, Patrick burst out laughing.

'Don't be selfish,' Raul drawled silkily. 'Share the joke with the rest of us.'

Clashing with shimmering dark eyes, Polly flushed. 'It wasn't really funny enough.'

'The English sense of humour isn't the same as ours,' Melina remarked sweetly. 'I've always found it rather juvenile.'

Patrick grinned. 'I have to confess I'm not into your wildly dramatic soap operas. Each to his own.'

Under cover of the ensuing conversation, Patrick murmured, 'See you tomorrow morning at six while Raul's out riding. I'll teach you enough to pass yourself, and then you can tell him you're just not very good and he can take over.'

'You're a saviour,' Polly muttered with real gratitude, and turned to address Rob Drydon.

After dinner, they settled down with drinks in the drawing room. Melina crossed the room with another one of her super-friendly smiles, saying in her clear, ringing voice, 'I want you to tell me all about yourself, Polly.'

Sinking deep into the sofa, to show the maximum possible amount of her incredibly long and shapely legs, Melina asked, 'So how's married life treating you?'

'Wonderfully well.' Polly emptied her glass in one gulp and prayed for deliverance, uneasily conscious that Raul was watching them both from the other side of the room. She wished she was feeling more herself.

'I don't think Raul likes to see you drinking so much. He rarely touches alcohol…the occasional glass of champagne on important occasions.' Registering Polly's surprise, Melina elevated a brow. 'So you didn't know? How couldn't you know something that basic about your own husband?'

Polly clutched her empty glass like a drunkard amongst teetotallers, bitterly, painfully resenting the fact that Melina could tell her anything she didn't know about Raul. It reminded her all over again that until very recently there had been nothing normal about her relationship with Raul.

'That's none of your business,' she told Melina flatly, determined not to play the blonde's spiteful double game. Now, when it was too late, she saw how foolish she had been not to tell Raul about her initial clash with Melina. If she tried to tell him now, he probably wouldn't believe her, not with Melina putting on the show of the century with her smiling friendliness.

'Raul *is* my business, and he always will be,' Melina said smugly. 'Did you make a huge scene when he came to see me that very same night?'

Polly froze and then slowly, jerkily turned her head, which was beginning to pound unpleasantly. 'What are you saying?'

'That even I wasn't expecting him quite *that* soon.' Glinting green eyes absorbed Polly's growing pallor with satisfaction. 'I didn't need ESP to realise that you'd obviously had a colossal row. It was your first night in your new home and yet Raul ended up with me.'

'You're lying...I don't believe you.' That night had been the equivalent of their wedding night. Raul couldn't have—he simply couldn't have gone to Melina beforehand! But he *had* gone out riding. In sick desperation, she strained to recall what he had told her. Hadn't he admitted calling in with a neighbour? Numbly, Polly let the maid refill her glass. Melina was a neighbour. Technically Raul hadn't lied to her...

'He came to me to talk. Raul needs a woman, not a little girl.'

Polly took a defiant slug of her drink. 'He needs you like he needs a hole in the head!' she said, and then frowned in confusion as Melina suddenly leant past her to start talking in low-pitched Spanish.

'I hope you're feeling better the next time I see you, Polly,' Melina then murmured graciously as she rose to her feet.

An icy voice like a lethal weapon breathed in Polly's shrinking ear, 'I'll see our guests out, *mi esposa*. Don't you dare get up. If you stand up, you might fall over, and if you fall over, I'll put you under a very cold shower!'

Devastated to realise that Raul must have overheard her last response to Melina, and doubtless believed that she had been inexcusably rude for no good reason, Polly sat transfixed while everyone took their leave, loads of sympathetic looks and concerned murmurs coming her way once Raul mentioned that she was feeling dizzy.

Patrick hung back to say with a frown, 'Do you think you'll make it down to the stables in the morning?'

Polly nodded with determination.

Recalling how wonderfully close she and Raul had been earlier in the day, Polly began to droop. *Had* Raul been with Melina that night? Only a fool would believe anything Melina said, she decided. But a split second later she was thinking the worst again, imagining how easy, how tempting it would have been for Raul in the mood he had been in to seek consolation with his mistress, a beautiful, self-assured woman whom he had known for so many years...

Two minutes later, Raul strode back in and scooped Polly off the sofa.

'I'm so miserable!' Polly suddenly sobbed in despair.

Taken aback, Raul tightened his arms around her and murmured what sounded like soothing things in Spanish.

'And I haven't had too much to drink...I just feel *awful*!' she wept, clutching at the lapel of his dinner jacket and then freeing him again, because she didn't want to touch him, didn't want to be close to him in any way if he was capable of such deception.

Raul carried her upstairs, laid her gently down on his bed and slipped off her shoes.

'I'm in agony with a headache!' Polly suddenly hurled.

'You're tipsy,' Raul murmured with total conviction as he unzipped her dress.

'My head's so sore,' Polly mumbled, drowning in self-pity.

Raul extracted her from her dress and deftly massaged her taut shoulders. 'You're so tense,' he scolded. 'Relax, I'll get some painkillers.'

Hadn't he heard what she had said to Melina after all? Had she jumped to conclusions? Surely he would have said something by now?

'Why were you angry with me?' she whispered.

'You were flirting like mad with Patrick.'

'I like him,' Polly muttered, distracted by that unexpected response.

'I *know*,' Raul growled, in an undertone that set up a chain reaction down her sensitive spine as he undid her bra and deftly disposed of it. 'I didn't realise you were feeling ill. I was surprised you were drinking so much.'

'I knew I had a bad head when I came downstairs,' Polly sighed, wriggling her way out of her tights at his behest. 'I felt rotten.'

'You should've told me,' Raul purred. 'Melina said you were talking about our annual fiesta here…were you?'

Polly tensed. 'Don't remember…my head was splitting. You seem to know her very well.'

'Inside out,' Raul agreed silkily.

'When did you invite Melina to dinner?'

'The same evening I visited my grandfather. Fidelio is the foreman of the ranch Melina rents,' Raul revealed.

'Oh... *Oh*...' Polly gasped slightly, slowly putting that together for herself.

Raul had called in with Fidelio that night to tell him he had a great-grandson. And that was why Raul had seen Melina. How silly she had been! And why hadn't it occurred to her before now that at some point Raul would have *had* to see Melina face to face to inform her of his marriage? As she came to terms with that rational explanation, a giant tide of relief started rolling over her.

'I'm awfully tired,' she confessed.

Raul tugged her up against him and gently slotted her into the silky pyjama jacket he had fetched. He carefully rolled up the sleeves. 'I have a villa on the coast. I think we should spend a few days there...'

'Sounds good,' Polly mumbled, and closed her eyes.

She slept like a log but she had the most terrifying dream. She was living in the house at the foot of the garden and Melina was queening it at the ranch. History repeating itself in reverse. She woke with a start, perspiring and shivering, just in time to see Raul reach the door in his riding gear.

'What time is it?'

'Only five-thirty...go back to sleep.'

Abruptly recalling the arrangement she had made with Patrick Gorman, Polly leapt out of bed the instant Raul closed the door behind him.

After a quick shower, she pulled on jeans and a T-shirt, frantic because she knew she was running late. She rushed down the corridor to see Luis, which was always the first thing she did in the morning. In the doorway of the nursery, she stopped dead in surprise and some dismay.

Raul was lounging back in a chair with Luis lying

asleep on top of him. Garbed in a little yellow sleepsuit and sprawled trustingly across his father's muscular chest, their son looked impossibly small in comparison.

'I thought you'd already left...' Her voice drained away again, because all of a sudden she felt the weight of her silly deception. It hit her the instant she registered what going behind Raul's back actually entailed.

Brilliant dark eyes veiled, Raul gave her a glinting smile that had the odd effect of increasing her discomfiture. 'If you feed him, Luis is very appealing at this hour.'

'You fed him yourself?' Polly was astonished.

'Since I woke him up by coming in, it didn't seem fair not to. He went through that bottle like he hadn't eaten in days!' Raul confided, smoothing light fingers down over his son's back as Luis snuffled and shifted his little froglike legs, content as only a baby with a full tummy can be. 'His nursemaid changed him for me. He looks so fragile stripped, I didn't want to run the risk of doing it myself.'

Polly reached down and stole Luis into her own arms, and lovingly rubbed her cheek against her son's soft, sweet-smelling skin before she reluctantly tucked him back into his cot.

'I gather the jeans mean you've finally decided to come out riding with me,' Raul drawled from the door. 'You won't find those jeans very comfortable...but then I assume you already know that.'

Still leaning over the cot with her back turned to him, Polly's jaw dropped.

'You're lucky I stopped off in here. You'd have missed me otherwise,' Raul added casually.

Outside the silent house, Polly clambered into the four-wheel drive with a trapped look in her eyes.

'It's been ages and ages since I've been on a horse, Raul,' she said, rather abruptly.

'It's a skill you never forget,' Raul asserted bracingly. 'A couple of hours in the saddle and you'll wonder how you ever lived without it.'

A couple of *hours*? Polly was aghast. Raul shot the vehicle to a halt at the side of the stables.

Patrick Gorman strolled out of the big tack room and then froze when he saw Raul.

'I'm not accustomed to seeing you abroad at this hour, Patrick. Polly's coming out with me this morning.'

'I'll be in the office if you want me.' Without even risking a glance in Polly's direction, Patrick strode off.

Polly stood like a graven image while a pair of grooms led out two mounts. El Lobo, Raul's big black stallion, and a doe-eyed bay mare—who looked, somewhat reassuringly, barely awake.

Raul planted a hard hat on her head and did up the strap. Then he extended a peculiarly shaped garment that reminded her of an oversized body warmer.

'Protection…since you mentioned being out of practice. If you take a toss, I don't want you hurt.' He fed her into the ugly bulky protector and deftly pushed home the clasps. It weighed her down like armour.

Sweeping her up, Raul settled her into the saddle, where she hunched in sudden complete terror.

'I can't ride… Raul, do you hear me? I can't ride!' Polly cried.

'I know…' Raul murmured, so softly she had to strain to hear him as he shortened the stirrups and slotted her feet into them. 'I'd have to be a complete idiot not to know.'

'You *kn-know*?' Polly gasped in disbelief as he swung up on El Lobo with fluid ease.

'*Dios mío*…how could I not guess? Your body language around the horses yesterday was not that of an experienced horsewoman. And I could hardly miss the fact that you hadn't a clue what I was talking about,' Raul delineated very drily.

Polly turned a dull red. 'I thought you'd find it a complete bore if I admitted I was a greenhorn.'

His stunning dark golden eyes gleamed with grim amusement. 'Are you really so naive about men? Is there any male who doesn't relish imparting his superior knowledge of a subject to a woman?'

'I told Patrick I couldn't ride last night…he offered to take me through the basics this morning,' she volunteered in an embarrassed rush. 'It was stupid of me.'

In response, Raul shot her a chilling glance as piercing as an arrow of ice. His lean, strong face was hard. '*Infierno!* I suspected something of the sort last night. Let me tell you now that I do not expect my wife to make furtive assignations with my employees!'

'It *wasn't* an assign—'

'And from now on you will ensure that you are never in Patrick Gorman's company without the presence of a third party.'

Thoroughly taken aback, Polly exclaimed, 'Don't be ridiculous!'

His brilliant eyes flashed. 'As your husband, I have the right to demand a certain standard of behaviour from you.'

Polly was outraged and mortified. 'But you're being totally unreasonable. ''The presence of a third party''!' she repeated in a fuming undertone of incredulity.

'If you disobey me, I'll dismiss him.'

Raul held her shaken eyes with fierce intensity, and then simply switched channels by telling her that she was sitting on the mare's back like a seasick sack of potatoes. The riding lesson which followed stretched Polly's self-discipline to the limits. She had to rise above that abrasive exchange and concentrate on his instructions, and Raul had high expectations.

Finally, Raul led her out onto the *llanos* at a walking pace. 'You're doing very well for a greenhorn, *mi esposa*,' he drawled, surprising her.

Polly focused on his darkly handsome features. As her tummy lurched with reaction, she despised herself. Not an hour ago Raul had been talking like a Middle Eastern potentate who thought no woman could be trusted alone with a man.

A frown line forming between his brows, Raul reined in his mount a few minutes later. A rider was approaching them—an elderly *llanero* with a bristling silver moustache, clad in an old-fashioned poncho and a wide-brimmed hat.

Raul addressed him in Spanish.

'My grandfather, Fidelio Navarro,' he told Polly flatly.

With a sober look of acknowledgement, his posture in the saddle rigid, the older man responded in softly spoken Spanish. He was as unyielding as Raul. Polly glanced between them in frustration. Raul and his grandfather greeted each other like strangers, each as scrupulously formal and rigid with unbending pride as the other.

Polly leant out of the saddle to extend her hand, a warm and determined smile on her face. After some hesitation, Fidelio Navarro moved his mount closer and briefly clasped her hand. 'It would please me very much if you came to see our son, Luis,' Polly said quietly.

'He doesn't speak English,' Raul breathed icily.

Not daring to look at him, conscious that he was angrily disconcerted by her intervention, Polly tilted her chin. 'Then please translate my invitation. And could you also tell him that as I have neither parents nor grandparents living, it would mean a great deal to me if Luis was given the chance to know his great-grandfather?'

Silence followed, a silence screaming with tension and Raul's outright incredulity.

Then Raul spoke at some length. His grandfather met Polly's hopeful gaze and sombrely replied.

'He thanks you for your warmth and generosity,' Raul interpreted woodenly. 'He will think the idea over.'

But there had been more than that in Fidelio's sun-creased dark eyes: a slight defrosting of his discomfiture, an easing of the rigidity round his unsmiling mouth. As they parted to ride off in different directions, she heard Raul release his breath in a stark hiss.

'*Caramba!* How can you justify such interference in what is nothing to do with you?' Raul gritted in a tone of raw disbelief that actually shook with the strength of his emotion. 'Do you think I have not already invited him to my home without success?'

'Well, if you glower at him like that when you ask, I'm not surprised. Maybe he thought you were only asking out of politeness, privately recognising the relationship without really wanting to get any closer...' Daringly, Polly proffered her own suspicions. 'I think you and Fidelio are both so scared of losing face that you're afraid to talk frankly to each other.'

'I am afraid of nothing, and how you can *dare*—'

'I did it for Luis,' Polly lied, because she had spoken up first and foremost for Raul's benefit—Raul, who definitely wanted closer ties with his grandfather. 'Neither of us have any other family to offer him.'

'What do *I* know about family?' Raul growled, spurring on El Lobo in the direction of the ranch.

'What do I know either?' Polly thought of her own less than perfect childhood, with her controlling, judgemental father. 'But we *are* a family now, and we can learn like everybody else!'

'A family?' Raul repeated in frowning acknowledgement, and with perceptible disconcertion. 'I suppose we are.'

Only sparing the time to inform her that they were leaving for his villa on the Caribbean coast that afternoon, Raul took his leave. Polly went for a bath to ease her tired muscles. It was all swings and roundabouts with Raul, she thought heavily. One moment he was alienating her with his tyrannical and utterly unreasonable threat to dismiss Patrick Gorman simply because *she* had unthinkingly stepped over the formal boundary lines Raul expected her to maintain. And the next?

The next, Raul was filling her with an almost overwhelming desire to close her arms round him in comfort and reassurance. For Raul, she recognised, the years between birth and adulthood had been dogged by traumatic experiences.

What had it been like for him? The son of Eduardo Zaforteza's mistress, his mother isolated by a relationship that had been flaunted rather than more acceptably concealed. Behind her lover's back, Pilar must have been shunned and despised, and how had that affected

Raul? Until his father had adopted him, nothing had been certain or safe in Raul's life.

Raul must have developed his own defences at an early age. After his mother's death, he'd lived as a bitter bone of contention in a destructive, acrimonious marriage. He had once remarked that in disputes between couples the child was often the weapon, that she had to know that as well as *he* did, only at the time she hadn't picked up on what he was telling her about his own background. In the same way, she remembered his unexpected outrage when she had made a crack about what he might consider a 'decent mother'. She had never dreamt what a sensitive subject that might be, and now winced at the recollection.

Finally she was beginning to understand the man she loved, but her dismay increased in proportion to that new understanding. At some stage in that damaged childhood and adolescence Raul had begun protecting himself, by keeping emotional ties that might threaten his equanimity on a superficial level. It showed in his relationships with women, even in his hopelessly defensive attitude to his estranged grandfather. He didn't risk himself, he held back, and yet he didn't hold back with Luis, Polly conceded painfully. He loved their son with unashamed intensity, and was content, indeed happy to focus his emotions on their child.

And that meant that she herself was still chasing hopes that were unattainable. Raul would never love her. If their marriage was to survive, she had to get her priorities in order and stop expecting more from Raul than he was capable of giving her. And yet, according to Melina, a little voice gibed with cruel effect, he had *loved* her...

*   *   *

Sprawled with elegant indolence on the rattan seating, a look of amusement on his bronzed features, Raul studied Polly while she watched the dancers on the beach with unconcealed fascination. The *tambores*—African drums made out of hollow logs—supplied the frenzied beat for the male and female figures twisting and shaking with abandonment.

'I thought you would enjoy this,' Raul murmured with lazy satisfaction. 'That's why I organised it.'

Meeting his stunning dark golden eyes, Polly burned. She had to drag her attention back to the dancers. The intensely sensual movements of the gyrating couples were becoming ever wilder.

Raul curved a long arm round her and she felt her whole body quicken with instant awareness. Over the past twelve days Raul had taught her to value every hour that they spent together, and every morning she got up, apprehensively waiting for him to announce that they were leaving the villa. After all, this coming weekend the fiesta would be held at the ranch. But right now Polly wanted time to stand still, because here nothing else seemed to touch them.

Raul made a lot of phone calls and used a computer to stay in touch with the world of business, but he was with her almost all the time, more relaxed and less restless and driven than she had ever known him to be. He never seemed bored. In fact he was rather like he had been in Vermont, she registered, with slight surprise at that acknowledgement. Talking to her, interested in her, amusing, entertaining, even tender, all the tension gone, the sole difference being that sexual intimacy now deepened their relationship.

As the dance appeared to be reaching a climax, Polly was astonished when another woman stepped in. With frantically twitching hips she shoved the original female dancer away from the male and triumphantly took her place.

'A comment on the fickleness of the male sex,' Raul drawled, amused at her bemused frown over such an unromantic development. 'You're so innocent, *querida*.'

Not so innocent, Polly reflected tensely, enervated by that unexpected change of partners that came too close for comfort to her own deepest fears.

How long was she going to live with the secret terror that Raul might some day return to his discreet liaison with Melina D'Agnolo? Melina had already made it abundantly clear that she was prepared to wait for him, and no doubt she was equally ready to do whatever it might take to get him back. When would fidelity become a challenge to a male who didn't love her? At what stage would her novelty value in the marital bed become boring and predictable? Disturbed by the insecure thoughts with which she was tormenting herself, Polly shut them down.

After thanking the dancers, they went back indoors to the marbled splendour of the spacious villa. Set beside a secluded palm-fringed beach of golden sand, complete with crystal-clear water to bathe in, the villa rejoiced in the surroundings of a tropical paradise.

They tiptoed in to see Luis, out for the count in his cot. Raul curved his arms round her from behind. 'He really *is* special,' he said huskily.

'Naturally...he's yours,' Polly teased. 'And because he's your son, he is the most super-intelligent and advanced baby on this planet!'

'You think so too, *querida*,' he reminded her in a sensual growl as he slowly spun her round to crush her soft, willing mouth hungrily under his own. Her body sang with feverish hot excitement.

He carried her through to their bedroom and settled her on the bed, standing over her, intent golden eyes roaming over her slender length with the bold and unashamed desire that never failed to ease her secret fears. How could Raul want her so much and have room to even think of any other woman? How could he make love to her day after day and night after night with a seemingly insatiable appetite for her body and find anything lacking in her?

In heaven, Polly closed her eyes as he peeled off her clothes, piece by tantalising piece, pausing to kiss and caress every newly revealed curve and line of her until there wasn't a single part of her quivering, wantonly aroused being that didn't ache for him to possess her.

'I'm going to teach you to dance like that with me,' Raul murmured.

Polly's eyes opened very wide on his devastatingly handsome face. He actually looked serious.

'But only in private. I don't want anyone else seeing the way you look at me, the way you move against me...' he admitted hoarsely.

He was so intense about sex. In fact, for someone who had informed her that sex was merely another physical appetite, Raul seemed to be set on proving that every time he touched her it was another variation on an endlessly fascinating theme that pretty much absorbed him more with every passing day. He couldn't keep his hands off her. He had gone from being a male who was not remotely tactile out of bed to a male who usually had her anchored in some way to him no matter where they were.

She framed his cheekbones with possessive hands

and let the tip of her tongue dart provocatively between his lips. With a groan of hunger, Raul practically flattened her to the bed and kissed her with a fierce sexual need that melted her skin over her bones. And all cool was abandoned at that point.

A long while later, she lay limp with satiation while Raul abstractedly wound a strand of her hair round a long brown forefinger. 'Tell me about the first time you fell in love,' he invited without warning.

Polly glanced at him in surprise. Raul didn't ask things like that. And it was an awkward question. One crush and one short-lived infatuation were all she had to talk about, barring himself.

He shrugged a bare bronzed shoulder. 'Curiosity.'

'He was called—'

'I don't want to know his name,' Raul intervened instantly, jawline hardening.

Somewhat disconcerted by that interruption, Polly breathed, 'Yes…er, well, he was another student—'

'I don't need to know that either…what I want to know is how you *felt*,' Raul stressed.

'How I…felt,' Polly echoed. 'Silly and dizzy, and then gutted about covers it. The minute I got to know what he was really like, I couldn't understand what I'd seen in him.'

'You fell out of love again that fast…what did he *do*?' Raul enquired darkly, raising himself up to stare down at her.

'He hustled me into a bedroom one lunchtime and told me it was my lucky day.'

She now had Raul's interest. 'You're kidding?'

'When I said no, he got abusive. He thought I'd be a push-over.'

'Major misjudgement,' Raul framed, a slight shake in his dark, deep voice. 'How old was this guy?'

'Nineteen.'

'All teenage boys think about is scoring.'

'You weren't much older when you and Melina…I mean—' Biting back the remainder of that impulsive remark, Polly coloured at the sudden narrowing of the shrewd dark eyes above hers. 'Well, she mentioned you'd once been an item.'

'Did she really?' His black spiky lashes screened his gaze, his wide, sensual mouth hardening on that information.

Polly lowered her eyes, more disturbed by that silence than she would have been by any explanation. Why was it that the unknown was always so much more threatening?

'We'll fly home on Friday morning,' Raul informed her.

'But the fiesta…' Polly groaned, torn between relief and anxiety. 'There must be loads of arrangements to make, and I haven't even made a start—'

'After all these years of practice, the staff could stage it on their own.' Rolling over onto his back, Raul reached for her again. His gleaming scrutiny raked over her pink face with unsettling efficiency. 'Have I ever told you how extraordinarily expressive those gorgeous blue eyes are, *mi esposa*?' he asked huskily. 'Do you know they close every time I kiss you?'

Polly studied him with the focused intensity of a woman in love, a kind of agony coiling tight as a spring inside her. If he betrayed her, she would die. If their marriage ended, her future would end with it. She could not bear to think of life without him. She wanted to cling like a vine, but clinging would be as much out of

order as probing personal questions which might well
have answers she'd be better off not hearing.

And suddenly he *was* kissing her again, evoking a
wild hunger that clawed at her slim body, awakening
all over again that frantic, feverish, elemental need that
overwhelmed every restraint and blanked out every
thought.

Polly woke up alone on the morning of their departure.
There was nothing unusual about that. It was a challenge to keep Raul in bed after dawn. Early rising and
a two-hour break at midday were the norm in
Venezuela. Trying not to feel sad that they were leaving
the villa, she went for a shower.

As she leafed through a wardrobe that had grown
mightily in size since leaving the ranch, she hugged
precious memories of their stay to herself. Strolling
hand in hand along the Paseo Colón boulevard in Puerta
la Cruz, enjoying the cool breezes coming in off the
ocean; speeding in a motor launch through the eerie
mangroves in the Mochina National Park; eating crispy
churros with hot chocolate for breakfast *and* supper on
Margarita Island; driving up to Caracas to shop in the
CCCT and Paseo las Mercedes malls, discovering that
there *was* such a thing as a male who loved shopping
and indeed that there were no greater worshippers of
the consumer society or the art of being beautiful than
the Venezuleans.

She was happy—yes, she had to admit it, she was
very, very happy. Feeling good in a beautifully tailored
leaf-green short skirt and top, she glanced into Luis's
room and smiled at the sight of the empty cot. Luis was
probably sitting in his infant seat watching his father

work and enjoying a somewhat one-sided conversation in between times.

She could already hear Raul talking as she reached the door of the room he had been using as an office.

'...am I bored?' Raul was saying with husky amusement. 'On my honeymoon, Melina?' And then, ruefully, 'I'm *thinking* in English these days!'

Polly froze in her tracks. Her heart was thumping so hard it felt as if it was banging in her ears, and she had to strain to hear. The silence went on and on. She peered round the door lintel and glimpsed Raul, poised with his back to the door, wide shoulders bunching with tension below the superb cut of his lightweight cream jacket, bronzed fingers beating out a rapid soundless tattoo on the edge of the desk.

'Of course I appreciate your loyalty, Melina,' Raul continued in a roughened sexy undertone. 'I'm looking forward to seeing you tonight too. No, I don't think it should be too difficult. I'm not on a leash yet.'

CHAPTER ELEVEN

'You still look rough. You should lie down,' Raul decreed as he walked Polly up the steps into the ranch.

'What about the fiesta...all the people coming?' Polly mumbled sickly, edging away from him as soon as she decently could.

'It's been happening for over a hundred years without you, *mi esposa*,' Raul responded in a teasing tone as he bent to lift her gently up into his arms and stride towards the magnificent staircase. 'Just go to bed and stay there until you feel better. That's the only important thing.'

Shock had unsettled her stomach. She had been sick during the flight, convincing Raul that she had caught some bug. He could not have been more caring and concerned had she developed a life-threatening illness. And she couldn't bear it, couldn't bear him near her, yet couldn't bear him out of her sight either for fear of what he might be doing or even thinking.

Listening to Raul on the phone to Melina D'Agnolo had shattered her. Now, as he carried her past the superb flower arrangements which had appeared everywhere, and the frantically busy staff excited about the party which kicked off the weekend festivities, Polly felt like the weakest of the weak. No way was she going to be lying in bed this evening like a party pooper while Melina held the floor!

Raul set her upright in their bedroom. Confront him, screamed through her mind in letters of taunting fire.

She walked over to the windows, torn by conflicting desires. She wanted to see them together first. She wanted to confront them. If she tried to confront Raul now, what did she base her accusations on? His appreciation of Melina's loyalty? Or that simple sentence 'I'm looking forward to seeing you tonight'?

It wasn't enough. It wasn't evidence of anything he couldn't explain away. But the very fact he had been on the phone talking to Melina like that…it ripped Polly apart. She had genuinely trusted him, sincerely come to believe that it was only her own insecurity which was tormenting her…

'Do you think a married man needs a mistress?' she asked abruptly.

Silence stretched.

Polly spun round. Raul looked slightly bemused, a frown line etched between his expressive brows. Then a splintering smile slashed his beautiful mouth. 'Not if he spends as much time in bed with his wife as I do!'

'It was a serious question, Raul.'

'Only not a very sensible one. With my background, the answer would be absolutely not. A divorce would be a better option,' Raul drawled reflectively.

Having invited that opinion, Polly's stomach curdled. She turned back to the windows on unsteady legs.

'Is there something you want to discuss with me?' Raul enquired in smooth invitation.

'Nothing.' Not without proof. She wasn't about to risk tearing their marriage apart without proper proof.

'I have this feeling that something is playing on your mind…it's not the first time I've had it.'

Taken aback by that assurance, Polly linked her unsteady hands tightly together and stared out of the window, seeing nothing. She might as well have been staring into space. Raul strolled to her side and followed the apparent path of her gaze.

Patrick Gorman was giving instructions to a group of workmen who were stringing up extra lighting in the gardens below.

'If I was the jealous type,' Raul breathed with sudden startling rawness, 'I'd go down there and kill him because you're looking at him!'

Polly focused on Patrick for the first time in complete bewilderment, like someone who had missed a crucial sentence that made sense of inexplicable behaviour. 'I wasn't looking at him…why would I want to look at him, for heaven's sake?'

Raul punched the button that closed the curtains with what struck her as quite unnecessary force. Polly surveyed him. A devastatingly handsome male in a seething rage. She blinked. He strode out of the room without a backward glance.

He's jealous of Patrick. Polly slowly shook her head at that strikingly obvious revelation. Why hadn't she made that connection before? Right from the minute he had seen her chattering happily to the young Englishman Raul had been warning her off him. Yet how could he possibly be jealous of another man when he was planning to continue his affair with Melina?

But then wasn't that men the world over? she reflected with newly learnt cynicism. Some men only valued a woman when another man admired her, or when they thought that they themselves were no longer desired. And then a man could be possessive without loving. Which category did Raul fall into? Or was it simply that, as his wife, he now regarded her in the light of a possession?

She sank down on the edge of the bed, dry-eyed but

pale as milk. Was Melina simply a habit with Raul? When he had told her that he appreciated her loyalty what had he meant? Had he been thanking her for patiently waiting for him? Did he honestly think he had a hope in hell of continuing such an affair without being found out?

The door opened again. Raul hovered for a split second, as if somewhat unsure of his welcome, and then extended his hand to her, one of his sudden flashing smiles driving all reserve from his lean bronzed features. 'We have a visitor, *gatita*,' he announced. 'My grandfather is here.'

Fidelio Navarro was stationed in the hall, curling his hat round and round between strained hands. Polly hurried down the stairs to greet him, breaking the ice by going straight up to him and leaning forward to kiss him on both cheeks, as one did with family members. He smiled and relaxed perceptibly while Raul translated her welcome with the air of a male grateful for the distraction.

Upstairs, Polly lifted Luis out of his cot and laid him in Fidelio's sturdy arms. The old man heaved a giant sigh and slowly shook his silvered head, openly overcome by the sight of his great-grandson.

'He says…Luis has my mother's eyes,' Raul translated gruffly.

Fidelio's eyes swam, his mouth tightening, his emotions too near the surface for him to say anything more. Polly accepted Luis back and looked at Raul hovering, her own gaze expectant. 'You go and have a celebration drink and talk now,' she instructed, knowing she had to spell it all out, afraid that, left to his own devices, Raul might duck the issue and take grateful refuge in polite conversation. 'You'll talk about your mother…and how much you loved her, and how good things are going to be now in this family.'

'*Sí...*' Raul dug his clenched fists tautly into his trouser pockets and bent his imperious dark head, swallowing hard.

Fidelio and Raul walked out of the room together about a foot apart.

Polly drew in a slow, deep breath and said a prayer that with a little give and take on both sides the barriers would finally come down between the two men. The older man needed to be completely sure of his welcome in this house. Without that confidence, he wouldn't visit again.

Two hours later, from the vantage point of an upper window, she watched Fidelio wrap his arms round Raul and hug him fiercely before he climbed back onto his horse outside the house. A tide of relief rolled over her. Clearly Raul hadn't backed off and stood on his dignity. She was satisfied then.

'I wouldn't call them gifts,' Raul delivered some hours later, looking deadly serious in the reflection Polly could see of him in the mirror as she dazedly fingered the fabulous diamond necklace and earrings he had just presented her with. 'They belonged to my mother, so now they're yours.'

Polly stared down at the fabulous river of diamonds and the teardrop earrings with a lump in her throat. 'They're out of this world.'

Lifting the necklace, Raul clasped it round her throat. 'No one but me ever saw her wear them. My father never took her out in public.'

Polly gulped. 'Oh, heavens…that's so sad!'

'No, *mi esposa*.' Raul watched her put on the earrings

and then stand up. 'We're a different generation, and the Zaforteza family has enjoyed a rebirth. I'm very grateful that the warmth I foolishly condemned you for has helped to heal the wounds of the past and persuade Fidelio to become a part of our lives.'

Wrinkling her nose to hold back tears in receipt of that surprisingly humble accolade, Polly turned to study her reflection in the cheval mirror. She looked elegant, with her hair swept up in a French roll, loose tendrils curling round her face. And then there was the dress, the designer sleeveless evening gown in green with the wonderful sweeping neckline and elaborate gilded embroidery, not to mention the spike-heeled shoes and all the diamonds catching fire under the lights. But none of that meant anything when set beside the burning sincerity she had glimpsed in Raul's stunning golden eyes. That filled her to bursting point with love.

Without the slightest warning, Raul reached for her hand and practically crushed the life from her fingers with the unwitting fierceness of his grip. He exhaled in a stark hiss. 'I think I love you...'

Polly's eyes opened very wide, and then flooded with pain. She hauled her fingers free in a gesture of repudiation. 'No, you don't. You're just feeling grateful and more emotional than usual,' she told him unevenly. 'Don't call that love.'

'I said it wrong, but I haven't had a lot of practice at this!' Raul gritted rawly. 'I shouldn't have said, I *think*—'

'You shouldn't have said anything. I'm sorry if I've made you feel that nothing short of true love will satisfy me,' Polly responded tautly, the stress and strain of the day mounting up to betray her into saying exactly what she was thinking. 'Actually, fidelity would do...so there, I've finally lowered my expectations to a more realistic level!'

His fabulous bone structure prominent with tension beneath his bronzed skin, Raul dealt her a thunderous look of disbelief that shook her. He parted his lips to respond at the same moment that an urgent knock sounded on the door.

'Our guests have begun to arrive,' he relayed seconds later.

Before he could leave the room, Polly rushed over to him, all cool abandoned in the growing awareness that she had reacted in the worst possible way, her blue eyes deeply troubled and full of guilt. 'Raul, I didn't mean...you took me by—'

'Relax...you've cured me of my delusional state,' he derided, silencing her, convincing her that he could only have spoken those words out of an impulsive need to reward her in some way for helping to bring him and his grandfather to a closer understanding.

It was not a good moment to go downstairs and discover that Melina D'Agnolo had arrived with the first wave of guests. Melina—spectacular in a glittering scarlet dress, blonde hair gleaming and a brilliant smile on her ripe pink mouth.

'What a lovely dress,' she said sweetly, and passed on.

Loads of baggage was being carried upstairs. Not everyone was staying the whole weekend, and not everyone was sleeping in the house. The equestrian centre had a spacious block of comfortable accommodation, used when Raul staged polo matches and occasional conferences, and many of their guests would be staying there. In the busy buzz of people, several different languages filling the air, Polly suffered a stark instant of panic, and then she drew in a deep, steadying breath and took her place at Raul's side.

Since being nice had never been a challenge for Polly—ironically with anyone but Raul—she soon found that natural friendliness was all that was required, and the approval in Raul's eyes soon dissolved her anxiety about socialising. Mid-way through the evening a fabulous fireworks display brought everyone out into the gardens. Polly was walking back indoors, hanging back to wait for Raul, who was chatting to a group of men, when Melina approached her.

'You watch him like an anxious mother, don't you?' It was an open sneer.

Polly coloured, suddenly painfully conscious that, whether she liked it or not, she *had* been sticking to Raul rather like superglue.

'Draped in diamonds worth millions,' Melina scorned with glittering green eyes. 'I hope they comfort you for sleeping alone at night.'

As Polly paled, the beautiful blonde flung her a triumphant look and strolled past her.

A pair of lean hands settled unexpectedly on her taut shoulders from behind. '*Dios mío*, how wonderfully friendly Melina's being!' Raul drawled above her slightly downbent head.

Polly jerked as if he had slapped her. 'Actually…'

'Actually?' Raul encouraged silkily.

'She was admiring my diamonds,' Polly completed dully.

'She's very fond of jewels…but not of her own sex.'

And who would know that best but him? That statement only served to remind Polly that Raul had intimate knowledge of Melina's character. It made her feel more isolated than ever.

The musicians began to play the haunting country music of the *llanos* and one of them began to sing. 'What is he singing about?' she whispered.

'A broken heart…it may well be mine,' Raul breathed with stark impatience, releasing her to stride back indoors.

Did he care about Melina? *Really* care? Might he only have realised that after their marriage? Stranger things had happened, and she could not say that Raul was a male noticeably in touch with his own feelings except where Luis was concerned. So why had he told *her* that he thought he loved her?

As a reward? Those words were so easy to say. Out of guilt? Knowing that he was about to betray her, had he tossed that declaration at her like a consolation prize? Or to take the edge off any suspicions she might develop about his fidelity? And yet, strangely, that was the second time Raul had invited her to talk to him about what she had on her mind. Raul knew something was wrong. He had freely admitted that Melina didn't like her own sex, almost as if he didn't trust the beautiful blonde…

Any more than *you* trust *him*? That accidental comparison shocked Polly. For trust had been there until she'd overheard that phone call. And before that call, whenever she'd thought of telling Raul all the horrible things which Melina had slung at her, she had remembered that nasty little scene on the jet, and then the way he had walked out on her that same day after calling her obsessively jealous. Furthermore, she had no evidence of anything that Melina had said. Was she now trying to work herself up to running and telling tales like an immature little girl? Or was she seriously waiting for Raul to make some sort of move on Melina, who already seemed so unbearably smug tonight? Like a temporarily forsaken mistress aware that her star was now in the ascendant again?

Patrick wandered over to speak to her. 'I thought I'd avoid you while Raul was around,' he shared in an undertone, glancing rather anxiously around himself, like a man watching out for trouble.

'Why's that?'

'Raul is a Latin American male to his fingertips. I used to think he wasn't, except when he was being a killer on the polo field. Then he married you, and all of a sudden that cool front is cracking. I honestly don't think he can stand another man within twenty feet of you.'

'Really?' Polly lifted her head, a fledgling smile curving her lips because she was ready at that moment to snatch at any straw.

'So, if you don't mind, I won't ask you to dance.'

'No problem. I want to dance with Raul.' Polly drifted off, her mind made up. Time to stop avoiding the issue and allowing Melina to make her miserable and call all the shots. It was time to fight back and do the sensible thing, which was to talk to Raul.

So, in the mood she was in, it wasn't pleasant to find Raul, standing in a corner with a brooding look of darkness on his starkly handsome features, and Melina, chattering in that covert, intimate way she always embraced around him, her exquisite face soft with a cloying smile.

But Polly walked right over. 'Would you like to dance, Raul?' she asked in a rather high-pitched voice, and with a sudden spooky horror that he might say no and humiliate her.

Melina raised a brow and averted her eyes, a self-satisfied little smile playing about her lips. Raul strode forward, eyes blazing hot gold as they whipped over his wife's flushed and unhappy expression.

He closed an arm around her, and instead of taking her onto the floor to dance, he guided her out into the softly lit greater privacy of the gardens.

'I didn't really want to dance,' Polly admitted unevenly, wondering why on earth he should look so scorchingly angry. 'I needed to talk to you in private. And if you're annoyed now, you're probably going to be even more annoyed when I've finished talking...so possibly we should take a raincheck on this until later...'

Polly got two steps away, and then was unceremoniously pulled back by the lean hand that closed round hers.

'No raincheck. You were saying?'

Polly breathed in deep to steady herself. She could not say that harsh tone was the most inviting she had ever heard. 'I heard you talking to Melina on the phone at the villa—'

'Did you indeed?' Raul threw that query like a gauntlet.

It wasn't quite the response she had expected.

Polly became even more flustered. 'I want you to know that up until that point I trusted you...and you may wonder why I should say that, but, you see, Melina told me she was your mistress the first day I came here, and she said that you'd go back to her...and that night you *did* go over there, and even though you *said* it was to see Fidelio—'

'One point at a time,' Raul intervened levelly. 'Melina called me at the villa to inform me that, after wrestling with her non-existent conscience, she had decided that it was her duty to tell me that you were meeting up with Patrick Gorman in secret.'

In shock at that news, Polly felt her mouth simply drop open.

Raul dealt her a grim look of amusement. 'I thought that would take the wind out of your sails.'

It did. Polly was poleaxed to realise that Melina had been working on both her and Raul.

'Divide and conquer. Not very original or clever, at least not clever enough to fool me,' Raul delineated grittily, shooting Polly a forbidding glance of reproach. 'I didn't believe a word of it, but I strung her along to see how far she was prepared to go in her determination to cause trouble between us. It also confirmed my suspicion that she had been working on you as well.'

He hailed a passing maid with a snap of his fingers and spoke to her in Spanish.

'I want to know everything that Melina told you,' he said next, his lean, strong face hard and unyielding.

'Maybe you should pull up a chair. She said a lot,' Polly muttered uncertainly, suddenly not knowing whether she was on her head or her heels, and getting the horrendous feeling that every time she parted her lips she was digging another foot of her own grave. There was no doubt that the more Raul heard, the angrier he became.

'Her poison couldn't have fallen on more fertile ground,' Raul remarked grimly when she had finished speaking. 'That first night she joined us for dinner I watched her with you, and I was immediately suspicious of her behaviour. She was too friendly towards you and too flirtatious with me...you should have come straight to me with the truth. When you said nothing, I thought I might've misjudged her.'

Polly grimaced, suddenly feeling such a total idiot. 'I didn't want you to think I was jealous again.'

Firmly closing a determined hand over hers, Raul took her back indoors through the entrance that led into his suite of offices.

'How much proof do you need to trust me?' Raul challenged. 'We are about to face Melina together!'

At that disconcerting announcement, Polly gulped.

'I sent the maid to tell Melina that I wanted to see her in private.'

Raul thrust open the door before them. Melina was inside, lounging back against Raul's desk. She straightened with a bright smile that froze round the edges, her brow furrowing, when she saw Polly.

'After all the lies you've told, I'm amazed that you can look either of us in the face,' Raul drawled in icy condemnation.

Taken aback by that direct opening, Melina's eyes rounded. 'What are you—?'

'I've been more than fair to you,' Raul cut in. 'When you came to me last year, distraught about your financial problems, I was sympathetic.'

Two high spots of red now burned in Melina's cheeks. 'I wanted more than sympathy, Raul!'

'I paid you to act as my hostess when I entertained here. You were excellent in the role, but it was strictly a business arrangement.'

Melina's face twisted with fury. 'If it hadn't been for her and that wretched child we would've ended up with a lot more than a business arrangement—'

'There was never any question of that,' Raul dismissed with stark impatience. '*Dios mío*...I learned my lesson with you at nineteen, but I was willing to help you as a friend. The lies you've fed Polly...and attempted to feed me…merely prove that you haven't changed at all, Melina.'

'I don't know what you *see* in her!' Melina raged at him incredulously. '*I* should have been your wife!'

'You wouldn't know love if it smacked you in the face,' Raul responded with contempt. 'Greed and ambition are no more attractive to me now than they were years ago.'

Melina reddened, sent him a look of loathing, and then seemed to collect herself. Tossing her head high, she parted her lips, but Raul got in first. 'I expect you to vacate your present accommodation by the end of the month. I won't be renewing the lease and you are no longer welcome here. A car will take you home.'

Without another word, Raul swept Polly back out of the room. Her legs felt hollow and butterflies were dancing in her tummy. She could not credit what a fool she had been to listen to the other woman's insidious lies. 'She's *never* been your mistress…'

'We had a brief affair when I was nineteen,' Raul admitted grimly. 'Although I didn't know it, I was far from being her only lover at the time. She's several years older than me. I *was* infatuated with her, but I wasn't a complete fool. Melina couldn't hide her greed. No matter what I gave her, she wanted more. When she realised I had no plans to marry her, she married a wealthy industrialist in his sixties—'

'And he died?'

'No, she's been married twice. Her first husband divorced her; the second died, leaving her in debt.'

'And that's when she came to you for help?'

Raul nodded, his jawline squaring. 'I should've known better than to take pity on her, *gatita*. She was always a bitch.'

'She resented me…she was just furious that you'd married me…'

'*Dios mío*, I didn't even realise that she was hoping I might become involved with her again. I'm not attracted to her now, but she can be amusing company.'

'I've been an idiot,' Polly mumbled ruefully.

'I should've made you tell me the truth. Your silence protected her.'

They returned to the party. Polly was light-headed with relief but thoroughly humbled by the awareness that she had been very naive in her dealings with Melina, and that it had taken Raul to sort it all out. OK, she had finally surrendered to the need to tell him the truth, but it had taken her too long to reach that point.

She wanted so much to be alone with Raul then, but it was impossible with so many people around. It was near dawn before the last of their guests dispersed. By then Polly felt stressed out emotionally, riven with guilt that she had so misjudged Raul and appalled that he knew of the suspicions she had cherished. And, worst of all, how could she have reacted as she had when he'd talked about loving her? Hadn't he already shown in lots of ways that he cared about her, desired her, enjoyed her company? So maybe that still didn't quite amount to her estimation of love, but it was probably as close as she was likely to get to being loved!

Raul thrust the bedroom door shut behind him, his screened gaze zeroing in on her aimless stance in the middle of the carpet. 'I wish every one of our guests would evaporate,' he admitted with real fervour.

'But—'

'No buts, *mi esposa*, privacy is at a premium this weekend, but thankfully we're leaving for London on

Sunday evening. I have a surprise for you. Monday *is* your birthday,' Raul reminded her.

'London…a *surprise*?' Polly's cup of guilt positively overflowed. 'I'm really sorry I listened to Melina.'

'You didn't know what you were up against.' Reaching for her, Raul eased her slowly into the circle of his arms. 'And now it's time for you to keep quiet and listen to me.'

Polly gazed up into clear dark golden eyes and her susceptible heart quickened.

'I fell in love with you in Vermont,' Raul delivered almost aggressively, strain hardening his sensual mouth. 'But I didn't realise that until recently. I basked in your response to me then. You asked nothing from me, but your love made you feel as much mine as the baby you carried.'

Polly was transfixed. 'Did it?'

'I felt very possessive of you even then. I'm not prone to analysing my emotions…I didn't have to,' Raul admitted bluntly. 'When you went missing, you went missing with my baby inside you, so I never had to question the strength of my need to find you both. I was always able to use Luis as a justification. And when I found it a challenge to keep our relationship impersonal, I told myself it was solely because you were the mother of my child.'

'You were pretty good at convincing yourself,' Polly whispered unevenly, almost afraid to believe in what he was trying to explain to her.

'I even had a good excuse to marry you—'

'I forced you into it.'

'I could've said no, and I didn't. You made it easy for me to avoid facing up to the fact that I wanted you on any terms…and then you vanished and I was climbing the walls with frustration again,' Raul confessed, and shifted a shoulder in a jerky shrug that signified unpleasant recollection. 'I was angrier than I've ever been in my life, and yet so scared that I wouldn't be able to find you a second time…'

She rested her brow against his broad chest, disturbed that she had caused him that much pain without even suspecting the fact. 'Oh, Raul…I thought it was only Luis you'd be worrying about and missing.'

'I didn't know what was happening inside my own head,' he confided grittily. 'I even assumed that once I'd satisfied my overpowering desire to make love to you I would go back to feeling like myself again. But it didn't work like that.'

'It doesn't,' Polly agreed shakily, eyes stinging with happiness because believing that Raul loved her was becoming easier with every word he spoke.

'When I came back in from that late-night ride and you weren't where I expected you to be I really lost it, and that's when I realised how much power you had over me…that was a very threatening discovery for me,' Raul conceded with driven honesty. 'And then it got worse…'

'*Worse?*' Falling in love wasn't always fun, but Raul was making it sound like being plunged into hell.

'With women, it was always easy come, easy go with me, and then you smiled at Patrick Gorman just the way you once smiled at me in Vermont, and I wanted to knock his teeth down his throat! It was so irrational, so childish, *querida*,' he grated, with a highly revealing combination of regret and embarrassment.

'I didn't really notice…I was too busy worrying about Melina and my own insecurities.' Polly winced at how blind she had been.

'It slowly dawned on me that this was what love felt like…all these crazy feelings, and rage and moments of weakness and fear, and just needing you there all the time…' His sculpted cheekbones were sharpened by a rise of dark colour. '*Infierno*…I can't believe I just said all that!'

'But it's like that for me too, and, believe me, loving you was not fun when we met up in London again, so I tried to tell myself I hated you,' Polly complained feelingly, but she wrapped her arms round him so tightly when she said it he wasn't in any danger of feeling rejected on the basis of his past sins.

'I wanted to haul you into my arms and I couldn't let myself…and now I can,' Raul appreciated, with a blazing smile of satisfaction and relief. He crushed her to him and proceeded to kiss her until her head swam. They ended up on the bed, discarding clothes with more haste than finesse, sealing their words of love with a passionate joining that released every last scrap of tension between them.

'Yes, you *do* like being loved,' Polly teased him as she smoothed possessive fingers through his damply tousled hair and met the tender look of satisfaction in his brilliant dark eyes.

'You should've guessed how I felt at the villa, *gatita*. I don't think I've ever felt that happy before…except now,' he conceded reflectively.

'Why are we going to London?'

'Surprise…'

'But I'm curious…' Polly ran a not entirely innocent hand down over a lean, hair-roughened thigh.

Raul gave her a wolfish grin even as he hauled her closer. 'You could torture me and I wouldn't tell you!'

'Am I going to be pleased?'

'You're worse than a child,' Raul groaned with vibrant amusement, and glanced at his watch. 'Are you aware that we have to rise to be hosts again in two hours?'

Polly was aghast.

'And if I fall asleep on El Lobo's back during the polo match, guess who I'm likely to blame?'

'It's only a game,' she said comfortingly.

Lowering his head, Raul studied her with frankly adoring but slightly pained eyes. 'I must be in love. Once I'd have slaughtered any woman for saying that...'

'Why are you bringing me here?' Polly exclaimed three days later as the limousine wafted them up the long driveway to Gilbourne, her late godmother's beautiful Georgian house in Surrey.

'Happy birthday. I bought Gilbourne months ago. A whim. Don't ask me why... I came here looking for you and I remembered how much you'd talked about this place in Vermont. The estate agent was showing the most obnoxious couple round the grounds, and they were giving forth about how they would rip out the rose garden where you used to sit with your godmother.'

It took Polly the entirety of that speech to catch her breath. 'You bought it for *me*?'

'When we come to England we can stay here,' Raul pointed out.

Polly was staring out at the other limousine already parked in front of the house, and then her eyes widened even more at the sight of the helicopter on the front lawn.

'Who's here?'

'Your friends, Maxie and Darcy—'

'Maxie and Darcy?' Polly gasped, barely over the first shock of discovering that she was now the owner of the gorgeous mansion she had always adored visiting as a child.

'I did try to bring them over for the fiesta, but Maxie's pregnant, and couldn't face the prospect of a long flight, so I decided to arrange the reunion here.'

Polly was touched, but she had also paled with dismay. 'Raul...the last time I was in the same room with Maxie and Darcy it was like holding off World War Three. We all used to be great friends, and then three years ago it all went wrong. Darcy was getting married and Maxie was her bridesmaid, and Darcy's bridegroom fell head over heels for Maxie. Relations have been strained ever since.'

'But not so strained that they weren't both prepared to come here to see you,' Raul countered reassuringly.

And, minutes after walking into the gracious drawing room where all three women had last met for the reading of Nancy Leeward's will, Polly was engulfed by a very warm welcome from her friends. Both Maxie and Darcy were chattering nineteen to the dozen—to her, to *each other*, and throwing stray comments in the direction of the men in the background.

'I recognise Angelos from his photo,' Polly whispered. 'But who's the other one?'

'My husband, Luca,' Darcy announced with lashings of pride. 'Gianluca Raffacani. He's Zia's father.'

Since Polly had entirely the wrong idea about who had fathered Darcy's little daughter, those twin announcements left her fairly bereft of speech.

'They're all listening, scared they're missing something. Look, what do you say we dump the men for half an hour?' Maxie suggested in a covert whisper.

So off they went on a supposed tour of the house. And Polly heard about how Darcy had called Maxie and had lunch with her a couple of weeks earlier.

'We made up,' Darcy completed.

Polly beamed. 'That's brilliant. So, congratulations on your marriage...and I hear you're pregnant, Maxie?'

'Never been so sick in my life,' Maxie moaned, her beautiful face a tinge paler than was the norm. 'But it should pass off in a couple of weeks. It'll be worth it if I land a cute little sprog like Luis.'

They stood looking down on the rose garden where they had often sat with their godmother, and finally settled in a row on the window seat.

'Do you think Nancy's pleased with us now?' Darcy said hopefully.

Maxie grinned. 'She did me a favour...I got Angelos.'

'Luca's changed my life,' Darcy confided.

Both women looked at Polly, and she went pink. 'Raul's fabulous.'

'Oh, *no!*' Maxie groaned with a comical expression of dismay. 'I just know the men think we're up here talking about them, and here we are actually doing it!'

Hours later, Polly climbed into the elegant, beautifully draped four-poster bed in the main bedroom, marvelling that Raul had simply bought the furniture with the house and engaged new staff. He hadn't worked it out yet, but she knew what had been going through his mind all those months ago. He had walked around Gilbourne, imagining her here, and he had bought the house as a result.

'So what *were* the three of you giggling like drains

over?' Raul persisted as he slid into bed beside her, all bronzed and gorgeous and sexy against the pale linen.

Pulses quickening, Polly gave him a secretive smile. 'That would be telling.'

'You were talking about us.' Raul lay back against the banked up pillows, his trust in that belief complete. '*We* talked business.'

'Get away—you were in the billiard room by the time we came back, but you hadn't closed the door, so we tiptoed up to see how the three of you were getting on without us around,' Polly confessed with a growing smile. 'And Angelos was talking about what a great mother Maxie was going to be, Luca was talking about Darcy's amazing knowledge of antiques. And *you* were talking about my inborn talent for horse-riding!'

Raul rolled over and trapped her beneath him, stunning golden eyes laughing down into hers. 'I may have exaggerated a little, but then it was male bragging session, and I couldn't say what I really wanted to say...'

'And what was that?' Polly enquired, scarcely able to breathe for excitement with him that close.

'I just adore you, *gatita*...'

'Me too.' Polly sighed ecstatically as he kissed her, closed her eyes the way she always did, and gave herself up without a care in the world to loving pleasure.

MARRIED TO A MISTRESS

MARRIED TO A MISTRESS

CHAPTER ONE

'AND since Leland has given me power of attorney over his affairs, I shall trail that little tramp through the courts and *ruin* her!' Jennifer Coulter announced with vindictive satisfaction.

Angelos Petronides surveyed his late mother's English stepsister with no more than polite attention, his distaste concealed, his brilliant black eyes expressionless. Nobody would ever have guessed that within the last sixty seconds Jennifer had made his day by putting him in possession of information he would've paid a considerable amount to gain. Maxie Kendall, the model dubbed the Ice Queen by the press, the one and only woman who had ever given Angelos a sleepless night, was in debt...

'Leland spent a fortune on her too!' As she stalked his vast and impressive London office, Jennifer exuded seething resentment. 'You should see the bills I've uncovered...you wouldn't *believe* what it cost to keep that little trollop in designer clothes!'

'A mistress expects a decent wardrobe...and Maxie Kendall is ambitious. I imagine she took Leland for everything she could get.' Angelos stoked the flames of his visitor's outrage without a flicker of conscience.

Unlike most who had witnessed the breakup of the Coulter marriage three years earlier, he had never suffered from the misapprehension that Leland had deserted a whiter than white wife. Nor was he impressed by Jennifer's pleas of penury. The middle-aged blonde

429

had been born wealthy and would die even wealthier, and her miserly habits were a frequent source of malicious amusement in London society.

'All that money gone for good,' Jennifer recounted tight-mouthed. 'And *now* I find out that the little tart got this huge loan off Leland as well—'

Imperceptibly, Angelos had tensed again. Trollop, tart? Jennifer had no class, no discretion. A mistress was a necessity to a red-blooded male, but a whore wasn't. However, Leland *had* broken the rules. An intelligent man did not leave his wife to set up home with his mistress. No Greek male would ever have been that stupid, Angelos reflected with innate superiority. Leland Coulter had made a fool of himself and he had embarrassed his entire family.

'But you have regained what you said you wanted most,' he slotted into the flood of Jennifer's financial recriminations. 'You have your husband back.'

The dry reminder made the older woman flush and then her mouth twisted again. 'Oh, yes, I got him back after his heart attack, so weak he's going to be recuperating for months! That bitch deserted him at the hospital...did I tell you that? Simply told the doctor to contact his wife and walked back out again, cool as a cucumber. Well, I *need* that money now, and whatever it takes I intend to get it off her. I've already had a lawyer's letter sent to her—'

'Jennifer...with Leland laid low, you have many more important concerns. And I assure you that Leland would not be impressed by the spectacle of his wife driving his former mistress into the bankruptcy court.' From below lush black lashes, Angelos watched the blonde stiffen as she belatedly considered that angle.

'Allow *me* to deal with this matter. I will assume responsibility for the loan and reimburse you.'

Jennifer's jaw slackened in shock. 'You...you *will*?'

'Are we not family?' Angelos chided in his deep, dark, accented drawl.

Slowly, very slowly, Jennifer nodded, fascinated against her will. Those incredible black eyes looked almost warm, and since warmth was not a character trait she had ever associated with Angelos Petronides before she was thrown off balance.

The head of the Petronides clan, and regarded with immense respect by every member, Angelos was ruthless, remorseless and coldly self-sufficient. He was also fabulously wealthy, flamboyantly unpredictable and frighteningly powerful. He scared people; he scared people just by strolling into a room. When Leland had walked out on his marriage, Angelos had silenced Jennifer's martyred sobs with one sardonic and deeply unsympathetic glance. Somehow Angelos had discovered that *her* infidelity had come first. Chagrined by that galling awareness, Jennifer had avoided him ever since...

Only the greater fear of what might happen to Leland's international chain of highly profitable casinos under her own inexpert guidance had driven her to approach Angelos for practical advice and assistance. Indeed, just at the moment Jennifer could not quite comprehend *how* she had been led into revealing her plans to destroy Maxie Kendall.

'You'll make her pay...?' Jennifer prompted drymouthed.

'My methods are my own,' Angelos murmured without apology, making it clear that the matter of the loan was no longer her province.

That hard, strikingly handsome face wore an expression that now chilled Jennifer. But she was triumphant. Clearly family ties, even distant ones, meant more to Angelos than she had ever dreamt. That little trollop would suffer; that was *all* Jennifer wanted.

When he was alone again, Angelos did something he had never been known to do before. He shattered his secretary by telling her to hold all his calls. He lounged indolently back in his leather chair in apparent contemplation of the panoramic view of the City of London. But his eyes were distant. No more cold showers. A sensual smile slowly formed on his well-shaped mouth. No more lonely nights. His smile flashed to unholy brilliance. The Ice Queen was *his*. After a three-year-long waiting game, she was finally to become *his*.

Mercenary and outwardly cold as she was…exquisite, though, indeed so breathtakingly beautiful that even Angelos, jaded and often bored connoisseur that he considered himself to be, had been stunned the first time he saw Maxie Kendall in the flesh. She looked like the Sleeping Beauty of popular fable. Untouchable, *untouched*… A grim laugh escaped Angelos. What nonsensical imagery the mind could serve up! She had been the mistress of a man old enough to be her grandfather for the past three years. There was nothing remotely innocent about the lady.

But for all that he would not use the loan like a battering ram. He would be a gentleman. He would be subtle. He would rescue her from her monetary embarrassments, earn her gratitude and ultimately inspire her loyalty as Leland had never contrived to do. She would not be cold with *him*. And, in reward, he would cocoon her in luxury, set the jewel of her perfection to a fitting frame and fulfil her every want and need. She would never have to work again. What more could any rational woman want?

Blissfully unaware of the detailed plans being formed on her behalf, Maxie climbed out of the cab she had caught from the train station. Every movement fluid with long-limbed natural grace, her spectacular trademark mane of golden hair blowing in the breeze, she straightened to her full five feet eleven inches and stared at her late godmother's home. Gilbourne was an elegant Georgian house set in wonderful grounds.

As she approached the front door her heart ached and she blinked back tears. The day she had made her first public appearance in Leland's company, her godmother, Nancy Leeward, had written to tell her that she would no longer be a welcome visitor here. But four months ago her godmother had come to see her in London. There had been a reconciliation of sorts, only Nancy hadn't said she was ill, hadn't given so much as a hint— nor had Maxie received word of her death until *after* the funeral.

So somehow it seemed all wrong to be showing up now for a reading of Nancy's last will and testament...and, worst of all, to be nourishing desperate prayers that at the last her godmother had somehow found it within her heart to forgive her for a lifestyle she had deemed scandalous.

In her slim envelope bag Maxie already carried a letter which had blown her every hope of future freedom to smithereens. It had arrived only that morning. And it had reminded her of a debt she had naively assumed would be written off when Leland severed their relationship and let her go. He had already taken three irreplaceable years of her life, and she had poured every penny she earned as a model into repaying what she could of that loan.

Hadn't that been enough to satisfy him? Right now she was homeless and broke and lurid publicity had severely curtailed her employment prospects. Leland had been vain and monumentally self-centred but he had never been cruel and he was certainly not poor. Why was he doing this to her? Couldn't he even have given her time to get back on her feet again before pressing her for payment?

The housekeeper answered the door before Maxie could reach for the bellpush. Her plump face was stiff with disapproval. 'Miss Kendall.' It was the coldest of welcomes. 'Miss Johnson and Miss Fielding are waiting in the drawing-room. Mrs Leeward's solicitor, Mr Hartley, should be here soon.'

'Thank you...no, there's no need to show me the way; I remember it well.'

Within several feet of the drawing-room, however, not yet ready to face the other two women and frankly nervous of the reception she might receive from one of them, Maxie paused at the window which overlooked the rose garden that had been Nancy Leeward's pride and joy. Her memory slid back to hazily recalled summer afternoon tea parties for three little girls. Maxine, Darcy and Polly, each of them on their very best behaviour for Nancy, who had never had a child of her own, had had pre-war values and expectations of her goddaughters.

Of the three, Maxie had always been the odd one out. Both Darcy and Polly came from comfortable backgrounds. They had always been smartly dressed when they came to stay at Gilbourne but Maxie had never had anything decent to wear, and every year, without fail,

Nancy had taken Maxie shopping for clothes. How shocked her godmother would've been had she ever learned that Maxie's father had usually sold those expensive garments the minute his daughter got home again...

Her late mother, Gwen, had once been Nancy's companion—a paid employee but for all that Nancy had always talked of her as a friend. Her godmother, however, had thoroughly disliked the man her companion and friend had chosen to marry.

Weak, selfish, unreliable... Russ Kendall was, unfortunately, all of those things, but he was also the only parent Maxie had ever known and Maxie was loyal. Her father had brought her up alone, loving her to the best of his ability. That she had never been able to trust him to behave himself around a woman as wealthy as Nancy Leeward had just been a cross Maxie had had to bear.

Every time Russ Kendall had brought his daughter to Gilbourne to visit he had overstayed his welcome, striving to butter her godmother up with compliments before trying to borrow money from her, impervious to the chill of the older woman's distaste. Maxie had always been filled with guilty relief when her father departed again. Only then had she been able to relax and enjoy herself.

'I thought I heard a car but I must've been mistaken. I wish Maxie would come...I'm looking forward to seeing her again,' a female voice said quite clearly.

Maxie twisted in surprise to survey the drawing-room door, only now registering that it was ajar. That had been Polly's voice, soft and gentle, just like Polly herself.

'That's one thrill I could live without,' a second female voice responded tartly. 'Maxie, the living doll—'

'She can't help being beautiful, Darcy.'

Outside the door, Maxie had frozen, unnerved by the biting hostility she had heard in Darcy's cuttingly well-bred voice. So Darcy *still* hadn't managed to forgive her, and yet what had destroyed their friendship three years earlier had been in no way Maxie's fault. Darcy had been jilted at the altar. Her bridegroom had waited until the eleventh hour to confess that he had fallen in love with one of her bridesmaids. That bridesmaid, entirely innocent of the smallest instant of flirtation *with* or indeed interest *in* the bridegroom, had unfortunately been Maxie.

'Does that somehow excuse her for stealing someone else's husband?'

'I don't think any of us get to choose *who* we fall in love with,' Polly stressed with a surprising amount of emotion. 'And Maxie must be devastated now that he's gone back to his wife.'

'If Maxie ever falls in love, it won't be with an ancient old bloke like that,' Darcy scorned. 'She wouldn't have looked twice at Leland Coulter if he hadn't been loaded! Surely you haven't forgotten what her father was like? Greed is in Maxie's bloodstream. Don't you remember the way Russ was always trying to touch poor Nancy for a loan?'

'I remember how much his behaviour embarrassed and upset Maxie,' Polly responded tautly, her dismay at the other woman's attitude audible.

In the awful pool of silence that followed Maxie wrapped her arms round herself. She felt gutted, totally gutted. So nothing had changed. Darcy was stubborn and never admitted herself in the wrong. Maxie had, however, hoped that time would've lessened the other woman's antagonism to the point where they could at least make peace.

'She *is* stunningly beautiful. Who can really blame her for taking advantage of that?' Darcy breathed in a grudging effort at placation. 'But then what else has Maxie got? I never did think she had much in the way of brains—'

'How can you say that, Darcy? Maxie is severely dyslexic,' Polly reminded her companion reproachfully.

Maxie lost all her natural colour, cringing at even this whispered reference to her biggest secret.

The tense silence in the drawing-room lingered.

'And in spite of that she's so wonderfully famous now,' Polly sighed.

'Well, if your idea of fame is playing Goldilocks in shampoo commercials, I suppose she is,' Darcy shot back crushingly.

Unfreezing, Maxie tiptoed back down the corridor and then walked with brisk, firm steps back again. She pushed wide the door with a light smile pasted to her unwittingly pale face.

'Maxie!' Polly carolled, and rose rather awkwardly to her feet.

Halfway towards her, Maxie stopped dead. Tiny dark-haired Polly was pregnant.

'When did you get married?' Maxie demanded with a grin.

Polly turned brick-red. 'I didn't...I mean, I'm *not*...'

Maxie was stunned. Polly had been raised by a fire-breathing puritanical father. The teenager Maxie recalled had been wonderfully kind and caring, but also extremely prim and proper as a result. Horribly aware that she had embarrassed Polly, she forced a laugh. 'So what?' she said lightly.

'I'm afraid the event of a child without a husband is not something as easily shrugged off in Polly's world as in yours.' Darcy stood by the window, her boyishly short auburn hair catching fire from the light behind her, aggressive green eyes challenging on the point.

Maxie stiffened at the reminder that Darcy had a child of her own but she refused to rise to that bait. Poor Polly looked strained enough as it was. 'Polly knows what I meant—'

'Does she—?' Darcy began.

'I feel dizzy!' Polly announced with startling abruptness.

Instantly Darcy stopped glaring at Maxie and both women anxiously converged on the tiny brunette. Maxie was the more efficient helper. Gently easing Polly down into the nearest armchair, she fetched a footstool because the smaller woman's ankles looked painfully swollen. Then, noting the untouched tea trolley nearby, she poured Polly a cup of tea and urged her to eat a digestive biscuit.

'Do you think you should see a doctor?' Darcy asked ruefully. 'I suppose I was lucky. I was never ill when I was expecting Zia.'

'What do you think, Polly?' Maxie prompted.

'I'm fine…saw one yesterday,' Polly muttered. 'I'm just tired.'

At that point, a middle-aged man in a dark suit was shown in with great ceremony by the housekeeper. Introducing himself as Edward Hartley, their godmother's solicitor, he took a seat, politely turned down the offer of refreshment and briskly extracted a document from his briefcase.

'Before I commence the reading of the will, I feel that I should warn you all beforehand that the respective monies will only be advanced *if* the strict conditions laid down by my late client are met—'

'Put that in English,' Darcy interrupted impatiently.

Mr Hartley removed his spectacles with a faint sigh. 'I assume that you are all aware that Mrs Leeward enjoyed a very happy but tragically brief marriage when she was in her twenties, and that the premature death of her husband was a lifelong source of sorrow and regret to her.'

'Yes,' Polly confirmed warmly. 'Our godmother often talked to us about Robbie.'

'He died in a car crash six months after they married,' Maxie continued ruefully. 'As time went on he became pretty much a saint in her memory. She used to talk to us about marriage as if it was some kind of Holy Grail and a woman's only hope of happiness.'

'Before her death, Mrs Leeward made it her business to visit each one of you. After completing those visits, she altered her will,' Edward Hartley informed them in a tone of wry regret. 'I advised her that the conditions of inheritance she chose to include might be very difficult, if not impossible for any one of you to fulfil. However, Mrs Leeward was a lady who knew her own mind, and she had made her decision.'

Maxie was holding her breath, her bemused gaze skimming over the faces of her companions. Polly wore an expression of blank exhaustion but Darcy, never able to hide her feelings, now looked worried sick.

In the pin-dropping silence, the solicitor began to read the will. Nancy Leeward had left her entire and extremely substantial estate evenly divided between her three goddaughters on condition that each of them married within a year and remained married for a minimum of six months. Only then would they qualify to inherit a portion of the estate. In the event of any one of them failing to meet the terms of the will, that person's share would revert to the Crown.

By the time the older man had finished speaking, Maxie was in shock. Every scrap of colour had drained from her face. She had hoped, she had *prayed* that she might be released from the burden of debt that had almost destroyed her life. And now she had learnt that, like everything else over the past twenty-two years, from the death of her mother when she was a toddler to her father's compulsive gambling addiction, nothing was going to be that easy.

A jagged laugh broke from Darcy. 'You've just got to be kidding,' she said incredulously.

'There's no chance of me fulfilling those conditions,' Polly confided chokily, glancing at her swollen stomach and looking away again with open embarrassment.

'Nor I...' Maxie admitted flatly, her attention resting on Polly and her heart sinking for her. She should have guessed there would be no supportive male in the picture. Trusting, sweet-natured Polly had obviously been seduced and dumped.

Darcy shot Maxie an exasperated look. 'They'll be queuing up for you, Maxie—'

'With my colourful reputation?'

Darcy flushed. 'All any one of us requires is a man and a wedding ring. Personally speaking, I'll only attract either by advertising and offering a share of the proceeds as a bribe!'

'While I am sure that that is a purely facetious comment, made, as it were, in the heat of the moment, I must point out that the discovery of any such artificial arrangement would automatically disqualify you from inheriting any part of your godmother's estate,' Edward Hartley asserted with extreme gravity.

'You may say our godmother knew her own mind… but I *think*…well, I'd better not say what I think,' Darcy gritted, respect for a much loved godmother evidently haltering her abrasive tongue.

Simultaneously, a shaken little laugh of reluctant appreciation was dredged from Maxie. *She* was not in the dark. The reasoning behind Nancy Leeward's will was as clear as daylight to her. Within recent months their godmother had visited each one of them…and what a severe disappointment they must all have been.

She had found Maxie apparently living in sin with an older married man. She had discovered that Polly was well on the road to becoming an unmarried mother. And Darcy? Maxie's stomach twisted with guilt. Some months after that day of cruel humiliation in the church, Darcy had given birth to a baby. Was it any wonder that the redhead had been a vehement man-hater ever since?

'It's such a shame that your godmother tied her estate up like that,' Maxie's friend, Liz, lamented the following afternoon as the two women discussed the solicitor's letter which had bluntly demanded the immediate settlement of Leland Coulter's loan. 'If she hadn't, all your problems would've been solved.'

'Maybe I should have told Nancy the real reason why I was living in Leland's house…but I couldn't have stood her thinking that I was expecting *her* to buy me out of trouble. It wouldn't have been fair to put her in that position either. She really did detest my father.' Maxie gave a fatalistic shrug. She had suffered too many disappointments in life to waste time crying over spilt milk.

'Well, what you need now is some good legal advice. You were only nineteen when you signed that loan agreement and you were under tremendous pressure. You were genuinely afraid for your father's life.' Liz's freckled face below her mop of greying sandy hair looked hopeful. 'Surely that *has* to make a difference?'

From the other side of the kitchen table, casually clad in faded jeans and a loose shirt, Maxie studied the friend who had without question taken her in off the street and freely offered her a bed for as long as she needed it. Liz Blake was the only person she trusted with her secrets. Liz, bless her heart, had never been influenced by the looks that so often made other women hostile or uneasy in Maxie's company. Blind from birth and fiercely independent, Liz made a comfortable living as a potter and enjoyed a wide and varied social circle.

'I signed what I signed and it did get Dad off the hook,' Maxie reminded her.

'Some thanks you got for your sacrifice.'

'Dad's never asked me for money since—'

'Maxie...you haven't *seen* him for three years,' Liz pointed out grimly.

Maxie tensed. 'Because he's ashamed, Liz. He feels guilty around me now.'

Liz frowned as her guide dog, Bounce, a glossy black Labrador, sprang up and nudged his head against her knee. 'I wonder who that is coming to the door. I'm not expecting anyone...and nobody outside the mail redirection service and that modelling agency of yours is supposed to know you're here!'

By the time the doorbell actually went, Liz was already in the hall moving to answer it. A couple of minutes later she reappeared in the doorway. 'You have a visitor...foreign, male, very tall, very attractive voice. He also says he's a very good friend of yours—'

'Of mine?' Maxie queried with a perplexed frown.

Liz shook her head. 'He *has* to be a good friend to have worked out where you're hiding out. And Bounce gave him the all-over suspicious sniff routine and passed him with honours so I put him in the lounge. Look, I'll be in the studio, Maxie. I need to finish off that order before I leave tomorrow.'

Maxie wondered who on earth had managed to find her. The press? Oh, dear heaven, had Liz trustingly invited some sneaky journalist in? Taut with tension, she hurried down the hall into the lounge.

One step into that small cosy room, she stopped dead as if she had run into a brick wall without warning. Smash, *crash*, her mind screamed as she took a sudden instinctive backward step, shock engulfing her in rolling waves of disorientation.

'Maxie...how are you?' Angelos Petronides purred as he calmly extended a lean brown hand in conventional greeting.

Maxie gaped as if a boa constrictor had risen in front of her, her heart thumping at manic speed and banging in her eardrums. A very good friend. Had Liz misheard him?

'Mr Petronides—?'

'Angelos, please,' he countered with a very slight smile.

Maxie blinked. She had never seen him smile before. She had been in this arrogant male's company half a dozen times over the past three years and this was the very first time he had deigned to verbally acknowledge that she lived and breathed. In her presence he had

talked around her as if she wasn't there, switching to
Greek if she made any attempt to enter the conversation,
and on three separate occasions, evidently responding
to his request, Leland had sent her home early in a taxi.

With rock-solid assurance, Angelos let his hand drop
again. Amusement at her stupefied state flashed openly
in his brilliant black eyes.

Maxie stiffened. 'I'm afraid I can't imagine what
could bring you here...or indeed how you found me—'

'Were you ever lost?' Angelos enquired with husky
innuendo while he ran heavily lidded heated dark eyes
over her lithe, slender frame with extraordinarily insulting thoroughness. 'I suspect that you know very well
why I am here.'

Her fair skin burning, Maxie's sapphire blue eyes
shuttered. 'I haven't the slightest idea—'

'You are now a free woman.'

This is not happening to me, a little voice screeched
in the back of Maxie's mind. She folded her arms, saw
those terrifyingly shrewd eyes read her defensive body
language and lowered her arms again, fighting not to
coil her straining fingers into fists.

One unguarded moment almost six months ago...
Was that all it had taken to encourage him? He had
caught her watching him and instantaneously, as if that
momentary abstraction of hers had been a blatant invitation, he had reacted with a lightning flash look of
primitive male sexual hunger. A split second later he
had turned away again, but that shatteringly unexpected
response of his had shaken Maxie inside out.

She had told herself she had imagined it. She had
almost cherished this arrogant Greek tycoon's indifference to her as a woman. OK, so possibly, once or twice,
his ability to behave as if she was invisible had irritated

and humiliated her, but then she had seen some excuse for his behaviour. Unlike Leland, Angelos Petronides would never be guilty of a need to show off a woman like a prize poodle at what was supposed to be a business meeting.

'And now that you *are* free, I want you in my life,' Angelos informed her with the supreme confident cool of a male who had never been refused anything he wanted by a woman. Not a male primed for rejection, not a male who had even contemplated that as a remote possibility. His attitude spoke volumes for his opinion of her morals.

And at that mortifying awareness Maxie trembled, her usual deadpan, wonderful and absolute control beginning to fray round the edges. 'You really believe that you can just walk in here and *tell* me—?'

'Yes,' Angelos cut in with measured impatience. 'Don't be coy. You have no need to play such games with me. I have not been unaware of your interest in me.'

Her very knees wobbled with rage, a rage such as Maxie had never known before. He had the subtlety of a sledgehammer, the blazing self-image of a sun god. The very first time she had seen Angelos Petronides she *had* had a struggle to stop staring. Lethally attractive men were few and far between; fiercely intelligent and lethally attractive men were even fewer. And the natural brute power Angelos radiated like an aura of intimidation executed its own fatal fascination.

He had filled her with intense curiosity but that was *all*. Maxie had never learnt what it was like to actually want a man. She didn't like most men; she didn't trust them. What man had ever seen her as an individual with emotions and thoughts that might be worth a moment's attention? What man had ever seen her as anything more than a glamorous one-dimensional trophy to hang on his arm and boast about?

As a teenager, Maxie had always been disillusioned, angered or frankly repelled long before she could reach the stage of reciprocating male interest. And now Angelos Petronides had just proved himself the same as the rest of the common herd. What she couldn't understand was why she should be feeling a fierce, embittered stab of stark disappointment.

'You're trembling...why don't you sit down?' Angelos switched into full domineering mode with the polished ease of a duck taking to water and drew up an armchair for her occupancy. When she failed to move, the black eyes beneath those utterly enviable long inky lashes rested on her in irritated reproof. 'You have shadows under your eyes. You have lost weight. You should be taking better care of yourself.'

She would *not* lose her temper; she would tie herself in knots before she exposed her outrage and he recognised her humiliation. How dared he...how *dared* he land on Liz's doorstep and announce his lustful intentions and behave as if he was awaiting a round of applause? If she spread herself across the carpet at his feet in gratitude, he would no doubt happily take it in his stride.

'Your interest in my wellbeing is unwelcome and unnecessary, Mr Petronides,' Maxie countered not quite levelly, and she sat down because she was honestly afraid that if she didn't she might give way to temptation and slap him across that insolent mouth so hard she would bruise her fingers.

He sank down opposite her, which was an instant relief because even when she was standing he towered over her. That was an unusual sensation for a woman as tall as Maxie, and one that with him in the starring role she found irrationally belittling.

For such a big, powerfully built man, however, he moved with the lightness and ease of an athlete. He was as dark as she was fair...quite staggeringly good-looking. Spectacular cheekbones, a strong, thin-bladed nose, the wide mouth of a sensualist. But it was those extraordinary eyes which held and compelled and lent such blazing definition to his fantastic bone structure. And there was not a soupçon of softness or real emotion in that hard, assessing gaze.

'Leland's wife was planning to take you to court over that loan,' Angelos Petronides delivered smoothly into the thumping silence.

Maxie's spine jerked rigid, eyes flying wide in shock as she gasped, 'How did you find out about the loan?'

Angelos angled a broad, muscular shoulder in a light, dismissive shrug, as if they were enjoying a light and casual conversation. 'It's not important. Jennifer will *not* take you to court. I have settled the loan on your behalf.'

Slowly, her muscles strangely unwilling to do her bidding, Maxie leant forward. 'Say that again,' she invited shakily, because she couldn't believe he had said what he had just said.

Angelos Petronides regarded her with glittering black unfathomable eyes. 'I will not hold that debt over you, Maxie. My intervention was a gesture of good faith alone.'

'G-good *faith*...?' Maxie stammered helplessly, her voice rising to shrillness in spite of her every effort to control it.

'What else could it be?' Angelos shifted a graceful

hand in eloquent emphasis, his brilliant gaze absorbing
the raw incredulity and shock which had blown a giant
smoking crater in the Ice Queen's famed façade of cool.
'What man worthy of the name would seek to blackmail
a woman into his bed?'

CHAPTER TWO

MAXIE leapt upright, her beautiful face a flushed mask of fury. 'Do you think I am a complete fool?' she shouted at him so loudly her voice cracked.

Unhurriedly, Angelos Petronides shifted his incredibly long legs and fluidly unfolded to his full height again, his complete control mocking her loss of temper. 'With regard to some of your past decisions in life…how frank am I allowed to be?'

Maxie sucked in oxygen as if she was drowning, clamped a hand to her already opening mouth and spun at speed away from him. She was shattered that he had smashed her self-discipline. As noise filtered through the open window she became dimly aware of the shouts of children playing football somewhere outside, but their voices were like sounds impinging from another world.

'You don't need to apologise,' Angelos drawled in a mocking undertone. 'I've seen your temper many times before. You go pale and you stiffen. Every time Leland put so much as a finger on you in public, I witnessed your struggle not to shrug him off. It must have been fun in the bedroom…'

Maxie's slender backbone quivered. Her fingernails flexed like claws longing to make contact with human flesh. She wanted to *kill* him. But she couldn't even trust herself to speak, and was all the more agitated by the simple fact that she had never felt such rage before and honestly didn't know how to cope with it.

'But then, it was always evident to me that Leland's biggest thrill was trotting you out in public at every possible opportunity. "Look at me, I have a blonde twice as tall as me and a third of my age,"' Angelos mused with earthy amusement. 'I suspect he might not have demanded intimate entertainment that often. He wasn't a young man...'

'And you are...without doubt...the most offensive, objectionable man I have ever met!' Maxie launched with her back still rigidly turned to him.

'I am a taste you will acquire. After all, you *need* someone like me.' A pair of strong hands settled without warning on her slim shoulders and exerted sufficient pressure to swivel her back round to face him.

'I need someone like you like I need a hole in the head!' Maxie railed back at him rawly as she tore herself free of that controlling hold. 'And keep your hands off me...I don't like being pawed!'

'Why are you so angry? I *had* to tell you about the loan,' Angelos pointed out calmly. 'I was aware that the Coulters' lawyer had already been in touch. Naturally, I wanted to set your mind at rest.'

The reminder of the debt that had simply been transferred acted like a drenching flood of cold water on Maxie's overheated emotions. Her angry flush was replaced by waxen pallor. Her body turned cold and weak and shaky and she studied the worn carpet at his feet. 'You've bought yourself a pup. I can't settle that loan...and right now I haven't even got enough to make a payment on it,' she framed sickly.

'Why do you get yourself so worked up about nothing?' Angelos released an extravagant sigh. 'Sit down before you fall down. Haven't I already given you my assurance that I have no intention of holding that former debt over your head in any way? But, in passing, may I ask what you needed that loan for?'

'I got into a real financial mess, that's all,' she muttered evasively, protecting her father as she always did, conscious of the derisive distaste such weakness roused in other, stronger men. And, drained by her outbursts and ashamed of them, she found herself settling back down into the chair again.

For the very first time she was genuinely scared of Angelos Petronides. He owned a piece of her, just as Leland once had, but he would be expecting infinitely more than a charade in return. She wasn't taken in by his reassurances, or by that roughly gentle intonation she had never dreamt he might possess. In the space of ten minutes he had reduced her to a babbling, screeching wreck and, for now, he was merely content to have made his domineering presence felt.

'Money is not a subject I discuss with women,' Angelos told her quietly. 'It is most definitely not a subject I ever wish to discuss with you again.'

Angelos Petronides, billionaire and benevolence personified? Maxie shuddered with disbelief. Did he ever read his own publicity? She had sat in on business meetings chaired by him, truly unforgettable experiences. The King and his terrified minions, who behaved as if at any moment he might snap and shout, 'Off with their heads!' Grown men perspired and stammered with nerves in his presence, cowered when he shot down their suggestions, went into cold panic if he frowned. He did not suffer fools gladly.

He had a brilliant mind, but that superior intellect had made him inherently devious and manipulative. He controlled the people around him. In comparison, Leland Coulter had been harmless. Maxie had *coped* with

Leland. And Leland, give him his due, had never tried
to pose as her only friend in a hostile world. But over
her now loomed a six-foot-four-inch giant threat without a conscience.

'I know where you're coming from,' Maxie heard
herself admit out loud as she lifted her beautiful head
again.

Angelos gazed down at her with steady black eyes.
'Then why all the histrionics?'

Maxie gulped, disconcerted to feel that awful surge
of temper rise again. With that admission she had expected to make him wary, force him to ease back. About
the last reaction she had expected was his cool acknowledgement that she was intelligent enough to recognise
his tactics for what they were. The iron hand in the
velvet glove.

'Have dinner with me tonight,' Angelos suggested
smoothly. 'We can talk then. You need some time to
think things over.'

'I need no time whatsoever.' Maxie stared back up
into those astonishingly dark and impenetrable eyes and
suffered the oddest light-headed sensation, as if the floor
had shifted beneath her. Her lashes fluttered, a slight
bemused frown line drawing her fine brows together as
she shook her head slightly, long golden hair thick as
skein on skein of silk rippling round her shoulders. 'I
will not be your mistress.'

'I haven't asked yet.'

A cynical laugh was torn from Maxie as she rose
restively to her feet again. 'You don't need to be that
specific. I certainly didn't imagine you were planning
to offer me anything more respectable. And, no, I do
not intend to discuss this any further,' she asserted
tightly, carefully focusing on a point to the left of him,

the tip of her tongue stealing out to moisten her dry lower lip in a swift defensive motion. 'So either you are a good loser or a bad loser, Mr Petronides...I imagine I'll find out which soon enough—'

'I do not lose,' Angelos breathed in a roughened undertone. 'I am also very persistent. If you make yourself a challenge, I will resent the waste of time demanded by pursuit but, like any red-blooded male, I will undoubtedly want you even more.'

Without even knowing why, Maxie shivered. There was the most curious buzz in the atmosphere, sending tiny little warning pulses of alarm through her tautening length. Her unsettled and bemused eyes swerved involuntarily back to him and locked into the ferocious hold of his compelling scrutiny.

'I will also become angry with you,' Angelos forecast, shifting soundlessly closer, his husky drawl thickening and lowering in pitch to a mesmeric level of intimacy. 'You made Leland jump through no hoops...why should I? And I would treat you *so* much better than he did. I know what a woman likes. I know what makes a woman of your nature feel secure and appreciated, what makes her happy, content, *satisfied...*'

Like a child drawn too close to a blazing fire in spite of all warnings, Maxie was transfixed. She could feel her own heartbeat accelerating, the blood surging rich and vibrantly alive through her veins. A kind of craving, an almost terrifying upswell of excitement potently and powerfully new to her gripped her.

'A-Angelos...?' she whispered, feeling dizzy and disorientated.

He reached out and drew her to him without once breaking that spellbinding appraisal. 'How easily you can say my name...'

And she said it again, like a supplicant eager to please.

Those stunning eyes of his blazed gold as a hot sun with satisfaction. She trembled, legs no longer dependable supports beneath her, and yet in all her life she had never been more shockingly aware of her own body. Her braless breasts were swelling beneath the denim shirt she wore, the tender nipples suddenly tightening to thrust with aching sensitivity against the rough grain of the fabric.

There was a sudden enormous jarring thud on the windowpane behind her. Startled, Maxie almost jumped a foot in the air, and even Angelos flinched.

'Relax...a football hit the window,' he groaned in apparent disbelief as he raised his dark, imperious head. 'It is now being retrieved by two grubby little boys.'

But Maxie wasn't listening. She had been plunged into sudden appalled confusion by the discovery that Angelos Petronides had both arms loosely linked round her and had come within treacherous inches of kissing her. Even worse, she realised, every fibre of her yearning body had been longing desperately for that kiss.

Jerking back abruptly from the proximity of his lean, muscular frame, Maxie pressed shaking hands against her hot, flushed cheeks. 'Get out of here and don't ever come back!'

Angelos grated something guttural in Greek, stood his ground and dealt her a hard, challenging look. 'What's the matter with you?'

And what remained of Maxie's self-respect drained away as she recognised his genuine bewilderment. Dear heaven, she had encouraged him. She had been straining up to him, mindlessly eager for his lovemaking, paralysed to the spot with excitement and longing, and he knew it too. And did his body feel as hers did now? Deprived, aching... As she registered such unfamiliar, intimate thoughts, Maxie realised just how out of control she was.

'I don't have to explain myself to you,' she gabbled in near panic as she rushed past him out into the hall to pull open the front door. 'I want you to leave and I don't want you to come back. In fact I'll put the dog on you if you ever come here again!'

In a demonstration of disturbing volatility, Angelos vented a sudden appreciative laugh, the sound rich and deep and earthy. His quality of dark implacability vanished under the onslaught of that amusement. Maxie stared. The sheer charisma of that wolfish grin took her by surprise.

'The dog's more likely to lick me to death...and you?' An ebullient ebony brow elevated as he watched the hot colour climb in her perplexed face.

'Leave!' The word erupted from Maxie, so desperate was she to silence him.

'And *you*?' Angelos repeated with steady emphasis. 'For some strange reason, what just happened between us, which on my level was nothing at all, unnerved you, scared you...embarrassed you...'

As he listed his impressions Maxie watched him with a sick, sinking sensation in her stomach, for never before had she been so easily read, and never before had a man made her feel like a specimen on a slide under a microscope.

'Now why should honest hunger provoke shame?' Angelos asked softly. 'Why not pleasure?'

'*Pleasure?*'

'I do not presume to know your every thought...as yet,' Angelos qualified with precision. His brilliant eyes intent, he strolled indolently back into the fresh air. 'But surely when ambition and desire unite, you should be pleased?'

He left her with that offensive suggestion, striding down the path and out to the pavement where a uniformed chauffeur waited beside a long, dark limousine. The two wide-eyed and decidedly grubby little boys, one of whom was clutching the football, were trying without success to talk to the po-faced chauffeur. She watched as Angelos paused to exchange a laughing word with them, bending to their level with disconcerting ease. Disturbed by her own fascination, she slammed shut the door on her view.

He would be back; she knew that. She couldn't explain how but she knew it as surely as she knew that dawn came around every morning. Feeling curiously like someone suffering from concussion, she wandered aimlessly back down into the kitchen and was surprised to find Liz sitting there, her kindly face anxious.

'Bounce started whining behind the studio door. He must've heard you shouting. I came back into the house but naturally I didn't intrude when I realised it was just an argument,' Liz confided ruefully. 'Unfortunately, before I retreated again, I heard rather more than I felt comfortable hearing. You're a wretched dog, Bounce...your grovelling greeting to Angelos Petronides affected my judgement!'

'So you realised who my visitor was—?'

'Not initially, but my goodness I should've done!' Liz exclaimed feelingly. 'You've talked about Angelos Petronides *so* often—'

'Have I?' Maxie breathed with shaken unease, her cheeks burning.

Liz smiled. 'All the time you were criticising him and

complaining about his behaviour, I could sense how attracted you were to him...'

A hoarse laugh erupted from Maxie's dry throat. 'I wish you'd warned me. It hit me smack in the face when I wasn't prepared for it. Stupid, wretched chemistry, and I never even realised... I feel such an idiot now!' Eyes prickling with tears of reaction, she studied the table, struggling to reinstate her usual control. 'And I've got the most banging headache s-starting up...'

'Of course you have,' Liz murmured soothingly. 'I've never heard you yelling at the top of your voice before.'

'But then I have never hated anyone so much in my life as I hate Angelos Petronides,' Maxie confessed shakily. 'I wanted to kill him, Liz...I really wanted to kill him! Now I'm in debt to *him* instead of Leland—'

'I did hear him say that you didn't have to worry about that.'

Maxie's eyes flashed. 'If it takes me until I'm ninety, I'll pay him back every penny!'

'He may have hurt your pride, Maxie...but he was most emphatic about not wanting repayment. He sounded sincere to me, and surely you have to give him some credit for his generosity whether you choose to regard it as a debt or otherwise?' Liz reasoned with an air of frowning confusion. 'The man has to be *seriously* interested in you to make such a big gesture on your behalf—'

'Liz—' Maxie broke in with a pained half-smile.

'Do you think he might turn out to be the marrying kind?' the older woman continued with a sudden teasing smile.

That outrageous question made Maxie's jaw drop. 'Liz, for heaven's sake...are you nuts?' she gasped. 'What put that in your mind?'

'Your godmother's will—'

'Oh, that…forget that, Liz. That's yesterday's news. Believe me when I say that Angelos Petronides was not thinking along the lines of anything as…well, anything as lasting as marriage.' Mindful of her audience, Maxie chose her words carefully and suppressed a sigh over the older woman's romantic imagination. 'He is not romantically interested in me. He is not that sort of man. He's hard, he's icy cold—'

'He didn't sound cold on my doorstep…he sounded downright *keen*! You'd be surprised how much I can pick up from the nuances in a voice.'

Liz was rather innocent in some ways. Maxie really didn't want to get down to basics and spell out just how a big, powerful tycoon like Angelos Petronides regarded her. As a social inferior, a beautiful body, a target object to acquire for his sexual enjoyment, a *live* toy. Maxie shrank with revulsion and hated him all over again. 'Liz…he would be offended by the very suggestion that he would even consider a normal relationship with a woman who's been another man's mistress—'

'But you haven't *been* another man's mistress!'

Maxie ignored that point. After the horrendous publicity she had enjoyed, nobody would ever believe that now. 'To be blunt, Liz…all Angelos wants is to get me into bed!'

'Oh…' Liz breathed, and blushed until all her freckles merged. 'Oh, dear, no…you don't want to get mixed up with a man like that.'

Maxie lay in bed that night, listening to the distant sound of the traffic. She couldn't forgive herself for being attracted to a male like Angelos Petronides. It was impossible that she could *like* anything about him. 'A woman of your nature,' he had said. His one little slip.

Wanton, available, already accustomed to trading her body in return for a luxurious lifestyle. That was what he had meant. Her heart ached and she felt as if she was bleeding inside. How had she ever sunk to the level where she had a reputation like that?

When Maxie had first been chosen as the image to launch a new range of haircare products, she had been a complete unknown and only eighteen years old. Although she had never had the slightest desire to be a model, she had let her father persuade her to give it a try and had swiftly found herself earning what had then seemed like enormous amounts of money.

However, once the novelty had worn off, she had loathed the backbiting pressure and superficiality of the modelling circuit. She had saved like mad and had planned to find another way to make a living.

But all the time, in the background of her life, her father had continued to gamble. Relying on her income as a safety net, he had, without her knowledge, begun playing for higher and higher stakes. To be fair, Leland's casino manager had cut off Russ Kendall's credit line the minute he'd suspected the older man was in over his head. Maxie had met Leland Coulter for the first time the day she settled her father's outstanding tab at his casino.

'You won't change the man, Maxie,' he had told her then. 'If he was starving, he would risk his last fiver on a bet. He has to be the one who wants to change.'

After that humiliating episode her father had made her so many promises. He had sworn blind that he would never gamble again but inevitably he had broken his word. And, barred from the reputable casinos, he had gone dangerously down-market to play high-rolling poker games in smoky back rooms with the kind of tough men who would happily break his fingers if he didn't pay his dues on time. That was when Maxie's life had come completely unstuck…

Having got himself into serious debt, and learning to his dismay that his daughter had no savings left after his previous demands, Russ had been very badly beaten up. He had lost a kidney. In his hospital bed, he had sobbed with shame and terror in her arms. He had been warned that if he didn't come up with the money he owed, he would be crippled the next time.

Distraught, Maxie had gone to Leland Coulter for advice. And Leland had offered her an arrangement. He would pay off her father's gambling debts and allow her to repay him at her leisure on condition that she moved in with him. He had been very honest about what he wanted. Not sex, he had insisted. No, what Leland had craved most had been the ego-boosting pleasure of being seen to possess a beautiful young woman, who would preside over his dinner table, act as his hostess, entertain his friends and always be available to accompany him wherever he went.

It hadn't seemed so much to ask. Nobody else had been prepared to loan her that amount of money. And she had been so agonisingly grateful that her father was safe from further harm. She hadn't seen the trap she was walking into. She hadn't even been aware that Leland was a married man until the headlines had hit the tabloids and taken her reputation away overnight. She had borne the blame for the breakup of his marriage.

'Jennifer and I split up because *she* had an affair,' Leland had admitted grudgingly when Maxie had roundly objected to the anomalous situation he had put her in. 'But this way, with you by my side, I don't feel like a fool...all right?'

And she had felt sorry for him then, right through the protracted and very public battle he and his wife had had over alimony and property. Jennifer and Leland had fought each other every inch of their slow path to the divorce court, yet a week before the hearing, when Leland had had a heart attack, the only woman he had been able to think about when he was convinced that he was at his last gasp had, most tellingly, been his estranged wife. 'Go away, leave me alone... I need Jennifer here... I don't want her seeing you with me now!' he had cried in pathetic masculine panic.

And that had hurt. In a crazy way she had grown rather fond of Leland, even of his silly showing-off and quirky little vanities. Not a bad man, just a selfish one, like all the men she had ever known, and she hoped he was happy now that he was back with his Jennifer. But he had used her not only to soothe his wounded vanity but also, and less forgivably, she recognised now, as a weapon with which to punish his unfaithful wife. And Maxie could not forget that, or forgive herself for the blind naivety that had allowed it to happen in the first place. Never, ever again, she swore, would she be *used*...

Early the next morning, Maxie helped Liz pack. Her friend was heading off to stay with friends in Devon. The fact that her house wouldn't be left empty during her absence was a source of great relief to Liz. The previous year her home had been burgled and her studio vandalised while she was away.

As soon as she had seen the older woman off, Maxie spent an hour slapping on make-up like war-paint and dressing up in style. Angelos Petronides needed a lesson and Maxie was determined to give it to him.

Mid-morning, she pawned the one piece of valuable jewellery she owned. She had been eleven when she'd found the Victorian bracelet buried in a box of cheap costume beads which had belonged to her mother. She had cried, guessing why the bracelet had been so well concealed. Even in the three short years of her marriage, her poor mother had doubtless learnt the hard way that when her husband was short of money he would sell anything he could get his hands on. Afterwards, Russ would be terribly sorry and ashamed, but by then it would be too late and the treasured possession would be gone. So Maxie had kept the bracelet hidden too.

And now it hurt so much to surrender that bracelet. It felt like a betrayal of the mother she could barely remember. But she desperately needed the cash and she had nothing else to offer. Angelos Petronides *had* to be shown that he hadn't bought her or any rights over her by settling Leland's loan. The sacrifice of her mother's bracelet, temporarily or otherwise, simply hardened Maxie's angry, bitter resolve.

Half an hour later, she strolled out of the lift on to the top floor of the skyscraper that housed the London headquarters of the vast Petronides organisation. She spared the receptionist barely a glance. She knew how to get attention.

'I want to see Angelos,' she announced.

'Miss…Miss Kendall?' The brunette was already on her feet, eyes opened wide in recognition: in a bold scarlet dress that caressed every curve, her spectacular hair rippling in a sheet of gold to her waist, and heels that elevated her to well over six feet, Maxie was extremely noticeable.

'I know where his office is.' Maxie breezed on down the corridor, the brunette darting after her with an incoherent gasp of dismay.

She flung wide his office door when she got there. Infuriatingly, it was empty. She headed for the boardroom, indifferent to the squawking receptionist, whose frantic pursuit had attracted the attention of another two secretarial staff.

Bingo! Maxie strolled through the boardroom's double doors. An entire room full of men in business suits swivelled at her abrupt entry and then gaped. Maxie wasn't looking at them. Her entire attention was for Angelos Petronides, already rising from his chair at the head of the long polished table, his expression of outrage shimmering in an instant into shocking impassivity. But she took strength from the stunned quality that had briefly lit those fierce black eyes of his.

'I want to see you now,' Maxie told him, sapphire-blue eyes firing a challenge.

'You could wait in Mr Petronides's office, just through here, Miss Kendall.' The quiet female intervention came from the slim older woman who had already rushed to cast invitingly wide the door which connected with her employer's office.

'Sorry, I don't want to wait,' Maxie delivered.

A blazing look of dark, simmering fury betrayed Angelos. It was the reaction of a male who had never before been subjected to a public scene. Maxie smiled sweetly. He couldn't touch her because she had nothing to lose. No money, no current employment, nothing but her pride and her wits. He should've thought of that angle. And, no matter what it took, she intended to make Angelos pay for the state he had put her in the day before.

In one wrathful stride, Angelos reached her side and closed a forceful hand round her narrow wrist. Maxie let out a squeal as if he had hurt her. Startled, he dropped her wrist again. In receipt of a derisive, unimpressed glance that would've made a lesser woman cringe, Maxie noted without surprise that Angelos was a quick study.

'Thank you,' she said, and meant it, and she strolled through to his big, luxurious office like a little lamb because now she knew he was coming too.

'Unexpected visitors with unpredictable behaviour are so enervating…don't you think?' Maxie trilled as she fell still by the side of his impressive desk.

Angelos swore in Greek, studying her with seething black eyes full of intimidation. 'You crazy—' His wide mouth hardened as he bit back the rest of that verbal assault with the greatest of visible difficulty. 'What the hell are you playing at?' he growled like a grizzly bear instead.

'I'm not playing, I'm *paying*!' With a flourish, Maxie opened her fingers above his desk and let drop the crushed banknotes in her hand. 'Something on account towards the loan. I can't be bought like a tin of beans off a supermarket shelf!'

'How dare you interrupt a business meeting?' Angelos launched at her full throttle. 'How *dare* you make a scene like that in my boardroom?'

Maxie tensed. She had never heard a man that angry. She had never seen a male with so dark a complexion look that pale. Nor had she ever faced a pair of eyes that slashed like bloodthirsty razors into her.

'You asked for it,' she informed him grittily. 'You embarrassed me yesterday. You made me feel *this* big…' With her thumb and her forefinger she gave him a literal demonstration. 'You made me feel powerless and this is payback time. You picked on the wrong woman!'

'Is this really the Ice Queen I'm dealing with?' Angelos responded very, very drily.

'You'd burn the ice off the North Pole!' Maxie sizzled back at him, wondering why he had now gone so still, why his naturally vibrant skin tone was recovering colour, indeed why he didn't appear to be in a rage any more.

'Do you suffer from a split personality?'

'Did you really think you *knew* me just because you were in the same room with me a handful of times?' Maxie flung her head back and was dumbstruck by the manner in which his narrowed gaze instantly clung to her cascading mane of hair, and then roved on down the rest of her with unconcealed appreciation. It struck her that Angelos Petronides was so convinced that he was an innately superior being and so oversexed that he couldn't take a woman seriously for five minutes.

Brilliant black eyes swooped up to meet hers again. 'No way did you ever behave like this around Leland—'

'My relationship with him is none of your business,' Maxie asserted with spirit. 'But, believe me, nobody has ever insulted me as much as you did yesterday.'

'I find that very hard to believe.'

Involuntarily, Maxie flinched.

Immensely tall and powerful in his superbly tailored silver-grey suit, Angelos watched her, not an informative glimmer of any emotion showing now on that lean, strong, hard-boned face. 'Since when has it been an insult for a man to admit that he wants a woman?' he demanded with derision.

'You frightened the life out of me telling me you'd

paid off that loan…you put me under pressure, then you
tried to move in for the kill like the cold, calculating
womaniser you are!' Maxie bit out not quite levelly,
and, spinning on her heel, she started towards the door.

'All exits are locked. You're trapped for the moment,' Angelos delivered softly.

Maxie didn't believe him until she had tried and
failed to open the door. Then she hissed furiously,
'Open this door!'

'Why should I?' Angelos enquired, choosing that exact same moment to lounge indolently back against the
edge of his desk, so cool, calm and confident that Maxie
wanted to rip him to pieces. 'Presumably you came here
to entertain me…and, although I have no tolerance for
tantrums, you *do* look magnificent in that dress, and
naturally I would like to know why I'm receiving this
melodramatic response to my proposition.'

In one flying motion, Maxie spun back. 'So you admit that that's what it was?'

'I want you. It's only a matter of time until I get what
I want,' Angelos imparted very quietly in the deadly
stillness.

Maxie shivered. 'When the soft soap doesn't work,
weigh in with the threats—'

'That *wasn't* a threat. I don't threaten women,'
Angelos growled with a feral flash of white teeth. 'No
woman has ever come to my bed under threat!'

Nobody could feign that much outrage. He was an
Alpha male and not one modestly given to underesti-
mating his own attractions. But then, he had it *all*, she
conceded bitterly. Incredible looks and sex appeal, more
money than he could spend in a lifetime and a level of
intelligence that scorched and challenged.

Maxie shot him a look of violent loathing. 'You think

you're so special, don't you? You thought I'd be flattered, ready to snatch at whatever you felt like offering...but you're no different from any of the other men who have lusted after me,' she countered with harsh clarity. 'And I've had plenty of practice dealing with your sort. I've looked like this since I was fourteen—'

'I'm grateful you grew up before our paths crossed,' Angelos breathed with deflating amusement.

At that outrageous comment, something inside Maxie just cracked wide open, and she rounded on him like a tigress. 'I shouldn't have had to cope with harassment at that age. Do you think I don't *know* that I'm no more real to a guy like you than a blow-up sex doll?' she condemned with raw, stinging contempt. 'Well, I've got news for you, Mr Petronides...I am not available to be any man's live toy. You want a toy, you go to a store and buy yourself a railway set!'

'I thought you'd respect the upfront approach,' Angelos confided thoughtfully. 'But then I could never have guessed that behind the front you put on in public you suffer from such low self-esteem...'

Utterly thrown by that response, and with a horrendous suspicion that this confrontation was going badly wrong shrilling through her, Maxie suddenly felt foolish.

'Don't be ridiculous...of course I don't,' she argued with ragged stress. 'But, whatever mistakes I've made, I have no intention of repeating them. Now, I've told you how I feel, so open that blasted door and let me out of here!'

Angelos surveyed her with burning intensity, dense lashes low on penetrating black eyes. 'If only it were that easy...'

But this time when Maxie's perspiring fingers closed

round the handle the door sprang open, and she didn't stalk like a prowling queen of the jungle on her exit, she simply fled, every nerve in her too hot body jangling with aftershock.

CHAPTER THREE

WHAT had possessed her, what on *earth* had possessed her? Maxie asked herself feverishly over and over again as she walked. The rain came heavily—long, lazy June days of sunshine finally giving way to an unseasonal torrent which drenched her to the skin within minutes. Since she was too warm, and her temples still pounded with frantic tension, she welcomed that cooling rain.

Something had gone wildly off the rails in that office. Angelos had prevented her quick exit. He had withstood everything she threw at him with provocative poise. In fact, just like yesterday, the more out of control she had got, the calmer and more focused he had become. And he zipped from black fury to outrageous cool at spectacular and quite unnerving speed.

Melodramatic, yes, Maxie acknowledged. She had been. Inexplicably, she had gone off the deep end and hurled recriminations that she had never intended to voice. And, like the shrewd operator he was, Angelos Petronides had trained those terrifyingly astute eyes on her while she recklessly exposed private, personal feelings of bitter pain and insecurity.

It was stress which had done this to her. Leland's heart attack, the sudden resulting upheaval in her own life, the dreadful publicity, her godmother's death. The pressure had got to her and blown her wide open in front of a male who zeroed in on any weakness like a predator. Low self-esteem…she did *not* suffer from low self-esteem!

469

A limousine drew up several yards ahead of her in the quiet side-street she was traversing. Alighting in one fluid movement, Angelos ran exasperated eyes over her sodden appearance and grated, 'Get in out of the rain, you foolish woman…don't you even know to take shelter when it's wet?'

Swallowing hard on that in-your-face onslaught, Maxie pushed shaking fingers through the wet strands of hair clinging to her brow and answered him with a blistering look of charged defiance. 'Go drop yourself down a drain!'

'Will you scream assault if I just throw you in the car?' Angelos demanded with raw impatience.

A kind of madness powered Maxie then, adrenaline racing through her. She squared up to him, scarlet dress plastered to her fantastic body, the stretchy hemline riding up on her long, fabulous legs. She dared him with her furious eyes and her attitude and watched his powerful hands clench into fists of self-restraint—because of course he was far too clever to make a risky move like that.

'Why are you following me?' she breathed.

'I'm not into railway sets…too slow, too quiet,' Angelos confessed.

'I'm not into egocentric dominating men who think they know everything better than me!' Maxie slung back at him, watching his luxuriant ebony hair begin to curl in the steady rain, glistening crystalline drops running down his hard cheekbones. And she thought crazily, He's getting wet for me, and she liked that idea.

'If this is my cue to say I might change…sorry, no can do. I am what I am,' Angelos Petronides spelt out.

Stupid not to take a lift when she could have one, Maxie decided on the spur of the moment, particularly when she was beginning to feel cold and uncomfortable in her wet clothing. Sidestepping him, enjoying the awareness that she was rather surprising him, she climbed into the limousine.

The big car purred away from the kerb.

'I decided to make you angry because I want you to leave me alone,' Maxie told him truthfully.

'Then why didn't you stay away from me? Why did you get into this car?' Angelos countered with lethal precision.

In answer, Maxie made an instinctive and instantaneous shift across the seat towards the passenger door. But, before she could try to jump back out of the car, a powerful hand whipped out to close over hers and hold her fast. The limousine quickened speed.

Black eyes clashed with hers. 'Are you suicidal?' Angelos bit out crushingly.

Maxie shakily pulled free of his grasp.

The heavy silence clawed at her nerves. Such a simple question, such a lethally simple, clever question, yet it had flummoxed her. If she had truly wanted to avoid him, why *had* she let something as trivial as wet clothes push her back into his company?

Angelos extended a lean brown hand again, with the aspect of an adult taking reluctant pity on a sulky child. 'Come here,' he urged.

Without looking at him again, Maxie curled into the far corner of the back seat instead. His larger-than-life image was already engraved inside her head. She didn't know what was happening to her, why she was reacting so violently to him. Her own increasing turmoil and the suspicion that she was adrift in dangerously unfamiliar territory frankly frightened her. Angelos Petronides was bad news in every way for a woman like her. Avoiding him like the plague was the only common sense response. And she should've been freezing him out, not screaming at him.

With a languorous sigh, Angelos shrugged fluidly out of his suit jacket. Without warning he caught her hand and pulled her to him. Taken by surprise, Maxie went crazy, struggling wildly to untangle herself from those powerful fingers. 'Let go! What are you trying to—?'

'Stop it!' Angelos thundered down at her, and he released her again in an exaggerated movement, spreading both arms wide as if to demonstrate that he carried no offensive weapon. 'I don't like hysterical women.'

'I'm not...I'm not like that.' Maxie quivered in shock and stark embarrassment as he draped his grey jacket round her slim, taut shoulders. The silk lining was still warm from his body heat. The faint scent of him clung to the garment and her nostrils flared. Clean, husky male, laced with the merest tang of some citrus-based lotion. She lowered her damp head and breathed that aroma in deep. The very physicality of that spontaneous act shook her.

'You're as high-strung as some of my racehorses,' Angelos contradicted. 'Every time I come close you leap about a foot in the air—'

'I didn't yesterday,' she muttered with sudden lancing bitterness.

'You didn't get the chance...I crept up on you.' With a tormentingly sexy sound of indolent amusement, Angelos reached out his hands and closed them over the sleeves of the jacket she now wore, tugging on them like fabric chains of captivity to bring her to him.

'No!' Maxie gasped, wide-eyed, her hands flying up, only to find that the only place she could plant her palms was against his broad, muscular chest.

'If you like, you can bail out after the first kiss—no questions asked, no strings attached,' Angelos promised thickly.

Even touching him through his shirt felt so incredibly intimate that guilty quivers ran through her tautening length. He was so hot. Her fingers spread and then shifted over the tactile silk barrier, learning of the rough whorls of hair below the fabric and enthralled. She was used to being around male models with shiny shaven chests. She shivered deliciously, appallingly tempted to rip open the shirt and explore.

Heavily lidded black eyes lambent with sensual indulgence intercepted hers. 'You look like a guilty child with her hand caught in the biscuit tin,' he confided with a lazy smile.

At the power of that smile, the breath tripped in Maxie's throat, her pupils dilating. His proximity mesmerised her. She could see tiny gold lights in his eyes, appreciate the incredible silky length and luxuriance of those black lashes and the faint blue shadow on his strong jawline. The potency of her own fascination filled her with alarm. 'You're all wrong for me,' she said in breathless panic, like a woman trying to run through a swamp and inexplicably finding herself standing still and sinking fast.

'Prove it,' Angelos invited in that velvet-soft drawl that fingered down her spine like a caress. A confident hand pushed into her drying hair and curved to the nape of her neck. 'Prove that anything that feels this good could possibly be wrong for either of us.'

He was so stunningly gorgeous, she couldn't think straight. Her heartbeat seemed to be racing in her tight throat. The insidious rise of her own excitement was like a drowning, overwhelming wave that drove all before it. He dropped his eyes to the pouting distended buds clearly delineated by the clinging bodice of her dress and her face burned red.

Slowly Angelos tilted her back, his arms banding round her spine to support her, and, bending his dark, arrogant head, he pressed the mouth she craved on hers to the thrusting sensitivity of an aching nipple instead. Her whole body jumped, throat arching, head falling back, teeth clenching on an incoherent whimper of shock.

Angelos lifted her up again, black eyes blazing with primal male satisfaction. 'It hurts to want this much. I don't think you were familiar with the feeling…but *now* you are.'

Trembling, Maxie stared at him, sapphire eyes dark with shaken arousal. Cold fear snaked through her. He was playing with her just as he might have played with a toy. Using his carnal expertise he was taunting her, winding her up, demonstrating his sexual mastery.

'Don't touch me!' Her hand whipped up and caught him across one hard cheekbone, and then she froze in dismay at what she had done.

With striking speed Angelos closed his fingers round that offending hand, and slowly he smiled again. 'Frustration *should* make you angry.'

Beneath her strained and bemused gaze, he bent his glossy dark head and pressed his lips hotly to the centre of her stinging palm. It was electrifying. It was as if every tiny bit of her body was suddenly programmed to overreact. And then, while she was still struggling to comprehend the incredible strength of his power over her, he caught her to him with indolent assurance and simply, finally, kissed her.

Only there was nothing simple about that long-awaited kiss. It blew Maxie away with excitement. It was like no kiss she had ever received. That hard, sensual mouth connected with hers and instantly she needed to be closer to him than his own skin. Pulses pounding at an insane rate, she clutched at him with frantic hands, reacting to the violent need climbing inside her, craving more with every passing second.

And then it was over. Angelos studied her with burnished eyes of appreciation, all virile male strength and supremacy as he absorbed the passion-glazed blankness of her hectically flushed and beautiful face.

'Come on,' he urged her thickly.

She hadn't even realised the limousine had stopped. Now he was closing his jacket round her again with immense care, practically lifting her back out into the rain and the sharp fresh air which she drank in great thirsty gulps. She felt wildly disorientated. For timeless minutes the world beyond the limousine just hadn't existed for her. In confusion, she curved herself into the support of the powerful arm welded to her narrow back and bowed her head.

Without warning, Angelos tensed and vented a crushing oath, suddenly thrusting her behind him. Maxie looked up just in time to see a photographer running away from them. Simultaneously two powerfully built men sprinted from the car behind the limo and grabbed him before he could make it across to the other side of the street.

Angelos untensed again, straightening big shoulders. 'My security men will expose his film. That photo of us will never see the light of day.'

In a daze, Maxie watched that promise carried out. As a demonstration of ruthlessness it took her breath away. She had often wished that she could avoid the intrusive cameras of the paparazzi, but she had never seen in action the kind of brute power which Angelos exercised to protect his privacy.

And it was *his* privacy that he had been concerned about, she sensed. Certainly not hers. Why was it that she suspected that Angelos would go to great lengths to avoid being captured in newsprint by her side? Why was it that she now had the strongest feeling that Angelos was determined not to be seen in public with her?

Shivering with reaction at that lowering suspicion, she emerged from her tangled thoughts to find herself standing in a stark stainless steel lift. 'Where are we?' she muttered then, with a frown of bewilderment.

The doors sped soundlessly back on a vast expanse of marble flooring.

'My apartment...where else?'

Maxie flinched in dismay, her brain cranking back into sudden activity. If that paparazzo had escaped, he would've had a highly embarrassing and profitable picture of her entering Angelos Petronides's apartment wrapped intimately in his jacket. No prizes for guessing what people would've assumed. She just could not believe how stupid she had been.

'I thought you were taking me back to Liz's,' she admitted rather unsteadily.

Angelos angled up a mocking brow. 'I never said I was...and, after our encounter in the car, I confess that I prefer to make love in my own bed.'

Maxie could feel her teeth starting to chatter, her legs shaking. Like a whore, that was how she would've looked in that photo, and that was exactly how he was treating her.

'Maxie...' Angelos purred, reading her retreat and

switching channel to high-powered sensual persuasion as he strolled with animal grace towards her, strong, hard-boned face amused. 'You think I'm likely to respect you more if you suggest that we should wait another week, another month? I have no time for outdated attitudes like that—'

'Obviously not.' Agreement fell like dropped stones from Maxie's tremulously compressed lips.

'And I cannot credit that you should feel any differently. We will still be together six months from now,' Angelos forecast reflectively. 'Possibly even longer. I burn for you in a way I haven't burned for a woman in a very long time.'

'Try a cold shower.' Ice-cool as her own shrinking flesh, Maxie stood there, chin tilting as high as she could hold it even though she felt as if she was falling apart behind her façade. She shrugged back her shoulders so that his jacket slid off and fell in a rejected heap on the floor. 'I'm not some bimbo you can bed before you even date me—'

'The original idea was only to offer you lunch...' A dark rise of blood accentuated the tautening slant of his bold, hard cheekbones as he made that admission.

'But why waste time feeding me?' Maxie completed for him, her distaste unconcealed. 'In my time I have met some fast movers, but you have to qualify as supersonic. A kiss in the limo and that was consent to the whole menu?'

Angelos flung his arrogant dark head back, black eyes thudding like steel arrows into a target. 'The desire between us was honest and mutual and very strong. Do you expect me to apologise for a hunger you answered with a passion as powerful as my own?'

Maxie flinched. 'No...I don't think you make a habit of apologising.'

'I'm very straight...what you see is what you get. You put out conflicting signals and then back off. You have the problem,' Angelos informed her in cool condemnation. 'Don't put it on me. When I became an adult, I put childish games behind me.'

Although every strained muscle in her taut length ached, Maxie remained as outwardly poised as a queen surveying a less than satisfactory subject. But violent loathing powered her now. It took its strength from her shame that she had allowed him to touch her at all.

'I won't say it's been nice getting to know you over the past twenty-four hours, Angelos...it's been lousy,' Maxie stated, and turned in the direction of the lift.

'Goddamn you...don't you dare walk away from me!' Angelos slashed across the distance that separated them. 'Who are you, Maxie Kendall, to speak to *me* like that?'

'No more...I don't want to hear it,' Maxie muttered shakily.

'This time you will listen to me,' Angelos raked at her in wrathful forewarning. In one powerful stride he imposed his intimidating size between her and the lift. His lean, strong face hard as steel, bold black eyes hurled a ferocious challenge. 'Do you think I don't know you moved in with Leland between one day and the next? You hardly knew him. You came out of nowhere into his life. Do you think I didn't notice that you weren't remotely attracted to him?'

Quite unprepared for that angle of attack, Maxie stammered, 'I...I—'

'In fact, Leland bored you to death and you couldn't hide it. You could hardly bear him to touch you but you stuck it for three years all the same. Does that strike you as the behaviour of a sensitive woman with principles? You sold yourself for a wardrobe of designer clothes—'

'No, I didn't!' Maxie gasped strickenly.

'At no stage did you wake up and say to yourself, "I could do better than this. I'm worth more than this. This isn't the way I should be living!"' Angelos roared at her in a rage of shockingly raw derision. 'So don't tell me I got the wrong impression. I trust the evidence of my own eyes and senses. You felt nothing for him. But you put yourself on the market and he was still able to buy!'

Nausea stirring in her stomach, Maxie was retreating deeper into the penthouse apartment, her hands coming up in a fluttering movement in front of her as if she could somehow ward him off. 'No...no,' she mumbled sickly.

'And I was the bloody fool who, even knowing all that, *still* wanted you!' Angelos slung, spreading his arms in an extravagant gesture of outrage at her, at himself. 'I didn't want to buy you...or maybe I wanted the cosy pretence that it didn't have to be like that between us...that because you lusted after me too I could gloss over the knowledge that my immense wealth might have anything to do with your presence in my life!'

Maxie was like a statue, terrified to risk a step in case she cracked and broke into shattered pieces. He had forced her into cruel confrontation with the image he had of her. Like an explosion of glass, countless shards pierced her cringing flesh as every painful word drew blood.

'I'll never forgive you for this,' she whispered, more

to herself than to him. 'But Leland was never my lover. We had an agreement. It was a charade we played—'

Angelos spat something guttural in Greek. 'Don't talk to me like I'm stupid!'

Maxie looked through him then, and despised herself for even attempting self-defence. It suggested a weakness inside her, a need for this arrogant Greek's good opinion that her savaged pride could not allow. 'You stay away from me from now on—'

'You made your choices in life long before you met me. What is it that you want now?' Angelos demanded contemptuously.

A semi-hysterical laugh erupted from Maxie and she choked it off, twisting her head away defensively before he could see the burning tears in her eyes. 'Just the usual things.' Then she whipped her golden head back, shimmering eyes as unwittingly bright as stars. 'And some day, when all this is behind me, I'll have them. I wouldn't have you as a gift, Angelos. I wouldn't make love with you unless you tied me to the bed and held me down and forced me…is that clear enough? What you want you will *never* have!'

Angelos stared at her as if he couldn't take his eyes off her and hated her for it.

Maxie stared back with a stab of malicious satisfaction new to her experience. 'Bad news, eh? I'll be the one who got away,' she breathed tautly, frighteningly aware of the thunderous charge of violence in the atmosphere but unable to silence her own tongue and her helpless need to taunt him. 'But then why should that bother you? It's not like you have a shred of *real* emotion in you—'

'What do you want from me?' Angelos ripped back

at her with suppressed savagery. 'I will not and could not love a woman like you!'

'Oh, that honesty…hits me right where it hurts,' Maxie trilled, a knife-like pain scything through her. She was shaking like a leaf without even being aware of it. 'But for all that you still want me, don't you? Do you know something, Angelos? I *like* knowing that.'

A muscle jerked at the corner of his wide, sensual mouth, his strong jawline clenching. Those stunning black eyes burned with rage and seething pride.

'Thanks, you've just done wonders for my low self-esteem,' Maxie informed him with a jagged catch in her voice.

'What a bitch you can be…I never saw that in you before.' His accent was so thick she could have sliced it up, but that contemptuous intonation would still have flamed over her like acid, hurting wherever it touched. 'So, quote me a price for one night in your bed. What do you think you would be worth?'

The derisive suggestion coiled like a whip around her and scarred her worse than a beating. Her backbone went rigid. Hatred fired her embittered gaze. 'You couldn't even make the bidding,' Maxie asserted, looking him up and down as if he had crawled out from under a stone. 'I'd want a whole lot more than a wardrobe of designer clothes. You see, I learn from my mistakes, Angelos. The next man I live with will be my husband…'

Shock turned Angelos satisfying pale. 'If you think for one *insane* second that I—'

'Of course you wouldn't,' Maxie slotted in, each word clipped and tight with self-control. 'But you must see now why I'm not available for lunch, in bed or out of it. A woman can't be too careful. Being associated with a randy Greek billionaire could be very harmful to my new image.'

'I will work this entire dialogue out of your wretched hide every day you are with me!' Angelos snarled at her with primal force, all cool abandoned.

'You are just so slow on the uptake. I am not ever going to be *with* you, Angelos,' Maxie pointed out, and with that last word she strolled past him, holding herself taut and proud to the last, and walked into the lift.

Outside in the street again, she discovered that she was trembling so violently it was an effort to put one leg in front of the other. For once disregarding her straitened circumstances, she chose to hail a cab. Her mind was working like a runaway express train, disconnected images bombarding her...

How *could* two people who scarcely knew each other spend so long tearing each other apart? How could she have been that bitchy? How could she have actually enjoyed striking back at him and watching him react with impotent black fury? And yet now she felt sick at the memory, and astonishingly empty, like someone who had learned to thrive on electric tension and pain...and who now could not see a future worth living without them.

Angelos Petronides had devastated her but he wouldn't bother her again now, she told herself in an effort at consolation. Even the toughest male wouldn't put himself in line for more of the same. And Angelos least of all. He had expected her to fall into his bed with the eagerness of an avaricious bimbo, scarcely able to believe her good fortune. Instead she had hit that boundless ego of his, watched him shudder in sheer shock from the experience...and yet inside herself she felt the most awful bewildering sense of loss.

Reluctant to dwell on reactions that struck her as peculiar, Maxie chose instead to look back on their brief acquaintance with self-loathing. She squirmed over her own foolishness. Like an adolescent fighting a first powerful crush, she had overreacted every step of the way.

She had fancied him like mad but, blind and naive as a headstrong teenager, she hadn't even admitted that to herself until it was too late to save face. 'I have not been unaware of your interest in me.' She shuddered with shame. Had she surrendered to that physical attraction, it would've been a one-way ticket to disaster. She knew she couldn't afford to make any more wrong choices. She hadn't needed *him* to tell her that. Dear heaven, as if becoming his mistress would've been any kind of improvement on the humiliating charade Leland had forced her to live for so long!

Angelos hadn't believed her about Leland, of course he hadn't—hadn't even paused to catch his breath and listen. And in pushing the issue she would've made an ass of herself, for nothing short of medical proof of her virginity, if there was such a thing, would've convinced him otherwise. In any case the level of her experience wouldn't count with a male like Angelos Petronides. He viewed her the same way people viewed a takeaway snack. As something quick and cheap to devour, not savour. Her stomach lurched sickly. Even had she been tempted, which she hadn't been, had he thought for one moment that she would've believed she was likely to hold his interest as long as six months?

'A man will tell a girl who looks like you *anything* to get her into the bedroom,' her father had once warned her grimly. 'The one who is prepared to wait, the one who is more interested in how you feel, is the one who *cares.*'

That blunt advice had embarrassed her at a time when she was already struggling to cope with the downside of the spectacular looks she had been born with. Girlfriends threatened by the male attention she attracted had dumped her. Grown men had leered at her and tried to touch her and date her. Even teenage boys who, alone with her, had been totally intimidated by her, had told crude lies about her sexual availability behind her back. Eight years on, Maxie was still waiting without much hope to meet a man who wasn't determined to put the cart before the proverbial horse.

An hour after she got back to Liz's house, the phone rang. It was Catriona Ferguson, who ran the Star modelling agency which had first signed Maxie up at eighteen.

'I've got no good news for you, Maxie,' she shared in her usual brisk manner. 'The PR people over at LFT Haircare have decided against using you for another series of ads.'

'We were expecting that,' Maxie reminded the older woman with a rueful sigh of acceptance.

'I'm afraid there's nothing else in the pipeline for you. Hardly surprising, really,' Catriona told her. 'You're too strongly associated with one brand name. I did warn you about that risk and, to be blunt, your recent coverage in the tabloids has done you no favours.'

It had been a month since Maxie had moved out of Leland's townhouse. She hadn't worked since then and now it looked as if she was going to have to find some other means of keeping herself. Her bank account was almost empty. She couldn't afford to sit waiting for work that might never come, nor could she blame Catriona for her lack of sympathy. Time and time again the older woman had urged Maxie to branch out into

fashion modelling, but Leland's frantic social life and
the demands he had made on her time had made that
impossible.

Hours later, Maxie hunched over both bars of the electric fire in Liz's lounge as she tried to keep warm while
she brooded. Angelos was gone. That was good, she
told herself, that was one major problem solved. She
scratched an itchy place on her arm and then gazed
down in surprise at the little rash of spots there.

What had she eaten that had disagreed with her? she
wondered, but she couldn't recall eating anything more
than half a sandwich since breakfast time. She just
couldn't work up an appetite. She fell asleep on the
settee and at some timeless stage of the night wakened
to feel her way down to the guest-room and undress on
the spot before sinking wearily into bed.

When she woke up late the next morning, she wasn't
feeling too good. As she cleaned her teeth she caught a
glimpse of her face in the tiny mirror Liz had on the
wall for visitors and she froze. There was another little
rash of spots on her forehead. It looked remarkably
like…chickenpox. And she itched, didn't she? But only
children got that, didn't they? And then she remembered
one of Liz's neighbours calling in a couple of weeks
back with a child in tow who had borne similiar spots.

'She's not infectious any more,' the woman had said
carelessly.

Lower lip wobbling, Maxie surveyed the possible
proof of that misapprehension. A dry cough racked her
chest, leaving her gasping for breath. Whatever she had,
she was feeling foul. Getting herself a glass of water,
she went back to bed. The phone went. She had to get
out of bed again to answer it.

'What?' she demanded hoarsely after another bout of coughing in the cold hall.

'Angelos here, what's wrong with you?'

'I have...I have a cold,' she lied. 'What do you want?'

'I want to see you—'

'No way!' Maxie plonked down the phone at speed.

The phone rang again. She disconnected it from its wall-point. A couple of hours later the doorbell went. Maxie ignored it. Getting out of bed yet again felt like too much trouble.

She dozed for the rest of the day, finally waking up shivering with cold and conscious of an odd noise in the dim room. Slowly it dawned on her that the rasping wheeze was the sound of her own lungs straining to function. Her brain felt befogged, but she thought that possibly she might need a doctor. So she lay thinking about that while the doorbell rang and rang and finally fell silent.

Fear got a healthy grip on her when she stumbled dizzily out of bed and her legs just folded beneath her. She hit the polished wooden floor with a crash. Tears welled up in her sore eyes. The room was too dark for her to get her bearings. She started to crawl, trying to recall where the phone was. She heard a distant smash. It sounded like glass breaking, and then voices. Had she left the television on? Trying to summon up more strength, she rested her perspiring brow down on the boards beneath her.

And then the floor lit up...or so it seemed.

CHAPTER FOUR

A DISTURBINGLY familiar male voice bit out something raw in a foreign language and a pair of male feet appeared in Maxie's limited view. Strong hands turned her over and began to lift her.

'You're all...*spotty*...' Angelos glowered down at her with unblinking black eyes, full of disbelief.

'Go away...' she mumbled.

'It just looks a little...strange,' Angelos commented tautly, and after a lengthy pause, while Maxie squeezed shut her eyes against the painful intrusion of that overhead light *and* him, he added almost accusingly, 'I thought only children got chickenpox.'

'Leave me alone...' Maxie succumbed weakly to another coughing fit.

Instead, he lifted her back onto the bed and rolled the bulky duvet unceremoniously round her prone body.

'What are you doing?' she gasped, struggling to concentrate, finding it impossible.

'I was on my way down to my country house for the weekend. Now it looks like I'll be staying in town and you'll be coming home with me,' Angelos delivered, with no visible enthusiasm on his strong, hard face as he bent down to sweep her up into his powerful arms.

Maxie couldn't think straight, but the concept of having nothing whatsoever to do with Angelos Petronides was now so deeply engrained, his appearance had set all her alarm bells shrieking. 'No...I have to stay here to look after the house—'

'I wish you could…but you can't.'

'I promised Liz…she's away and she might be burgled again…put me down.'

'I can't leave you alone here like this.' Angelo stared down at her moodily, as if he was wishing she would make his day with a sudden miraculous recovery but secretly knew he didn't have much hope.

Maxie struggled to conceal her spotty face against his shoulder, mortified and weak, and too ill to fight but not too ill to hate. 'I don't want to go anywhere with you.' Gulping, she sniffed.

'I don't see any caring queue outside that door ready to take my place…and what have you got to snivel about?' Angelos demanded with stark impatience as he strode down the hall. Then he stopped dead, meshing long fingers into her hair to tug her face round and gaze accusingly down into her bemused eyes. 'I smashed my way in only because I was aware that you were ill. Decency demanded that I check that you were all right.'

'I do not snivel,' Maxie told him chokily.

'But the only reason I came here tonight was to return your "something on account' and to assure you that it would be a cold day in hell before I ever darkened your door again—'

'So what's keeping you?'

But Angelos was still talking like a male with an ever-mounting sense of injustice. 'And there you are, lying on the floor in a pathetic shivering heap with more spots than a Dalmatian! What's fair about that? But I'm not snivelling, am I?'

Maxie opened one eye and saw one of his security men watching in apparent fascination. 'I do not snivel…' she protested afresh.

Angelos strode out into the night air. He ducked

down into the waiting limousine and propped Maxie up in the farthest corner of the seat like a giant papoose that had absolutely nothing to do with him.

Only then did Maxie register that the limousine was already occupied by a gorgeous redhead, wearing diamonds and a spectacular green satin evening dress which would've been at home on the set of a movie about the Deep South of nineteenth-century America. The other woman gazed back at Maxie, equally nonplussed.

'Have you had chickenpox, Natalie?' Angelos enquired almost chattily.

Natalie Cibaud. She was an actress, a well-known French actress, who had recently won rave reviews for her role in a Hollywood movie. It had not taken Angelos long to find other more entertaining company, Maxie reflected dully while a heated conversation in fast and furious French took place. Maxie didn't speak French, but the other woman sounded choked with temper while Angelos merely got colder and colder. Maxie curled up in an awkward heap, conscious she was the subject under dispute and wishing in despair that she could perform a vanishing act.

'Take me home!' she cried once, without lifting her sore head.

'Stay out of this...what's it got to do with you?' Angelos shot back at her with positive savagery. 'No woman owns me...no woman ever has and no woman ever will!'

But Angelos was fighting a losing battle. Natalie appeared to have other ideas. Denied an appropriately humble response, her voice developed a sulky, shrill edge. Angelos became freezingly unresponsive. Strained silence finally fell. A little while later, the limousine came to a halt. The passenger door opened. Natalie swept out with her rustling skirts, saying something acid in her own language. The door slammed again.

'I suppose you thoroughly enjoyed all that,' Angelos breathed in a tone of icy restraint as the limousine moved off again.

Opening her aching eyes a crack, Maxie skimmed a dulled glance at the space Natalie had occupied and recently vacated. She closed her eyes again. 'I don't understand French...'

Angelos grated something raw half under his breath and got on the phone. He had been ditched twice in as many days. And, wretched as she was, Maxie was tickled pink by that idea. Angelos, who got chased up hill and down dale by ninety-nine out of a hundred foolish women, had in the space of forty-eight hours met two members of the outstanding and more intelligent one per cent minority. And it was good for him—really, really good for him, she decided. Then she dozed, only to groggily resurface every time she coughed. Within a very short time after that, however, she didn't know where she was any more and felt too ill to care.

'Feeling a bit better, Miss Kendall?'

Maxie peered up at the thin female face above hers. The face was familiar, and yet unfamiliar too. The woman wore a neat white overall and she was taking Maxie's pulse. Seemingly she was a nurse.

'What happened to me?' Maxie mumbled, only vaguely recalling snatches of endless tossing and turning, the pain in her chest, the difficulty in breathing.

'You developed pneumonia. It's a rare but potentially

serious complication,' the blonde nurse explained. 'You've been out of it for almost five days—'

'Five…days?' Maxie's shaken scrutiny wandered over the incredibly spacious bedroom, with its stark contemporary furniture and coldly elegant decor. She was in Angelos's apartment. She knew it in her bones. Nowhere was there a single piece of clutter or feminine warmth and homeliness. His idea of housing heaven, she reflected absently, would probably be the wide open spaces of an under-furnished aircraft hangar.

'You're very lucky Mr Petronides found you in time,' her companion continued earnestly, dragging Maxie back from her abstracted thoughts. 'By recognising the seriousness of your condition and ensuring that you got immediate medical attention, Mr Petronides probably saved your life—'

'No…I don't want to owe him *anything*…never mind my life!' Maxie gasped in unconcealed horror.

The slim blonde studied her in disbelief. 'You've been treated by one of the top consultants in the UK…Mr Petronides has provided you with the very best of round-the-clock private nursing care, and you say—?'

'While Miss Kendall is ill, she can say whatever she likes,' Angelos's dark drawl slotted in grimly from the far side of the room. 'You can take a break, Nurse. I'll stay with your patient.'

The woman had jerked in dismay at Angelos's silent entrance and intervention. Face pink, she moved away from the bed. 'Yes, Mr Petronides.'

In a sudden burst of energy, Maxie yanked the sheet up over her head.

'And the patient is remarkably lively all of a sudden,' Angelos remarked as soon as the door closed on the nurse's exit. 'And ungrateful as hell. Now, why am I not surprised?'

'Go away,' Maxie mumbled, suddenly intensely conscious of lank sweaty hair and spots which had probably multiplied.

'I'm in my own apartment,' Angelos told her drily. 'And I am not going away. Do you seriously think that I haven't been looking in on you to see how you were progressing over the past few days?'

'I don't care…I'm properly conscious now. If I was so ill, why didn't you just take me to hospital?' Maxie demanded from beneath the sheet.

'The top consultant is a personal friend. Since you responded well to antibiotics, he saw no good reason to move you.'

'Nobody consulted me,' Maxie complained, and shifted to scratch an itchy place on her hip.

Without warning, the sheet was wrenched back.

'No scratching,' Angelos gritted down at her with raking impatience. 'You'll have scars all over you if you do that. If I catch you at that again, I might well be tempted to tie your hands to the bed!'

Aghast at both the unveiling and the mortifying tone of that insultingly familiar threat, Maxie gazed up at him with outraged blue eyes bright as jewels. 'You pig,' she breathed shakily, registering that he was getting a kick out of her embarrassment. 'You had no right to bring me here—'

'You're in no fit state to tell me what to do,' Angelos reminded her with brutal candour. 'And even I draw the line at arguing with an invalid. If it's of any comfort to your wounded vanity, I've discovered that once I got used to the effect the spotty look could be surprisingly appealing.'

'Shut up!' Maxie slung at him, and fell back against the pillows, completely winded by the effort it had taken to answer back.

While she struggled to even out her breathing, she studied him with bitter blue eyes. Angelos looked soul-destroyingly spectacular. He wore a beige designer suit with a tie the shade of rich caramel and a toning silk shirt. The lighter colours threw his exotic darkness into prominence. He exuded sophistication and exquisite cool, and at a moment when Maxie felt more grotty than she had ever felt in her life, she loathed him for it! Rolling over, she presented him with her back.

Maddeningly, Angelos strolled round the bed to treat her to an amused appraisal. 'I'm flying over to Athens for the next ten days. I suspect you'll recover far more happily in my absence.'

'I won't be here when you get back...oh, no, Liz's house has been left empty!' Maxie moaned in sudden guilty dismay.

'I had a professional housesitter brought in.'

Maxie couldn't even feel grateful. Her heart sank even further. He had settled Leland's loan. He had paid for expensive private medical care within his own home. And now he had shelled out for a housesitter as well. If it took her the rest of her life, she would still be paying off what she now had to owe him in total!

'Thanks,' she muttered ungraciously, for her friend's sake.

'Don't mention it,' Angelos said with considerable irony. 'And you *will* be here when I return. If you're not, I'll come looking for you in a very bad mood—'

'Don't talk like you own me!' she warned him in feverish, frantic denial. 'You were with that actress only a few days ago…you were never going to darken my door again—'

'You darkened mine. Oh…yes, before I forget…' Angelos withdrew something small and gold from his pocket and tossed it carelessly on the bed beside her.

Stunned, Maxie focused on the bracelet which she had pawned.

'*'Ice Queen in pawnshop penury'* ran the headline in the gossip column,' Angelos recounted with a sardonic elevation of one ebony brow as he watched Maxie turn brick-red with chagrin. 'The proprietor must've tipped off the press. I found the ticket in your bag and had the bracelet retrieved.'

Wide-eyed and stricken, Maxie just gaped at him.

Angelos dealt her a scorching smile of reassurance. 'You won't have to endure intrusive publicity like that while you are with me. I will protect you. You will never have to enter a pawnshop again. Nor will you ever have to shake your tresses over a misty green Alpine meadow full of wildflowers…unless you want to do it for my benefit, of course.'

Maxie simply closed her eyes on him. She didn't have the energy to fight. He was like a tank in the heat and fury of battle. Nothing short of a direct hit by a very big gun would stop his remorseless progress.

'Silence feels good,' Angelos remarked with silken satisfaction.

'I hate you,' Maxie mumbled, with a good deal of very real feeling.

'You hate *wanting* me,' Angelos contradicted with measured emphasis. 'It's poetic justice and don't expect sympathy. When I had to think of you lying like a block of ice beneath Leland, I did not enjoy wanting you either!'

Maxie buried her burning face in the pillow with a hoarse little moan of self-pity. He left her nothing to hide behind. And any minute now she expected to be hauled out of concealment. Angelos preferred eye-to-eye contact at all times.

'Get some sleep and eat plenty,' Angelos instructed from somewhere alarmingly close at hand, making her stiffen in apprehension. 'You should be well on the road to recovery by the time I get back from Greece.'

Maxie's teeth bit into the pillow. Her blood boiled. For an instant she would have sacrificed the rest of her life for the ability to punch him in the mouth just once. She thought he had gone, and lifted her head. But Angelos, who never, ever, it seemed, did anything she expected, was still studying her from the door, stunning dark features grave. 'By the way, I also expect you to be extremely discreet about this relationship—'

'We don't have a relationship!' Maxie bawled at him. 'And I wouldn't admit to having been here in your apartment if the paparazzi put thumbscrews on me!'

Angelos absorbed that last promise with unhidden satisfaction. And then, with a casual inclination of his dark, arrogant head, he was gone, and she slumped, weak and shaken as a mouse who had been unexpectedly released from certain death by a cat.

Maxie finished packing her cases. While she had been ill, Angelos had had all her clothes brought over from Liz's. The discovery had infuriated her. A few necessities would have been sensible, but *everything* she possessed? Had he really thought she would be willing to stay on after she recovered?

For the first thirty-six hours after his departure she had fretted and fumed, struggling to push herself too far too fast in her eagerness to vacate his unwelcome hospitality.

The suave consultant had made a final visit to advise her to take things slowly, and the shift of nursing staff had departed, but Maxie had had to face that she was still in no fit state to look after herself. So she *had* been sensible. She had taken advantage of the opportunity to convalesce and recharge her batteries while she was waited on hand and foot by the Greek domestic staff…but now she was leaving before Angelos returned. In any case, Liz was coming home at lunchtime.

Two of Angelos's security men were hovering in the vast echoing entrance hall. Taut with anxiety, they watched her stagger towards them with her suitcases. Neither offered an ounce of assistance.

'Mr Petronides is not expecting—' the bigger, older one finally began stiffly.

'If you know what's good for you, you'll stay out of this!' Maxie thumped the lift button with a clenched fist of warning.

'Mr Petronides doesn't want you to leave, Miss Kendall. He's going to be annoyed.'

Maxie opened dark blue eyes very, very wide. *'So?'*

'We'll be forced to follow you, Miss Kendall—'

'Oh, I wouldn't do that, boys,' Maxie murmured gently. 'I would hate to call in the police because I was being harassed by stalkers. It would be sure to get into the papers too, and I doubt that your boss would enjoy *that* kind of publicity!'

In the act of stepping forward as the lift doors folded back, both men froze into frustrated stillness. Maxie dragged her luggage into the lift.

'A word of advice,' the older one breathed heavily. 'He makes a relentless enemy.'

Maxie tossed her head in a dismissive movement. Then the doors shut and she sagged. No wonder Angelos threw his weight around so continually. Everybody was terrified of him. Unlimited wealth and power had made him what he was. His ruthless reputation chilled, his lethal influence threatened. The world had taught him that he could have whatever he wanted. Only not her...never ever *her*, she swore vehemently. Her mind was her own. Her body was her own. She was inviolate. Angelos couldn't touch her, she reminded herself bracingly.

The housesitter vacated Liz's house after contacting her employer for instructions. Alone then, and tired out by the early start to the day, Maxie felt very low. Making herself a cup of coffee, she checked through the small pile of post in the lounge. One of the envelopes was addressed to her; it had been redirected.

The letter appeared to be from an estate agent. Initially mystified, Maxie struggled across the barrier of her dyslexia to make sense of the communication. The agent wrote that he had been unable to reach her father at his last known address but that she had been listed by Russ as a contact point. He required instructions concerning a rental property which was now vacant. Memories began to stir in Maxie's mind.

Her father's comfortably off parents had died when she was still a child. A black sheep within his own family even then, Russ had inherited only a tiny cottage on the outskirts of a Cambridgeshire village. He had been even less pleased to discover that the cottage came with an elderly sitting tenant, who had not the slightest intention of moving out to enable him to sell up.

Abandoning the letter without having got further than the third line, Maxie telephoned the agent. 'I can't tell

you where my father is at present,' she admitted ruefully. 'I haven't heard from him in some time.'

'The old lady has moved in with relatives. If your
father wants to attract another tenant, he'll have to
spend a lot on repairs and modernisation. However,' the
agent continued with greater enthusiasm, 'I believe the
property would sell very well as a site for building development.'

And of course that would be what Russ would want,
Maxie reflected. He would sell and a few months down
the road the proceeds would be gone again, wasted on
the racecourse or the dog track. Her troubled face stiffening with resolve, Maxie slowly breathed in and found
herself asking if it would be in order for her to come
and pick up the keys.

She came off the phone again, so shaken by the ideas
mushrooming one after another inside her head that she
could scarcely think straight. But she *did* need a home,
and she had always loved the countryside. If she had
the courage, she could make a complete fresh start. Why
not? What did she have left in London? The dying rem-
nants of a career which had done her infinitely more
harm than good? She could find a job locally. Shop
work, bar work; she wasn't fussy. As a teenager Maxie
had done both, and she had no false pride.

By the time Liz came home, Maxie was bubbling
with excitement. In some astonishment, Liz listened to
the enthusiastic plans that the younger woman had already formulated.

'If the cottage is in a bad way, it could cost a fortune
to put it right, Maxie,' she pointed out anxiously. 'I
don't want to be a wet blanket, but by the sound of
things—'

'Liz...I never did want to be a model and I'm not

getting any work right now,' Maxie reminded her rue-fully. 'This could be my chance to make a new life and, whatever it takes, I want to give it a try. I'll tell the agency where I am so that if anything does come up they can contact me, but I certainly can't afford to sit around here doing nothing. At least if I start earning again, I can start paying back Angelos.'

If Maxie could've avoided telling Liz about the housesitter and her own illness, she would've done so. But Liz had a right to know that a stranger had been looking after her home. However, far from being trou-bled by that revelation, Liz was much more concerned to learn that Maxie had been ill. She was also morti-fyingly keen to glean every detail of the role which Angelos Petronides had played.

'I swear that man is madly in love with you!' Liz shook her head in wonderment.

Maxie vented a distinctly unamused laugh, her eyes incredulous. 'Angelos wouldn't know love if it leapt up and bit him to the bone! But he will go to any lengths to get what he wants. I suspect he thinks that the more indebted he makes me, the easier he'll wear down my resistance—'

'Maxie...if he'd left you lying here alone in this house, you might be dead. Don't you even feel the slightest bit grateful?' Liz prompted uncomfortably. 'He could've just called an ambulance—'

'Thereby missing out on the chance to get me into his power when I was helpless?' Maxie breathed cyni-cally. 'No way. I know how he operates. I *know* how he thinks.'

'Then you must have much more in common with him than you're prepared to admit,' Liz commented.

* * *

Maxie arrived at the cottage two days later. With dire mutters, the cabbie nursed his car up the potholed lane. In the sunshine, the cottage looked shabby, but it had a lovely setting. There was a stream ten feet from the front door and a thick belt of mature trees that provided shelter.

She had some money in her bank account again too. She had liquidated a good half of her wardrobe. Ruthlessly piling up all the expensive designer clothes which Leland had insisted on buying her, Maxie had sold them to a couple of those wonderful shops which recycle used quality garments.

Half an hour later, having explored her new home, Maxie's enthusiasm was undimmed. So what if the accommodation was basic and the entire place crying out for paint and a seriously good scrub? As for the repairs the agent had mentioned, Maxie was much inclined to think he had been exaggerating.

She was utterly charmed by the inglenook fireplace in the little front room and determined not to take fright at the minuscule scullery and the spooky bathroom with its ancient cracked china. Although the furnishings were worn and basic, there were a couple of quite passable Edwardian pieces. The new bed she had bought would be delivered later in the day.

She was about a mile from the nearest town. As soon as she had the bed made up, she would call in at the hotel she had noticed on the main street to see if there was any work going. In the middle of the tourist season, she would be very much surprised if there wasn't an opening somewhere…

Five days later, Maxie was three days into an evening job that was proving infinitely more stressful than she had anticipated. The pace of a waitress in a big, busy bar was frantic.

And why, oh, why hadn't she asked whether the hotel bar served meals *before* she accepted the job? She could carry drinks orders quite easily in her head, but she had been driven into trying to employ a frantic shorthand of numbers when it came to trying to cope at speed with the demands of a large menu and all the innumerable combinations possible. She just couldn't write fast enough.

Maxie saw Angelos the minute he walked into the bar. The double doors thrust back noisily. He made an entrance. People twisted their heads to glance and then paused to stare. Command and authority written in every taut line of his tall, powerful frame, Angelos stood out like a giant among pygmies.

Charcoal-grey suit, white silk shirt, smooth gold tie. He looked filthy rich, imposing and utterly out of place. And Maxie's heart started to go bang-bang-bang beneath her uniform. He had the most incredible traffic-stopping presence. Suddenly the crowded room with its low ceiling and atmospheric lighting felt suffocatingly hot and airless.

For a split second Angelos remained poised, black eyes raking across the bar to close in on Maxie. She had the mesmerised, panicked look of a rabbit caught in car headlights. His incredulous stare of savage impatience zapped her even at a distance of thirty feet.

Sucking in oxygen in a great gulp, Maxie struggled to finish writing down the order she was taking on her notepad. Gathering up the menus again, she headed for the kitchens at a fast trot. But it wasn't fast enough. Angelos somehow got in the way.

'Take a break,' he instructed in a blistering undertone.

'How the heck did you find out where I was?'

'Catriona Ferguson at the Star modelling agency was
eager to please.' Angelos watched Maxie's eyes flare
with angry comprehension. 'Most people are rather reluctant to say no to me.'

In an abrupt move, Maxie sidestepped him and hurried into the kitchen. When she re-emerged, Angelos
was sitting at one of *her* tables. She ignored him, but
never had she been more outrageously aware of being
watched. Her body felt uncoordinated and clumsy. Her
hands perspired and developed a shake. She spilt a drink
and had to fetch another while the woman complained
scathingly about the single tiny spot that had splashed
her handbag.

Finally the young bar manager, Dennis, approached
her. 'That big dark bloke at table six...haven't you noticed him?' he enquired apologetically, studying her
beautiful face with the same poleaxed expression he had
been wearing ever since he'd hired her. With an abstracted frown, he looked across at Angelos, who was
tapping long brown fingers with rampant impatience on
the tabletop. 'It's odd. There's something incredibly familiar about the bloke but I can't think where I've seen
him before.'

Maxie forced herself over to table six. 'Yes?' she
prompted tautly, and focused exclusively on that expensive gold tie while all the time inwardly picturing
the derision in those penetrating black eyes.

'That uniform is so short you look like a bloody
French maid in a bedroom farce!' Angelos informed her
grittily. 'Every time you bend over, every guy in here

is craning his neck to get a better view! And that practice appears to include the management.'

Maxie's face burned, outrage flashing in her blue eyes. The bar had a Victorian theme, and the uniform was a striped overall with a silly little frilly apron on top. It did look rather odd on a woman of her height and unusually long length of leg, but she had already let down the hemline as far as it would go. 'Do you or do you not want a drink?' she demanded thinly.

'I'd like the table cleared and cleaned first,' Angelos announced with a glance of speaking distaste at the cluttered surface. 'Then you can bring me a brandy and sit down.'

'Don't be ridiculous...I'm working.' Maxie piled up the dishes with a noisy clatter, and in accidentally slopping coffee over the table forced him to lunge back at speed from the spreading flood.

'You're working for me, and if I say you can sit down, I expect you to do as you're told,' Angelos delivered in his deep, dark, domineering drawl.

Engaged in mopping up, Maxie stilled. 'I beg your pardon? You said...I was working for *you*?' she queried.

'This hotel belongs to my chain,' Angelos ground out. 'And I am anything but impressed by what I see here.'

Maxie turned cold with shock. Angelos *owned* this hotel? She backed away with the dishes. As she was hailed from the kitchen, she watched with a sinking stomach as Angelos signalled Dennis. When she reappeared with a loaded tray, Dennis was seated like a pale, perspiring graven image in front of Angelos.

She hurried to deliver the meals she had collected but

there was a general outcry of loud and exasperated complaint.

'I didn't order this…' the first customer objected. 'I asked for salad, not French fries—'

'And I wanted garlic potatoes—'

'This steak is *rare*, not well-done—'

The whole order was hopelessly mixed up. A tall, dark shadow fell menacingly over the table. In one easy movement, Angelos lifted Maxie's pad from her pocket, presumably to check out the protests. 'What *is* this?' he demanded, frowning down at the pages as he flipped. 'Egyptian hieroglyphics…some secret code? Nobody could read this back!'

Maxie was paralysed to the spot; her face was bone-white. Her tummy lurched with nausea and her legs began to shake. 'I got confused, I'm sorry. I—'

Angelos angled a smooth smile at the irate diners and ignored her. 'Don't worry, it will be sorted out as quickly as possible. Your meals are on the house. Move, Maxie,' he added in a whiplike warning aside.

Dennis, she noticed sickly, was over at the bar using the internal phone. He looked like a man living a nightmare. And when she came out of the kitchen again, an older man, whom she recognised as the manager of the entire hotel, was with Angelos, and he had the desperate air of a man walking a tightrope above a terrifying drop. Suddenly Maxie felt like the albatross that had brought tragedy to an entire ship's crew. Angelos, it seemed, was taking out his black temper on his staff. Her own temper rose accordingly.

How the heck could she have guessed that he owned this hotel? She recalled the innumerable marble plaques in the huge foyer of the Petronides building in London. Those plaques had listed the components of Angelos's vast and diverse business empire. Petronides Steel, Petronides Property, and ditto Shipping, Haulage, Communications, Construction, Media Services, Investments, Insurance. No doubt she had forgotten a good half-dozen. PAI—Petronides Amalgamated Industries—had been somewhat easier to recall.

'Maxie…I mean, Miss Kendall,' Dennis said awkwardly, stealing an uneasy glance at her and making her wonder what Angelos had said or done to make him behave like that. But not for very long. 'Mr Petronides says you can take the rest of the night off.'

Maxie stiffened. 'Sorry, I'm working.'

Dennis looked aghast. 'But—'

'I was engaged to work tonight and I need the money.' Maxie tilted her chin in challenge.

She banged a brandy down in front of Angelos. 'You're nothing but a big, egocentric bully!' she slung at him with stinging scorn.

A lean hand closed round her elbow before she could stalk away again. Colour burnished her cheeks as Angelos forced her back to his side with the kind of male strength that could not be fought without making a scene. Black eyes as dark as the legendary underworld of Hades slashed threat into hers. 'If I gave you a spade, you would happily dig your own grave. Go and get your coat—'

'No…this is my job and I'm not walking out on it.'

'Let me assist you to make that decision. You're sacked…' Angelos slotted in with ruthless bite.

With her free hand, Maxie swept up the brandy and upended it over his lap. In an instant she was free. With an unbelieving growl of anger, Angelos vaulted upright.

'If you can't stand the heat, stay out of the kitchen!' Maxie flung fiercely, and stalked off, shoulders back, classic nose in the air.

CHAPTER FIVE

DENNIS was waiting for Maxie outside the staff-room when she emerged in her jeans and T-shirt. Pale and still bug-eyed with shock, he gaped at her. 'You must be out of your mind to treat Angelos Petronides like that!'

'Envy me...I don't work for him any more.' Maxie flung her golden head high. 'May I have my pay now, please?'

'Y-your pay?' the young bar manager stammered.

'Is my reaction to being forcibly held to the spot by the owner of this hotel chain sufficient excuse to withhold it?' Maxie enquired very drily.

The silence thundered.

'I'll get your money...I don't really think I want to raise that angle with Mr Petronides right now,' Dennis confided weakly.

Ten minutes later Maxie walked out of the hotel, grimacing when she realised that it was *still* pouring with rain. It had been lashing down all day and she had got soaked walking into town in spite of her umbrella. Every passing car had splashed her. A long, low-slung sports car pulled into the kerb beside her and the window buzzed down.

'Get in,' Angelos told her in a positive snarl.

'Go take a hike! You can push around your staff but you can't push *me* around!'

'Push around? Surely you noticed how sloppily that bar was being run?' Angelos growled in disbelief.

Thrusting open the car door, he climbed out to glower down at her in angry reproof. 'Insufficient and surly staff, customers kept waiting, the kitchens in chaos, the tables dirty and even the carpet in need of replacement! If the management don't get their act together fast, I'll replace them. They're not doing their jobs.'

Taken aback by his genuine vehemence, Maxie nonetheless suppressed the just awareness that she herself had been less than impressed by what she had seen. He had changed too, she noticed furiously. He must have had a change of clothes with him, because now he was wearing a spectacular suit of palest grey that had the exquisite fit of a kid glove on his lean powerful frame.

Powered by sizzling adrenaline alone, Maxie studied that lean, strong face. 'I hate you for following me down here—'

'You were waiting for me to show up...'

Her facial muscles froze. The minute Angelos said it, she knew it was true. She had *known* he would track her down and find her.

'I'm walking home. I'm not getting into your car,' she informed him while she absently noted that, yet again, he was getting wet for her. Black hair curling, bronzed cheekbones shimmering damply in the street lights.

'I have not got all night to waste, waiting for you to walk home,' Angelos asserted wrathfully.

'So you know where I'm living,' Maxie gathered in growing rage, and then she thought, What am I doing here standing talking to him? 'Well, don't you dare come there because I won't open the door!'

'You could be attacked walking down a dark country road,' Angelos ground out, shooting her a flaming look of antipathy. 'Is it worth the risk?'

Angling her umbrella to a martial angle, Maxie spun on her heel and proceeded to walk. She hadn't gone ten yards before her flowing hair and long easy stride attracted the attention of a bunch of hard-faced youths lounging in a shop doorway. Their shouted obscenities made her stiffen and quicken her pace.

From behind her, she heard Angelos grate something savage.

A hand came down without warning on Maxie's tense shoulder and she uttered a startled yelp. As she attempted to yank herself free, everything happened very fast. Angelos waded in and slung a punch at the offender. With a menacing roar, the boy's mates rushed to the rescue. Angelos disappeared into the fray and Maxie screamed and screamed at the top of her voice in absolute panic.

'Get off him!' she shrieked, laying about the squirming clutch of heaving bodies with vicious jabs of her umbrella and her feet as well.

Simultaneously a noisy crowd came out of the pub across the street and just as suddenly the scrum broke and scattered. Maxie knelt down on the wet pavement beside Angelos's prone body and pushed his curling wet black hair off his brow, noting the pallor of his dark skin. 'You stupid fool…you stupid, stupid fool,' she moaned shakily.

Angelos lifted his head and shook it in a rather jerky movement. Slowly he began to pick himself up. Blood was running down his temples. 'There were five of them,' he grated, with clenched and bruised fists.

'Get in your car and shut up in case they come back,' Maxie muttered, tugging suggestively at his arm. 'Other people don't want to get involved these days. You could've been hammered to a pulp—'

'*Them and who else?*' Angelos flared explosively, all male ego and fireworks.

'The police station is just down the street—'

'I'm not going to the police over the head of those little punks!' Angelos snarled, staggering slightly and spreading his long powerful legs to steady himself. 'I got in a punch or two of my own—'

'Not as many as they did.' Maxie hauled at his sleeve and by dint of sustained pressure nudged him round to the passenger side of his opulent sports car.

'What are you doing?'

'You're not fit to drive—'

'Since when?' he interrupted in disbelief.

Maxie yanked open the door. 'Please, Angelos…you're bleeding, you're probably concussed. Just for once in your wretched life, do as someone else asks.'

He stood there and thought about that stunning concept for a whole twenty seconds. There was a definite struggle taking place and then, with a muffled curse, he gradually and stiffly lowered himself down into the passenger seat.

'Can you drive a Ferrari?' he enquired.

'Of course,' Maxie responded between clenched teeth of determination, no better than him at backing down.

The Ferrari lurched and jerked up the road.

'Lights,' Angelos muttered weakly. 'I think you should have the lights on…or maybe I should just close my eyes—'

'Shut up…I'm trying to concentrate!'

Having mastered the lights and located the right gear, Maxie continued, 'It was typical of you to go leaping in, fists flying. Where are your security guards, for goodness' sake?'

'How *dare* you?' Angelos splintered, leaning forward with an outrage somewhat tempered by the groan he emitted as the seat belt forced him to rest back again. 'I can look after myself—'

'Against five of them?' Maxie's strained mouth compressed, her stomach still curdling at what she had witnessed. Damn him, damn him. She felt so horribly guilty and shaken. 'I'm taking you to Casualty—'

'I don't need a doctor…I'm OK,' Angelos bit out in exasperation.

'If you drop dead from a skull fracture or something,' she said grimly, 'I don't want to feel responsible!'

'I have cuts and bruises, nothing more. I have no need of a hospital. All I want to do is lie down for a while and then I'll call for a car.'

He sounded more like himself. Domineering and organised. Maxie mulled over that unspoken demand for a place to lie down while she crept along the road in the direction of the cottage at the slowest speed a Ferrari had probably ever been driven at. Then the heavy rain was bouncing off the windscreen and visibility was poor. 'All right…I'll take you home with me—but just for an hour,' she warned tautly.

'You are so gracious.'

Maxie reddened, conscience-stricken when she recalled the amount of trouble he had taken to ensure that she was properly looked after when she was ill. But then Angelos had not been personally inconvenienced; he had paid others to take on the caring role. In fact, as she drove up the lane to the cottage, she knew she could not imagine Angelos allowing himself to be inconvenienced.

Her attention distracted, she was wholly unprepared to find herself driving through rippling water as she began to turn in at the front of the cottage. In alarm, she braked sharply, and without warning the powerful car went into a skid. 'Oh, God!' she gasped in horror as the front wheels went over the edge of the stream bank. The Ferrari tipped into the stream nose-first with a jarring thud and came to rest at an extreme angle.

'God wasn't listening, but at least we're still alive,' Angelos groaned as he reached over and switched off the engine.

'I suppose you're about to kick up a whole macho fuss now, and yap about women drivers,' Maxie hissed, unclamping her locked fingers from the steering wheel.

'I wouldn't dare. Knowing my luck in your radius, I'd step out of the car and drown.'

'The stream is only a couple of feet deep!'

'I feel so comforted knowing that.' With a powerful thrust of his arm, Angelos forced the passenger door open and staggered out onto the muddy bank. Then he reached in to haul her out with stunning strength.

'I'm sorry… I got a fright when I saw that water.'

'It was only a large puddle. What do you do when you see the sea?'

'I thought the stream had flooded and broken its banks, and I wanted to be sure we didn't go over the edge in the dark…that's *why* I jumped on the brakes!' Fumbling for her key, not wishing to dwell on quite how unsuccessful her evasive tactics had been, Maxie unlocked the battered front door and switched on the light.

Angelos lowered his wildly tousled dark head to peer, unimpressed, into the bare lounge with its two seater hard-backed settee. Without the fire lit or a decorative face-lift, it didn't look very welcoming, she had to admit.

'All right, upstairs is a bit more comfortable. You can lie down on my bed.'

'I can hardly believe your generosity. Where's the phone?'

Maxie frowned. 'I don't have one.'

Tangled wet black lashes swept up on stunned eyes. 'That's a joke?'

'Surely you have a mobile phone?'

'I must've dropped it in the street during the fight.' With a mutter of frustrated Greek, Angelos started up the narrow staircase.

He was a little unsteady on his feet, and Maxie noted that fact anxiously. 'I think you need a doctor, Angelos.'

'Rubbish…just want to lie down—'

'Duck your head!' she warned a split second too late as he collided headfirst with the lintel above the bedroom door.

'Oh, no,' Maxie groaned in concert with him, and shot out both arms to support him as he reeled rather dangerously on the tiny landing. Hurriedly she guided him into the bedroom before he could do any further damage to himself.

'There's puddles on the floor,' Angelos remarked, blinking rapidly.

'Don't be silly,' Maxie told him, just as a big drop of water from somewhere above splashed down on her nose.

Aghast, she tipped back her head to gaze up at the vaulted wooden roof above, which she had thought was so much more attractive and unusual than a ceiling. Droplets of water were suspended in several places and there *were* puddles on the floorboards. The roof was leaking.

'I'm in the little hovel in the woods,' Angelos framed.

Maxie said a most unladylike word and darted over to the bed to check that it wasn't wet. Mercifully it appeared to be occupying the only dry corner in the room, but she wrenched back the bedding to double-check. Angelos dropped down on the edge of the divan and tugged off his jacket. It fell in a puddle. She snatched up the garment and clutched it as she met dazed black eyes. 'I shouldn't have listened you. I should've taken you to Casualty.'

'I have a very sore head and I am slightly disorientated. That is *all*.' Angelos coined the assurance with arrogant emphasis. 'Stop treating me like a child.'

'How many fingers do you see?' In her anxiety, Maxie stuck out her thumb instead of the forefinger she had intended.

'I see one thumb,' he said very drily. 'Was that a trick question?'

Flushing a deep pink, Maxie bridled as he yanked off his tie. 'Do you have to undress?'

'I am not lying down in wet clothes,' Angelos informed her loftily.

'I'll leave you, then...well, I need to get some bowls for the drips anyway,' Maxie mumbled awkwardly on her passage out through the door.

Just the thought of Angelos unclothed shot a shocking current of snaking heat right through her trembling body. It was only nervous tension, Maxie told herself urgently as she went downstairs, the result of delayed shock after that horrendous outbreak of masculine violence in the street. *She* had been really scared, but Angelos was too bone-deep macho and stupid to have been scared. However, she should have forced him to go to the local hospital…but how did you force a male as spectacularly stubborn as Angelos to do something he didn't want to do, and surely there couldn't be anything really serious wrong with him when he could still be so sarcastic?

In the scullery, she picked up a bucket and a mop, and then abandoned them to pour some disinfectant into a bowl of water instead. She needed to see close up how bad that cut was. Had he been unconscious for several seconds after the youths had run off? His eyes had been closed, those ridiculously long lashes down like black silk fans and almost hitting his cheekbones. Dear heaven, what was the matter with her? Her mind didn't feel like her own any more.

Angelos was under her rosebud-sprigged sheets when she hesitantly entered the bedroom again. His eyes seemed closed. She moistened her lower lip with a nervous flick of her tongue. She took in the blatant virility of his big brown shoulders, the rough black curls of hair sprinkling what she could see of his powerful pectoral muscles and that vibrant golden skintone that seemed to cover all of him, and which looked so noticeable against her pale bedding…

'You're supposed to stay awake if you have concussion,' she scolded sharply in response to those unnecessarily intimate observations. Stepping close to the bed, she jabbed at a big brown shoulder and swiftly withdrew her hand from the heat of him again as if she had been scalded, her fair skin burning.

Those amazing black eyes snapped open on her.

'You're bleeding all over my pillow,' Maxie censured, her throat constricting as she ran completely out of breath.

'I'll buy you a new one.'

'No, you buy nothing for me…and you lie still,' she instructed unevenly. 'I need to see that cut.'

With an embarrassingly unsteady hand and a pad of kitchen towelling, Maxie cleaned away the blood. As she exposed the small seeping wound, a beautifully shaped brown hand lifted and closed round the delicate bones of her wrist. 'You're shaking like a leaf.'

'You might've been knifed or something. I still feel sick thinking about it. But I could've dealt with that kid on my own—'

'I think not…his mates were already moving in to have some fun. Nor would it have cost them much effort to drag you round the corner down that alleyway—'

'Well, I'm not about to thank you. If you had stayed away from me, it wouldn't have happened,' Maxie stated tightly. 'I'd have stayed in the hotel until closing time and got a lift home with the barman. He lives a couple of miles on down the road.'

With that final censorious declaration, Maxie pulled herself free and took the bowl downstairs again. She would have to go back up and mop the floor but it was true, she *was* shaking like a leaf and her legs felt like jelly. Unfortunately it wasn't all the result of shock. Seeing Angelos in her bed, wondering like a nervous adolescent how much, if anything, he was wearing, hadn't helped.

Five minutes later she went back up, with a motley collection of containers to catch the drips and the mop and bucket. In silence, she did what had to be done, but she was horribly mortified by the necessity, not to mention furious with herself for dismissing the agent's assessment of the cottage's condition on the phone. This was the first time it had rained since she had moved in and clearly either a new roof or substantial repairs would be required to make the cottage waterproof before winter set in. It was doubtful that she could afford even repairs.

As each receptacle was finally correctly positioned to catch the drips from overhead, a cacophany of differing noises started up. Split, splat, splash, plop…

'How are you feeling?' Maxie asked thinly above that intrusive backdrop of constant drips.

'Fantastically rich and spoilt. Indoors, water belongs in the bathroom or the swimming pool,' Angelos opined with sardonic cool. 'I can't credit that you would prefer to risk drowning under a roof that leaks like a sieve sooner than come to me.'

'Credit it. Nothing you could do or say would convince me otherwise. I don't want to live with any man—'

'I wasn't actually asking you to live with me,' Angelos delivered in gentle contradiction, his sensual mouth quirking. 'I like my own space. I would buy you your own place and visit—'

An angry flush chased Maxie's strained pallor. 'I'm not for sale—'

'Except for a wedding ring?' Angelos vented a roughened laugh of cynical amusement. 'Oh, yes, I got the message. Very naive, but daring. I may be obsessed with a need to possess that exquisite body that trembles with sexual hunger whenever I am close,' he murmured silkily, reaching up with a confident hand to close his fingers over hers and draw her down beside him before she even registered what he was doing, 'but, while I will fulfil any other desire or ambition with pleasure, that one is out of reach, *pethi mou*. Concentrate on the possible, not the wildly improbable.'

'If you didn't already have a head injury, I'd swing for you!' Maxie slung fiercely. 'Let go of me!'

In the controlled and easy gesture of a very strong male, Angelos released her with a wry smile. 'At the end of the day, Leland did quite a number on your confidence, didn't he? Oh, yes, I know that *he* dispatched *you* from the hospital and screeched for Jennifer. Suddenly you found yourself back on the street, alone and without funds. So I quite understand why you should decide that a husband would be a safer bet than a lover next time around. However, I am *not* Leland...'

Maxie stared down into those stunning dark golden eyes. Fear and fascination fought for supremacy inside her. She could feel the raw magnetism of him reaching out to entrap her and she knew her own weakness more and more with every passing second in his company. She hated him but she wanted him too, with a bone-deep yearning for physical contact that tormented her this close to him. She was appalled by the strength of his sexual sway over her, shattered that she could be so treacherously vulnerable with a male of his ilk.

'Come here...stop holding back,' Angelos urged softly. 'Neither of us can win a battle like this. Do we not both suffer? I faithfully promise that I will never, ever take advantage of you as Leland did—'

'What are you trying to do right now?' Maxie condemned strickenly.

'Trying to persuade you that trusting me would be in your best interests. And I'm not laying a finger on you,' Angelos added, as if he expected acclaim for that remarkable restraint.

And the terrible irony, she registered then, was that she *wanted* him to touch her. Her bright eyes pools of sapphire-blue dismay and hunger, she stared down at him. Reaching up to loosen the band confining her hair to the nape of her neck, Angelos trailed it gently free to wind long brown fingers into the tumbling strands and slowly tug her down to him.

'But that's not what you want either, is it?' he said perceptively.

'No…' Her skin burning beneath the caress of the blunt forefinger that skated along her tremulous and full lower lip, she shivered violently. 'But I won't give in. This attraction means nothing to me,' she swore raggedly. 'It won't influence my brain—'

'What a heady challenge…' Black eyes flaring with golden heat held her sensually bemused gaze.

'I'm not a challenge, I'm a woman…' Maxie fumbled in desperation to make her feelings clear but she didn't have the words or, it seemed, the self-discipline to pull back from his embrace.

'A hell of a woman, to fight me like this,' Angelos confirmed, with a thickened appreciation that made her heart pound like mad in her eardrums and a tide of disorientating dizziness enclose her. 'A woman worth fighting for. If you could just rise above this current inconvenient desire to turn over a new leaf—'

'But—'

'No buts.' Angelos leant up to brush his lips in subtle glancing punishment over her parted ones, scanning her with fierce sexual hunger and conviction. 'You *need* me.'

'No…' she whispered feverishly.

'*Yes…*' Dipping his tongue in a snaking explorative flick into her open mouth, Angelos jolted her with such an overpowering stab of excitement, she almost collapsed down on top of him.

Pressing his advantage with a ruthless sense of timing, Angelos tumbled her the rest of the way and gathered her into his arms. She gasped again, 'No.'

The palm curving over a pouting, swollen breast stilled. Her nipple was a hard, straining bud that ached and begged for his attention, and she let her swimming head drop down on the pillow while she fought desperately for control. She focused on him. The brilliant eyes, the strong nose, the ruthless mouth. And that appalling tide of painful craving simply mushroomed instead of fading.

'No?' Angelos queried lazily.

She inched forward like a moth to a candle flame, seeking the heat and virility she could not resist, all thought suspended. He recognised surrender when he saw it, and with a wolfish smile of reward he closed his mouth hungrily over hers and she burned up like a shooting star streaking through the heavens at impossible speed, embracing destruction as if she had been born to seek it.

He curved back from her when her every sense was thrumming unbearably, her whole body shaking on a peak of frantic anticipation, and eased one hand beneath the T-shirt to curve it to her bare breasts. She whimpered and jerked, the most terrifying surge of hunger taking over as his expert fingers tugged on her tender nipples and then his caressing mouth went there instead. For long, timeless minutes, Maxie was a shuddering wreck of writhing, gasping response, clutching at him, clutching at his hair, her denim-clad hips rising off the bed in helpless invitation.

Abruptly Angelos tensed and jerked up his dark head, frowning. 'What's that?' he demanded.

'W-what's what?' she stammered blankly.

'Someone's thumping on the front door.'

By then already engaged in gaping down at her own shamelessly bared breasts, the damp evidence of his carnal ministrations making the distended pink buds look even more wanton, Maxie gulped. With a low moan of distress she threw herself off the bed onto quaking legs.

'You swine,' she accused shakily, hauling down her T-shirt, crossing trembling arms and then rushing for the stairs.

She flung open the front door. Her nearest neighbour, Patrick Devenson, who had called in to introduce himself the day before, stared in at her. 'Are you aware that you have a Ferrari upended in your stream?'

Dumbly, still trembling from the narrowness of her escape from Angelos and his seductive wiles, Maxie nodded like a wooden marionette.

The husky blond veterinary surgeon frowned down at her. 'I was driving home and I saw this strange shape from the road, and, knowing you're on your own here, I thought I'd better check it out. Are you OK?'

'The driver's upstairs, lying down,' Maxie managed to say.

'Want me to take a look?'

'No need,' she hastened to assert breathlessly.

'Do you want me to ring a doctor?'

Maxie focused on the mobile in its holder at his waist. 'I'd be terribly grateful if you'd let me use that to make a call.'

'No problem...' Patrick said easily, and passed the phone over. 'Mind if I step in out of the rain?'

'Sorry, not at all.'

Maxie walked upstairs rigid-backed, crossed the room and plonked the phone down on the bed beside Angelos. 'Call for transport out of here or I'll throw you out in the rain!'

His stunningly handsome features froze into impassivity, but not before she saw the wild burn of outrage flare in the depths of his brilliant eyes. He stabbed the buttons, loosed a flood of bitten-out Greek instructions and then, cutting the connection, sprang instantly out of bed. Maddeningly, he swayed slightly.

But Maxie was less affected by that than by her first intimidating look at a naked and very aroused male. Colouring hotly, she dragged her shaken scrutiny from him and fled downstairs again.

'Thanks,' she told Patrick.

'Had a drink or two, had he? Wicked putting a machine like that in for a swim,' Patrick remarked with typical male superiority as he moved very slowly back to the door. 'Your boyfriend?'

'No, he's not.'

'Dinner with me then, tomorrow night?'

Words of automatic refusal brimmed on Maxie's lips, and then she hesitated. 'Why not?' she responded after that brief pause for thought. She was well aware that Angelos had to be hearing every word of the conversation.

'Wonderful!' Patrick breathed with unconcealed pleasure. 'Eight suit you?'

'Lovely.'

She watched him swing cheerfully back into his four-wheel drive and thought about how open and uncomplicated he was in comparison to Angelos, who was so devious and manipulative he would contrive to zigzag down a perfectly straight line. And she hated Angelos, she really did.

Hot tears stung her eyes then, and she blinked them back furiously. She hated him for showing her all over again how weak and foolish she could be. She hated that cool, clever brain he pitted against her, that brilliantly persuasive tongue that could make the unacceptable sound tempting, and that awesome and terrifying sexual heat he unleashed on her whenever she was vulnerable.

Barely five minutes later, Angelos strode fully dressed into the front room where she was waiting. He radiated black fury, stormy eyes glittering, sensual mouth compressed, rock-hard jawline at an aggressive angle. His hostile vibrations lanced through the already tense atmosphere, threatening to set it on fire.

'You bitch...' Angelos breathed, so hoarsely it sounded as if he could hardly get the words out. 'One minute you're in bed with me and the next you're making a date with another man within my hearing!'

'I wasn't in bed with you, not the way you're implying.' Her slender hands knotted into taut fists of determination by her side, Maxie stood her ground, cringing with angry self-loathing only inside herself.

'You don't *want* any other man!' Angelos launched at her with derisive and shocking candour. 'You want *me*!'

Maxie was bone-white, her knees wobbling. In a rage, Angelos was pure intimidation; there was nothing he would not say. 'I won't be your mistress. I made that clear that from the start,' she countered in a ragged rush. 'And even if I had slept with you just now, I would still have asked you to leave. I will not be cajoled, manipulated or seduced into a relationship that I would find degrading—'

'Only an innocent can be seduced.' His accent harshened with incredulity over that particular choice of word. '*Degrading?*' Outrage clenched his vibrant dark features hard. 'Fool that I am, I would have treated you like a precious jewel!'

Locked up tight somewhere, to be enjoyed only in the strictest privacy, Maxie translated, deeply unimpressed.

'I know you don't believe me, but I was never Leland's mistress—'

'Did you call yourself his lover instead?' Angelos derided.

Maxie swallowed convulsively. 'No, I—'

Grim black eyes clashed with hers in near physical assault. '*Theos*...how blind I have been! All along you've been scheming to extract a better offer from me. One step forward, two steps back. You run and I chase. You tease and I pursue,' he enumerated in harsh condemnation. 'And now you're trying to turn the screw by playing me off against another man—'

'No!' Maxie gasped, unnerved by the twisted light he saw her in.

Angelos growled, 'If you think for one second that you can force me to offer a wedding ring for the right to enjoy that beautiful body, you are certifiably insane!'

His look of unconcealed contempt sent scorching anger tearing through Maxie. 'Really...? Well, isn't that just a shame, when it's the only offer I would ever settle for,' she stated, ready to use any weapon to hold him at bay.

Evidently somewhat stunned to have his worst suspicions so baldly confirmed, Angelos jerked as if he had run into a brick wall. He snatched in a shuddering breath, his nostrils flaring. 'If I ever marry, my wife will be a lady with breeding, background and a decent reputation.'

Maxie flinched, stomach turning over sickly. She had

given him a knife and he had plunged it in without compunction. But ferocious pride as great as his own, and hot, violent loathing enabled her to treat him to a scornful appraisal. 'But you'll still have a mistress, won't you?'

'Naturally I would choose a wife with my brain, not my libido,' Angelos returned drily, but he had ducked the question and a dark, angry rise of blood had scoured his blunt cheekbones.

Maxie gave an exaggerated little shiver of revulsion. The atmosphere was explosive. She could feel his struggle to maintain control over that volatile temperament so much at war with that essentially cool intellect of his. It was etched in every restive, powerfully physical movement he made with his expressive hands and she rejoiced at the awareness, ramming down the stark bitterness and sense of pained inadequacy he had filled her with. 'You belong in the Natural History Museum alongside the dinosaur bones.'

'When I walk through that door I will never come back...how will you like that?'

'Would you like to start walking now?'

'What I would *like* is to take you on that bed upstairs and teach you just once exactly what you're missing!'

Wildly unprepared for that roughened admission, Maxie collided with golden eyes ablaze with frustration. It was like being dragged into a fire and burned by her own hunger. She shivered convulsively. 'Dream on,' she advised fiercely, but her voice shook in self-betrayal.

The noise of a car drawing up outside broke the taut silence.

Angelos inclined his arrogant dark head in a gesture of grim dismissal that made her squirm, and then he walked.

CHAPTER SIX

MAXIE drifted like a sleepwalker through the following five days. The Ferrari was retrieved by a tow-truck and two men who laughed like drains throughout the operation. She contacted a builder to have the roof inspected and the news was as bad as she had feared. The cottage needed to be reroofed, and the quote was way beyond her slender resources.

She dined out with Patrick Devenson. No woman had ever tried harder to be attracted to a man. He was good-looking and easy company. Desperate to feel a spark, she let him kiss her at the end of the evening, but it wasn't like falling on an electric fence, it was like putting on a pair of slippers. Seriously depressed, Maxie made an excuse when he asked when he could see her again.

She didn't sleep, *couldn't* sleep. She dreamt of fighting with Angelos. She dreamt of making wild, passionate love for the first time in her life. And, most grotesque of all, she dreamt of drifting down a church aisle towards a scowling, struggling Greek in handcuffs. She felt like an alien inside her own head and body.

She sat down and painstakingly made a list of every flaw that Angelos possessed. It covered two pages. In a rage with herself, she wept over that list. She loathed him. Yet that utterly mindless craving for his enlivening, domineering Neanderthal man presence persisted, killing her appetite and depriving her of all peace of mind.

How could she miss him, how could she possibly? How *could* simple sexual attraction be so devastating a leveller? she asked herself in furious despair and shame. And, since she could only be suffering from the fallout of having repressed her own physical needs for so long, why on earth hadn't she fancied Patrick?

At lunchtime on the fifth day, she heard a car coming up the lane and went to the window. A silver Porsche pulled up. When Catriona Ferguson emerged, Maxie was startled. She had never in her life qualified for a personal visit from the owner of the Star modelling agency and couldn't begin to imagine what could've brought the spiky, city-loving redhead all the way from town.

On the doorstep, Catriona dealt her a wide, appreciative smile. 'I've got to hand it to you, Maxie...you have to be the Comeback Queen of the Century.'

'You've got some work for me?' Maxie ushered her visitor into the front room.

'Since the rumour mill got busy, you're really *hot*,' Catriona announced with satisfaction. 'The day after tomorrow, there's a Di Venci fashion show being staged in London...a big splashy charity do, and your chance to finally make your debut on the couture circuit.'

'The rumour mill?' Maxie was stunned by what the older woman was telling her. One minute she was yesterday's news and the next she was being offered the biggest break of her career to date? That didn't make sense.

Having sat down to open a tiny electronic notepad, Catriona flashed her an amused glance. 'The gossip columns are rumbling like mad...don't you read your own publicity?'

Maxie stiffened. 'I don't buy newspapers.'

'I'm very discreet. Your private life is your own.' However, Catriona still searched Maxie's face with avid curiosity. 'But what a coup for a lady down on her luck, scandalously maligned and dropped into social obscurity... Only one of the richest men in the world—'

Maxie jerked. 'I don't know what you're talking about.'

Catriona raised pencilled brows. 'I'm only talking about the guy who has just single-handedly relaunched your career without knowing it! The paparazzo who had his film exposed howled all over the tabloids about who he had seen you with—'

'You're talking about Angelos...'

'And when I received a cautious visit from a tight-mouthed gentleman I know to be close to the Greek tycoon himself, I was just totally *amazed*, not to mention impressed to death,' Catriona trilled, her excitement unconcealed. 'So I handed over your address. They say Angelos Petronides never forgets a favour...or, for that matter, a slight.'

Maxie had turned very pale. 'I...'

'So why are you up here vegetating next door to a field of sheep?' Catriona angled a questioning glance at her. 'Treat 'em mean, keep 'em keen? Popular report has it that this very week he dumped Natalie Cibaud for you. Whatever you're doing would appear to be working well. And he's an awesome catch, twenty-two-carat gorgeous, and as for that delicious *scary* reputation of his—'

'There's nothing between Angelos and me,' Maxie cut in with flat finality, but her head buzzed with the information that Angelos had evidently still been seeing the glamorous French film actress.

The silence that fell was sharp.

'If it's already over, keep it to yourself.' Catriona's disappointment was blatant. 'The sudden clamour for your services relates very much to *him*. The story that you've captured his interest is enough to raise you to celebrity status right now. So keep the people guessing for as long as you can...'

When Maxie recalled how appalled she had been at the threat of being captured in newsprint with Angelos and being subjected to more lurid publicity, she very nearly choked at that cynical advice. And when she considered how outraged Angelos must be at the existence of such rumours, when he had demanded her discretion, she sucked in a sustaining breath.

Catriona checked her watch. 'Look, why don't I give you a lift back to town? I suggest you stay with that friend in the suburbs again. The paparazzi are scouring the pavements for you. You don't want to be found yet. You need to make the biggest possible impact when you appear on that catwalk.'

It took guts, but Maxie nodded agreement. The old story, she thought bitterly. She needed the money. Not just for the roof but also to pay off Angelos as well. Yet the prospect of all those flashing cameras and the vitriolic pens of the gossip columnists made her sensitive stomach churn. Money might not buy happiness, but the lack of it could destroy all freedom of choice. And Maxie acknowledged then that the precious freedom to choose her own way of life was what she now craved most.

Scanning Maxie's strained face, Catriona sighed. 'Whatever *has* happened to the Ice Queen image?'

As she packed upstairs, Maxie knew the answer to that. Angelos had happened. He had chipped her out from behind the safety of her cool, unemotional façade

by making her feel things she had never felt before…painful things, hurtful things. She wanted the ice
back far more desperately than Catriona did.

Maxie came off the catwalk to a rousing bout of thunderous applause. Immediately she abandoned the strut-
ting insolent carriage which was playing merry hell with
her backbone. Finished, *at last*. The relief was so huge,
she trembled. Never in her life had she felt so exposed.

Before she could reach the changing room, Manny
Di Venci, a big bruiser of a man with a shaven head
and sharp eyes, came backstage to intercept her. 'You
were brilliant! Standing room only out there, but now
it's time to beat a fast retreat. No, you don't need to
get changed,' the designer laughed, urging her at a fast
pace down a dimly lit corridor that disorientated her
even more after the glaring spotlights of the show.
'You're the best PR my collection has ever had, and a
special lunch-date demands a touch of Di Venci class.'

Presumably Catriona had set up lunch with some VIP
she had to impress.

Thrust through a rear entrance onto a pavement
drenched in sunlight, Maxie was dazzled again.
Squinting at the open door of the waiting vehicle, she
climbed in. The car had pulled back into the traffic before she registered that she was in a huge, opulent limo
with shaded windows, but she relaxed when she saw
the huge squashy bag of her possessions sitting on the
floor. She checked the bag; her clothes were in it too.
Somebody had been very efficient.

Off the catwalk, she was uncomfortable in the daring
peacock-blue cocktail suit. She wore only skin below
the fitted jacket with its plunging neckline, and the skirt
was horrendously tight and short. She would have pre-

ferred not to meet a potential client in so revealing an outfit, but she might as well make the best of being sought after while it lasted because it wouldn't last long. The minute Angelos appeared in public with another woman, she would be as 'hot' as a cold potato. But oh, how infuriating it must be for Angelos to have played an accidental part in pushing her back into the limelight!

When the door of the limo swung open, Maxie stepped out into a cold, empty basement car park. She froze in astonishment, attacked by sudden mute terror, and then across the vast echoing space she recognised one of Angelos's security men, and was insensibly relieved for all of ten seconds. But the nightmare image of kidnapping which had briefly gripped her was immediately replaced by a sensation of almost suffocating panic.

'Where am I?' she demanded of the older man standing by a lift with the doors wide in readiness.

'Mr Petronides is waiting for you on the top floor, Miss Kendall.'

'I didn't realise that limo was *his*. I thought I was meeting up with my agent and a client for lunch…this is o-outrageous!' Hearing the positively pathetic shake of rampant nerves in her own voice, Maxie bit her lip and stalked into the lift. She was furious with herself. She had been the one to make assumptions. She should have spoken to the chauffeur before she got into the car.

Like a protective wall in front of her, the security man stayed by the doors, standing back again only after they had opened. Her face taut with temper, Maxie walked out into a big octagonal hall with a cool tiled floor. It was not Angelos's apartment and she frowned, wondering where on earth she was. Behind her the lift whirred downward again and she stiffened, feeling ludicrously cut off from escape.

Ahead of her, a door stood wide. She walked into a spacious, luxurious reception room. Strong sunlight was pouring through the windows. The far end of the room seemed to merge into a lush green bank of plants. Patio doors gave way into what appeared to be a conservatory. Was that where Angelos was waiting for her?

Her heart hammered wildly against her ribs. Utterly despising her own undeniable mix of apprehension and excitement, Maxie threw back her slim shoulders and stalked out into...*fresh air*. Too late did she appreciate that she was actually out on a roof garden. As she caught a dizzy glimpse of the horrific drop through a gap in the decorative stone screening to her right, her head reeled. Freezing to the spot, she uttered a sick moan of fear.

'Oh, hell...you're afraid of heights,' a lazy drawl murmured.

A pair of hands closed with firm reassurance round her whip-taut shoulders and eased her back from the parapet and the view that had made her stomach lurch to her soles. 'I didn't think of that. Though I suppose I could keep you standing out here and persuade you to agree to just about anything. Sometimes it's *such* a challenge to be an honourable man.'

Shielding her from the source of her mindless terror with his big powerful frame, Angelos propelled her back indoors at speed. Appalled by the attack of panic which had thrown her off balance, Maxie broke free of him then, on legs shaking like cotton wool pins, and bit out accusingly, 'What would *you* know about honour?'

'The Greek male can be extremely sensitive on that

subject. Think before you speak,' Angelos murmured in chilling warning.

Maxie stared at him in surprise. Angelos stared levelly back at her, black eyes terrifyingly cold.

And it tore her apart just at that moment to learn that she couldn't *bear* him to look at her like that. As if she was just anybody, as if she was nobody, as if he didn't care whether she lived or died.

'You get more nervy every time I see you,' Angelos remarked with cruel candour. 'Paler, thinner too. I thought you were pretty tough, but you're not so tough under sustained pressure. Your stress level is beginning to show.'

Colour sprang into Maxie's cheeks, highlighting the feverish look in her gaze. 'You're such a bastard sometimes,' she breathed unevenly.

'And within itself, that's strange. I've never been like this with a woman before. There are times when I aim to hurt you and I shock myself,' Angelos confided, without any perceptible remorse.

Yet he still looked so unbelievably good to her, and that terrified her. She couldn't drag her attention from that lean, strong face, no matter how hard she tried. She couldn't forget what that silky black hair had felt like beneath her fingertips. She couldn't stop herself noticing that he was wearing what had inexplicably become the colour she liked best on him. Silver-grey, the suit a spectacular fit for that magnificent physique. And how had she forgotten the way that vibrant aura of raw energy compelled and fascinated her? Cast into deeper shock by the raging torrent of her own frantic thoughts, Maxie felt an intense sense of her own vulnerability engulf her in an alarming wave.

'Relax…I've got a decent proposal to put on the table

before lunch,' Angelos purred, strolling soundlessly forwards to curve a confident arm round her rigid spine and guide her across the hall into a dining-room. 'Trust me...I think you'll feel like you've won the National Lottery.'

'Why won't you just leave me alone?' Maxie whispered, taking in the table exquisitely set for two, the waiting trolley that indicated they were not to be disturbed.

'Because you don't want me to. Even the way you just looked at me...' Angelos vented a soft husky laugh of very masculine appreciation. 'You really *can't* look at me like that and expect me to throw in the towel.'

'How did I look?'

'Probably much the same way that I look at you,' he conceded, uncorking a bottle of champagne with a loud pop and allowing the golden liquid to foam expertly down into two fluted glasses. 'With hunger and hostility and resentment. I am about to wipe out the last two for ever.'

Angelos slotted the moisture-beaded glass between her taut fingers. Absorbing her incomprehension, he dealt her a slashing smile. 'The rumour that Angelos Petronides cannot compromise is a complete falsehood. I excell at seeing both points of view and a period of reflection soon clarified the entire problem. The solution is very simple.'

Maxie frowned uneasily. 'I don't know what you're driving at...'

'What *is* marriage? Solely a legal agreement.' Angelos shrugged with careless elegance but she was chilled by that definition. 'Once I recognised that basic truth, I saw with clarity. I'll make a deal with you now that suits us both. *You* sign a prenuptial contract and I *will* marry you...'

'S-say that again,' Maxie stammered, convinced she was hallucinating.

Angelos rested satisfied eyes on her stunned expression. 'The one drawback will be that you won't get the public kudos of being my wife. We will live apart much of the time. When I'm in London and I want you here, you will stay in this apartment. I own this entire building. You can have it all to yourself, complete with a full complement of staff and security. The only place we will share the same roof will be on my island in Greece. How am I doing?'

Maxie's hand was shaking so badly, champagne was slopping onto the thick, ankle-deep carpet. Was he actually asking her to marry him? Had she got that right or imagined it? And, if she was correct and hadn't misunderstood, why was he talking about them living apart? And what had that bit been concerning 'public kudos'? Her brain was in a hopelessly confused state of freefall.

Angelos took her glass away and set it aside with his own. He pressed her gently down onto the sofa behind her and crouched down at her level to scan her bewildered face.

'If a marriage licence is what it takes to make you feel secure and bring you to my bed, it would be petty to deny you,' Angelos informed her smoothly. 'But, since our relationship will obviously not last for ever, it will be a private arrangement between you and I alone.'

Maxie stopped breathing and simply closed her eyes. He had hurt her before but never as badly as this. Was her reputation really *that* bad? In his eyes, it evidently was, she registered sickly. He didn't want to be seen with her. He didn't want to be linked with her. He would go through the motions of marrying her only so long as it was a 'private arrangement'. And a temporary one.

Cool, strong hands snapped round her straining fingers as she began to move them in an effort to jump upright. 'No...think about it, don't fly off the handle,' Angelos warned steadily. 'It's a fair, realistic, what-you-see-is-what-you-get offer—'

'A mockery!' Maxie contradicted fiercely.

And that had to be the most awful moment imaginable to realise that she was very probably in love with Angelos. It was without doubt her lowest hour. Devastated to suspect just how and why he had come to possess this power to tear her to emotional shreds, Maxie was shorn of her usual fire.

'Be reasonable. How do I bring Leland's former mistress into my family and demand that they accept her as my wife?' Angelos enquired with the disorientating cool of someone saying the most reasonable, rational things and expecting a fair and understanding hearing. 'Some things one just does not do. How can I expect my family to respect me if I do something I would kill any one of them for doing? The family look to me to set an example.'

Maxie still hadn't opened her eyes, but she knew at that instant how a woman went off the rails and killed. There was so much pain inside her and so much rage—at her, at him—she didn't honestly know how she *could* contain it. Mistress within a marriage that nobody would ever know about because she was too scandalous and shameful a woman to deserve or indeed expect ac-

ceptance within the lofty Petronides clan…that was
what he was offering.

'I feel sick…' Maxie muttered raggedly.

'No, you do not feel sick,' Angelos informed her with
resolute emphasis.

'I…feel…sick!'

'The cloakroom is across the hall.' Angelos withdrew
his strong hands from hers in a stark demonstration of
disapproval. Only when he did so did she realise how
tightly she had been holding onto him for support. The
inconsistency of such behaviour in the midst of so devastating a dialogue appalled her. 'I didn't expect you to
be so difficult about this. I can appreciate that you're a
little disappointed with the boundaries I'm setting, but
when all is said and done, it is *still* a marriage proposal!'

'Is it?' Maxie queried involuntarily, and then, not
trusting herself to say anything more, she finally, mercifully made it into the sanctuary of the cloakroom.

She locked the door and lurched in front of a giant
mirror that reflected a frightening stranger with the
shocked staring eyes of tragedy, pallid cheeks and a
horribly wobbly mouth. You do *not* love that swine—
do you hear me? she mouthed with menace at the alien
weak creature in the reflection. The only thing you're
in love with is his *body*! She knew as much about love
as a fourteen-year-old with a crush! And she could not
imagine where that insane impulsive idea that she might
love such a unreconstructed pig could've come from…it
could only have been a reaction to overwhelming shock.

She wanted to scream and cry and break things and
she knew she couldn't, so she hugged herself tight instead and paced the floor. As there was a great deal of
floor available, in spite of the fact it was only a cloakroom, that was not a problem.

He's prepared to give you a whole blasted building to yourself. But then he does like his own space. He's prepared to do virtually anything to get you into bed except own up to you in public. Love and hate. Two sides of the same coin. A cliché but the brief, terrifying spasm of that anguished love feeling had now been wholly obliterated by loathing and a desire to hit back and hurt that was ferocious.

A *marriage* proposal? A bitter laugh erupted from Maxie. Angelos was still planning to use her, still viewing her as a live toy to be acquired at any cost for his bedroom. And evidently her reluctance had sent what he was prepared to pay for that pleasure right through the roof! Grimacing, she could not help thinking about the two men before Angelos who had most influenced her life. Her father and Leland. For once she thought about her father without sentimentality…

Russ had gambled away her earnings and finally abandoned her, leaving her to work off *his* debts. Leland had stolen three years of her life and destroyed her reputation. How often had she sworn since never to allow any man to use her for his own ends again?

Like a bolt from the blue an infinitely more ego-boosting scenario flashed into Maxie's mind. She froze as the heady concept of turning the tables occurred to her. What if *she* were to do the using this time around?

Didn't she require a husband to inherit a share of her godmother's estate? When she had heard that news, she had taken disappointment on the chin. She had not foreseen the remotest possibility of a husband on the horizon, and the concept of looking for one with the sole object of collecting that inheritance had made her cringe.

Only no longer did Maxie feel so nice in her notions.

Angelos had done that to her. He was a corrupting influence and no mistake. He had distressed her, humiliated her, harassed her, not to mention committed the ultimate sin of taking the holy bond of matrimony and twisting it into a sad, dirty joke.

Angelos saw her as an ambitious, money-grabbing bimbo without morals. No doubt he despised what he saw. He probably even despised his own obsessive hunger to possess her. The marriage, if it could be called such, wouldn't last five minutes beyond the onset of his boredom.

But what if she were to take the opportunity to turn apparent humiliation into triumph? She *could* break free of everything that had ruined her life in recent years. That debt to Angelos, a career and a life she hated, Angelos himself. If she had the courage of her convictions, she could have it *all*. Yes, she really could. She could marry him and walk out on him six months later. She pictured herself breezily throwing Angelos a cheque and telling him no, she didn't need his money, she now had her own. She looked back in the mirror and saw a killer bimbo with a brain and not a hint of tears in her eyes any more.

Maxie was surprised to find Angelos waiting in the hall when she emerged.

'Are you OK?' he enquired, as if he really cared.

Her lip wanted to curl but she controlled it. The rat. An extraordinarily handsome rat, but a rat all the same.

'I was working out my conditions of acceptance.' Maxie flashed him a bright smile of challenge.

Angelos tensed.

'I'll need to be sure I *will* feel like a Lottery winner at the end of this private arrangement,' she told him for good measure.

Angelos frowned darkly. 'My lawyer will deal with such things. Do you have to be so crude?'

Crude? My goodness, hadn't he got sensitive all of a sudden? He didn't want to be forced to dwell on the actual cost of acquiring her. And even if she didn't go for the whole package, and indeed considered herself insulted beyond belief, it *was* quite a hefty cost on his terms, Maxie conceded grudgingly. A marriage licence as the ultimate assurance of financial security—the life-style of a very wealthy woman and no doubt a very generous final settlement at the end of the day.

Mulling over those points, Maxie decided that he certainly couldn't accuse her of coming cheap, but she was entranced to realise that Angelos had no desire to be reminded of that unlovely fact. Just like everybody else, it seemed, Angelos Petronides preferred to believe that he was wanted for himself. She stored up that unexpected Achilles' heel for future reference.

Maxie widened her beautiful eyes at his words. 'I thought you admired the upfront approach?'

'I brought you here to celebrate a sane and sensible agreement, not to stage another argument.'

With that declaration, heated black eyes watched her flick her spectacular mane of golden hair over her slim shoulders and stayed to linger on her exquisite face. As his intent appraisal slowly arrowed down over the deep shadowy vee of her neckline, Maxie stiffened. At an almost pained pace of ever-deepening lust, his appreciative gaze wandered on down to take in the full effect of her slim hips and incredibly long legs. 'No, definitely not to have another argument,' Angelos repeated rather hoarsely.

'If your idea of celebration encompasses what I think it might, I'm afraid no can do.' Maxie swept up her glass of champagne with an apologetic smile pasted on her lips and drank deep before continuing at a fast rate of knots, 'I'll share your bed on our wedding night, but not one single second, minute, hour or day before. I suggest that we have lunch—'

'Lunch?' Angelos repeated flatly.

'We might as well do lunch because we are not about to do anything else,' Maxie informed him dulcetly.

'*Theos*...come here,' Angelos groaned. He hauled her resisting frozen length into his arms. 'Why are you always so set on punishing me?' He gave her a frustrated little shake, black eyes blazing over her mutinous expression. 'Why do you always feel the need to top everything I do and turn every encounter into a fight? That is not a womanly trait. Why cannot you just one time give me the response I expect?'

'I suppose I do it because I don't like you,' Maxie admitted, with the kind of impulsive sincerity that was indisputably convincing.

In an abrupt movement, Angelos's powerful arms dropped from her again. He actually looked shocked. 'What do you mean you don't *like* me?' he grated incredulously. 'What sort of a thing is that to say to man who has just asked you to marry him?'

'I wrote two whole pages on the subject last week...all the things I don't like...but why should you let that bother you? You're not interested in what goes on inside my head...all you require is an available body!'

'You're overwrought, so I won't make an issue of that judgement.' Angelos frowned down into her beautiful face with the suggestion of grim self-restraint. 'Let's have lunch.'

As she sat down at the table Maxie murmured

sweetly, 'One more little question. Are you planning to generously share yourself between Natalie Cibaud and me?'

Angelos glared at her for a startled second. 'Are you out of your mind?'

'That's not an answer—'

Angelos flung aside his napkin, black eyes glittering hard and bright as diamonds. 'Of course I do not intend to conduct a liaison with another woman while I am with you,' he intoned in a charged undertone.

Relaxing infinitesimally, Maxie said flatly, 'So when will the big event be taking place?'

'The wedding? As soon as possible. It will be very private.'

'I think it is so sweet that you had not a single doubt that I would say yes.' Maxie stabbed an orange segment with vicious force.

'If you want me to take you to bed to close that waspish mouth, you're going the right way.'

Looking up, Maxie clashed with gleaming black eyes full of warning. She swallowed convulsively and coloured, annoyed that she was unable to control her own fierce need to attack him.

'You told me yourself that the one offer you would settle for is marriage. I have delivered…stop using me as target practice.'

Maxie tried to eat then, but she couldn't. All appetite had ebbed, so she tried to make conversation, but it seemed rather too late for that. Angelos now exuded brooding dissatisfaction. She saw that she had already sinned. He had expected to pour a couple of glasses of champagne down her throat and sweep her triumphantly off to bed. She felt numb, for once wonderfully untouched by Angelos's incredibly powerful sexual presence.

'Are you aware that all those rumours about you and I have actually relaunched my career?' she murmured stiffly.

'Today was your swansong. I don't want you prancing down a catwalk half-naked and I don't want you working either,' Angelos framed succinctly.

'Oh,' Maxie almost whispered, because it took so much effort not to scream.

'Be sensible...naturally I want you to be available when I'm free.'

'Like a harem slave—'

'Maxie...' Angelos growled.

'Look, I've got a ripping headache,' Maxie confessed abruptly and, pushing her plate away, stood up. 'I want to go home.'

'This will be your home in London soon,' he reminded her drily.

'I don't like weird pictures and cold tiled floors and dirty great empty rooms with ugly geometric furniture...I don't want to live in a building with about ten empty floors below me!' Maxie flung, her voice rising shrilly.

'You're just overexcited—'

'Like one of your racehorses?'

With a ground-out curse, Angelos slung his napkin on the table and, thrusting his chair back, sprang to his full commanding height. As he reached for her she tried to evade him, but he simply bent and swept her up into his powerful arms and held her tight. 'Maxie...why are you suddenly behaving like a sulky child?'

'How *dare*—?'

In answer, Angelos plunged his mouth passionately

hard down on hers and smashed his primal passage through every barrier. Her numbness vanished. He kissed her breathless until she was weak and trembling with tormented need in his arms. Then he looked down at her, and he stared for a very long while.

The silence unnerved her, but she was too shaken by the discovery that even a few kisses could reduce her to wanton compliance to speak.

His bronzed face utterly hard and impassive, he finally murmured flatly, 'I'll call the car for you and I'll be in touch. I don't feel like lunch now either.'

Maxie registered his distance. The sense of rejection she felt appalled her. And she thought then, If I go through with this private arrangement, if I try to play him at his own game, I will surely tear myself apart...

No—no, she wouldn't, she told herself urgently, battening down the hatches before insidious doubt could weaken her determination. One way or another she would survive with her pride intact. Wanting Angelos was solely a physical failing. Ultimately she would overcome that hunger and look forward to the life she would have *after* him.

CHAPTER SEVEN

'So, EVEN though it was a rather unconventional proposal, Angelos *did* have marriage in mind,' Liz finally
sighed with satisfaction.

'Only when he saw it was his only hope.'

'I hear a lot of men are like that. Angelos is only
thirty-three, but he's bound to be rather spoilt when it
comes to his...well, when many other women would be
willing to sleep with him without commitment,' Liz extended with warming cheeks. 'I expect you've been
something of a learning experience for him, and if *you*
were more sensible, he could learn a lot more.'

'Meaning?'

'This marriage will be what you make of it.'

'Haven't you been listening to what I've been saying?' Maxie muttered in confusion. 'It isn't going to *be*
a proper marriage, Liz.'

'Right now you are very angry with Angelos. I refuse
to credit that you could really go through with walking
out on your marriage in six months' time,' Liz told her
with a reproving shake of her head.

'I will, Liz...believe me, I *will*—'

'This time I'm definitely not listening,' Liz asserted
wryly. 'And as for Angelos's apparent fantasy that he
can marry you and live with you on an occasional basis
without people finding out that he's involved with
you...he's almost as off the wall on this as you are,
Maxie!'

'No, he knows exactly what he's doing. He just doesn't expect me to be in his life for very long.'

Liz compressed her lips. 'I have only one real question to ask you. Why can't you just sit down and tell Angelos the whole truth about Leland?'

Taken aback, Maxie protested, 'He didn't want to listen when I did try—'

'You could've made him listen. You are no shrinking violet.'

'Do you seriously think that Angelos is likely to believe that Leland took advantage of me in every way but the *one* in which, of course, everyone thinks he did, even though he didn't?' Maxie was shaken into surprised defensiveness by Liz's attitude.

'Well, your silence on the subject has defined your whole relationship with Angelos. Indeed, I have a very strong suspicion that you don't really *want* him to know the real story.'

'And why on earth would I feel like that?'

'I think that *you* think you're a much more exciting proposition as a bad girl,' Liz admitted reluctantly, and Maxie turned scarlet. 'You get all dolled up in your fancy clothes and you flounce about getting a bitter thrill out of people thinking you're a real hard, grasping little witch—'

Maxie was aghast. 'Liz, *that's*—'

'Let me finish,' the older woman insisted ruefully. 'I believe that that's the way you've learnt to cope with those who have hurt you, not to mention all the mud you've had slung at you. You hide away inside that fancy shell and sometimes you get completely carried away with pretending to be what you're not…so ask yourself—is it any wonder that Angelos doesn't know you the way he should? He's never seen the real you.'

The *real* me, Maxie reflected, cringing where she sat. He would be bored stiff by the real Maxie Kendall, who, horror of horrors, couldn't even read or write properly. And was it really likely that a male as sexually experienced as Angelos would be equally obsessed with possessing a woman who turned out to be just one big pathetic bluff? A woman who had never yet shared a bed with any man? A virgin?

Unaware of the younger woman's hot-cheeked distraction, Liz was made anxious by the lingering silence. 'You're the closest thing to a daughter I'll ever have,' she sighed. 'I just want you to be happy…and I'm afraid that if you keep up this front with Angelos, you'll only end up getting very badly hurt.'

Her eyes prickling, Maxie gave her friend a hug. She blamed herself for being too frank and worrying Liz. From here on in, she decided shamefacedly, she would keep her thoughts and her plans to herself.

Angelos phoned her at six that evening. He talked with the cool detachment of someone handing out instructions to an employee. She knew herself unforgiven. His London lawyer would visit her with the prenuptial contract. The ceremony would take place the following week in the north of England.

'*Next week?*' Maxie exclaimed helplessly.

'I'm organising a special licence.'

'Why do we have to go north?'

'We couldn't marry in London without attracting attention.'

Maxie bit her lower lip painfully. So, Liz innocently assumed that such secrecy couldn't be achieved? She didn't know Angelos. Employing his wealth in tandem with his naturally devious mind, Angelos clearly intended to take every possible precaution.

'Do we travel up together in heavy disguise?'

'We'll travel separately. I'll meet you up there.'

'Oh…' Even facetious comments were squashed by such attention to detail.

'I'm afraid that I won't be seeing you beforehand—'

'Why *not*?' Maxie heard herself demand in disbelief, and then was furious with herself for making such an uncool response.

'Naturally I intend to take some time off. But in order to free that space in a very tight schedule, I'll be flying to Japan later this evening and moving on to Indonesia for the rest of the week.'

'You'll be seriously jet lagged by the time you get back.'

'I'll survive. I suggest you disengage yourself from your contract with the modelling agency—'

'I was on the brink of signing a new one,' Maxie admitted.

'Excellent. Then you can simply tell them that you have changed your mind.'

Maxie was still recovering from Catriona Ferguson's angry incredulity at their brief and unpleasant interview when she was subjected to the visit from Angelos's lawyer.

At her request the older man read out the document she was expected to sign. If Maxie had been as avaricious as Angelos apparently believed, she would've been ecstatic. In return for her discretion she was offered a vast monthly allowance on top of an all-expenses-paid lifestyle, and when the marriage ended she was to receive a quite breathtaking settlement.

By the time he had finished speaking, Maxie's nails were digging into her palms like pincers and she was

extremely pale. She signed, but the only thing that gave
her the strength to do so was the bitter certainty that in
six months' time she would tear up her copy of that
agreement and throw the pieces scornfully back at
Angelos's feet. Only then would he appreciate that she
could neither be bought nor paid off.

The church sat on the edge of a sleepy Yorkshire ham-
let. Mid-morning on a weekday, the village had little
traffic and even fewer people. Maxie checked her watch
for the tenth time. Angelos was *now* eleven minutes
late.

Having run out of casual conversation, the elderly
rector and his wife were now uneasily anchored in the
far corner of the church porch while Maxie hovered by
the door like a pantomime bride, on the watch in terror
that the groom had changed his mind. And it *was* possible, wasn't it? The arrangements had been so detached
they now seemed almost surreal.

A car had picked her up at a very early hour to ferry
her north. And Angelos had phoned only twice over the
past week. He would have been better not phoning at
all. Her spontaneity vanished the instant she recognised
her own instinctive physical response to that rich, dark
drawl. It had not made for easy dialogue.

Today, I am getting married. This is my wedding day,
she told herself afresh in a daze of disbelief, and of
course he would turn up, but he would get a tongue-
lashing when he did. Angelos… Hatred was so incredibly enervating, Maxie conceded grimly. He kept her
awake at night and he haunted her dreams. That infuriated and threatened her.

In defiance of the suspicion that she was taking part
in some illegal covert operation, she was wearing her

scarlet dress. A scarlet dress for a scarlet woman. No doubt that would strike Angelos as an extremely appropriate choice.

Hearing the sound of an approaching car, Maxie tensed. A gleaming Mercedes closely followed by a second car pulled up. Angelos emerged from the Mercedes. Sheathed in a wonderfully well-cut navy suit, pale blue tie and white silk shirt, he looked stupendous. As his London lawyer appeared from the second car, Angelos paused to wait for him. As if he had all the time in the world, Maxie noted incredulously. Her ready temper sizzled. How *dared* Angelos keep her waiting and then refuse to hurry himself?

Stepping into full view, her attention all for Angelos as he mounted the shallow steps to the door, Maxie snapped, 'And what sort of a time do you call this? Where the heck have you been?'

As his lawyer froze into shattered stillness, Angelos's black eyes lit on Maxie like burnished blazing gold. And then a funny thing happened. A sudden scorching smile of raw amusement wiped the disturbing detachment from his savagely handsome features. 'We had to wait thirty minutes for a landing slot at the airport. Short of a parachute jump, there wasn't much I could do about that.'

Suddenly self-conscious, her cheeks flaming, Maxie shrugged. 'OK.'

'Thanks for wearing my favourite outfit. You look spectacular,' Angelos murmured huskily in her ear, before he moved smoothly forward to offer his apologies to the rector for his late arrival.

Minutes later, they were walking down the aisle. As the ceremony began Maxie looked tautly around herself and then down at her empty hands. Not even a flower to hold. And her dress—so inappropriate, so strident against the timeworn simplicity of the church and its quiet atmosphere of loving piety. But then what did love have to do with her agreement with Angelos?

Suddenly she felt the most terrible fraud. Like any other woman, she had had wedding day dreams. Not one of them had included marrying a man who didn't love her. Not one of them had included the absence of her father and of even a single friend or well-wisher. Her eyes prickled with tears. Finding herself all choked up, Maxie blinked rapidly, mortified by her own emotionalism. A ring was slid onto her wedding finger. And then it was over. When Angelos tried to kiss her, she twisted her golden head away and presented him with a cool, damp cheek.

'What's the matter with you?' Angelos demanded as he strode down the steps, one big hand stubbornly enclosing hers in spite of her evasive attempts to ease free of him. 'Why the tears?'

'I feel horribly guilty…we just took vows we didn't mean.'

Maxie climbed into the Mercedes. After a brief exchange with his lawyer, Angelos swung into the driver's seat and slammed the door. Starting the engine, he drove off. The silence between them screeched louder with every passing minute.

'Tell me, is there the slightest hope of any bridal joy on the horizon?' Angelos finally enquired in a charged and sardonic undertone.

'I don't feel like a bride,' Maxie responded flatly. 'I thought you'd be pleased about that.'

Angelos brought the Mercedes to a sudden halt on the quiet country road. As he snapped free his seat belt Maxie turned to look at him, wondering why he had stopped. With a lack of cool that took her completely by surprise, Angelos pulled her into his powerful arms and sealed his mouth to hers in a hot, hard, punishing kiss. Maxie struck his broad muscular back with balled fists of outrage, but all that pent-up passion he unleashed surged through her like a lightning bolt of retribution.

Her head swam; her heartbeat thundered insanely fast. Her fists uncoiled, her fingers flexed and then rose to knot round the back of his strong neck. She clung. He prised her lips apart and with a ragged groan of need let his tongue delve deep. Excited beyond belief at that intensely sexual assault, Maxie reacted with a whimpering, startled moan of pleasure, and then as abruptly as he had reached for her Angelos released her again, his hard profile taut.

'We haven't got time for this. I don't want to have to hang around at the airport.'

Maxie's swollen mouth tingled. She lowered her head, but as Angelos shifted restlessly on the seat and switched the engine back on she could not help but notice that he was sexually aroused. Her face burning from that intimate awareness, she swiftly averted her attention again. He seemed to get that way very easily, she thought nervously. And only then did Maxie admit to herself that her own lack of sexual experience had now become a source of some anxiety to her.

For a cool, sophisticated male, Angelos had seemed alarmingly close to the edge of his control. If he could react like that to one kiss, what would he be like tonight?

That Greek temperament of his was fiery. Virile, overwhelming masculinity powered his smouldering passion to possess, which she had already frustrated more than once. And, since he believed that she had had other lovers, maybe he wouldn't bother too much with preliminaries. Maybe he would just expect her to be as hot and impatient as he was for satisfaction...

For goodness' sake, Angelos wasn't a clumsy teenager, she told herself in exasperation. As experienced as he undoubtedly was in the bedroom, he was sure to be a skilled and considerate lover. And he would never guess that she was inexperienced. She had once read on a problem page that most men couldn't even tell whether a woman was a virgin or not.

Honestly, she was being ridiculous! Embarrassed for herself, Maxie stared stonily out at the passing scenery and forced her mind blank. She smothered a yawn. As the ferocious tension drained gradually out of her muscles, tiredness began to creep in to take its place.

Angelos helped her out of the car at the airport. He frowned down at her pale, stiff face. 'Are you OK?'

'I'm just a bit tired.'

They were flying straight to Greece and they were able to board his private jet immediately. He tucked her into a comfortable seat and, after takeoff, a meal was served. Maxie had about two mouthfuls and a glass of wine. In the middle of the conversation Angelos was endeavouring to open, she noticed that she still had the wedding ring on her finger.

He *is* my husband, Maxie suddenly registered in shock. And then, just as suddenly, she erased that thought. She didn't want to think of him as her husband because she was all too well aware that he did not think of her as his wife. A private arrangement, a temporary one, not a normal marriage, she reminded herself. Her troubled eyes hardened. Sliding the slender band from her finger, she studied it with a slightly curled lip before leaning forward to set it down on the table between them.

'You'd better take that back,' she told him carelessly.

Angelos stared at her as if she had slapped him. A faint arc of colour scored his high cheekbones. His fulminating gaze raked over her. 'You are a ravishingly beautiful woman…but sometimes you drive me clean up the wall!' he admitted grittily. 'Why should you remove that ring now, when we are alone?'

'Because I don't feel comfortable with it.' To evade that hard, assessing scrutiny, Maxie rested her head back and closed her eyes. He was acting as if she had mortally insulted him. But she had no intention of sporting a ring that she would eventually have to take off. On that awareness, she fell asleep.

Angelos shook her awake just after the jet had landed at Athens.

'You've been tremendous company,' he drawled flatly.

Maxie flushed. 'I'm sorry, I was just so tired I crashed.'

'Surprisingly enough, I did get that message.'

They transferred from the jet onto a helicopter for the final leg of their journey to the island. As the unwieldy craft rose into the air and then banked into a turn, providing Maxie with a frighteningly skewed panoramic view of the city far below, her stomach twisted sickly. She focused on the back of the pilot's seat, determined not to betray her fear to Angelos. A long, timeless period of mute suffering followed.

'We're almost there. I want you to see the island as we come in over the bay,' Angelos imparted. His warm breath fanned her cheekbone as the helicopter gave an alarming lurch downward and she flinched. 'Go on…*look*.' Angelos strove to encourage her while she shut her eyes tight and her lips moved as she prayed.

'I totally forgot you were afraid of heights,' he murmured ruefully as he lifted her down onto solid ground again and steadied her with both hands. 'I always come to Chymos in the helicopter. You'll have to get used to it some time.'

All Maxie could think about was how soon she would have to undergo that ordeal again.

'What you need is more of the same,' Angelos announced in a tone of immoveable conviction. 'I have a pilot's licence. I'll take you up in the helicopter every day for longer and longer periods and you'll soon get over your phobia.'

Welded to the spot by such a threat, Maxie gave him an aghast look. 'Is it your mission in life to torture me?'

Angelos dealt her a smouldering appraisal, his hard, sensual mouth curving in consideration while his black eyes glittered over her with what could only be described as all-male anticipation. 'Only with pleasure, in my bed, *pethi mou*.'

CHAPTER EIGHT

WARM colour fingered into Maxie's pale cheeks.

Thirty yards from them a long, low white villa sprawled in isolated splendour across the promontory. It overlooked a pale sandy beach, and the rugged cliffs and dark blue sea supplied a majestic backdrop for Angelos's island home.

'I was born on Chymos. As a child I spent all my vacations here. Although I was an only child, I was never lonely because I had so many cousins. Both my parents came from large families. Since my father died, this island has become my retreat from the rest of the world.' Dropping an indolent and assured arm round her stationary figure, Angelos guided her towards the villa. 'You're honoured. I have never brought a woman here before, *pethi mou*.'

As they entered the charming hall she saw into the spacious lounge opposite. In one glance she took in the walls covered with pictures, the photographs scattered around, the shelves of books and the comfortable sofas and rugs. It was full of all the character of a family home. 'It's not like your apartment at all!' Maxie surprise was unconcealed.

'One of my cousins designed my London apartment. I did tell her what I wanted but it didn't quite turn out the way I had imagined it would.' Angelos closed his arms round her from behind. 'We're alone here. I gave the staff some time off.'

Maxie tensed. He pressed his wickedly expert mouth

to the smooth skin just below her ear. Every treacherous pulse jumped in response. Maxie quivered, knees wobbling. With an earthy chuckle of amusement, Angelos scooped her off her feet as if she weighed no more than a doll and strode out of the hall down a long tiled corridor.

It was the end of the line of restraint and Maxie knew it. She parted her dry lips nervously. 'Angelos?' she muttered urgently. 'I know you think I've slept with—'

'I do *not* want to hear about the other men who have preceded me,' Angelos interrupted with ruthless precision, glowering down at her in reproof. 'Why do women rush to make intimate revelations and then lie like mad about the number of lovers they've had? Why can't you just keep quiet?'

Not unnaturally silenced by that unexpected attack, Maxie chewed her lower lip uncertainly as he settled her down on the thick carpet in a beautifully furnished bedroom. Her entire attention immediately lodged on the bed.

Seemingly unable to tolerate an instant of physical separation, Angelos encircled her with his arms again and loosed a husky sigh of slumberous pleasure above her head. Curving her quiescent length into glancing contact with his hard, muscular physique, Angelos tugged down the zip on her dress. As cooler air hit her taut shoulder-blades, followed by the sensual heat of Angelos's exploring mouth, Maxie braced herself and surged back into speech.

'Actually,' she confided in an uneven rush, 'all I wanted to say is that I'm really not that experienced!'

'*Theos…*' Angelos ground out, abruptly dropping his arms from her and jerking away to stride across the room. Peeling off his jacket and pitching it aside under her bemused gaze, he sent her a look as dark and threatening as black ice under spinning wheels.

'Sorry, what—?' Maxie began.

'Why are you *doing* this to me?' Angelos demanded rawly as he wrenched at his tie with an exasperated hand. 'Why tell me these foolish lies? Do you think I need to hear them? Do you honestly believe that I could credit such a plea from you for one second?'

Marooned in the centre of the carpet, her dress lurching awkwardly off one bare and extremely taut shoulder, Maxie let her gaze fall from his in a mixture of fierce embarrassment and resentment. If that was his response to the mere admission that she was not a bedroom sophisticate likely to wow him with the unexpected, or possibly even with moves he *did* expect, she could only cringe from the possibility of what an announcement of complete inexperience would arouse. And she did not want to go to bed with an angry man.

'No doubt next you will be offending me beyond belief by referring to the man who kept you for three years…don't *do* it,' Angelos told her in emphatic warning. 'I do not wish to hear one more word about your past. I accept you as you are. I have no choice but to do otherwise.'

Maxie tried to shrug her dress back up her arm.

'And why are you standing there like a child put in the corner? Are you trying to make me feel bad?'

Hot colour burnished her cheeks. 'You're in a very volatile mood—'

'Put it down to frustration…you've done nothing but freeze me out since I married you this morning,' Angelos drawled with raw impatience.

'And you have done nothing but think about sex.'

Having made that counter-accusation, Maxie collided

with scorching black eyes of outrage and tilted her chin. Like a child in a corner, was she? How *dare* he? Her bright eyes blazed. The silence thundered. She shrugged her slim shoulders forward and extended her slender arms.

Angelos tensed, eyes narrowing. The scarlet dress shimmied down to Maxie's feet, unveiling her lithe, perfect figure clad in a pair of minuscule white panties and a no more substantial gossamer-fine bra. Angelos looked as if he had stopped breathing. Stepping out of the dress, she slung him a catwalk model's look of immense boredom and, strolling over to the bed, kicked off her shoes and folded herself down on it.

'What are you waiting for? A white flag of surrender?' Maxie enquired drily, pride vindicated by the effect she had achieved.

'Something rather less choreographed, a little warmer and more enthusiastic,' Angelos purred with sudden dangerous cool, strolling over to the side of the bed to stare down at her with slumberous eyes of alarming shrewdness. 'I'm developing a strong suspicion that to date your bedroom forays have been one big yawn, because you really *don't* understand how I feel, do you?'

Face pink, and uneasy now, Maxie levered herself up on one elbow. 'What are you trying to imply?'

'You're about to find out.' Disorientatingly, his bold black eyes flamed with amusement as he began unbuttoning his shirt.

'Is that a threat?' Maxie said breathlessly.

'Is that fear or hope I hear?' With a soft, unbearably sexy laugh, Angelos dispensed with his shirt and gazed down mockingly into very wide blue eyes. 'Your face...the expression is priceless!'

Maxie veiled her scrutiny, her fair complexion reddening.

Angelos strolled across the room, indolent now that he had her exactly where he wanted her, fully in control. 'As for me thinking about sex all the time...don't you know men? I've been celibate for many weeks. I've wanted you for an incredibly long time. I'm not used to waiting and fighting every step of the way for what I want. When you have everything, what you cannot have naturally assumes huge importance—'

'And when you finally get it, I suppose it means next to nothing?' Maxie slotted in tightly.

Angelos elevated a slanting ebony brow. 'Lighten up,' he advised, not even pretending not to comprehend her meaning. 'Only time will decide that. I live in the present and so should you, *pethi mou*.'

He undressed with fluid ease. She watched him. Ever since that night at the cottage, his powerful image had been stamped into her brain like a Technicolor movie still. But she was still hopelessly enthralled, shaken by the extent to which she responded to his intensely physical allure. Yet she had never seen beauty in the male body until he came along. But from his wide brown shoulders, slim hips and long, powerful hair-roughened thighs, Angelos made her mouth run dry, her pulses race and her palms perspire.

'You've been so quiet since that ceremony...and now you recline like a very beautiful stone statue on my bed.' Angelos skimmed off his black briefs in one long, lazy movement. 'If it wasn't so ridiculous, I would think you were scared of me.'

Maxie managed to laugh but her throat was already constricting with nerves. He was so relaxed about his nudity, quite unconcerned that he was hugely aroused.

And while common sense was telling her that of course
God had fashioned men and women to fit, Maxie just
could not begin to imagine *how* at that moment.

Angelos came down on the wide bed beside her. He
scanned the sudden defensive upward tilt of her perfect
profile, trailed a slow and appreciative hand through the
lush tumble of golden strands of hair cascading off the
pillows. He threw himself back and closed his hands
round her slender forearms to bring her gently down to
him. 'And now my reward for waiting,' he breathed
with indolent satisfaction. 'Nothing can disturb or part
us here.'

Maxie gazed down into smouldering golden eyes full
of expectancy. 'Angelos...'

He reached up to run the tip of his tongue erotically
along the tremulous line of her generous mouth. 'You
feel like ice. I'll melt you,' he promised huskily, deft
fingers already engaged in releasing the catch on her
bra.

Maxie trembled, feeling her whole body filled with
delicious tension. She closed her eyes. He kissed her,
and every time he kissed her it got just that little bit
more tormenting, and she would open her lips wider,
needing more pressure, more passion, begging for it as
the floodtide of unstoppable hunger began to build and
race through her veins.

He rolled her over and closed a hand over the pouting
swell of one pale breast. Her taut body jumped as he
smiled brilliantly down into her shaken eyes. 'And yet
you are so red-hot, responsive when I touch you. Every
time that gives me a high,' Angelos confessed thickly.
'I love seeing you out of control.'

Threatened by that admission, Maxie shifted uneasily. 'I don't like that—'

'You'll have to learn to like it.' Angelos bent his dark, arrogant head over a pink straining nipple and laved that achingly tender tip with his tongue, engulfing her in sensation that she now struggled instinctively to resist.

'No...' she gasped.

'Don't fight what I can make you feel...' he urged hoarsely, employing expert fingers on her sensitive flesh, making her squirm in breathless, whimpering excitement.

Her body wasn't her own any more, but by then she didn't want it to be. With every atom of her being she craved those caresses. Wild sensation was addictive. She was hooked between one second and the next, her mind wiped clean of all thought. The hot wire of his seduction pulled tight as heat flared between her shifting thighs. She moaned his name low in her throat.

He took her mouth with a hot, sexual dominance then. He sealed her to the abrasively masculine angles of his hard, hungry body. She panted for breath when he released her swollen lips, sensually bemused eyes focusing on the brooding intensity of that darkly handsome face now curiously stilled above hers.

'Angelos...?' she mumbled, her fingers rising without her volition to trace the unremittingly harsh compression of his mouth.

He jerked back his head, so that she couldn't touch him. In pained bewilderment Maxie lowered her hand again and stared up at him.

'You used to watch me all the time,' he breathed grimly. 'But the instant I turned in your direction, you looked away...except that once, seven months ago. Then I knew you were mine, as much *mine* as if I had a brand on you!'

Stricken by that assurance slung at her out of the blue, Maxie twisted her head away, feeling naked, exposed. Even then Angelos had been able to see inside her, see below the surface which had dazzled other men. And, worst of all, he had immediately recognised the hunger she had refused to recognise within herself.

'So I waited for you to make your move,' Angelos admitted in a tone of growing condemnation. 'I waited and I waited for you to dump him. But you still stayed *with* him! I began to wonder if you had a single living brain cell inside that gorgeous head!'

He was talking about Leland. Shocked rigid by what he was telling her, Maxie muttered, 'But I...I didn't—'

Angelos vented a harsh, cynical laugh. 'Oh, I know why you stayed with him *now*! You owed him too much money to walk out. Did you think I hadn't worked that out yet? But that's when you reduced yourself to the level of a marketable commodity, and when I think about that it makes me want to smash things! Because, having learnt that wonderful lesson with him, you then sold yourself to me for an even higher price.'

'How *can* you—?'

'What else is this marriage but the price I had to pay for you?'

'You...swine,' Maxie whispered brokenly, white as death as the contempt he had concealed from her sank into her sensitive flesh like poison.

'And I'll get you out of my system soon if it kills me,' Angelos swore with ragged force as he gazed broodingly down at her.

'Start by letting me out of this bed,' she demanded unevenly.

'No way...I paid with a wedding ring and millions of pounds for this pleasure.'

'No!'

'But you're no good at saying no to me,' Angelos murmured with roughened menace against her tremulous lips. 'Sexually you are one very weak reed where I'm concerned. It's my one and only consolation while I'm making a bloody fool of myself over a woman like you!'

'How dare you?' Maxie gulped.

But Angelos skimmed an assured hand down the taut length of one quivering thigh and kissed her with fierce, angry hunger. And it was like instantaneous combustion. She went up in flames. He didn't hold her down. He didn't pin her to the mattress. He kissed her into submission, tormented her with every erotic trick in his extensive repertoire and the most overpowering physical passion. He swept away her defences with terrifying ease.

Stroking apart her slender thighs, Angelos traced the swollen, moist sensitivity at the very heart of her with knowing fingers. With a strangled moan, Maxie clutched at him in desperation. He controlled her with the hunger she could not deny and made her ache for him. That ache for satisfaction tortured her. He groaned something in Greek, pushing her tumbled hair back off her brow with an unsteady hand, circling her mouth caressingly with his one more time.

As Angelos shifted over her she couldn't get him there fast enough. Her own urgency was as screamingly intense as his. And then she felt him, hot and hard and gloriously male, seeking entrance, and she shivered convulsively, on a high of such anticipation and excitement she was mindless.

So when he thrust hungrily into her willing body she was quite unprepared for the jagged pain of that forceful intrusion. Pain ripped apart the fog of sensual sensation and made her jerk and cry out in shock as she instinctively strove to push him away from her. But Angelos had already stilled to frown down at her with stunned, disbelieving black eyes. 'Maxie—?'

'What are you looking at me like that for?' Maxie whispered in stricken embarrassment, utterly appalled and outraged that her own body could have betrayed her to such an extent.

With a sudden shift of his hips, Angelos withdrew from her again. But he kept on staring down at her in the most mortifying way, his bewilderment blatant. A damp sheen accentuated the tautness of the bronzed skin stretched over his hard cheekbones and the pallor spreading beneath. '*Cristo*…a virgin…' he breathed, not quite levelly.

Maxie lay there, feeling horribly rejected and inadequate and wishing she could vanish.

'And I really hurt you,' Angelos groaned even more raggedly, abruptly levering his weight from her, black eyes holding hers with the same transfixed incredulity with which he might have regarded the sudden descent of an alien spaceship in his bedroom. 'Are you in a lot of pain?'

In one driven movement Maxie rolled off the bed and fled in the direction of the bathroom. Dear heaven, he had been so repulsed he had just abandoned their lovemaking.

'Maxie?' Angelos murmured grimly. 'I think *this* is something we definitely need to talk about—'

Maxie slammed the bathroom door so loudly it rocked on its hinges and then she depressed the lock double-quick. Bang went the image of the cool sophisticate! And without that glossy image she felt naked and exposed. The last thing she could've faced right then was awkward questions. And as she turned on the bath taps she recalled his swinging verbal attack on her before they made love and she burst into gulping tears.

Angelos banged on the door. 'Maxie? Come out of there!'

'Go to hell!' she shouted, cramming her hand to her wobbling mouth before a sob could escape and betray her.

'Are you all right?'

'I'm having a bath, Angelos…not drowning myself! Although with that technique of yours, I understand your concern!'

But no sooner had Maxie hurled those nasty words than she was thoroughly ashamed of herself. He hadn't meant to hurt her, he hadn't known, and lashing out in retaliation because she felt horribly humiliated was unjust and mean. Silence fell. Slowly, miserably, Maxie climbed into the bath.

Only then did it occur to her that it was foolish to be distressed by what Angelos had said in temper earlier. After all, he had now discovered that she could not possibly have been Leland's mistress. So that had to make a difference to the light in which he saw her, *surely*? Only what she had been given with one hand had seemingly been taken with the other. Angelos had been repulsed by her inexperience.

Devastated by that awareness, Maxie thought back seven months to that single exchanged glance with Angelos across that long table in the Petronides boardroom, that charged clash of mutual awareness which seemed to have changed her entire life. Angelos had actually been waiting for her to ditch Leland on his behalf and he had been furious when she hadn't.

Furthermore, Angelos could not now bring himself to speak Leland Coulter's name out loud. In fact he had said she would offend him beyond belief with any reference to Leland before they'd even got into bed. Yet Angelos had been in no way that sensitive to that former relationship when he'd first come to announce his intentions at Liz's house... Men were strange, Maxie decided limply, and none more strange than Angelos.

It took her a long time to emerge from the bathroom, but when she did, wrapped in an over-large short silk robe she had found, the bedroom was empty. It was something of an anticlimax. Maxie got back into bed, not remotely sleepy and very tense, while she waited and waited for Angelos to reappear. A postmortem to end all postmortems now threatened. Having emerged from shock, Angelos would take refuge in anger, she forecast glumly. He would demand to know why she hadn't told him the truth about Leland. He would utterly dismiss any claim that he would never have believed her.

She lay back, steeling herself for recriminations as only Angelos could hurl them. Like deadly weapons which struck a bull's-eye every time. He never missed. And she hadn't been fair to him; she knew now that she hadn't been fair. Liz had been right. She *had* reaped a twisted kind of relish out of pretending to be something she wasn't while she goaded Angelos on and taunted him. And so why had she reacted to him in a way she had never reacted to any other man? Maxie discovered that she was miserable enough without forcing herself to answer that question.

The door opened. She braced herself. Angelos stood poised in the doorway. Barefoot, black hair tousled, strong jawline already darkening with stubble, he looked distinctly unfamiliar in a pair of black tight-fitting jeans, with a black shirt hanging loose and un-buttoned on his bare brown hair-roughened chest.

'I now know *everything*...' he announced in the most peculiar slurred drawl. 'But I am too bloody drunk to fly!'

Maxie sat up. Eyes huge, she watched Angelos collide with the door and glower at it as if it had no business being there in his path. He was drunk all right. And he just looked so helpless to Maxie at that moment that she abandoned her stony, defensive aspect. Concern for him took over instead.

Leaping out of bed and crossing the room, she put her hand on his arm. 'Come and lie down,' she urged.

'Not on that bed.' As he swayed Angelos surveyed the divan with an extraordinary force of antagonism. 'Right at this moment I want to burn it.'

Assuming that her vindictive comment on his technique had struck home with greater force and efficacy than she could ever have imagined, Maxie paled with guilt but continued to try and ease him in the same direction. Was that why he had gone off to hit the bottle? Some intrinsically male sense of sexual failure because he had inadvertently hurt her? Maxie endeavoured to drag him across the carpet. He was obstinate as ever.

'Lie down!' she finally launched at him in full-throttle frustration.

And Angelos *did* lie down. Maxie couldn't believe it but he sprawled down on the bed as if she had a gun trained on him. And he looked so utterly miserable. It was true, she decided in fascination, women were definitely the stronger sex. Here was the evidence. Disaster had befallen Angelos when he had least expected it in

a field he prided himself on excelling in and he couldn't
handle it.

Crawling onto the bed beside him, Maxie gazed down
at him until her eyes misted over. She was shattered to
discover that all she wanted to do was cocoon him in
lashings of TLC.

'You were really great until the last moment,' she
told him in tender consolation. 'I didn't mean what I
said. You mustn't blame yourself—'

'I blame Leland,' Angelos gritted.

In complete confusion, Maxie frowned. 'You
blame…you blame *Leland*?' she stressed, all at seas as
to his meaning.

Angelos growled something in Greek that broke from
him with the aggressive force of a hurricane warning.

'English, Angelos…'

'He's a slime-bag!'

Focusing on her properly for the first time, Angelos
dug a hand into the pocket of his jeans and withdrew a
great wodge of crumpled fax paper.

Maxie took it from him and spread the paper out. It
was so long it kept on spreading, across his chest and
finally right off the edge of the bed. She squinted down
and recognised her own signature right at the very foot.
In such dim light, it left her little the wiser as to its
content, and in his presence she didn't want to be seen
peering to comprehend all that tiny type.

'Leland took advantage of your stupidity—'

'Excuse me?' Maxie cut in, wide-eyed.

'Only a financially *very* naive person would've
signed that loan contract,' Angelos extended, after a
long pause during which he had visibly struggled to
come up with that more diplomatic term. 'And a mon-

eylender from a backstreet would've offered more generous terms than that evil old bastard!'

Clarity shone at last for Maxie. Angelos had somehow obtained a copy of the loan agreement she had signed three years earlier. That was what was on the fax paper. 'Where did you get this from?'

'I got it,' Angelos responded flatly.

'Why did you say I was stupid…? Because I'm *not*!'

'You'd still have been paying that loan off ten years from now.' He got technical then, muttering grimly about criminal rates of interest and penalty clauses. She couldn't bring herself to tell him that she had become trapped in such an agreement because she had been too proud to ask someone else to read the small print out and explain the conditions.

'You were only nineteen,' Angelos grated finally. 'You signed that the day before you moved in with Leland. He blackmailed you—'

'No…I agreed. There was never any question of us sharing a bedroom or anything like that. All he ever asked for was the right to show me off. I was just an ego-trip for him but I didn't know what I was getting into until it was too late to back out,' Maxie muttered tightly, squashing the fax paper into a big crunched-up ball again and throwing it away.

'And Leland was getting his own back on an unfaithful wife,' Angelos completed grimly.

Unsurprised that he should have known about Jennifer Coulter's affair, Maxie breathed in deep and decided to match his frankness. 'My father is a compulsive gambler, Angelos. He got into trouble with some very tough men and he couldn't pay up what he owed them. It was nothing to do with Leland but I went to him for advice, and that's when he told me he'd loan me the money if I moved in with him.'

'Lamb to the slaughter,' Angelos groaned, as if he was in agony. 'Compulsive gambler?' he queried in sudden bemusement.

'Dad would sell this bed out from under you if he got the chance.'

'Where have you kept this charming character concealed?'

'I don't know where he is right now. We haven't been close...well, not since I took on that loan to settle his debts. Naturally Dad feels bad about that.'

'The debt was *his*?' Angelos bit out wrathfully as that fact finally sunk in. 'Your precious father stood back and watched you move in with Leland just so that he could have his gambling debts paid?'

'It was life or death, Angelos...it *really* was,' Maxie protested. 'He'd already been badly beaten up and he was terrified they would kill him the next time around. Leland gave me that money when nobody else would have. It saved Dad's life.'

'Dad doesn't sound like he was worth saving—'

'Don't you dare say that about my father!' Maxie censured chokily. 'He brought me up all on his own!'

'Taught you how to go to the pawnshop? Flogged anything he could get his hands on? Your childhood must've been a real blissfest, I *don't* think!'

'He did his best. That's all anyone can do,' Maxie whispered tautly. 'Not everyone is born with your advantages in life. You're rich and selfish. Dad's poor and selfish, but, unfortunately for him, he has too much imagination.'

'So have I...oh, *so* have I. I imagined you,' Angelos confided, his deep dark drawl slurring with intense bitterness. 'The only quality I imagined right was that you *do* need me. But all the rest was my fantasy. Tonight…deservedly…it exploded right in my face.'

Maxie slumped as if he had beaten the stuffing out of her. She wanted to tell him that she *didn't* need him but her throat was so clogged up with tears she couldn't trust herself to speak. A fantasy? He had *imagined* her? That was even worse than being a one-dimensional trophy, she realised in horror. At the end of the day, when fantasy met reality and went bang, there was just nothing left, was there?

'I don't want to sober up,' Angelos admitted morosely. 'The more I find out about you, the worse I feel. I don't like regret or guilt. Some people love to immolate themselves in their mistakes. I don't. How could I have been so bloody stupid?'

'Sex,' Maxie supplied, even more morosely.

Angelos shuddered. It was a very informative reaction.

'Was it that bad?' she couldn't help asking.

'Worse,' Angelos stressed feelingly. 'I felt like a rapist.'

'Silly…just bad luck…life kicking you in the teeth…you get used to it after a while…least, I do,' Maxie mumbled, on the brink of tears again.

'You should be furious with me—'

'No point…you're drunk. I like you better drunk than I like you sober,' she confided helplessly. 'You're more human.'

'*Christos*…when you go for the deathblow, you don't miss, do you?' Unhealthily pale beneath his bronzed skin, Angelos let his tousled head fall heavily back on the pillows. His lashes swept down on his shadowed black eyes. 'So now I know where I stand with you...basement footing—possibly even right down level with the earth's core,' he muttered incomprehensibly.

'Go to sleep,' Maxie urged.

'When one is that far down, one can only go up,' Angelos asserted with dogged resolution.

Well, at least he wasn't talking about flying again. With a helicopter parked thirty yards away that had been a genuine cause for concern. She ought to hate him. She knew she ought to hate him for breaking her heart with such agonising honesty. But the trouble was, she loved him in spite of that two-page list of flaws. She didn't know why she loved him. She just did. And she was in really deep too. He had just rejected her in every possible way and all she wanted to do was cover him up and hug him to death. Flaked out, silenced and vulnerable, Angelos had huge appeal for Maxie.

Why had she spent so long telling herself that she hated this guy? She had been cleverer than she knew, she conceded. Loving him hurt like hell. She felt as if she had lost an entire layer of skin and every inch of her was now tender and wounded. There she had been, naively imagining that he might have been upset because his sexual performance had not resulted in her impressed-to-death ecstasy. And all the time he had been ahead of her, whole streets ahead of her...

The minute he had found out that *he* was her first lover, he had fairly leapt into seeking out what her relationship with Leland had been based on, since it had self-evidently not been based on sex. Naturally he had immediately thought of that loan and probed deeper. And now he knew the whole sorry story and her name had been cleared. But much good it seemed to have done her...

Liz had said Maxie enjoyed pretending to be what she had called a 'bad girl'. Maxie suppressed a humourless laugh. Poor Liz had never allowed for the painful possibility that Angelos, who had exceedingly poor taste in women, was more excited by bad girls than he was by virgins.

CHAPTER NINE

MAXIE wakened the next morning in the warm cocoon of Angelos's arms. It felt like heaven.

Some time during the night he had taken off his shirt. She opened her lips languorously against a bare brown shoulder and let the tip of her tongue gently run over smooth skin. He tasted wonderful. She breathed in the achingly familiar scent of him with heady pleasure. Hot husky male with a slight flavour of soap. She blushed for herself, but the deep, even rise and fall of his broad chest below her encircling arm soothed her sudden tension. He was still out for the count.

And she would probably never lie like this with Angelos again. He was only here now because he had fallen asleep. She had plummeted from the heights of obsessive desirability like a stone. She had lost him but then she had never really had him. He had craved the fantasy, the Ice Queen, not the ordinary woman, and when in so many ways she had played up to that fantasy of his, how could she really blame him for not wanting her any more?

Easing back her arm, she let her palm rest down on that hair-roughened expanse of chest which drew her attention like a magnet. Her fingertips trailed gently through black springy curls, delicately traced a flat male nipple, slid downward over the rippling muscular smoothness of his abdomen, discovering a fascinating little furrow of silky hair that ran...and then she tensed in panic as she recognised the alteration in his breathing pattern. She was waking him up!

And just at that moment Maxie didn't feel strong enough to face Angelos waking up, sober and restored to intimidating normality. Angelos would bounce back from last night's shock and humility like a rubber ball aiming for the moon. Lying absolutely still, she waited until his breathing had evened out again and then, sidling out from under his arm, she slid off the bed.

Gathering up her discarded garments, she crept out into the corridor. Through the open doorway of the bedroom opposite she could see her single suitcase sitting at the foot of the bed. And that sight just underlined Maxie's opinion of her exact marital status. She had *no* status whatsoever. Her possessions belonged in a guest-room because she was supposed to be a casual visitor, not a wife.

Pulling out a white shift dress, fresh lingerie and strappy sandals, Maxie got dressed at speed. It was only seven but the heat was already building. The house was silent. Finding her way into a vast, gleaming kitchen, she helped herself to a glass of pure orange juice and swiped a couple of apples from a lush display of fruit. Determined not to face Angelos until she had sorted herself out, she left the house. Traversing the beautiful gardens, she wandered along the rough path above the beach.

Then she let her thoughts loose, and she winced and she squirmed and she hurt. Their wedding night had been a disaster. And how much of that final confessional dialogue would Angelos recall when he woke up? Would he remember the stupid, soppy way she had hung over him? Would he recognise the pain she had not been able to conceal for what it was? The mere idea that Angelos might guess that she was in love with him was like the threat of death by a thousand cuts for Maxie.

Last night, for the very first time, Angelos hadn't treated her as an equal. Maxie shrank from that lowering awareness. Funny how she hadn't really noticed or even appreciated that Angelos had *always* met her on a level playing field until he suddenly changed tack. Now everything was different. She had been stripped of her tough cookie glossy image and exposed as a pathetic fraud. A virgin rather than a sultry, seductive object of must-have desire. A blackmail victim rather than a calculating gold-digger and the former mistress of an older man.

And who would ever have guessed that Angelos Petronides had a conscience? But, amazingly, he *did*. Angelos had been appalled by what he'd discovered. Even worse, he had pitied her for her less than perfect childhood and her gullible acceptance of that hateful loan agreement. *Pitied*. That acknowledgement was coals of fire on Maxie's head.

Angelos now regretted their strange marriage but he felt guilty. Maxie didn't want his guilt or his pity, and suddenly she saw how she could eradicate both. It would be so simple. All she had to do was tell Angelos about the conditions of Nancy Leeward's last will and testament. When Angelos realised that she had had an ulterior motive in marrying him, he would soon stop feeling sorry for her…at least she would retain her pride that way.

As Maxie rounded a big outcrop of rock, she saw two little boys trying to help a fisherman spread a net on the beach below. As she watched, unseen, their earnest but clumsy efforts brought a warm, generous smile to her lovely face.

'You have never once shown me that ravishing smile.' Maxie was startled into a gasp by the intervention of that soft, rich, dark drawl, and her golden head spun.

Angelos stood several feet away. Clad in elegant chinos and a white polo shirt, he stole the very breath from Maxie's lungs. Her heart crashed violently against her breastbone. He looked drop-dead gorgeous. But her wide eyes instantly veiled. She knew how clever he was. She was terrified he would somehow divine her feelings for him.

'But then possibly I have done nothing to inspire such a reward,' Angelos completed tautly.

He stared at her, black eyes glittering and fiercely intent. In the brilliant sunlight, with her hair shimmering like a veil of gold and the simple white dress a perfect foil for her lithe figure, she was dazzling. Moving forward slowly, as if he was attuned to her pronounced tension, he closed a lean hand over one of hers and began to walk her back along the foreshore.

'From today, from this moment, *everything* will be different between us,' Angelos swore with emphasis.

'Will it be?' Briefly, involuntarily, Maxie stole a glance at him, nervous as a cat on hot bricks.

'You should have told me the truth about Leland the very first day—'

'You wouldn't have believed me...'

His long brown fingers tightened hard on hers. He looked out to sea, strong profile rigid. He released his breath in a sudden driven hiss. 'You're right. I wouldn't have. Nothing short of the physical proof you gave me last night would've convinced me that you weren't the woman I thought you were.'

'At least you're honest,' Maxie muttered tautly.

Apparently enthralled by the view of the single caique anchored out in the bay, Angelos continued to stare out over the bright blue water. 'Considering that there were so many things that didn't add up about you, I can't say that I can pride myself on my unprejudiced outlook...or my judgement. You asked me to stay away from you and I wouldn't. You even left London...'

He was talking as if someone had a knife bared at his throat. Voice low, abrupt, rough, every word clenched with tension and reluctance.

'I have never treated a woman as badly as I have treated you...and in the manner of our marriage I really did surpass myself, *pethi mou.*'

He sounded like a stranger to Maxie. Angelos having a guilt trip. She trailed her fingers free of his, cruel pain slashing at her. It was over. She didn't need to hear these things when she had already lived them, and most of all she did not want *him* feeling sorry for *her.* In fact that humiliation stung like acid on her skin.

'Look, I have something to tell you,' Maxie cut in stiffly.

'Let me speak...do you think this is *easy* for me?' Angelos slung at her in a gritty undertone of accusation. 'Baring my feelings like this?'

'You don't have any feelings for me,' Maxie retorted flatly, her heart sinking inside her, her stomach lurching.

'You seem very sure of that—'

'Get real, Angelos. There are rocks on this beach with more tender emotions than you've got!' Having made that cynical assurance, Maxie walked on doggedly. 'And why should you feel bad for trying to use me when I was planning to use you too? It's not like I'm madly in love with you or anything like that!' She paused to stress that point and vented a shrill laugh for good measure. 'I only married you because it *suited* me to marry you. I needed a husband for six months...'

Against the soft, rushing backdrop of the tide, the silence behind her spread and spread until it seemed to echo in her straining ears.

'What the hell are you talking about?' Angelos finally shattered the seething tension with that harsh demand.

Maxie spun round, facial muscles tight with self-control. 'My godmother's will. She was a wealthy woman but I can't inherit my share of her estate without a marriage licence. All I wanted was access to my own money, not yours.'

Angelos stood there as if he had been cast in granite, black eyes fixed to her with stunning intensity. 'This is a joke...right?'

Maxie shook her golden head in urgent negative. She was so tense she couldn't get breath enough to speak. Angelos was rigid with incredulity and in the stark, drenching sunlight reflecting off the water he seemed extraordinarily pale.

'You do realise that if what you have just told me is true, I am going to want to kill you?' Angelos confided, snatching in a jagged breath of restraint.

'I don't see why,' Maxie returned with determined casualness. 'This marriage wasn't any more real to you than it was to me. It was the only way you could get me into bed.' His hard dark features clenched as if she had struck him but she forced herself onward to the finish. 'And you didn't expect us to last five minutes beyond the onset of your own boredom. So that's why I decided I might as well be frank.'

Turning on her heel, trembling from the effect of that confrontation, Maxie walked blindly off the path and up through the gardens of the house. He wasn't going to be feeling all sorry and superior now, was he? The biter bit, she thought without any satisfaction as she crossed the hall. Now they would split up and she would never see him again…and she would spend the rest of her life being poor and wanting a man she couldn't have and shouldn't even want.

'Maxie…?'

She turned, not having realised in her preoccupation that Angelos was so close behind her. The world tilted as he swept her off her startled feet up into his powerful arms. A look of aggressive resolution in his blazing golden eyes, Angelos murmured grittily, 'It should've occurred to you that I might not be bored yet, *pethi mou*!'

'But—'

The kiss that silenced her lasted all the way down to the bedroom. It was like plunging a finger into an electric socket. Excitement and shock waved through her. He brought her down on the bed. Surfacing, Maxie stammered in complete bewilderment, 'B-but you don't want me any more…you imagined me—'

Engaged in ripping off his clothes over her, Angelos glowered down at her. 'I didn't *imagine* that clever little brain or that stinging tongue of yours, did I?'

'What are you *doing*?' she gasped.

'What I should have done when I woke up this morning to find you exploring me like a shy little kid…I didn't want to embarrass you.' Angelos focused on her, his sheer incredulity at that decision etched in every line of his savagely attractive features. 'How could I possibly have dreamt that you *could* be embarrassed?

Beneath that angelic, perfect face you're as tough as Teflon!'

Maxie was flattered to be called that tough. She didn't mind being told she was clever, or that she had a sharp tongue either. This was respect she was getting. It might not be couched in terms most women would've recognised but she knew Angelos well enough to see that she had risen considerably in his estimation since the previous night. Indeed, it crossed her mind that Angelos responded beautifully to a challenge, and that acknowledgement shone a blinding white light of clarity through her thoughts. She sat there transfixed.

'Why are you so quiet?' Angelos enquired suspiciously. 'I don't trust you quiet.'

Maxie cast him an unwittingly languorous smile over one shoulder. 'I presume we're not heading for a divorce right at this moment...?'

'*Theos*, woman...we only got married yesterday!'

The heat of his hungry gaze sent wild colour flying into her cheeks. He still wanted her. He still seemed to want her every bit as much as he had ever wanted her, she registered in renewed shock. And then he brought his mouth to hers again and her own hunger betrayed her. Her hands flew up to smooth through his hair, curve over his hard jawline. The need to touch, to hold was so powerful it made her eyes sting and filled her with instinctive fear.

'I won't hurt you this time...I promise,' Angelos groaned against her reddened mouth while he eased her out of her dress virtually without her noticing. He cupped her cheekbones to stare down into her sensually bemused eyes, his own gaze a tigerish, slumberous gold. 'To be the first with you...that was an unexpected gift. And telling me crazy stories in an effort to level some imaginary score is pointless. You ache for me too...do you think I don't see that in you with every look, every touch?'

Crazy stories? The will, her godmother's will. Ob viously, after a moment of reflection, he hadn't believed her after all. But Maxie couldn't keep that awareness in mind. She did part her lips, meaning to contradict him, but he kissed her again and she clutched at him in the blindness of a passion she could not deny.

'Why should you still fight me?' Angelos purred as he freed her breasts from the restraint of her bra and paused to run wondering dark eyes over her. He brushed appreciative fingers over the engorged tip of one pale breast and then lingered there in a caress that stole the very breath from her quiveringly responsive body. 'Why should you even *want* to fight me?'

There was something Maxie remembered that she needed to tell him, but looking up into those stunning golden eyes she could barely recall what her own name was, never mind open a serious conversation. Angelos angled a blinding megawatt smile of approval down at her and it was as if she had been programmed from birth to seek that endorsement. She reached up and found his lips again, a connection she now instinctively craved more than she had ever craved anything in her life before.

His tongue played with hers as he lay half over her. He smoothed a hand down over her slim hips and eased off the scrap of lace that still shielded her from him. With skilled fingers he skimmed through the golden curls at the apex of her slender thighs and sought the hot, moist centre of her. A whimper of formless sound was torn from Maxie then. Suddenly she was burning all over and she couldn't stay still.

And, as straying shards of sunlight played over the bed, Angelos utilised every ounce of his expertise to fire her to the heights of anguished desire. When she couldn't bear it any more, he slid over her. He watched her with hungry intimacy as he entered her, the fierce restraint he exercised over his own urgency etched in every taut line of his dark, damp features.

The pleasure came to her then, in wave after drugging wave. In the grip of it, she was utterly lost. 'Angelos...' she cried out.

And he stilled, and Maxie gasped in stricken protest, and with an earthy sound of amusement he went on. She didn't want him ever to stop. The slow, tormenting climb to fevered excitement had raised her to such a pitch, she ached for more with every thrust of his possession. And when finally sensation took her in a wild storm of rocketing pleasure, she uttered a startled moan of delight. As the last tiny quiver of glorious fulfilment evaporated she looked up at him with new eyes.

'Wow,' she breathed.

Struggling to catch his breath, Angelos dealt her a very male smile of satisfaction. 'That was the wedding night we should have had.'

Maxie was still pretty much lost in wonder. Wow, she thought again, luxuriating in the strong arms still wrapped around her, the closeness, the feeling of tenderness eating her up alive and threatening to make her eyes overflow. Oh, yes, wouldn't tears really impress him? Blinking rapidly, she swallowed hard on the surge of powerful emotion she was struggling to control.

'I think it's time I made some sort of announcement about this marriage of ours,' Angelos drawled lazily.

Maxie's lashes shot up, eyes stunned at all that went unsaid in that almost careless declaration. Evidently

Angelos no longer saw the slightest need to keep their true relationship a secret from the rest of the world.

'Don't you think?' he prompted softly, and then with a slumberous sigh he released her from his weight and rolled off the bed in one powerfully energetic movement. 'Shower and then breakfast…I don't think I've ever been so hungry in my life!'

Only then did Maxie recall what he had said about 'crazy stories' before they'd made love. Her face tensed, her stomach twisting. 'Angelos…?'

He turned his tousled dark head and he smiled at her again.

Her fingers knotted nervously into a section of sheet. 'What I mentioned earlier…what I said about my god-mother's will…that *wasn't* a story, it was the truth.'

Angelos stilled, his smile evaporating like Scotch mist, black eyes suddenly level and alert.

Maxie explained again about the will. She went into great detail on the subject of her godmother's lifelong belief in the importance of marriage, the older woman's angry disapproval when Maxie had moved in with Leland. But Maxie didn't look at Angelos again after that first ten seconds when she had anxiously registered the grim tautening of his dark features.

'You see, at the time…after the way you proposed…I mean, I was angry, and I didn't see why I shouldn't make use of the fact that you were actually offering me exactly what I required to meet that condition of inheritance…' Maxie's voice petered out to a weak, uncertain halt because what had once seemed so clear now seemed so confused inside her own head. And the decision which once had seemed so simple and so clever mysteriously took on another aspect altogether when she attempted to explain it out loud to Angelos.

The silence simmered like a boiling cauldron.

Slowly, hesitantly, Maxie lifted her head and focused on Angelos.

Strong face hard with derision, black eyes scorching slivers of burning gold, he stared back at her. 'You are one devious, calculating little vixen,' he breathed with raw anger. 'When I asked you to marry me, I was honest. Anything *less* than complete honesty would've been beneath me because, unlike you, I have certain principles, certain standards!'

Maxie had turned paper-pale. 'Angelos, I—'

'Shut up…I don't want to hear any more!' he blazed back at her with sizzling contempt. 'I'm thinking of the generous financial settlement you were promised should our marriage end. You had neither need nor any other excuse to plot and plan to collect on some trusting old lady's will as well!'

A great rush of hot tears hit the back of Maxie's aching eyes. Blinking rapidly, she looked away. He was looking at her as if she had just crawled out from under a stone and sudden intense shame engulfed her.

'How could you be so disgustingly greedy?' Angelos launched in fierce condemnation. 'And how could you try to use me when I never once tried to use you?'

'It wasn't like that. You've got it all wrong,' Maxie fumbled in desperation, deeply regretting her own foolish mode of confession on the beach when saving face had been uppermost in her mind. 'It was a spur-of-the-moment idea…I was hurt and furious and I—'

'When a man gives you a wedding ring, he is honouring you, *not* using you!' Angelos gritted between clenched teeth.

Maxie started to bristle then. 'Well, I wouldn't know

about that…I only had the supreme honour of wearing that ring for about five minutes—'

'You gave it back—'

Maxie lifted shimmering blue eyes and tilted her chin. 'You *took* it!' she reminded him wrathfully. 'And I don't want it back either…and I don't want you making any announcement to anybody about our marriage…because I wouldn't want anybody to know I was *stupid* enough to marry you!'

'That cuts both ways,' Angelos asserted with chilling bite, temper leashed back as he squared his big shoulders. 'And I'll be sure to ditch you before the six months is up!'

He strode into the bathroom.

Maxie flung herself back against the pillows, rolled over and pummelled them with sheer rage and frustration. Then she went suddenly still, and a great rolling breaker of sobs threatened because just for a little while she had felt close to Angelos and then, like a fairy-tale illusion, that closeness had vanished again…driven away by her own foolish, reckless tongue.

Yes, sooner or later she would naturally have had to tell Angelos about Nancy Leeward's will. But on the beach she had blown it, once and for all. After all, who was it who had told him that she had planned to use him? And the whole thing had struck him as so far-fetched that within minutes of being told he had decided it wasn't true. Indeed he had assumed that she was childishly trying to 'level the score.' Maxie shivered, belatedly appalled by the realisation that Angelos could understand her to that degree…

That was exactly what she had been doing. Believing that their relationship was over, she had been set on saving face and so she had told him about the will in the most offensive possible terms. Now that she had convinced him that she was telling him the truth, she was reaping the reward she had invited…anger, contempt, distaste.

And how could she say now, I wanted to marry you anyway and I needed a good excuse to allow myself to do that and still feel that I was control? There was no way that she could tell Angelos that she loved him. There was no way she could see herself *ever* telling Angelos that she loved him…

When he came out of the bathroom, a towel knotted round his lean brown hips, Maxie studied him miserably. 'Angelos, I was going to tear up that prenuptial contract—'

'You should be writing scripts for Disney!' Angelos countered with cutting disbelief, and strode towards the dressing-room.

'You said…you said you couldn't pride yourself on your judgement where I was concerned,' Maxie persisted tightly, wondering if what she was doing qualified as crawling, terrified that it might be.

'I'm back on track now, believe me.' Angelos sent her an icy look of brooding darkness. 'I'm also off to London for a couple of days. I have some business to take care of.'

Business? What business? They had only arrived yesterday. Maxie wasn't stupid. She got the message. He just didn't want to be with her any more.

'Are you always this unforgiving in personal relationships?' Maxie breathed a little chokily when he had disappeared from view, but she knew he could still hear her.

'I love that breathy little catch in your voice but it's

wasted on me. You wouldn't cry if I roasted you over a bonfire!'

'You're right,' Maxie said steadily, hastily wiping the tears dripping down her cheeks with the corner of the sheet.

Angelos reappeared, sheathed in a stupendous silver-grey suit. Lean, dark face impassive, he looked as remote as the Himalayas and even colder.

Maxie made one final desperate attempt to penetrate that armour of judgemental ice. 'I really don't and never did want your money, Angelos,' she whispered with all the sincerity she could muster.

Angelos sent her a hard, gleaming scrutiny, his expressive mouth curling. 'You may not be my conception of a wife but you will make the perfect mistress. In that role you can be every bit as mercenary as you like. You spend my money; I enjoy your perfect body. Randy Greek billionaires understand that sort of realistic exchange best of all. And at least this way we both know where we stand.'

Maxie gazed back at him in total shock. Every scrap of colour drained from her cheeks. But in that moment the battle lines were drawn...if Angelos wanted a mistress rather than a wife, a mistress, Maxie decided fierily, was what he was jolly well going to get!

'Angelos doesn't *know* where you are? You mean he's not aware that you're back in London yet?' Liz breathed in astonishment when the fact penetrated.

Maxie took a deep breath. 'I came straight here from the airport. I'm planning to surprise him,' she said, with more truth than the older woman could ever have guessed.

'Oh...yes, of course.' Liz relaxed again and smiled.

'What a shame business concerns had to interrupt your honeymoon! It must've been something terribly important. When was it you said Angelos left the island?'

'Just a few days ago...' Maxie did not confide that she had left on the ferry exactly twenty-four hours later—the very morning, in fact, when her credit cards had been delivered. Credit cards tellingly made out in her maiden name. The die had been cast there and then. Angelos's goose had been cooked to a cinder.

And, faced with that obvious invitation to spend, spend, spend, as any sensible mistress would at the slightest excuse, Maxie had instantly risen to the challenge. She had flown to Rome and then to Paris. She had had a whale of a time. She had repaired the deficiencies of her wardrobe with the most beautiful designer garments she could find. And if she had seen a pair of shoes or a handbag she liked, she had bought them in every possible colour...

Indeed, she could now have papered entire walls with credit card slips. If Angelos had been following that impressive paper trail of gross extravagance and shameless avarice across Rome and Paris, he would probably still think she was abroad, but he wouldn't know where because she had deliberately used cash to pay for flights and hotel bills.

'Are you happy?' Liz pressed anxiously.

'Incredibly...' Well, about as happy as she could be when it had been six days, fourteen hours and thirty-seven minutes since she had last laid eyes on Angelos, Maxie reflected ruefully. But to vegetate alone, abandoned and neglected on Chymos, would've been even worse.

'Do you think Angelos might come to love you?'

Maxie thought about that. She had set her sights on

him loving her but she wasn't sure it was a very realistic goal. Had Angelos ever been in love? It was very possible that she might settle for just being *needed*. Right now, all she could accurately forecast was that Angelos would be in a seething rage because she had left the island without telling him and hadn't made the slightest effort to get in touch.

But then that was what a mistress would do when the man in her life departed without mention of when he would return. A mistress was necessarily a self-sufficient creature. And if Angelos hadn't yet got around to putting in place the arrangements by which he intended to see her and spend time with her, then that was his oversight, not hers. No mistress would tell her billionaire lover when *she* would be available...that was *his* department.

Maxie had tea with Liz and then she called a cab. With the mountain of luggage she had acquired, it was quite a squeeze. She directed the driver to the basement car park of the building Angelos had informed her was to be exclusively hers. She was a little apprehensive about how she was to gain entry. After all, Angelos didn't even know she was back in London yet, and possibly the place would be locked up and deserted.

But on that point she discovered that she had misjudged him. There was a security man in the lift.

'Miss Kendall...?'

'That's me. Would you see to my luggage, please?' Maxie stepped into the lift to be wafted upwards and wondered why the man was gaping at her.

When the doors slid back, she thought she had stopped on the wrong floor. The stark modern decor had been swept away as if it had never been. In growing amazement, Maxie explored the spacious apartment.

The whole place had been transformed with antique furniture, wonderful rugs and a traditional and warm colour scheme. King Kong on stilts couldn't have seen over the barriers ringing the roof garden and, just in case she still wasn't about to bring herself to step out into the fresh air, a good third of the space now rejoiced in being a conservatory.

The apartment was gorgeous. No expense had been spared, nothing that might add to her comfort had been overlooked, but, far from being impressed by Angelos's consideration of her likes and dislikes, and even her terror of heights, Maxie was almost reduced to grovelling tears of despair. Angelos had had all this done just so that they could live *apart*. Looked at from that angle, the lengths he had gone to in his efforts to make her content with her solitary lot seemed like a deadly insult and the most crushing of rejections.

Maxie unpacked. That took up what remained of the evening and her wardrobe soon overflowed into the guest-room next door. She took out the two-page list of Angelos's flaws that had become her talisman. Whenever she got angry with him, whenever she missed him, she took it out and reminded herself that while she might not be perfect, he was not perfect either. It was a surprisingly comforting exercise which somehow made her feel closer to him.

How long would it take him to work out where she was? She lay in her sunken bath under bubbles, miserable as sin. She wanted to phone him but she wouldn't let herself. The perfect mistress did not phone her lover. That would be indiscreet. She put on a diaphanous azure-blue silk nightdress slit to the thigh and curled up on the huge brass bed in the master suite.

The arrival of the lift was too quiet and too far away

for her to hear. But she heard the hard footsteps ringing down the corridor. Maxie tensed, anticipation filling her. The bedroom door thrust wide, framing Angelos.

In a black dinner jacket that fitted his broad shoulders like a glove, and narrow black trousers that accentuated the long, long length of his legs, he was breathtakingly handsome. Her heart went thud…and then *thud* again. His bow tie was missing; the top couple of studs on his white dress shirt were undone to reveal a sliver of vibrant brown skin.

Poised in the doorway, big hands clenched into fists and breathing rapidly as if he had come from somewhere in a heck of a hurry, he ran outraged golden eyes over her relaxed pose on the brass bed as she reclined back against the heaped-up luxurious pillows as if she hadn't a single care in the world.

'You're here on my first night back…what a lovely surprise!' Maxie carolled.

CHAPTER TEN

MOMENTARILY disconcerted by that chirpy greeting, Angelos stilled. His lush black lashes came down and swept up again as if he wasn't quite sure what he was seeing, never mind what he was hearing.

Having learned some very good lessons from him, Maxie took the opportunity to sit forward, shake back her wonderful mane of golden hair and stretch so that not one inch of the remarkably sexy nightdress hugging her lithe curves could possibly escape his notice.

'What do you think?' she asked gaily. 'I bought it in—'

His entire attention was locked on her, darker colour highlighting his taut high cheekbones and the wrathful glitter of incredulity in his brilliant eyes. 'Where the hell have you been for the past week?' he launched at her with thunderous aggression as he strode forward. 'Do you realise that I flew back to Chymos before I realised you'd left the island?'

'Oh, *no*,' Maxie groaned. 'I would've felt awful if I'd known that!'

'Why the blazes didn't you phone me to tell me what you were thinking of doing?' Angelos demanded with raw incredulity. 'You can shop any time you like but you don't need to do it in time that you could be with me!'

'Why didn't you phone me to tell me that you were coming back?' Maxie's eyes were as bright as sapphires. 'You see, I couldn't phone you. None of the villa staff spoke a word of English and I don't have your phone number—'

Angelos froze. 'What do you mean you don't have my number?'

'Well, you're not in the directory and I'm sure your office staff are very careful not to hand out privileged information like that to just anybody—'

'*Theos*...you're not just anybody!' Angelos blazed, in such a rage he could hardly get the words out. 'I expect to know where you are every minute of the day! And the best I could do was follow your credit card withdrawals as they leapfrogged across Europe!'

What Maxie was hearing now was bliss. She had been missed. 'I think it really would be sensible for you to give me a contact number,' she said gently. 'I'm sorry, but I honestly never realised how possessive you could be—'

'*Possessive?*' Angelos snatched in a shuddering breath of visible restraint, scorching golden eyes hot as lava. 'I am *not* possessive. I just wanted to know where you were.'

'Every minute of the day,' Maxie reminded him helplessly. 'Well, how was I to know that when you didn't tell me?'

Angelos drove raking fingers through his luxuriant black hair. 'You do not *ever* take off anywhere again without telling me where you're going...is that clear?' he growled, withdrawing a gold pen from the inside pocket of his well-cut jacket and striding over to the bedside table.

To her dismay he proceeded to use the blank back page of her list of his flaws to write on. She had left it lying face-down on the table. 'What are you doing?'

'I am listing every number by which I can be reached.

Never again will you use the excuse that you couldn't contact me! My portable phone, my confidential line, the apartment, the car phones, and when I'm abroad…'

And he wrote and he wrote and he wrote while Maxie watched in fascination. He had more access numbers than a telecommunications company. It was as if he was drawing up a network for constant communication. Mercifully it had not occurred to him, however, to take a closer look at what he was writing on.

'I got the news that you had reappeared while I was entertaining a group of Japanese industrialists,' Angelos supplied grittily. 'I had to sit through the whole blasted evening before I could get here!'

'If only I'd known,' Maxie sighed, struggling to keep her tide of happiness in check. Angelos was no longer cold and remote. He had been challenged by the shocking discovery that she did not sit like an inanimate object stowed on a shelf when he was absent. He had been frustrated by not knowing where she was or exactly when or where she might choose to show up again. As a result, Angelos had had far more to think about than the argument on which they had parted on Chymos.

Angelos was still writing. He stopped to sling her a penetrating look of suspicion. 'You were in Rome…you were in Paris…who were you with?' he demanded darkly.

'I was on my own,' Maxie responded with an injured look of dignity.

Angelos's intent gaze lingered. A little of his tension evaporated. Dense lashes screened his eyes. 'I was pretty angry with you…'

She knew that meant he had been thumping walls and raising Cain. From the instant he'd found her absent without leave from the island, he had been a volcano smouldering, just longing for the confrontational moment of release when he could erupt.

'I'd offer you a drink but I'm afraid all the cupboards are bare,' Maxie remarked.

'Naturally…I wasn't expecting you to move in here.'

Maxie frowned. 'How can you say that when this entire apartment has obviously been remodelled for my occupation?'

Setting down his pen, Angelos straightened and settled gleaming dark eyes on her. 'Look, that was *before* we got married…you might not have noticed, but things have changed since then.'

Maxie looked blank. 'Have they?'

Angelos's beautiful mouth compressed hard. 'I've been thinking. You might as well come home with me. I'll stick a notice about our marriage in the paper—'

'No…I like things the way they are.' Saying that was the hardest thing Maxie had ever done, but pride would not allow her to accept the role of wife when it was so grudgingly offered. 'I love this apartment and, like you, I really do appreciate my own space. And there is no point in firing up a media storm about our marriage when it's going to be over in a few months.'

Angelos studied her intently, like a scientist peeling layers off an alien object to penetrate its mysteries. And then, without the slightest warning, his brilliant eyes narrowed and the merest hint of a smile lessened the tension still etched round his mouth. 'OK…fine, no problem. You're being very sensible about this.'

Inside herself, Maxie collapsed like a pricked balloon. He sounded relieved by her decision. He saw no point in them attempting to live as a normal married couple. Evidently he still saw no prospect of them having any kind of a future together. But Maxie wanted him *begging* her to share the same roof. Clearly she had a long way to go if she was to have any hope of achieving that objective.

'But I would appreciate an explanation for your sudden departure from Chymos,' Angelos completed.

Maxie tautened. 'I didn't know when you were coming back. You were furious. It seemed a good idea to let the dust settle.'

'Do you know *why* I came back to London?' Strong face taut, Angelos drew himself up to his full commanding height, the two-page list still clasped in one hand and attracting her covert and anxious attention.

'I haven't a clue.'

'I had to sort out Leland.'

Quite unprepared for that announcement, Maxie gasped. *'Leland?'*

With an absent glance at the loose pages in his hand, Angelos proceeded to fold them and slot them carelessly into the pocket of his jacket. Utterly appalled by that development, and already very much taken back by his reference to Leland Coulter, Maxie watched in sick horror as her defamatory list disappeared from view.

'Leland had to be dealt with. Surely you didn't think I planned to let him get away with what he did to you?' Angelos drawled in a fulminating tone of disbelief. 'He stole a whole chunk of your life and, not content with that, he ripped you off with that loan—'

'Angelos…L-Leland is a sick man—'

'Since he had the bypass op he is well on the road to full recovery,' Angelos contradicted grimly. 'But he's thoroughly ashamed of himself now, and so he should be.'

'You actually confronted him?' Maxie was still reeling in shock.

'*And* in Jennifer's presence. Now that she knows the real story of your dealings with her husband, she's ecstatic. Leland had no plans to confess the truth and his punctured vanity will be his punishment. He trapped you into a demeaning, distressing charade just to hit back at Jennifer!' Angelos concluded harshly.

'I never dreamt you would feel so strongly about it,' Maxie admitted tautly.

'You're mine now,' Angelos countered with indolent cool. 'I look after everything that belongs to me to the very best of my ability.'

'I don't belong to you…I'm just passing through…' Hot, offended colour had betrayingly flushed Maxie's cheeks. She wanted to hit him but, surveying him, she just gritted her teeth because she *knew* that the instant she got that close she would just melt into his arms and draw that dark, arrogant head down to hers. Almost seven days of sensory and emotional deprivation were making her feel incredibly weak.

Poised at the foot of the bed, lean brown hands flexing round the polished brass top rail, Angelos rested slumbrous yet disturbingly intent dark eyes on her beautiful face. 'Leland and Jennifer *do*, however, lead one to reflect on the peculiarity of the games adults play with each other,' he commented levelly. 'What a mistake it can be to underestimate your opponent…'

A slight chill ran down Maxie's backbone. Games? No, surely he couldn't have recognised what she was trying to do, she told herself urgently, for, apart from anything else, she did not consider herself to be playing a game. 'I don't follow…'

'Leland neglected his wife. Jennifer had a silly affair. She wouldn't say sorry. He was too bitter to forgive her. So they spent three years frantically squabbling over the terms of their divorce, enjoying a sort of twisted togetherness and never actually making it into court. Neither one of them allowed for the other's intransigence or stamina.'

'Crazy,' Maxie whispered very low.

'Isn't it just?' Angelos agreed, flicking a glance down at the thin gold watch on his wrist. He released a soft sigh of regret. 'I'd love to stay. However, I did promise to show my face at my cousin Demetrios's twenty-first celebration at a nightclub...and it's getting late.'

Maxie sat there as immobile as a stone dropped in a deep pond and plunged into sudden dreadful suffocating darkness. 'You're...*leaving*?' she breathed, not quite levelly.

'I lead a fairly hectic social life, *pethi mou*. Business, family commitments,' Angelos enumerated lazily. 'But the pressure of time and distance should ensure that the snatched moments we share will be all the more exciting—'

'Snatched moments?' Maxie echoed in a strained and slightly shrill undertone as she slid off the bed in an abrupt movement. 'You think I am planning to sit here and wait for ''snatched moments'' of your precious time?'

'Maxie...you're beginning to sound just a little like a wife,' Angelos pointed out with a pained aspect. 'The one thing a mistress must never ever do is nag.'

'*Nag?*' Maxie gasped, ready to grab him by the lapels of his exquisitely tailored dinner jacket and shake him until he rattled like a box of cutlery in a grinding machine.

'Or sulk, or shout or look discontented...' Angelos warmed to his theme with a glimmering smile of satisfaction. 'This is where I expect to come to relax and shrug off the tensions of the day… I'll dine here with you tomorrow night—'

Maxie was seething and ready to cut off her nose to spite her face. 'I'm going out.'

'Maxie…' Angelos shook his imperious dark head in reproof. 'Naturally I expect your entire day to revolve round being available when I want you to be.'

'For snatched moments?' Maxie asserted in outrage. 'What am I supposed to do with myself the rest of the time?'

'Shop,' Angelos delivered with the comforting air of a male dropping news she must be dying to hear. 'Any woman who can spend for an entire week without flagging once is a serious shopaholic.'

Maxie flushed to the roots of her hair, assailed by extreme mortification. She had spent an absolute fortune.

'And if it's a phobia, you should now be very happy,' Angelos continued bracingly. 'With me bankrolling you, you won't ever need to take the cure.'

Maxie was mute. Her every objective, her script, everything she had dreamt up with which to challenge him over the past week now lay in discarded tatters round her feet. As yet she couldn't quite work out how that had happened. Angelos had started out angry, fully meeting her expectations, but he was now in a wonderfully good mood…even though he was about to walk out on her.

During that weak moment of inattention, Angelos reached out to tug her into his arms with maddeningly confident hands. Maxie was rigid, and then she just drooped, drained of fight. He curved her even closer, crushing her up against him with a groan of unconcealed pleasure and sending every nerve in her body haywire with wanton longing.

'If it wasn't for this wretched party, I'd stay...' Angelos pushed against her with knowing eroticism, shamelessly acquainting her with the intensity of his arousal. Maxie's heartbeat went from a race into an all-out sprint. Heat surged between her thighs, leaving her weak with lust.

'I could throw you down on the bed and sate this overpowering ache for fulfilment—'

Maxie said, 'Yes...'

'But it would be wicked and unforgivable to make a snack out of what ought to be a five-course banquet.' Even as he talked Angelos was tracing a passage down her extended throat with his mouth in hot, hungry little forays. He slid a long, powerful thigh between hers to press against the most sensitive spot in her entire shivering body. 'I really do have to go...'

'Kiss me,' Maxie begged.

'Absolutely not...I'd go up in flames,' Angelos groaned with incredulous force, tearing himself back from her with shimmering golden eyes full of frustration.

Maxie clutched the bed to stay upright. Angelos backed away one slow step at a time, like a recovering alcoholic struggling to resist the temptation of a drink. '*Christos*...you're so beautiful, and so totally perfect for me,' he murmured with hoarse satisfaction.

Maxie blinked. All she could focus on was the fact that he was leaving. Everything that mattered to her in the whole world was walking out, and it felt as if it was for ever. The shock of separation from him was so painful it swallowed her alive. And a kind of terror swept over her then, because for the first time she tasted the full extent of her own agonising vulnerability.

She watched him until the last possible moment. She listened to him striding fast down the corridor. She even strained to hear the lift but she couldn't. And then she collapsed in a heap on the soft thick carpet and burst into floods of tears. Dear heaven, what an idiot she had been to set out to provide Angelos with a challenge! All of a sudden she could not credit that she had been so insane as to refuse the chance of making something of their marriage.

He had said that he hadn't expected her to move into this apartment. He had said that she might not have noticed but things had changed. He hadn't even mentioned that wretched argument over that equally wretched will of her godmother's. 'You might as well come home with me,' he had drawled. Her stupid, stupid pride had baulked; he had sounded for all the world like a disgruntled male grudgingly facing up to an inevitable evil. But no matter how half-hearted that offer had seemed, shouldn't she have accepted it?

She would've had something to build on then. Her rightful place as his wife. Instead, she had turned it down, gambled her every hope of happiness on the slender hope that Angelos would learn to love her and want her to be more than a mistress in his life. But, judging by his behaviour in the aftermath of that refusal, she appeared to have offered Angelos exactly what *he* wanted.

No, she had *not* made a mistake in rejecting that offer, she conceded heavily. How long would it have been before he resented the restraints of such a marriage? He had only married her for sex. She shuddered. There had to be a lot more than that on offer before she would risk figuring in the tabloids as the ultimate discarded bimbo yet again.

Angelos certainly wouldn't have been offering a wife snatched moments of his time…nor would he have been taking off for a nightclub on his own. Maxie sobbed her heart out and then, after splashing her swollen face with loads of cold water, she surveyed her weak reflection in the mirror with loathing and climbed into her lonely bed.

Tonight she had got some things wrong, but ultimately she had still made the right decision. She had played right into his hands but it was early days yet, she reminded herself bracingly. Stamina—she needed buckets of stamina to keep up with Angelos. It was so strange, she reflected numbly, every time she rejoiced in the belief that she had got Angelos off balance, he retaliated by doing the exact same thing to *her*…

The instant Maxie was engulfed by the hard heat of a hair-roughened male body, she came awake with a start. Pulling away with a muffled moan of fright, she sat up in a daze. Dawn light was filtering through the curtains.

'I didn't mean to wake you up…' Angelos murmured.

Utterly unconvinced by that plea of innocence, Maxie struggled to focus on him in the dim light. Against the pale bedlinen, he was all intriguing darkness and shadow. Her heart was still palpitating at such a rate, she pressed a hand to her breast and suppressed the lowering suspicion that Angelos might have more stamina than she had. 'What are you d-doing here?' she stammered helplessly.

'It was a long drive home…what do you *think* I'm doing here?' Angelos demanded with sudden disturbing amusement. He rolled over to her side of the bed at the speed of light to haul her back into his arms and seal her into all-pervasive contact with every charged line of his big, powerful frame.

'*Oh…*' Maxie said breathlessly.

'I know anticipation is supposed to be the cutting edge of erotic pleasure but I am not really into self-denial, *agape mou*,' Angelos confided huskily, his warm breath fanning her cheekbone. 'It's been a hell of a week…seven very rough days of wondering if you had left me and found another man.'

As it had genuinely not occurred to her that Angelos might interpret her departure from Chymos in that melodramatic light, Maxie was shaken. 'But—'

'The thought of you out there…*loose*,' Angelos framed with a hoarse edge to his dark, deep drawl.

'What do you mean by…''loose'?'

'The world is full of men like me. If I saw a ravishing beauty like you walking down a street alone, I'd make a move on her like a shot!'

Maxie was not best pleased by that assurance. 'If I ever have the slightest reason to think you're two-timing me, I'll be out of here so fast—'

'How can a husband two-time his wife?'

'He has an affair…*or* a mistress.'

'Well, you've got the market cornered there, haven't you?' Angelos breathed with galling amusement, running his hands down to the curvaceous swell of her hips to cup them and urge her even closer.

Maxie quivered, her body responding with a wanton life all of its own, but she struggled desperately to keep on talking because potential infidelity was an extremely important subject, to be tackled and dealt with on the

spot. 'Wh-who was it said that when the mistress becomes the wife, a vacancy is created?'

'Some guy who hadn't had the good fortune to discover you,' Angelos growled with blatant satisfaction.
'You are not like other women.'

Maxie blossomed at what sounded like a true compliment. 'Did you have a good time at the club?'

'What do *you* think?' Angelos nipped at the tender
lobe of her ear in sensual punishment and curved her
suggestively into contact with the straining evidence of
his arousal. 'I've been like this all night, hot and hungry
and *aching*—''

Maxie kissed him to shut him up; he was embarrassing her. He seized on that invitation with a fervour that
fully bore out his frustration. She came up for air again,
awash with helpless tenderness. He was irredeemably
oversexed but she just adored him. Something to build
on. Obviously being a sex object was the something to
build on. How the mighty had fallen, she conceded, and
then Angelos kissed her again and all rational thought
was suspended...

Maxie crept out of bed and tiptoed across the carpet to
the chair where she could see Angelos's clothing
draped. She would get the list back before he found it.
The very last thing their relationship needed now was
the short, sharp shocking result of Angelos seeing that
awful list of all that she had once thought was wrong
with him. That list had been a *real* hatchet job. After
all, when she had written it, she'd been trying to wean
herself off him.

Maxie couldn't believe her eyes when she discovered
that the jacket she was searching *wasn't* his dinner
jacket! Before he had returned to her at dawn, Angelos

had evidently gone back to his own apartment to change. She could've screamed... *Stamina*, she reminded herself, but her nerves were already shot to hell.

'Maxie...what are you doing?'

Maxie jerked and dropped his jacket as if she had been burnt. 'Nothing!'

'What time is it?' he queried softly.

'Eight...'

'Come back to bed, *agape mou*.'

Maxie was so relieved he hadn't noticed what she was doing, she responded with alacrity.

An hour and a half later she sat across the dining-room table while breakfast was served by Angelos's manservant, Nikos. He had imported his own staff to remedy the empty cupboards in the kitchen. His efficiency in sweeping away such problems just took her breath away. Now he lounged back, skimming through a pile of newspapers and onto his third cup of black coffee.

He was a fantastic lover, she thought dreamily. He could be so gentle and then so...so wild. And he ought to be exhausted after only a couple of hours of sleep, but instead Angelos emanated a sizzling aura of pent-up energy this morning. I'm never, ever going to get over him, she thought in sudden panic. I *need* my list back to deprogramme myself from this dependency.

Without warning, Angelos bit out something raw and incredulous in Greek and sprang upright, sending half his coffee flying. Volatile, volcanic, like a grizzly bear, Maxie reminded herself studiously. He strode across the dining-room, swept up the phone, punched out some numbers and raked down the line, 'That piece on Maxie Kendall on the gossip page...who authorised that? You print a retraction tomorrow. And after that she's the invisible woman…you tell that malicious poison-pen artist to find another target. She's supposed to be writing up society stuff, not trawling the gutter for sleaze!'

About thirty seconds later, Angelos replaced the receiver. Maxie was suffering from dropped-jaw syndrome. Only Nikos, evidently inured to the liveliness of life with Angelos, was functioning normally. Having mopped up the split coffee, he had brought a fresh cup, and he now removed himself from the room again with admirable cool.

Angelos slapped the offending newspaper down in front of Maxie. 'This is what happens when you stroll round Paris without protection,' he informed her grimly. 'You didn't even realise you'd been caught on camera, did you?'

'No,' she confided, and swallowed hard, still in shock from that startling knee-jerk demonstration of male protectiveness. She cast a brief glance at the photo. 'But do you really think that newspaper is likely to pay the slightest heed to your objections?'

'I *own* that newspaper,' Angelos breathed flatly, his lean face sardonic. 'And just look at what that stupid columnist has written!'

Maxie obediently bent her head. She put a finger on the lines of italic type to the right of the photo. The tiny words blurred and shifted hopelessly because she couldn't even begin to concentrate with Angelos standing over her as he was.

The silence thundered.

Then a lean brown forefinger came down to shift hers to the section of type *below* the photograph. 'It's that bit, actually,' Angelos informed her, half under his breath.

Maxie turned white, her stomach reacting with a violent lurch. 'I never read this kind of stuff…and you've caught me out. I'm horribly long-sighted…

The silence went on and on and on. She couldn't bring herself to look up to see whether or not he had been fooled by that desperate lie.

In an abrupt movement, Angelos removed the newspaper. 'You shouldn't be looking at that sort of sleazy trash anyway. It's beneath your notice!'

The sick tension, the shattering fear of discovery drained out of Maxie, but it left her limp, perspiration beading her short upper lip. How *could* she tell him? How could she admit a handicap like dyslexia to someone like Angelos? Like many, he might not even believe that the condition really existed; he might think that it was just a fancy name coined to make the not very bright feel better about their academic deficiencies. Over the years Maxie had met a lot of attitudes like that, and had learnt that any attempt to explain the problems she had often resulted in contempt or even greater discomfiture.

'Maxie…' Angelos cleared his throat with rare hesitancy. 'I don't think there's anything wrong with your eyesight, and I don't think it's a good idea at this stage in our relationship to pretend that there is.'

As that strikingly candid admission sank in, appalled humiliation engulfed Maxie. This was her worst nightmare. Angelos had uncovered her secret. She could have borne anybody but him seeing through the lying excuses that came so readily to her lips when her reading or writing skills were challenged. She sat there just staring into space, blocking him out.

'Maxie…I don't like upsetting you but I'm not about to drop the subject.' Angelos bent and hauled the chair around by the arms, with her still sitting in it. 'You are very intelligent so there has to be a good reason why you can't read ten lines in a newspaper with the same ease that I can. And, you see, I remember your notebook when you were waitressing…like a type of shorthand instead of words.'

Maxie parted compressed lips like an automaton. 'I'm dyslexic…OK?'

'OK…do you want some more coffee?' Angelos enquired without skipping a beat as he straightened.

'No, I've had enough…I thought you'd want to drag it all out of me,' she said then accusingly.

'Not right now, if it's upsetting you to this degree,' Angelos returned evenly.

'I'm *not* upset!' Maxie flew upright and stalked across the room in direct contradiction of the statement. 'I just don't like people prying and poking about in what is my business and nobody else's!'

Angelos regarded her in level enquiry. 'Dyslexia is more widespread than perhaps you realise. Demetrios, whose twenty-first I attended last night, is also dyslexic, but he's now in his second year at Oxford. His two younger brothers also have problems. Didn't you get extra tuition at school to help you to cope?'

Relaxing infinitesimally, Maxie folded her arms and shook her head dully. 'I went to about a dozen different schools in all—'

'A dozen?' Angelos interrupted in astonishment.

'Dad and I never stayed in one place for long. He always ended up owing someone money. If it wasn't the landlord it was the local bookie, or some bloke he had laid a bet with and lost…so we would do a flit to pastures new.'

'And then the whole cycle would start again?' Angelos questioned tautly.

'Yes...' Maxie pursued her lips, her throat aching as she evaded his shrewd appraisal. 'I was ten before a teacher decided that there might be an explanation other than stupidity for my difficulties and I was assessed. I was supposed to get extra classes, but before it could be arranged Dad and I moved on again.' She tilted her chin, denying her own agonising self-consciousness on the subject. 'In the next school, after I'd been tested, they just stuck me in the lowest form alongside the rest of the no-hopers.'

Angelos actually winced. 'When did you leave school?'

'As fast as my legs could carry me at sixteen!' Maxie admitted with sudden explosive bitterness. 'As my godmother once said to me, "Maxie, you can't expect to be pretty *and* clever."'

'I don't think I like the sound of her very much.'

'She was trying to be kind but she thought I was as thick as a brick because I was such a slow reader, and my writing was awful and my spelling absolutely stinks!' Feeling the tears coming on, Maxie shot across the room like a scalded cat and fled back to the bedroom.

Angelos came down on the bed beside her.

'And don't you dare try to pretend that you don't see me differently now!' Maxie sobbed furiously.

'You're right. You are incredibly brave to cope with something like that all on your own and still be such a firecracker,' Angelos breathed grittily. 'And if I'd known this when I had Leland in my sights, I'd have torn him limb from limb...because you couldn't *read* that bloody loan contract, could you?'

'Bits of it...I can get by...but it takes me longer to

read things. I didn't want to show myself up, so I just signed.'

'Demetrios was fortunate. His problems were recognised when he was still a child. He got all the help he needed but you were left to suffer in frustration…you shouldn't be—you *mustn't* be ashamed of the condition.'

Tugging her back against him, Angelos smoothed her hair off her damp brow as if he was comforting a distressed and sensitive child, and she jerked away from him. He persisted. Out of pride, she tried to shrug him off again, but it was a very half-hearted gesture and recognised as such. Somehow, when Angelos closed his powerful arms round her, she discovered, nothing could possibly feel that bad.

'What did that piece in the gossip column say anyway?' Maxie wiped her eyes on her sleeve.

'That the rumours about you and I were complete nonsense. But that it looked like you had attracted another wealthy "friend"—the implication being that he was another married man.'

'The columnist got that bit right.' An involuntary laugh escaped Maxie.

Angelos's grip tightened. 'It didn't amuse me.'

Maxie then dug up the courage to ask something that had been puzzling her all night. 'Why aren't you still furious about me deciding to marry you because of my godmother's will?'

'In your position, I might have reacted the same way. I fight fire with fire too,' Angelos admitted reflectively. 'I don't surrender, I get even. But, you see, there comes a time when that can become a dangerously destructive habit…'

'I'll stop trying to top everything you do,' Maxie promised tautly.

'I'll stop trying to set you up for a fall,' Angelos swore, and then he surveyed her with sudden decision. 'And we'll fly back the island to enjoy some privacy.'

'You really are a fabulous cook,' Angelos commented appreciatively as Maxie closed the empty picnic hamper.

Maxie tried to look modest and failed. In the most unexpected ways, Angelos was a complete pushover. With all those servants around, and the ability to eat every meal at five-star locations if he chose, no woman had ever, it seemed, made the effort to cook for him, and he was wildly and unduly impressed by the domestic touch. If she cracked an egg, he made her feel like Mother Earth.

'You could make some lucky guy a really wonderful wife,' Angelos drawled indolently.

Maxie leant over him and mock-punched him in the ribs. Bronzed even deeper by the sun, narrow hips and long powerful thighs sheathed in a pair of low-slung cut-off jeans, Angelos was all lean, dark, rampantly virile male. She stared down at him, entrapped, heart thumping, breathing constricted. He threaded a lean hand into her tumbling hair to imprison her in that vulnerable position.

Disturbingly serious black eyes focused on her. 'Tell me, have you *ever* trusted a member of my sex?'

'No,' Maxie admitted uneasily.

'I feel as if I'm on trial. We're married. You won't wear my ring. You still don't want anyone to know you're my wife—'

'You made the offer to announce our marriage out of guilt.'

'I'm not that big a fool. I think you're paying me back for refusing to do it the right way from the start,' Angelos countered steadily. 'I hurt you and I'm sorry, but we have to move on from there.'

Maxie's gaze was strained, wary. 'I'm not ready for that yet.'

'Thanks for that vote of faith.' Releasing her with startling abruptness, Angelos sprang upright and strode up the beach.

Fighting a sensation of panic, and the urge to chase after him, Maxie hugged her knees tightly and stared out at the sun-drenched blue of the sea. The first row since they had left London. It totally terrified her. She could not overcome the fear that she was just a fascinating interlude for Angelos, that she did not have what it would take to hold him. She could not face the prospect of being his wife in public and then being dumped a few months down the line when he lost interest...

And yet, to be fair, so far Angelos had not shown the slightest sign of becoming bored with her. In fact, with every passing day Angelos made her feel better about herself, so much more than a beautiful face and body—something no man had ever achieved or even *tried* to achieve.

Yesterday he had had to fly to Athens for the day on business. Three gorgeous bouquets of the white lilies she loved had been flown in during his absence. And every one of them had carried a personal message, carefully block-printed by his own hand. 'Missing you.' 'Missing you more.' 'Missing you even more,' Maxie recalled headily. So impractical, so over-the-top. Not bad for a guy she had believed didn't have a romantic,

imaginative, thoughtful, sensitive or tender bone in his
entire beautiful body.

But for the past ten days Angelos had been proving
just how wrong she had been to attribute such flaws to
him. The list? Well, as yet, since that dinner jacket was
still in London, she hadn't had a chance to get hold of
it, and the list might well have been dumped by Nikos
or trashed at the dry-cleaners or some such thing by
now. She knew Angelos *couldn't* have found it before
they left London. He couldn't possibly have kept his
mouth shut on the subject if he had.

He had presented her with a laptop computer with a
wonderful spellcheck mechanism on it so that she could
write things with ease. He read newspapers with her.
He was so patient with her efforts and, as her confidence
had risen from absolute rock-bottom inadequacy, she
had improved amazingly. How had she ever imagined
he was selfish and inconsiderate? And how had she ever
thought she could bask in such generosity and not be
expected to give something back? And she knew what
he wanted back. Total, unconditional surrender. That
was what trust was. She was being such a terrible, selfish coward...

Maxie found him in the airy lounge. Hovering in the
doorway, she studied him, her heart jumping worse than
it did when he took her up in the helicopter most morn-
ings. 'I trust you,' she said tautly, a betraying shimmer
brightening her eyes.

Angelos dealt her a pained, unimpressed look, and
then he groaned with suppressed savagery. Striding
across the room, he pulled her into his arms in one
powerful motion. '*Christos*...don't look at me like that,
agape mou!' he urged ruefully. 'Forget that whole con-

versation. I'm just not very good at patience…not a lot
of practice and too big an ego.'

'I like you the way you are.'

'The lies women tell in certain moods,' Angelos
sighed with an ironic look.

'It's *not* a lie, Angelos—'

'Possibly it won't be…some time in the future.' And
with that last word he sealed his sensual mouth to hers
with a kind of hungry desperation.

The ground beneath Maxie's feet rocked. In that one
way Angelos controlled her. He understood that. He
used it. She accepted it; the passion he unleashed inside
her was more than she could withstand. But, most importantly of all, it was the one time she could show him
affection without the fear that she might be revealing
how much she loved him. And if anything, after the
past ten days, she loved him ten times more.

She was enslaved, utterly, hopelessly enslaved. So
the minute Angelos touched her she let all that pent-up
emotion loose on him. She clutched, she clung, she
heaved ecstatic sighs and she hugged him tight. And he
responded with a flattering amount of enthusiasm every
time.

Probing her mouth with hot, sexual intimacy,
Angelos unclipped her bikini bra. As her breasts spilt
full and firm into his palms, he uttered a hungry sound
of pleasure. He let his thumbs glance over her urgently
sensitive pink nipples. Maxie moaned, her spine arching
as he used his mouth to torment those straining buds.
She was so excited she couldn't breathe. Reaching
down, he unclipped the bikini briefs clasped at her slim
hips and pulled them free, leaving her naked.

'I love exciting you,' Angelos confided hoarsely, and
he kissed her again, slowly, sensually this time. A long,

powerful thigh nudged hers apart. A surge of unbearable heat left her boneless as he bent her back over his supporting arm, splaying his hand across the clenched muscles of her stomach. His skilled fingers skated through the cluster of damp golden curls and into the hot, melting warmth beneath. She whimpered and squirmed under his mouth, and at the exact moment when her legs began to buckle he picked her up with easy strength and carried her down to the bedroom.

He stood over her, unzipping the cut-offs, peeling them off. And then he came down to her. 'Angelos...' she pleaded, aroused beyond bearing.

Answering the powerful need he had awakened, he took her hard and fast, as always disturbingly attuned to the level of her need. And then there was nothing, nothing but him and the wild sensation that controlled her as surely as he did. She cried out as he drove her to a peak of exquisite pleasure and then slumped, absolutely, totally drained.

'Have you ever been in love?' Angelos asked lazily then.

Unprepared for serious conversation, Maxie blinked and met brilliant assessing eyes. 'Yes.'

'What happened?'

Maxie lowered her lashes protectively. 'He didn't love me back...er, what about you?'

'Once...'

Maxie opened her eyes wide. *'And?'*

Angelos focused on her swollen mouth, ebony lashes screening his gaze. 'I fell victim to a feminist with high expectations of the man in her life. She thought I was great in bed but that was kind of it.'

'Tart!' Maxie condemned without hesitation, absolutely outraged to discover he had loved somebody else and, worst of all, somebody wholly undeserving of the honour. There was just so much more to Angelos than his ability to drive her crazy with desire, she thought furiously. He was highly entertaining company and such a wretched tease sometimes...

Dark eyes met hers with disturbing clarity. 'She wasn't and isn't a tart...is that jealousy, I hear?'

'I'm not the jealous type,' Maxie lied, and, snaking free of him with the Ice Queen look she hadn't given him in weeks, she slid off the bed. 'I feel like a shower.'

On the flight back to London, Maxie contemplated the wedding ring now embellishing her finger. It was new, a broad platinum band. It was also accompanied by a gorgeous knuckleduster of sapphires and diamonds.

'An engagement ring?' she had asked him incredulously.

'A *gift*,' Angelos had insisted. But he had produced both at spectacular speed.

Indeed, her finger was now so crowded, a glance at a hundred yards would give the news that she was married to even the most disinterested onlooker. But why couldn't Angelos mention the prospect of having children...or something, *anything* that would make her feel like a really permanent fixture in his life? she wondered ruefully. Maybe he didn't want children. Or maybe he just couldn't contemplate the idea of having children with her. Certainly he hadn't taken a single risk in that department.

They parted at the airport. Angelos headed for the Petronides building and Maxie travelled back to *his* apartment, her new home. Barely stopping to catch her breath, she found the main bedroom, went into the dressing-room and searched through wardrobe after wardrobe of fabulous suits in search of that dinner jacket with her list in the pocket. She found half a dozen dinner jackets, but not one of them contained what she sought. Obviously that list had been dumped. She relaxed.

Angelos called her at lunchtime. 'Something's come up. I may be very late tonight,' he informed her.

Maxie's face fell a mile but her response was upbeat. 'Don't worry, I'll amuse myself—'

'*How?*' Angelos interrupted instantaneously.

'I'll have an early night.' Maxie worked hard to keep the amusement out of her voice.

'I have this recurring image of you hitting the town on your own.'

'Because you know you got away with going to that nightclub by yourself, but you won't ever again,' Maxie murmured with complete sincerity.

Maxie couldn't believe how much she missed him that night. She thought she would turn over at some stage and find him there in the bed beside her, and it was something of a shock to wake up at eight and discover she was still alone.

By the time she sat down to breakfast, however, the table was rejoicing in a huge bunch of white lilies. 'Missing you too much,' the card complained. Maxie heaved a happy sigh, consoled by the sight. Her portable phone buzzed.

'Thank you for the flowers,' she said, since nobody else but Angelos had her number. 'Where are you?'

'The office. I was out of town last night. It was too late to drive back and I didn't want to wake you up by phoning in the early hours.'

'The next time, phone,' Maxie urged.

'What are you wearing, *agape mou*?' Angelos enquired huskily.

Maxie gave a little shiver and crammed the phone even closer to her ear. The sound of that honeyed drawl just knocked her out. 'Shocking pink…suit…four-inch stilettos,' she whispered hoarsely. 'I can't wait to take them all off.'

'How am I supposed to concentrate when you say things like that?' Angelos demanded in a driven undertone.

'I want you to miss me.'

'I'm missing you…OK?'

'OK…when can I expect a snatched moment?'

'Don't go out anywhere. I'll pick you up at eleven. I've got a surprise for you.'

Maxie flicked through the topmost newspaper and went as usual to the gossip column. She saw the picture of Angelos instantly. Her attention lodged lovingly on how wonderfully photogenic he was, and then her gaze slowly slewed sideways to take in the woman who occupied the photo with him, the woman whose hand he was intimately clasping across a table.

Aghast, she just stared for a full count of ten seconds. Her stomach twisted, her brow dampened. She felt sick. Natalie Cibaud, the movie actress…

CHAPTER ELEVEN

Fresh from reports of an on-off affair with the model Maxie Kendall, Greek tycoon Angelos Petronides, our all-time favourite heartbreaker, seen dining last night with the ravishing actress Natalie Cibaud. Is it off with Maxie and on with Natalie again? Or is this triangle set to run and run?

Last night? Dear heaven, Angelos had been with another woman? With Natalie Cibaud? Maxie just couldn't believe it. She kept on laboriously re-reading the column and staring an anguished hole into the photo. Then her stomach got the better of her. She lost her breakfast in the cloakroom.

Sick and dizzy, she reeled back to the table to study the card she had received with her flowers. 'Missing you *too* much.' There was a certain appalling candour in that admission, wasn't there? Evidently Angelos couldn't be trusted out of her sight for five minutes. And, trusting woman that she was, Angelos had been out of her sight for almost *twenty-four* hours...

Maxie asked Nikos to have the car brought around. She swept up her portable phone. No, she wasn't going to warn Angelos. Nor was she about to sit and wait for him to arrive with whatever surprise his guilty conscience had dreamt up. She would confront him in the Petronides building. Her phone buzzed in the lift. She ignored it.

The phone went again in the limousine. Angelos trying to call her. She switched the phone off with trembling fingers. Offered the car phone some minutes later, she uttered a stringent negative. Getting a little nervous, was he? By now, Angelos would've been tipped off about that piece in the gossip column. He knew he had been caught out. He had been unfaithful to her. He *must* have been. He had been out all night. *All night*. Maxie shivered, gooseflesh pricking her clammy skin. She was in sick shock. Why…*why*? was all she could think.

Until now she hadn't appreciated just how entirely hers Angelos had begun to seem. She had trusted him one hundred per cent. And now she couldn't comprehend how her trust had become so unassailable. He had never mentioned love, never promised to be faithful. On the very brink of making a public announcement of their marriage, Angelos had betrayed her. Why? Was this one of those male sexual ego things women found so incomprehensible? Or was an adulterous fling his revealing reaction to the prospect of fully committing himself to her?

Magnificent in her rage, Maxie stalked into the Petronides building. Every head in the vicinity seemed to turn. They did a double-take at the bodyguards in her wake. Maxie stepped into the executive lift.

Angelos had to be gnashing his teeth. Famous for his discretion in his private life, and his success in keeping his personal affairs out of the gossip columns, he would've assumed he was safe from discovery. Or had he deliberately sought to be found out? Was she becoming paranoid? The simplest explanations were usually the most likely, she reflected wretchedly. Had Angelos just met up with Natalie Cibaud again and suddenly realised that *she* was the woman he really wanted?

The receptionist on the top floor stared and rose slowly to her feet.

Maxie strode on past, the stillness of her pale features dominated by eyes as brilliant as sapphires. Agog faces appeared at doorways. Without breaking her stride, Maxie reached the foot of the corridor and, thrusting wide the door of Angelos's office, she swept in and sent the door slamming shut behind her again.

Angelos was standing in the centre of the room, lean, hard-boned face whip-taut, black eyes shimmering.

A pain as sharp as a knife cut through Maxie. She could read nothing but angry frustration in those startlingly handsome features. That neither shame nor regret could be seen savaged her. 'Before I walk out of your life for ever, I have a few things to say to you—'

Angelos moved forward and spread silencing hands. 'Maxie—'

'Don't you dare interrupt me when I'm shouting at you!' Maxie launched. 'And don't say my name like that. The only way you could get around me at this moment is with a rope! When I saw that photo of you with Natalie Cibaud, I couldn't believe my eyes—'

'Good,' Angelos slotted in fiercely. 'Because you shouldn't have believed what you were seeing. That photo was issued by Natalie's agent *three* months ago! That dinner date took place *three* months ago!'

'I don't believe you,' Maxie breathed jerkily, studying him with stunned intensity.

'Then call my lawyer. I've already been in touch with him. I intend to sue that newspaper.'

Maxie's lashes fluttered. Her legs trembled. She slumped back against the door. Widening blue eyes dazed, she framed raggedly, 'Are you saying that…you *weren't* with Natalie last night?'

'Maxie, I haven't laid eyes on Natalie since the night you took ill. We did not part the best of friends.'

The tremble in Maxie's lower limbs was inexorably spreading right through her entire body. 'But I thought you saw her after that—'

'You thought wrong. I have neither seen nor spoken to her since that night, and as far as I'm aware she's not even in the UK right now. Maxie...you should know I haven't the smallest desire for any other woman while you are in my life,' Angelos swore, anxiously searching her shaken face and then lapsing into roughened Greek as he reached for her and held her so tight and close she couldn't breathe.

'You s-said if you saw a beautiful woman walk down the street—'

'No, I said, "a ravishing beauty like *you*",' Angelos contradicted with strong emphasis. 'And there *is* no other woman like you. When I realised you must've seen that picture, it was like having my own heart ripped out! I can't bear for you to be hurt—not by me, not by anyone, *agape mou*.'

Strongly reassured by that unexpectedly emotional speech, Maxie gazed wordlessly up at him. Angelos breathed in deep and drew back from her. Black eyes meeting her bemused scrutiny, he murmured tautly, 'I have so much I want to say to you...but there is someone waiting to see you and it would be cruel to keep him waiting any longer. Your father is already very nervous of his reception.'

'My...my father?' Maxie whispered shakily. 'He's *here*?'

'I put private detectives on his trail and they contacted me as soon as they found him. I went to see him yesterday. I had planned to bring him back to the apartment to surprise you.' Angelos guided her over to one of the comfortable armchairs and settled her down carefully, seeming to recognise that she was in need of that assistance. 'I'll send him in…'

Stiff with strain, Maxie breathed unevenly, 'Just tell me one thing before you go…has Dad asked you for money?'

'No. No, he hasn't. He's cleaned up his act, Maxie. He's holding down a job and trying to make a decent life for himself.' Angelos shrugged. 'But he would be the first one to admit that he still has to fight the temptation to go back to his old habits.'

Her troubled eyes misted with tears. As Russ Kendall stepped uncertainly through the door through which Angelos had just departed, Maxie slid upright. Her father looked older, his hair greyer, and he had put on weight. He also looked very uncertain of himself.

'I wasn't sure about coming here after what I did,' her father admitted uncomfortably. 'It's very hard for me to face you now. I let you down the whole time I was bringing you up but I let you down worst of all three years ago, when I left you to pay the price for my stupidity.'

Maxie's stiffness gave way. Closing the distance between them, she gave the older man a comforting hug. 'You loved me. I *always* knew that. It made up for a lot,' she told him frankly. 'You did the best you could.'

'I hit rock-bottom when I saw you having to dance to the tune of that old coot, Leland Coulter.' Russ Kendall shook his head with bitter regret. 'There was no way I could avoid facing up to how low I'd sunk and how much I'd dragged you down. I leeched off you, off everyone. All I lived for was the next game, the next bet—'

Maxie drew him up short there. 'Angelos says you've got a job. Tell me about that,' she encouraged.

For the past year he had been working as a salesman for a northern confectionery firm. It was now eighteen months since he had last laid a bet. He still attended weekly meetings with other former gamblers.

Maxie told him that the cottage no longer had a sitting tenant. Her father frowned in surprise, and then slowly he smiled. Rather apprehensively, he then admitted that he had met someone he was hoping to marry. He would sell the cottage and put the proceeds towards buying a house. Myrtle, he explained, had some savings of her own, and it was a matter of pride that he should not bring less to the relationship.

Now he was middle-aged, she registered, her father finally wanted the ordinary things that other people wanted. Security, self-respect, to be loved, appreciated. And wasn't that exactly what *she* had always wanted for herself? Her father had needed her forgiveness and she had needed to shed her bitter memories. As they talked, her gratitude to Angelos for engineering such a reconciliation steadily increased. Russ had built a new life and she wished him well with her whole heart.

'You've got yourself a good bloke in Angelos,' her father commented with a nod as he took his leave. 'I shouldn't like to cross him, though.'

Maxie was mopping her eyes when Angelos reappeared. She didn't look at him. 'This has been a heck of morning...but I'm really grateful that you found Dad for me. It's like a whole big load of worry has dropped off my shoulders. Tell me, would you have brought us together again if he'd still been down on the skids?'

From the corner of her eye, she saw Angelos still. 'Not immediately,' he confessed honestly. 'I would have tried to get him some help first. But he wouldn't have come if he hadn't sorted himself out. He wouldn't have had the courage to face you.'

Angelos curved a supportive hand round her spine and walked her towards the door. 'We have a helicopter to catch.'

'Where on earth are we going?'

'Surprise…'

'I thought Dad was my surprise.'

'Only part of it.' He urged her up a flight of stairs and they emerged onto the roof, where a helicopter waited. Maxie grimaced and gave him a look of reproach which he pretended not to notice.

He held her hand throughout the flight. Maxie was forced to admit that it wasn't so bad. She was even persuaded to look out of the windows once or twice. But she still closed her eyes and prayed when they started coming in to land. Angelos restored her to solid ground again with careful hands. 'You're doing really great,' he told her admiringly.

Only then did Maxie open her eyes. She gaped. A hundred yards away stood a very large and imposing nineteenth-century country house surrounded by a gleaming sea of luxury cars. Three other helicopters were parked nearby. 'Where are we? What's going on?'

'I did once mention having a house in the country but you were ill at the time,' Angelos conceded with a wolfish smile. 'Welcome to the wedding reception you never had, Mrs Petronides…'

'I beg your pardon?' Maxie prompted unevenly.

'All my relatives and all my friends are waiting to meet you,' Angelos revealed. 'And the advantage of inviting them for lunch is that they all have to go home before dinner. Two weeks ago, the only reason I agreed to hold fire on announcing our marriage was that I hadn't the *slightest* desire to share you with other people. I wanted you all to myself for a while—'

'*All* your relatives…*all* your friends?'

'Maxie…this little celebration has been in the pipeline for two weeks. The invitations went out while we were in Greece.' He hesitated and cast her a rueful glance. 'I did ask your father to join us but he preferred not to.'

Maxie nodded without surprise and wondered absently why they were dawdling so much on their passage towards the house. 'Was Dad the something that came up yesterday?'

'I went up to Manchester to see him. That took up quite a few hours and then I came back here for the night. I wanted to check everything was ready for us.' Angelos stilled her steps altogether, casting an odd, frustrated glance of expectancy up at the sky.

'What's wrong…?'

The whine of an aircraft approaching brought a smile back to Angelos's impatient dark features. As a low-flying plane approached over the trees, he banded both arms round Maxie and turned her round. 'Look up,' he urged.

Maxie's eyes widened. In the wake of the strange trail of pink smoke left by the plane, words appeared to be forming.

'That's an I,' Angelos informed her helpfully. 'And that's an L and an O and a V—'

'Even I can read letters that big!' Maxie snapped.

The words 'I love you' stood there in the sky, picked out in bright pink. Maxie's jaw dropped.

Somewhat pained by this lack of response, Angelos breathed, 'I wanted you to know that I am proud of my feelings for you…and it was the only way I could think of doing it.'

Never in Maxie's wildest dreams would it have occurred to her that Angelos would do something so public and so deeply uncool. 'You love me?' she whispered weakly.

'You ought to know that by now!' Angelos launched in frustration. 'I've been tying myself in knots for weeks trying to *show* you how much I care!'

Maxie surveyed him with eyes brimming with happiness, but was conscious of a very slight sense of female incomprehension. 'Angelos…couldn't you just *say* the words?'

'You weren't ready to hear them. You had a very low opinion of me…and, let me tell you, few men would've emerged from reading that written character assassination of yours with much in the way of hope!' Angelos asserted with a feeling shudder.

Maxie was aghast. 'You *found* my list—?'

'How could you write all those things about me?'

'There was no name on it, so if you recognised the traits…' Maxie fell silent and studied him with dismayed and sympathetic eyes. 'Oh, Angelos…you kept quiet all this time, and that must've killed you—'

'I used that list as a blueprint for persuading you that I wasn't the man you imagined I was.'

'And you improved so much,' Maxie completed rather tactlessly.

With a helpless groan, Angelos hauled her close and kissed her with devouring passion. Maxie's impressionable heart went crazy. She submitted to being crushed with alacrity and hugged him tight, finally resting her golden head down on his broad shoulder as she struggled to catch her breath again. 'Oh, dear, *I* was the tart who thought you were great in bed and that was all...you were playing games with me when you said that, Angelos!' she condemned.

'That is really rich...coming from a wife who announced she preferred to be a mistress—'

'Only after being told she would be perfect in that role—'

'Perfect wife, perfect mistress, perfect...you are the love of my life,' Angelos confessed rather raggedly. 'Why the hell did I arrange the reception for today?'

Maxie squinted across the sea of big cars at the house. A lot of faces were looking out of the windows. But she didn't squirm. She threw her head high. Angelos *loved* her. The one and only love of his life? She felt ten feet tall. She would never, ever, no matter how long she lived, tell him how utterly naff that pink trail in the sky had been—particularly not when he was so pleased with himself for having come up with the idea.

'I love you too,' she confided as they threaded a passage through the parked cars on their way to the impressive front doors that already stood wide for their entrance. 'I really don't think I ought to tell you, but it wasn't the new improved you that did the trick entirely. I got sort of irrationally attached to you even before I wrote the list.'

'How can you tell me you love me with all these people hovering?' Angelos slung in a gritty hiss of reproach, but he smiled and their eyes met and that devastating smile of his grew even more brilliant.

'I want you to meet my wife,' Angelos announced a few minutes later, with so much pride and pleasure that Maxie felt her eyes prickle.

A whole host of people lined up to greet them. They

were mobbed. At one stage it was something of a surprise to find herself looking down on Leland Coulter's balding little head, and then meeting his faded, discomfited blue eyes. 'I'm sorry,' he breathed tightly.

'I made him sorry,' his wife, Jennifer, said very loudly, and Leland flinched and seemed to shrink into himself. 'Everyone knows the whole story now. There's no fool like an old fool.'

The older woman shook hands with brisk efficiency and passed on.

Somewhat paralysed by that encounter, Maxie whispered to Angelos, 'I feel so sorry for him now.'

'Don't you dare...if it hadn't been for Leland, we'd have been together three years sooner!' Angelos responded without pity.

'I couldn't have coped with you at nineteen.'

'I never knew anyone learn to cope with me faster,' Angelos countered, guiding her through the crush to a quiet corner.

Maxie focused on her friend, Liz, in delighted surprise. Petting Bounce, she sat down beside her. 'How did you get here?' she demanded.

'Angelos phoned me last night. We travelled down in a limousine this morning. Bounce was most impressed. Now, didn't I tell you that man loved you? Oh, dear, is he listening?' Liz said with comic dismay.

'Your senses are so much more acute than Maxie's,' Angelos told Liz cheerfully. 'To convince her, I had to hire a plane to spell out "I love you' in the sky.'

'How did that feel?' Liz asked Maxie eagerly.

'It felt...it *felt* absolutely fantastic,' Maxie swore. 'It was so imaginative, so unexpected, so—'

'Naff?' Angelos slotted in tautly.

'No, it was the moment I realised that I loved you

most.' And truthfully it had been, when he had unerringly betrayed to her just how hard he found it to put his pride on the line and say those three little words before she said them.

Lunch was a vast buffet served in the ballroom by uniformed waiters. Maxie sipped champagne and drifted about on an ecstatic cloud with Angelos's arm curved possessively round her. She met his aunts and his uncles and his cousins and his second cousins and his third cousins, and all the names just went right over her head.

And then, when the band struck up the music, rising to the role expected of the bridal couple, they circled the floor and the dancing began. Given an excuse to remain constantly within Angelos's hold, Maxie was initially content. Curving herself round him like a vine, she breathed in the hot, familiar scent of his body and inevitably turned weak with longing. 'Any sign of anyone leaving yet?' she kept on asking hopefully.

At last a trickle of departures led to a generalised flood. They saw Liz back out to the limo. Then Maxie and Angelos mounted the stairs hand in hand at a stately pace. 'When did you realise you were in love with me?' she pressed.

'When you had the chickenpox and I still couldn't wait to take you home.'

'But you weren't prepared to admit it—'

'Torture wouldn't have made me confess I was that vulnerable. This is our bedroom.' Angelos cast wide a door with a flourish.

'"Our" has a warm sound,' Maxie savoured. 'I still can't believe you love me...'

'You wouldn't have had to wait so long to find out if you had kept quiet on the beach the morning after I got drunk.' In exasperation Angelos framed her surprised face with loving hands. 'I was ready to tell you. Since I was painfully aware that I had got everything wrong, and I was feeling unusually humble, I was planning to go for the sympathy vote…and what did *you* do?'

'I told you about my godmother's will… I think I'll give my share to Nancy's favourite children's charity.' She stared dizzily into dark eyes blazing with love and gave him a glorious smile. 'I had to tell you about the will some time, but I was just trying to save face. I didn't want you to realise how much I loved you—'

'You're a total dreamer.'

'I'm the love of your life,' Maxie reminded him rather smugly as she flicked loose his tie and slid his jacket down off his broad shoulders with the intent air of one unwrapping a wonderful parcel. 'And you're the love of mine.'

Angelos brought her down on the four-poster bed with a husky laugh of amusement. 'Let me remind you of what you said in your list. Chauvinistic, bad-tempered, selfish, unromantic, insensitive, domineering—'

'A woman always reserves the right to change her mind,' Maxie inserted before he could get really warmed up.

Black eyes were burnished to pure gold as he met her dancing eyes. 'You may be gorgeous…but I think it was your mind I fell in love with…all those snappy replies and sneaky moves, *agape mou.*'

'To think I once thought you were cold.' Maxie ran a tender loving hand over his hair-roughened chest. 'How many children are we going to have?' she asked.

Angelos gave her a startled smile of appreciation that

turned her heart over and inside out. 'You want my baby?'

Maxie nodded. The prospect just made her melt.

'You really are tremendous,' Angelos breathed hoarsely.

And then he took her readily parted lips with urgent, speaking hunger and the passion took over, gloriously reaffirming their love for each other.

Ten months later, they had their first child. Maxie gave birth to a baby girl with blue eyes as bright and bossy as her own. Angelos took one look at his daughter and he just adored her too.

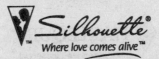

If you enjoyed what you just read,
then we've got an offer you can't resist!

Take 2
bestselling novels FREE!
Plus get a FREE surprise gift!

Clip this page and mail it to The Best of the Best™

IN U.S.A.	**IN CANADA**
3010 Walden Ave.	P.O. Box 609
P.O. Box 1867	Fort Erie, Ontario
Buffalo, N.Y. 14240-1867	L2A 5X3

YES! Please send me 2 free Best of the Best™ novels and my free surprise gift. After receiving them, if I don't wish to receive anymore, I can return the shipping statement marked cancel. If I don't cancel, I will receive 4 brand-new novels every month, before they're available in stores! In the U.S.A., bill me at the bargain price of $4.74 plus 25¢ shipping and handling per book and applicable sales tax, if any*. In Canada, bill me at the bargain price of $5.24 plus 25¢ shipping and handling per book and applicable taxes**. That's the complete price and a savings of over 20% off the cover prices—what a great deal! I understand that accepting the 2 free books and gift places me under no obligation ever to buy any books. I can always return a shipment and cancel at any time. Even if I never buy another The Best of the Best™ book, the 2 free books and gift are mine to keep forever.

185 MDN DNWF
385 MDN DNWG

Name	(PLEASE PRINT)	
Address	Apt.#	
City	State/Prov.	Zip/Postal Code

* Terms and prices subject to change without notice. Sales tax applicable in N.Y.
** Canadian residents will be charged applicable provincial taxes and GST.
All orders subject to approval. Offer limited to one per household and not valid to current The Best of the Best™ subscribers.
® are registered trademarks of Harlequin Enterprises Limited.

BOB02-R   ©1998 Harlequin Enterprises Limited

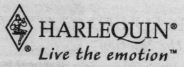

USA TODAY *bestselling author*

JULIE
KENNER

Brings you a supersexy tale of love and mystery...

Silent CONFESSIONS

A BRAND-NEW NOVEL.

Detective Jack Parker needs an
education from a historical sex
expert in order to crack his
latest case—and bookstore
owner Veronica Archer is just
the person to help him. But
their private lessons give
Ronnie some other ideas on
how the detective can help
her sexual education....

"JULIE KENNER JUST
MIGHT WELL BE THE MOST
ENCHANTING AUTHOR
IN TODAY'S MARKET."
—THE ROMANCE
READER'S CONNECTION

Look for
SILENT CONFESSIONS,
available in April 2003.

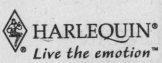

HARLEQUIN®
Live the emotion™

Visit us at www.eHarlequin.com

PHSC